OCEANS RISING

OCEANS RISING

D. M. Baker

ISBN: 061593692X
ISBN 13: 9780615936925
Library of Congress Control Number: 2015903821
Mark D. Baker, Butler, PA

CHAPTER ONE

Friday, May 7
6:23 a.m.

What a mess he had gotten himself into, he thought as he sat on the edge of the bed and looked out the window at the first crimson streaks of the morning sky. Not to mention that his life had probably been at risk. He shouldn't have been anywhere near that place, he thought as he slowly stood, checking his balance before taking his first step toward the bathroom.

He felt dizzy, and his knee hurt as he limped across the room. He'd struck it on the bathroom door when he was trying to get out of the bar. It hadn't felt that bad last night, but this morning it was stiff and sore. He stopped in the stream of light coming from the bathroom to take a better look at the purplish discoloration over his knee. It hurt worse than it looked, he told himself. He looked back over his shoulder at his wife to make sure she was still sleeping, before entering the bathroom and closing the door.

Didn't want to wake her...had too much else on his mind to have to deal with her gibberish this morning. He didn't want to have a long, strung-out conversation with her about all their personal problems, he thought, rubbing his bruised knee and bending it a couple of times, trying to loosen it up.

He should never have been at that bar...that seedy strip joint with the terrible reputation, he told himself. Drugs, gambling, prostitution...probably...who knew what went on at the bar? He didn't even want to know, he thought as he looked at his reflection in the mirror, at his thinning gray hair and the wrinkles around his lifeless eyes. He looked older than he was, he thought as he opened up the medicine cabinet, exposing the two rows of bottles. Medicines and vitamins, all lined up like soldiers. Thirteen bottles in all: five on the top shelf, the important ones—the generals—pills for his high blood pressure and cholesterol. Eight bottles on the bottom shelf—the foot soldiers— mostly vitamins and supplements...who knew the difference? A, C, D, E, folic acid, and niacin...couldn't even remember them all. And saw palmetto, a small green pill that was supposed to keep his prostate from getting any bigger than it already was. All of them were supposed to make him live a longer and happier life...with more vim and vigor, he thought as he started the tedious routine of unscrewing the caps on each of the bottles and fishing out one pill from each.

On the very bottom shelf sat the expensive tube of hair restorer. Didn't work...wasn't restoring anything but the company's profits, he thought as he squeezed a ribbon of cream from the tube into the palm of his hand and then massaged it into his scalp, around the little hair that hadn't abandon him...fertilizer.

He hadn't slept a wink thinking about his mess...his potential dilemma. Now he was dead tired, had a migraine, and still had a long, stressful day in front of him, he thought as he lathered shaving cream over his face.

How would it look if everyone found out that a well-known and respected physician in the community had been in a strip club seeing one of the strippers? A happily married man—a good, clean Christian; a prominent physician; a professor emeritus at the university with a respected reputation—sneaking around in a strip club, dating one of the strippers. Wouldn't look good, he thought as he made the first pass with his razor.

Everyone in town knew him, and now everyone might find out about the sordid side of his miserable life. The part of his life that he had tried so hard to keep concealed. What would people think if they found out that he had been having an affair with a stripper who was half his age?

Just hanging out with the rest of the lowlifes in the city…at a sleazy strip bar in one of the worst sections of the city…drug addicts, alcoholics, hookers, criminals. "Who knew what lived there?" he mumbled to himself as he felt the sharp pain of the razor cutting into his chin. What would everyone think about that? More, what would his wife think? What would he tell her? Worse, what would he tell his mother? They'd probably all think that he was just some kind of a sex pervert, he imagined. He could have been in there selling bible covers and it wouldn't have mattered. Everyone would still think he was some kind of a pervert, he figured.

He shook his head pitifully as he rinsed his razor. He knew something like this might happen to expose him, he thought as he grabbed a piece of toilet paper to stop the razor cut from bleeding. He had always feared that some night the police would raid the place, for one reason or another, and arrest him and everyone else, put them all in handcuffs and then parade them out the front door of the bar, in front of bright lights and TV cameras. Then he would be on the eleven o'clock news, standing there in line with the tattooed lot of them all—lined up as the camera panned down the row: two drug addicts, a prostitute, a stripper in some absurd outfit, and then the well-known doctor—the respected surgeon—Dr.

Benjamin Weed. None other than Dr. Benjamin Weed, standing in line with all the other lowlifes in the community…That would be a great image.

And then the whole event would be smeared across the front page of the newspaper and across every television station in the city. He feared that possibility every time he was in that bar. He'd even dreamed about it a couple of times. And as with his luck, he was just about ready to leave the damned bar before it all happened, he remembered as he turned on the shower, waiting for the water to warm up before stepping in.

He had just left the main bar area to walk down a long hallway to the men's room. He recalled looking into that dirty, cracked mirror hanging over the sink before he sat down in one of the two stalls—the lesser of the two evils.

That's when he heard what had to have been a gunshot—a loud, deafening sound.

And that's when he jumped up and hit his knee on the damn stall door, realizing immediately what had just happened, or at least thinking he knew what had just happened. That Tatter's son had just shot his dad. It was the only logical explanation.

He had seen them fighting in the bar just before he left for the men's room.

The son—whatever they called him—had some strange name like Peanuts or something. He was a big, burly, scary-looking guy covered with tattoos and piercings, arguing with his dad—a small, thin, emaciated man with bad emphysema. They had been arguing for almost an hour as the girls danced, he remembered…yelling, cussing, making threats and shaking their fists at each other.

"Fuck this…fuck that…fuck you!"

He'd seen them fighting before, but this fight seemed more intense. He could even hear them arguing with the door shut in the men's room…something about stolen money, he thought.

That was the only thing that made sense, but he couldn't be certain because he hadn't actually seen a thing. He had just heard the shot and then maybe some sounds that you would expect after someone was shot—some moans and groans—and then a few muffled screams, chairs sliding across the floor, and perhaps glass breaking. Maybe he had even heard someone mumble the words, "He shot him!" It had all happened so unexpectedly that he didn't really know what had just taken place.

That's when he panicked and bolted out of the restroom and out the back door of the bar, stumbling around with his pants still half dragging on the floor. And he hadn't even really thought about the crazy lunatic doing the shooting. Just knew he didn't want to be there when the police arrived…couldn't risk that, he thought as he rinsed the soap from his hair. That was his main concern.

The thought still sent a chill up his spine, thinking about how close he had been to a shooting. He could have gotten shot. He didn't even want to think about that. He was never going back there, he told himself as he stepped out of the shower.

But if his assumption was correct and Tatter's son had shot him, then the police would be investigating and looking for witnesses… maybe. Police could be looking for him right now, he imagined. And an investigation could open up a big can of worms, he thought as he dried off. This little incident could destroy his life…could destroy his career…could destroy his reputation, he feared.

He had at least gotten away cleanly for the time being…and maybe he would get lucky. Maybe the police would never find out that he had been in the bar.

Then again, maybe he was wrong about the whole thing. Maybe Tatter's son had just fired a warning shot into the wall or something. Maybe he hadn't shot anyone at all. But Tatter's son had already spent time in jail for shooting someone. Can, the dancer he was seeing—known as Candy—had told him that. She had told him to "stay away from that psycho" because he was crazy and had spent a lot of time in a psychiatric hospital.

Then too, the police might not even care that he was there. There were plenty of other people in the bar for them to question. There must have been at least twenty patrons there at that time—maybe more. Even taking into account all the people that had run out of the bar with him, surely there had to have been a few bar flies still there when the police arrived, he thought as he looked at his pathetic reflection in the mirror.

Let those people tell the police what happened. Why would they even want to talk to him when they already had a bunch of eyewitnesses to the shooting? Witnesses who actually saw what happened. They wouldn't even need to talk to him, he hoped.

The police wouldn't know he had been in the bar anyway...unless someone told them. And who knew him at the bar? Not many. He made sure of that. He always kept a low profile...always wore sunglasses and a baseball cap to shield his identity. And he hadn't seen anyone in the bar that he knew who could identify him. Not like the night he had run into two nurses from the hospital. And Candy wouldn't say anything to the police. He had told her many times about hiding his identity, he thought as he gingerly removed the small pieces of toilet paper from his chin. But he couldn't be certain...She had done some pretty stupid things in the past. He would just have to remind her later.

When he was finished in the bathroom, he slowly opened the door and looked across the room at his wife to make sure she was still sleeping. Then he quietly left the room, walking down the hallway to his closet.

Even if the police found out that he had been there, it might not matter. He still might be all right. He could answer a few questions... tell them that he didn't know anything...hadn't seen anything. And that would be the end of it—maybe. His wife, his mother, and all the people he knew would never be the wiser. That was a possibility, but it would be cutting it pretty close.

Yes, he had been there that night. And maybe he had heard a gunshot, but he wasn't even sure about that, he could tell the police. He didn't have to tell them anything about seeing Pickles and his dad fighting in the bar, he thought as he picked out a suit... finally remembered what they called Tatter's son. Pickles.

Yes, he could tell the police that he had just gone in to see one of the dancers. Might have to, at least, tell the police that...could tell them that they were just friends. He didn't need to get into any specifics about their relationship. They didn't need to know that he was having an affair with her. That was personal. That was his business. Didn't have any relevance to the shooting anyway. There wasn't anything illegal about going into a bar to have a drink with someone, he reasoned as he tightened the knot in his tie—the noose around his neck, he imagined.

Then there was Sandy. If she found out about the bar shooting, he would be in real trouble. Their marriage was already in trouble. He would have to come up with a good, believable explanation for her, just in case. Maybe that he had gone into the bar to meet a friend... maybe Bob Seymour. Bob would cover for him, he was sure. Could tell Sandy that Seymour had just asked him to meet him there... didn't know why. That he really didn't know much about that particular bar. Yes, he had seen the ad in the paper with the strippers, with all the young girls in seductive, suggestive poses, but he didn't even know that was the bar he was going to. It was Bob's idea that they meet there. Doubted that Bob even knew what kind of a bar it was, he could tell her...that Bob had some kind of an emergency that he needed to talk to him about. He would work on a better story to tell her later when his mind was clearer, he thought.

She was always suspicious of his lies. None of his explanations ever sounded believable. Just a bad liar...always saying something to give it away. Sometimes he felt that his whole life was just one big lie anyway. Acting like—pretending like—he was someone he wasn't. Sandy was unlikely to believe whatever he told her. Might be the event that finally pushed their marriage off the bridge, he thought as he checked his appearance in the mirror. They were already seeing a marriage counselor who had made a big deal about having an open and honest relationship. Counselor had even made them both sign some kind of crazy bullshit contract about being honest with one another not more than a month earlier. How would he explain all this mess to her, after that?

Sandy would take him to the cleaners over something like this if she found out.

Being caught in that damn strip bar...stupid, just stupid. Now the whole world could find out about what kind of a person he really was. That he was not a very nice person...a philandering sex addict who liked to hang out at strip bars. That he wasn't the clean-living, happily married success that he led everyone to believe he was. All of it...out in the open for the public to view...to review... to judge...to form scathing opinions about. How degrading...how embarrassing...Might as well just have rolled around naked like a raving lunatic on Main Street. People probably wouldn't think any less of him if he had.

Not a bad guy, really. Probably pretty normal, he told himself as he looked in the mirror again. People went into stripper bars all the time and no one ever found out about it...probably. People had affairs. People had secrets...secret lives, he justified as he started toward the stairs, satisfied that he hadn't awakened his wife. Had all just been bad timing—bad luck.

He didn't need any more embarrassment...intimidation...stress in his life. Not now, anyway.

Maybe he would get away with it. He didn't know...how did anyone ever know, he wondered as he slowly walked down the squeaky steps and into the kitchen. Maybe he was already out of the woods and the police already knew what had happened, and maybe they didn't even need to do an investigation. And maybe he had dodged the proverbial bullet and had made a clean getaway. The way he looked at it, his chances were pretty good. It was highly unlikely that anyone would ever discover that he had been in the bar, he concluded as he opened the front door and picked up the morning newspaper from the front porch.

Christ, he still wasn't sure that anything had even happened at the bar. Still wasn't sure that anyone had even gotten shot.

Bad thing was—the really bad thing—he figured as he carried the newspaper into the house, was that this incident—this shooting—if there was a shooting—this mess that he had potentially gotten himself into, couldn't have come at a worse time in his life.

CHAPTER TWO

Friday, May 7
7:04 a.m.

He didn't need another mess like this to further complicate his already complicated life. Not now. Not when he already had one mess that he was trying to clean up. Not when he was already under the public's scrutiny for something else almost as equally embarrassing—and almost as equally likely to ruin his life.

He was already involved with an embarrassing legal battle (with some pain-in-the-ass, wealthy, well-known socialite who had sued him for malpractice). A law suit that was being played out publicly in all the newspapers and on all the TV stations in the city for everyone to experience firsthand. A frivolous lawsuit that was making him look like a complete fool.

One mess was enough, he thought disgustedly as he quickly scanned the front page of the newspaper for any articles about shootings in the city. And just in time for the start of the trial—the main event that everyone had been anxiously waiting for.

Now, if the public caught wind that he had been in some sleazy strip club and that he was having an affair with one of the strippers, there wouldn't be a snowball's chance in hell that he would win his case. That revelation would destroy his image and reputation completely. And his image and reputation were about all he had left. They had been the better part of his defense and had already been weakened enough. A story like this would just validate all those accusations about his character...and weaken him even more, he knew as he drank some coffee and ate a stale donut.

The lawsuit had started almost two years ago. He had been at a restaurant late, having dinner...with Liz...eating and...drinking a little...but not as much as the attorney had intimated.

He had just gotten home when he got the call from the hospital.

A woman had struck a parked car and had sustained two large facial lacerations that needed surgical repair, and it just so happened he was the "lucky doctor" on call that night, the ER doctor had reminded him.

It was 3:00 a.m. by the time he arrived at the hospital. The patient was exactly what he had expected—an obnoxious drunk...causing havoc...teetering precariously through the ER, like a wind-up tin toy...dressed only in a hospital gown, baring her ass for everyone to see. Her head wrapped like a mummy...with an unlit cigarette dangling from the mouth hole that had been cut into the bandages...a cervical collar around her neck, tethered to oxygen tubing...and dragging an IV bag behind her on the floor as she shouted inappropriate profanities and demands.

Foulmouthed. A constant stream of "Shit this!" and "Fuck that!" Most of it made little sense...she was pissed that no one would light her cigarette...and shit-faced drunk, Weed remembered.

He was furious at the misery she had caused him and already had a guttural dislike for the obnoxious drunk, he remembered, perhaps more than usual.

When she staggered close enough, he pulled the cigarette from her mouth and told her to get her ass back up on the stretcher before he stitched her "foul mouth shut." At least that's how he thought their initial encounter had started…He couldn't really remember all the details about that night or all the things her attorneys had alluded to when they took his deposition.

He told her that he was tired of treating fat, obnoxious drunks. He did remember that.

But they had argued pretty much the whole time he repaired her lacerations…couldn't even remember about what now. The accident…her stupidity…his stupidity…his insensitivity…the car… flagrant insults that even then seemed juvenile…fighting over something so ridiculous and then thinking that he had won. It seemed as if they had always been mortal enemies but had only now found each other, he thought.

Two drunks fighting it out, he mused, but then he forced that bothersome thought into denial.

But their protracted fight had taken place before he discovered who the patient was. "Do you know who that woman is?" the nurse had queried, incredulous. The question still shocked him when he thought about it. He recalled fearing the answer that she was about to give him, hoping it was some nobody, but knowing it was someone important. "That's Gertrude Hileman." It was an answer he didn't want to hear…an answer that made him dizzy as he stood there dumbfounded…realizing that he had just pissed off the one of the few people in the city that you didn't want to piss off.

Too impatient and ignorant to even realize who he had been treating, he thought. A golden opportunity to impress someone important…turned into a tragedy.

He had tried to walk it all back that night, to make some kind of a recovery with a forced apology, but that attempt had been embarrassingly awkward. He tried to convince her that he was looking out for her best interests, somehow. That it was all just a joke…to try and break the tension…to try and calm her down…to take her mind off of her injuries. Explanations that didn't sound convincing or make much sense—even to him. He even tried to convince her that she had suffered a concussion and was confused. But it all sounded like the big fabrication that it was, and it had probably made the whole fight seem worse. The damage had been done… The die had been cast.

Gertrude P. Hileman. He knew all about Gertrude P. Hileman… who didn't? Granddaughter of Simon Hileman…founder of the multimillion-dollar Hileman's Mustards Co. Hands-down the richest and most influential family in the city. There was no doubt about that. There were Hileman streets, Hileman buildings, Hileman foundations, and Hileman parks…all over town. And Hileman's Mustard in every store. Fifty-six varieties to be exact. Half the city's population seemed to work for the company.

He had even talked to her a couple of times in the past, and even taken her on as a close acquaintance that he could proudly brag to friends about, as if they had been close personal friends for years.

Was almost a year later before the seven-million-dollar lawsuit was dropped at his doorstep—a medical-malpractice lawsuit…for negligence in repairing her two facial lacerations that had resulted in two painful and unsightly scars—the result of Dr. Weed's incompetence…the apparent bones of the case. But there were twenty-seven other injuries she had come up with to add substance to her case, injuries that had magically appeared to make her suit seem more credible: nerve damage in her neck and back, post-concussive depression and memory loss, anxiety, and others that he couldn't think of now…all also claimed to be the result of Dr. Weed's incompetence and gross negligence…and all mostly ridiculous fabrications, he knew.

But it became embarrassing and degrading when the news media found out about the case…after all the articles started to appear in the newspapers and the TV stations started following the case. A few stories at first...maybe once a week...but later almost every day some scathing article or report about him and the case. Reports that questioned his professional ability and competence as a surgeon.

And if the articles and reports weren't directly about the case, they were about some related topic...with subtle references to his case...interviews with other doctors...neurologists...plastic surgeons...giving their expert opinions of what he had done wrong... and then some investigative reports about "egregious medical errors" one night, and "the pervasive malpractice problem" the next...And then the following week a two-hour report entitled "The Epidemic of Poor Care and Incompetent Doctors" one night on one station and the next a "confession from a drug-abusing physician." The case had snowballed out of control and had quickly gained attention in the city. They had even dug up two previous law suits that he had lost...dragging them both through the mud again... business as usual.

"The case" had become serialized...dramatized for everyone in the city to anxiously follow. The main topic of conversation, he knew. Had almost wished something else terrible would happen. His picture had appeared countless times...seemed like everyone knew who he was.

And then more articles about Hileman's struggle to recover and how brave she had been and what a nightmare it had all been for her...And then articles about all her philanthropy and good things she had done for the city. Was difficult to read and listen to anything anymore, he thought.

But never one word said or printed about how drunk and obnoxious she had been that night. And no lengthy investigative reports about all the unruly alcoholic patients that pollute the ERs.

Every article was slanted and spun to make him the villain and Hileman the innocent victim.

But then the lawsuit was never about her injuries or his incompetence. It was just payback for him bruising her fragile ego…for pissing her off…for telling her the truth. Just a means to make his life miserable. To destroy him completely. Seven million dollars was meaningless to her. And the scars would have needed to be revised later anyway. All her other complaints were from her accident… They weren't the result of his negligence…They were caused by her hitting a parked car when she was drunk…And there was not a thing he could do about that.

And seven million dollars…an amount craftily figured to ensure his complete financial demise. An amount that would leave him penniless. And that's what had really fascinated the public; the possibility that everyone could witness the total destruction of someone other than themselves. That misery loved company…And he had plenty of company.

That's what had really piqued the public's interest. That's what they were all waiting to see…rooting for, he knew. His demise…his fall…was this year's entertainment, and it all pissed him off as he continued to search the newspaper.

Probably wouldn't matter what had happened at the bar…dating a stripper half his age…witnessing a shooting…probably just flies in the ointment, considering everything else. The case might already be lost…didn't know. Maybe it was just the validation that a story like that would provide…a story that would confirm and validate his true character. To let everyone know that Hileman had been right about him all along…That he wasn't such a good person, that he wasn't what he appeared to be…that he was a fraud. An upstanding citizen with a reputation as a good surgeon…was all an act. What he really was, was a sexual pervert that dated strippers half his age even when he was married. To validate all the things that had already been said about him.

An event so strategically placed—so perfectly timed—that it seemed almost supernatural…God getting even for all his transgressions…That would be his mother's explanation, he knew. A sort of an exclamation mark on the sentence of misfortune.

But when he thought about it…losing the case and all his money and respect wasn't near as bad as letting the whole world know how stupid he had been. The stupidity of putting himself into such a situation at such a critical time…when so many people were watching. That's what would really hurt. To expose his stupidity. Now that would be embarrassing, he thought. Hilarious…would be the laughing stock for years, he realized as he slid the newspaper aside and sat for a minute to collect his thoughts.

If he lost the case, then he was just going to close up the office and retire anyway…He had already sort of made up his mind about that…He wasn't going to put up with this bullshit any longer…this aggravation…He didn't have the energy to start over penniless. Not at his age. He would just pack it in and live on whatever money he could find, he thought as he looked under the sink for one of the bottles of bourbon he had placed there a week ago. He didn't want to run out now. Not with all this mess and stress to deal with, he thought, putting the bottle of bourbon in the inside pocket of his suit jacket. Part of it was burn-out, he knew. He was disgusted with his life even before this all started…He didn't want to be here anymore…He wanted a new life…a fresh life with new friends, he thought.

But maybe he could still catch a break…and find out that nothing serious had actually taken place at the bar and that the police hadn't even been called. And that Pickles had fired his gun into the ceiling or wall or floor. That was still a remote possibility, he imagined…as he listened to the painful squeaking sound of his wife coming down the steps.

CHAPTER THREE

Friday, May 7
7:12 a.m.

He watched out of the corner of his eye as Sandy entered the kitchen, poured herself a cup of coffee, and stood for an annoyingly long time looking down at the box of stale donuts before choosing one and sitting down at the table across from him...all done in silence.

"Couldn't sleep...worrying about everything," she garbled somewhat around the mouthful of donut. "Was awake half the night thinking about your meeting today with the attorneys," she said, but he didn't respond. "That and everything else...the party, the trial, the banquet...has me all nervous and anxious," she added, taking a sip of coffee.

"Everything go all right last night?" she asked after a long pause as he continued to stare blankly at the newspaper. And for a second, he thought that she was asking him about the shooting at the bar, before he realized that she was asking him about the emergency surgery he had told her that he had to perform at the hospital. That was the excuse he had made up so that he could go watch Candy dancing at the bar.

"Yeah, okay I guess…"

"Yeah, you smelled like smoke again…Makes me nauseated when you smell like smoke."

"Some asshole puffing on a cigar at the gas station, I guess…I don't know. I don't know," he told her without looking up from the newspaper.

"But before I forget, you're going to have to drive the MG for another couple of days," she said as she stood in front of the refrigerator looking at a to-do list that was hanging there. "They can't find the part yet for the Mercedes…I guess."

"Three weeks and they can't find a part? Where the hell are they looking? 'Cause I'm not sure the MG's going to hold out much longer. Sounds like it's about ready to fall apart," he said, taking a sip of coffee. The antique 1953 MG—another one of his great ideas gone south—hadn't run right since he bought it.

"The caterer and the lawn service need paid, too" she continued, still looking at the list. "Is there any money left in the account?"

"I don't know. Should be," he said while watching her take the list down from the refrigerator to hold it in front of her.

"Caterers are being a pain in the ass," she added, sounding pissed. "Should have gone with someone else, but they were the only ones that could do that Hawaiian-theme thing," she said as she scratched something off the list with a stubby pencil.

"And the pool needs to be looked at…still has that leak thing going on," she added. "We're going to have to have that fixed before the party. You call the pool service yet?" she asked, looking over at him for an answer.

"Don't even know if we should have the party. Maybe we should just cancel the whole damn thing. It's all turning into one big pain in the ass, and I don't even like half the people you invited. They're just a bunch of losers…social climbers looking for a handout…coming to see if the rumors of our impending demise are true. And I don't feel like being pleasant and acting happy around a bunch of annoying bums. Not now!"

"Well, it's a little late for that. The food and drinks have all been paid for," she fired back, looking over at him before crossing another item off the list. "And I want to have it anyway. It will be fun, and it might dispel some of the rumors about the lawsuit and us running out of money and rumors that we're getting a divorce," she said with a sarcastic tone to her voice. "I'm going to lay it on heavy. I'm just tired of all the innuendos and rumors. Everything at the party is going to be top shelf: food, decorations, wine…just the best. And we're going to act happy…even if we're not. Show everyone that everything is just fine," she added, "and that we couldn't be any happier."

The rumors just might all come true, he thought but feared to bring that topic up again.

"That's why it's important that we act happy. We have to put up a good image for everyone to see. Act like everything is okay," she said while he searched a kitchen drawer for the keys to the MG. "Oh, I almost forgot…Helen's coming over tonight."

"Great. I thought that we were finished with Helen? Thought that the twelve weeks of counseling were all that was required?"

"Yeah, but she's our friend now, and I guess she wants to check up on us to see how we've been doing. We're one of her biggest successes…and she's proud. She says that it's just routine that she checks up on us every so often. And she hasn't been charging us for all the extras, anyway. Besides, she's a nice person, and I think she feels that she's responsible for saving our marriage…just doesn't want us to have any relapses. You know, we have been under a lot of stress lately. It wouldn't hurt us to have a little tune -up."

"I don't know…"

"Well, I do know, for a fact, that she spent a whole lot of money on the gift she's giving us for our anniversary…money that she probably couldn't afford to spend…maybe a couple of hundred dollars," she said, pushing the paper aside. "She got us one of those expensive anniversary clocks…I think."

"Yeah, well, she's still a strange person."

"She's not that strange. I know you don't like her, but she's not that bad. Anyway, what was I supposed to do? Tell her no…that we didn't want her coming over?"

"That would have been okay," he said and shrugged.

"And plus, everyone's strange to you. And I'm serious…I think we're making definite progress. Helen thinks so too, and I believe it's all going to work out. All relationships go over rough roads. It's just a normal process," she said, leaning forward to give him a kiss, "just another bump in the road. And a lot of it's because of all the trouble we've been having…all the stress from this lawsuit. We just have to get organized…get oriented…and get our lives back in order…then things will all work out. In two weeks it will be our tenth wedding anniversary. There's no reason that it can't work for another ten years…maybe another hundred years, for that matter," she said, echoing the irritating words Helen had used numerous times.

"Well, tell me how she's supposed to straighten out our lives when her life is such a mess," he said.

"You say that all the time, but her life is not such a mess."

"She's been divorced, and her kids hate her and they won't talk to her…And what's with all the crying she was doing the last time she was here?"

"I don't know. You were divorced and your kids don't talk to you. You told me they don't like you, but that doesn't mean that your life is a mess. Things happen," she added, pausing to take a sip of her coffee. "And anyway, she was just happy for us. I guess they were just tears of joy, that's all. I told you, we're friends. She cares about us. Can't you understand that? She wants us to be happy… wants to be our friend, that's all. Is that asking too much? I'll tell her how excited you are about her coming," she said sarcastically after a short pause.

"Is Frank coming too?"

"Probably...I mean...I suppose. She didn't tell me differently."

"Great! That will make it a whole lot more enjoyable," he said acerbically. "Thought that he was all busy setting up his booth at the arts festival to sell his crappy paintings, and that he was too busy to do anything else?"

"Yeah well, I don't know. Maybe he won't come. What's the difference?"

"I can't stand being around him either...is the difference," he answered. "He just grates on my nerves with all of his babble. He thinks he knows everything about everything, you know? He has an answer for every question. And he thinks he's related to Andy Warhol, and I'll have to listen to that story again."

"Well, that part is probably true. His great grandmother was a Warholinski. I mean, that's not a common name in this city...And he's traced it all the way back. He said Andy's not a close relative, but he's like a third or fourth cousin...or something. So what's the big deal?" she said flippantly.

"Doesn't matter who he's related to, he still can't paint."

"He's proud of his work. You tried to paint once...You know how hard it is to paint. Yours weren't that much better, you know. Sure you're not just a little jealous?" she added after a long pause.

"Yeah, that's probably it...*pffft!*" he snorted.

"And there's the sarcasm again...like Helen said. You can't say a thing without being sarcastic...And people don't like sarcasm...it's cheap...it's outdated...passé."

He shook his head but didn't say anything more. They had already discussed his sarcasm problem.

"And you know I have that meeting with Hileman's attorneys today...And you do something like this...The day just keeps getting better," he said as he fought to fold the newspaper.

On top of everything else, he had to meet Liz for dinner after his meeting with the attorneys, he remembered. Just another pain-in-the-ass relationship that he had to deal with, he thought as Sandy droned on. Maybe tonight he would just tell Liz that it was over between them. That it just wasn't working out. If he could only get up the nerve...hadn't been able to so far...worrying about what she might do if he did break it off...like maybe calling Sandy and telling her all about their relationship. No, too much stress in his life right now to try and manage another crisis with Liz.

"You concentrating? You hear what I just told you?" Sandy said, irritated and interrupting his thoughts. "You mumble and then you can't concentrate!" she said after he shook his head. "We're just having steaks on the grill tonight. No big deal, and I'll wait to put yours on—if you're late," she said, pausing to sigh. "And I think they're going to take the money and settle the case anyway. It's the only thing that makes any sense. How can they pass up getting a million dollars for a couple of scars? You watch. Her attorneys will take the money and run, and it will all be over...all be behind us," she said confidently.

He knew that there was no way Hileman and her attorneys would settle. Hileman wouldn't agree to settle anything until she had destroyed him completely. She didn't need the money anyway...wasn't even about the money...was about destroying him, he knew, but he didn't say anything to Sandy. That argument was old and stale.

"Anything in the newspaper today?" she asked.

"Didn't see anything."

"Well, at least that's some good news. Three days without one mention of the trial. It's a pain worrying about it all the time—especially now with the Spring Fling and our anniversary party and everything else we have planned. Why couldn't the trial have been last month when nothing was going on—instead of now? Seems like it was all coordinated so that it would come at the most inappropriate time for us. We'll probably end up being the main topic of conversation at the Spring Fling. You know how people are, especially with both you and Hileman being there. Could be a pretty awkward situation...could be pretty embarrassing...for both of us."

"I don't know. I still might not go. I don't know if I can stand being in the same room with that annoying bitch."

"Well, not going is pretty much out of the question," she shot back. "Would make you look even worse...like you were guilty... just draw more attention to yourself. We need to be there to defend ourselves, even if it's just for a little while."

"And I don't care what all the people who hang out at the country club think about me anyway. It's just an excuse for all the social climbers to get together and try to outdo each other with all their designer clothes and big diamonds. A night of nauseating, pretentious excess," he said, but he knew his words sounded hypocritical.

The Spring Fling. Even the name was nauseating, he thought. Some sort of yearly benefit for the needy, but no one really gave a shit about the needy. And this year, Hileman could show off her scars for everyone to see: sitting there, at the head table, where everyone important in the community could get a good, long look at her. So everyone could see firsthand the reason why Dr. Weed was going to lose his house and cars and end up in the gutter. To verify what a terrible surgeon he really was, and to warn everyone to steer clear of Dr. Weed—unless they wanted to look like her, he thought as Sandy continued to babble on about something.

"You know how people are. No one ever says anything to your face, but you know that they're all talking about you behind your back, about Hileman and all her scars, and how you were the surgeon that did that to her. It's like that proverbial elephant in the room," she said, "until you bring it up, and then they act like they don't know what the hell you're talking about. Don't like it that everyone's talking about us behind our backs...that we're the laughing stock of the party—the town—whatever. I even think that a lot of them would like to see you lose. I don't like to believe it, but I do.

They want us to lose the case. Like, they think they're actually going to march us off to some poorhouse. Disgusting! I would never feel that way about anyone," she said and paused for a few moments. "I don't even think there is a poor house anymore," she mumbled. "And Helen told me she overheard someone talking about us but wouldn't tell me what they said. Wouldn't even tell me after I told her I didn't care…didn't want to hurt my feelings. She's such a nice person…probably the best friend I have right now," she continued, looking distantly and teary-eyed out the kitchen window. "This could be our Waterloo, you know?" she added. "The thing that destroys us," she said as she looked under the table for the part of her donut that had broken away and fallen to the floor.

"Hileman's just trying to destroy me. Something deep inside her…something visceral that she just doesn't like about me," he said when she reappeared above the table. "And actually, I think she likes having the scars…just to make me look bad. Not because they make *her* look bad, but because they make *me* look bad. The only thing that makes any sense," he said. "Because if she was really concerned about the scars, she would have had them repaired a long time ago. A plastic surgeon could easily repair them so you wouldn't even notice. So, there's really no other explanation," he said, pausing to think. "And another thing I realized the other day when I saw her picture in the newspaper…I actually think that she may be doing something to make the scars look worse than they really are."

"What's that?" she asked distractedly.

"The scars! I think that she's using some kind of make-up to make her scars look worse, because there's no way they could look *that* bad…They just look unnatural."

"I don't know. Unnatural-looking scars? Would she do that?"

"Absolutely! She's crazy, I told you. At this point, I think she would do just about anything to make me look bad. All that neck pain and back pain that she cooked up…all a bunch of lies…You know that!" He sat there at the table, already exhausted, before forcing himself to stand.

"I just hope we don't lose…" she said, sipping her coffee. "I can't imagine what it would be like. How can someone work all his life and have so much…and then lose it all in the blink of an eye?" she asked rhetorically, almost in tears.

"We're not going to lose everything. Maybe a little…But no jury in the world is going to give her anywhere near seven million dollars. That's ridiculous! Maybe a couple hundred thousand…I mean…that's about all it's worth. No way that a jury will give her more than my insurance coverage. I'm really not even that concerned about it," he told her—even though he was.

"It just bothers me what Mordy says. Says that he knows more than one doctor who has lost everything…for doing a lot less than you did."

"Mordy's an idiot! He's the same person who sunk his hundred-thousand-dollar boat the first time he took it out…fifteen minutes, and it was at the bottom of the lake…and he almost killed his whole family in the process. And anyway, I told you…He talks too much. He's a lousy attorney who gives us lousy advice," he said, pausing before adding, "And he likes to see me suffer. I told you that. Probably as much as Hileman likes to see me suffer…maybe more…just a sadistic bastard," he told her but then thought about his plans to call Mordy later to ask him about the potential legal implications of the mess at the bar. Wouldn't give Mordy any specifics…just make him think that it was an off-the-cuff question.

"Mordy says that it's his job to get people prepared for the worst possible consequences," she added as he walked toward the front door. "And don't forget to call the pool guy…I don't want a half-full pool for our anniversary party," she said, looking at her list as she followed him to the door. "And remember, Mother's Day is Sunday, so don't forget to pick up some flowers or something for your mother. You remember the fuss she put up last year when you forgot."

"Yeah, I will," he told her, waving back in her direction as he left the house…if he remembered.

CHAPTER FOUR

Friday, May 7
7:25 a.m.

He never would have gotten sued if the patient hadn't been such an irresponsible asshole that night, he knew as he ground the MG to a start.

Couldn't imagine losing everything. All that he had worked for over the last twenty-five years...all the blood, sweat, and tears... stolen away from him by some insane person, he thought, looking back at the house and drifting the car down the long driveway. His two-million-dollar brick colonial home getting smaller...shrinking...drifting prophetically away.

He was fighting for his life all because of some insignificant chance encounter—and a few misplaced comments. "From the penthouse to the outhouse," Mordy had said. Losing it all to some obnoxious bitch. Could be evicted from my own house...forced to live at the Holiday Inn. Hileman would love to see that, he thought as he pushed in the clutch with his sore leg, putting the car into gear and sending it jumping down the street a few feet before it started moving smoothly.

It wasn't as if something like this hadn't happened before. Mordy had been right about that. Jim Peterson, an anesthesiologist, had lost everything in an ugly lawsuit just two years ago. That suit had destroyed Jim. Now, Jim was walking around all morose...on antidepressants...like a zombie. *I could end up like him. And to think, I thought it was funny at the time. Not so funny now,* he thought as he drove toward the hospital and tried to locate a clear radio station through the static on the worn-out radio. Maybe he could find out if there was any news about a shooting, he thought as he turned the dial—slowly—as if he were trying to open a safe.

And juries were crazy these days with their astronomical awards for even minor injuries. A jury, seeing Hileman's scars and hearing about all the other injuries she claimed to have, might just give her the seven million dollars she was demanding, he thought as he tried to listen to a station over the din of the rattling MG and static. A jury could award her even more than the seven million since there was no cap on awards, he imagined. Seven million dollars wasn't much today when it came to malpractice awards, he thought as he pulled onto the freeway behind a long line of slow-moving traffic.

When you analyzed the case, there really wasn't much credence to the physical damages, he knew. The only credible claim was the scarring, and even that wasn't all that credible. The scars could be easily repaired by a plastic surgeon to make them look almost unnoticeable. Hileman's scars could have already been repaired. But then, she couldn't do that. To have the scars repaired would destroy her entire case. Without the scars, she had nothing, really. The other injuries—the back pain, the neck pain, the depression, and all the other alleged complaints that her lawyers had come up with—were all fabricated, just to try to increase the legitimacy of an otherwise weak case. That, and to increase the amount of money that the jury might award them. Just the standard operating procedure today, he knew.

Maybe today at the pretrial hearing, the judge would realize that Hileman's case was flimsy and force her attorneys to reach an out-of-court settlement. Convince them that taking the money the insurance company was offering was their only option, he thought as he sat in traffic. That's what he was hoping would happen…But he seriously doubted it would.

Had to be at least one news station where he could actually hear the news over all the static and rattling…that didn't fade out completely, he thought as he adjusted the radio dial again and pulled off the highway into the line at the McDonald's drive-thru.

He didn't need to get drawn into some sticky, bullshit police investigation for everyone to find out about either. Not now. But then he didn't want to even think about that possibility.

Didn't need the hospital to find out about any shooting, either. They didn't need to know that he had been in some lowlife strip bar—seeing one of the strippers. The board was already on his ass for pissing off Hileman, one of their biggest contributors, and for drawing the hospital into a messy lawsuit with a lot of bad press. The case was hurting the hospital's image, and they didn't want Hileman taking her money across town to one of the other hospitals.

He had become a liability to the hospital, and liabilities had a way of getting kicked off the hospital's medical staff. That possibility was in the air—he could feel it—floating around, walking beside him, and waiting to strike. And that possibility was almost a certainty if this bar thing reared its ugly head. And if he got kicked off the medical staff—he was finished. He wouldn't be able to practice medicine anywhere…his whole career over…down the drain… all because of some frivolous lawsuit and a shooting at a bar—which he knew nothing about.

He adjusted the radio again, finally finding a station that he thought he could hear, as the clerk at the window gave him his change and his large Coke.

As he sat at a red light, he drank some of the Coke and then took the bottle of bourbon out from under the car's front seat and filled the Coke cup back up to the top. He took a couple of satisfying sips before the person in the car behind him blew his horn to let him know that the light had changed. When he looked up, the line of traffic was now far ahead of him.

The bourbon tasted good, he thought as he drove. The valium and the bourbon would make him more relaxed…more able to deal with all the bullshit he was going to have to deal with today, he concluded as he turned down the street that ran behind the hospital.

Would just run the whole damn bar mess past Mordy. Just wouldn't give him many details, he thought as he dialed him on his cell phone and sat in his parked car behind the hospital. Mordy had worked as a criminal attorney years ago. He would know about things like this. Maybe Mordy could give him some advice that— for once—would be of some value. Maybe help him to prevent it all from spinning out of control. But Mordy would have a field day if he told him what really happened. Mordy liked to rub salt in the wounds of his misfortunate clients…make them suffer…make it all sound even worse than it really was—if that was possible. And Mordy would probably keep his mouth shut about the whole mess, but then he wasn't really sure about that.

He would be pretty vague about what he told Mordy, anyway. No names—no places, he thought.

When Mordy didn't answer, he left a message for him to call back. Then he dialed Candy's number as he sipped at the comforting bourbon and Coke. She would likely know what happened at the bar last night…She was still there when it happened, he thought. He listened to the phone ring and ring—unanswered.

Might be easier to just run off with Candy to some tropical island and avoid it all, he imagined as he took another drink of his bourbon and Coke and then left a message on her cell.

Could always move back home with his mother if he lost everything. Would be nice, living like he did when he was young... no worries...no responsibilities...not a care in the world. When life was good...when everything was new and exciting...when emotions felt real. The best time of his life, he thought, taking another sip.

One thing was certain, he wasn't going to start all over. He wasn't going to spend the rest of his life paying off some bitch like Hileman. If he lost the case, things were going to change, he thought as some voices started coming from the radio for a short time before fading out again.

Was still early...still had a half hour before his first surgery was scheduled, he thought, finally finding a radio station that he could hear clearly. He sat in his car, under the shade of some large oak trees in front of the hospital, and listened to the news while he sipped his drink.

A bad accident in Larimore; the city council was planning a new tax on bars; the weather; a stock market report...But there was no news about any shooting—at any bar—anywhere in the city. Surely, if someone had gotten shot, it would have been on the news by now, he thought somewhat relieved before reaching down and turning off the radio.

Maybe Pickles had only fired a shot into the wall or the ceiling, he told himself before drinking the last of the Coke and bourbon and feeling cautiously relieved. Maybe his run of bad luck had changed and nothing at all would come of his probably imagined shooting. Maybe it wasn't going to be as bad of a day as he thought.

"Ben!" someone called out and then started tapping lightly on his window.

When he looked, Henry Pisor was standing at the passenger side window, looking in at him and making a motion with his arm for him to roll down the window.

Pisor was one of the psychiatrists at the hospital. A friend that always wanted to help people with their problems, even when they didn't want help, and even when they didn't have problems. Pisor had been offering him advice about the trial. He wanted to make sure that he wasn't depressed and wasn't going to do anything stupid—like slitting his wrists. Useless advice, Weed thought as he reached across the seat and rolled down the window a crack, hoping that Pisor wouldn't smell the bourbon he had been drinking.

"I just got a couple of minutes," Pisor told him as he sat his briefcase down on the hood of the car. "Have to get to an ethics meeting. Linn told me that you're having some kind of a get-together at your house next week sometime?" he asked as he brushed what looked like donut powder off his bow tie.

"Yeah, our tenth anniversary party. You get the invitation?" Weed asked as he tried to loosen up his sore knee before getting out of the car.

"Yeah, we got it, but Linn can't find it to send it back. She lost it and then forgot about it, and then remembered about it this morning and told me to tell you, if I saw you, that we were coming."

"That's good. The more the merrier," Weed answered, limping slightly as they started walking across the parking lot toward the hospital. "Yeah, she had to have a tenth anniversary party, but then, who celebrates their tenth anniversary? I can see, maybe, having a party on your twenty-fifth, but not after just ten years. That's bullshit. Just a lot of aggravation," he said, hoping that Pisor wouldn't ask him how he was "holding up"—again.

"Today's ten is yesterday's twenty-five," Pisor said, laughing.

"Seems like fifty," Weed said, but Pisor didn't seem to pick up on the joke that he was trying to make. "Sandy has some crazy idea that it will help resuscitate our marriage. We're supposed to be taking

31

our wedding vows again at the party. Was Helen's idea, mostly. Put Sandy up to the whole thing."

"You hurt your knee?" Pisor asked, backing away to watch Weed limp forward a couple of steps.

"Just old age," he answered as he tried to correct his gait.

"Linn said the party's supposed to be a pretty big deal?"

"Yeah, I guess. Sandy's pulling out all the stops. She hired a band and an expensive caterer, put up a lot of decorations, and invited a lot of people. I don't even know half the people that she invited. Party's going to cost me a bundle."

"Yeah, Linn's the same way. Never cares about how much anything costs," he said, laughing. "We supposed to dress up like Hawaiians?"

"Yeah, I guess. The caterers are supposed to make our back yard look like you're in Hawaii."

"Hawaii sounds fun."

"People will all get to see how we're 'holding up' under all the stress. See how people act, right before they lose everything," Weed said sarcastically. "Might even be evicted by then," he laughed, but was upset that he had been the one to bring up the lawsuit.

"Not as bad as that. You could win or at least not lose much. Your case isn't that bad. I told you about how you should handle the stress…You have to keep a level head. It's just a tempest in a tea pot. Starts Monday?" Pisor asked, pulling open the hospital door.

"Supposed to start then. Pretrial hearing's today, though…me and the judge and Hileman and all the attorneys. Last chance to settle before the trial actually starts, but I don't hold out much hope for that. Hileman's crazy, you know that? She doesn't want to settle, just wants to make my life even more miserable than it already is."

"Who knows? Seems like they always settle these cases at the last minute."

"It's all bullshit. A few scars…big fuckin' deal. But how am I supposed to get a fair trial when they print all that stuff that makes me look like an incompetent hack? She has the damn newspaper in her back pocket. Wasn't one thing printed about how drunk and obnoxious *she* was that night. Not one word about what *I* had to put up with that night."

"People only believe half of what they see and nothing that they hear. You know that! Anyway, I wouldn't worry. It will all blow over soon," he said as Weed followed him down a long corridor inside the hospital. "Couple of months, no one will even remember anything about it. That's the way it is these days," he added. "Hey, I'm sort of in a hurry right now, but if you need to talk, let me know. That's what I'm here for," he said apologetically, waving back as he hurried off in a different direction.

CHAPTER FIVE

Friday, May 7
10:12 a.m.

By the time Weed had finished his three cases in the OR, his knee was swollen twice its normal size and throbbing like a toothache. The pain—a constant reminder of all his problems—a punishment, even if nothing did come of the shooting, he thought as he pushed open the door, limped out of the OR and down the hallway.

He rode the elevator down two floors and then watched the noon news on the television in the ER. There still wasn't anything about any shooting anywhere in the city being reported, he thought, feeling more relieved now.

He had just overreacted again, like he always did, he imagined as he tried Candy's cell phone again. She could confirm his belief that nothing serious had taken place at the bar last night—if she would ever answer her phone, he thought as he walked out of the hospital and into the blinding sun. He stood there, somewhat disoriented, looking out at the sea of cars and trying to remember where he had parked.

He searched up one aisle and then the next, thinking for a few minutes that maybe his car had been stolen—before realizing that he was looking for the wrong car—that this morning he had been driving the MG and not the Mercedes—and then wondered if he might just be slipping a little mentally. Making sure that no one could see him, he took another drink of bourbon as he sat in the car and then slid the bottle back under the car seat.

He had also had trouble finding his car in the parking lot of the Venus Lounge the night of Hileman's accident, he remembered as he started his drive to the courthouse downtown. The night all his troubles began...

He had been drinking at the Venus Lounge a couple of hours before he had arrived at the hospital. But when Hileman's attorneys had questioned him about whether he had been under the influence, he denied it vehemently. He still feared that maybe the accusation would grow legs and destroy his reputation even further, along with any chance he had of winning the case. There were plenty of potential witnesses at the bar that night, but as far as he knew, Hileman's attorneys hadn't found any of them. Nor, for that matter, had they discovered where he had been drinking that night, or with whom he had been drinking. But if they tracked down Liz, she would tell them everything, because Liz was just the kind of person that wouldn't lie about anything... some damn religious thing, he thought as he moved his car slowly through traffic.

And he hadn't really been drunk that night. Yeah, maybe he'd had four or five drinks over a three-hour period before the accident, but he was nowhere near the legal limit of intoxication. He hadn't drunk nearly enough to affect his medical ability—he was certain—he thought as he pulled into the parking lot of Clancy's Restaurant.

He still had plenty of time before the pretrial hearing with Hileman and the attorneys, he figured after checking the time on his cell phone. One last chance to relax before the inquisition, he thought as he walked through the restaurant and sat down at the bar. He sat there for a while eating before noticing his darkened image in the mirror behind the bar. How quickly he had grown old: his eyes lifeless and thin hair graying. How fast time had passed. How he had mostly wasted his life. How stupid that person in the mirror was for getting into such a mess. It was an unpleasant image staring back at him, he thought as he looked away and consciously attempted to avoid eye contact with that person again—a person that he wasn't even sure he liked anymore.

The sun had turned to clouds and a brisk wind was blowing when he left the bar. He would still be a little early for his meeting, but he pulled his car into traffic anyway and slowly inched his way toward the courthouse.

Almost two o'clock in the afternoon and not one indication from any source that there had been a shooting anywhere in the city, he thought as he listened to another newscast on the radio. And as a bonus, Mordy hadn't called him back. For once, Mordicah's incompetence had paid off. Now he wouldn't have to deal with Mordy's harassment at all, he thought as he pulled the MG into the parking lot directly across from the courthouse and waited.

It had been almost two years since he had been inside the courthouse to sign off on one of his other malpractice cases. He had felt like a criminal that day too, he remembered as he watched a flock of pigeons circle and drop shit bombs on the two bronze WWI soldiers standing guard in front of the courthouse.

This was the place he would be spending the better part of the next two weeks of his life, he knew as he took another couple of sips of bourbon.

He watched as some workers in the park next to the courthouse struggled with some wind-blown tents they were constructing for this year's arts festival. Rows of colorful tents that, in a couple of days, would be filled with artists and their paintings, or sculptures, or jewelry they had made…or anything else they could think up to create and call art…but mostly crafts that they were all trying to get art prices for. There were some pretty bizarre creations, he knew. Delusional artisans like Helen's husband Frank, he thought as he watched a truck loaded with shaking porto-johns back over a high curb and into the park.

He had tried his hand at painting, for a short while. He wasn't sure why, now. Maybe to calm his nerves—like Sandy had said—but he doubted that. Maybe because he'd hoped to be a famous painter someday or maybe it was to create some meaning in his life…never really figured it out. He had even considered bringing some of his paintings down to the festival one year but then thought better of that idea. When he stood back and looked at what he'd created, he realized that most of it wasn't very good…just like everything else in his life…a painting that just wasn't right—wrong colors, wrong shapes, dull, unnatural, and as lifeless as lifeless art could be, he realized. The paintings were a lot like his own life, he supposed: unable to see the true nature of his work, unable to see the true nature of his life. That's when he realized he was probably just another delusional artist trying to find his way, he remembered pensively as he drained the last of the bourbon.

His life had become like one of his paintings: dull and lifeless, monotonous and tedious, and smothered by its own foibles, he thought. Nothing seemed real, exciting, or interesting to him anymore. It was as if he were slowly fading away…slowly disappearing.

It was a feeling he couldn't really explain and one that he didn't really understand. Some new emotion that there was no name for—that had never been described—that he had discovered. An emotion that was, maybe, a combination of melancholy and depression, and maybe a few other things too; a feeling of despair, disinterest, and disgust all rolled into one. What name could he come up with for that emotion, he wondered? Maybe it's a feeling you get when you start to get old and irrelevant; when you realize that everything good is behind you; when no one really cares any longer—the song of the aged and lost. It was hard for him to see the relevance of anything anymore, anyway. He might soon lose everything, and for some reason he didn't really seem to care all that much.

Maybe it was like the feeling of love, an emotion too complicated to understand or describe. He remembered what Helen had said to him in one of their counseling sessions: that he didn't know the meaning of love. Maybe she was right, and he didn't know what love was...He was just a defective human being who had never received the gene needed for that emotion, he thought, feeling a little lightheaded as he took the first sip out of a fresh bottle of bourbon. After ten years, he still didn't know if he loved Sandy. He didn't know if he loved Candy either. He didn't know if he had ever really loved anyone or if anyone had ever loved him. Maybe love was nothing more than a nice word for lust and sex.

He shut his eyes, put his head back, and tried to relax while sipping his bourbon, thinking about the meeting with Hileman's attorneys. He listened to the plaintive whine of an electric saw echoing through the park. At least the arts festival would be a distraction while the trial was in progress.

He sat in his car for another couple of minutes thinking before walking across the street to the courthouse.

"Ben!" Morgan said, startled that Weed was apparently standing so close. Morgan was the attorney that the insurance company had assigned to his case.

Morgan stood and gathered up his loose papers and put them back into his briefcase before he leaned forward and shook Weed's hand.

"We can talk down here," he said, motioning for Weed to follow. "I have some papers I need you to sign." Weed followed him down one of the corridors and into a men's room.

"More insurance company paperwork," he said apologetically as he laid the papers out on top of a sink before handing Weed a pen. "Went back to Henderson, the insurance adjuster down at the office, and he told me that I could up the offer to seven hundred thousand dollars, but that's it. Says that he doesn't think the case is worth anything more. But it probably won't matter, since Hileman's attorneys are pretty fixed on their seven million dollars."

"Henderson's the guy who sold me the defective one-million-dollar policy in the first place! He's why I'm in this mess to begin with!"

"Yeah, you told me that before, but anyway...I figure Hileman's attorneys might consider three or four million if you can figure a way to come up with the difference...property or any other assets you might be able to get a loan on. It might save you a ton of money in the long run, especially since juries are pretty unpredictable with their awards these days. Could give her ten million...for all I know. I mean, the scars look bad, but how much can a couple of scars be worth? And her attorneys are going to have to depend on their expert witness to convince the jury that all Hileman's other bullshit complaints are legitimate...which might not be that easy for them to do," Morgan told him as he took the papers Weed had signed and put them back into his brief case.

"They're not interested in settling," Weed said. "She just wants to see me suffer. Make me look as incompetent and heartless as she possibly can. Embarrass me as much as possible. Wouldn't matter if I offered her a hundred million...She wouldn't settle. It's just a game to her. I mean, she has more money than God!"

"Yeah, certainly seems like that's part of their game, but you never know," Morgan added, looking over at Weed as he wiped the sweat from his forehead with a paper towel.

"And to tell you the truth, I'd just as soon burn my house down, with everything in it, before I'd let her get it. She was just as much at fault for her injuries that night as I was. She's only lucky that someone was there to take care of her…that I got up at three in the morning to save her sorry ass. She could have died if it hadn't been for me…But I guess that doesn't matter. Should have just let her bleed to death."

"Yeah, I understand. I know how you feel."

"The scars are bullshit anyway. You know that, and our experts said the same thing. She could have had them revised so they wouldn't even be noticeable. And her neck injury, and back injury, and concussions, and depression, and whatever else she claims I'm responsible for—are just malicious fabrications to give the damn case some credibility. And anyway, if I lose, it won't matter because I'm just going to quit practicing medicine altogether and move on with my life in a different direction. It's all that I can do to keep my head above water financially, right now anyway, with all the business I'm losing from all the bad press she's spreading about how incompetent I am. There's a new revelation almost every day. Patients are running away like rats from a sinking ship. If things continue the way they're going right now, I'll have no business at all by the end of the year," Weed said, even though Morgan didn't seem to be all that interested. "I used to see fifty patients a week. You know how many people I saw last week?" he asked, as Morgan shook his head that he didn't. "I saw seven patients, and three of them were on welfare. I can't survive just seeing seven patients! And I'm certainly not going to work like a slave to pay off some ludicrous malpractice award to some insane person!"

"Yeah, you already told me about your plans," Morgan said. "You may reconsider later, though. You know how these things are. Hard to change directions."

"And that asshole Mordy, that attorney of mine that you said you knew. Well, he's been telling Sandy all kind of crazy stuff. He told her that if I lose, Hileman's attorneys could take all our possessions and evict us from our own house—the next day—if they wanted to. Now she's getting so paranoid that she's been taking chairs, tables, dishes—and anything else she can pick up and carry—out of our house and down to her mother's house. At least that's where I think she's taking it. Every time I go into the house, there's something else missing. Hardly anything left right now, actually. I have to look all over sometimes just to find a place to sit down. Scares me because I think she might actually be going a little crazy, and now she won't take her medication. I told her to take some extra Valium, but she tells me she's fine," Weed said, though he wasn't sure why he was telling Morgan about his personal problems.

"Yeah, Mordy was always like that. Even in law school, I remember how strange he was. How'd you ever get him as your personal attorney, anyway? You should just tell him to keep his mouth shut. And tell her not to give up the ship. We could still win. Stanger things have happened," Morgan added as they finally reached the conference room.

"You don't really believe that, do you? She has too much influence in this shit town."

"Well, it will all be over in a couple of weeks anyway. And in a couple of months, no one will remember a thing about it and then you can get back to your life…whatever that might be. Anyway, don't get upset today," Morgan said. "Her attorneys might get pretty nasty, so just ignore it all, and let me do the explaining. Just sit there and act like you care and that you're sympathetic about Hileman's injuries and all her pain and suffering," he said somewhat sarcastically as he pushed open the door to the conference room.

CHAPTER SIX

Friday, May 7
3:37 p.m.

When Weed entered the conference room, Gertrude Hileman was sitting at a large mahogany table and leaning slightly forward in a wheelchair, wearing sunglasses and a thick cervical collar around her neck, the two long, unnatural-appearing purple scars tracking torturously across the left side of her forehead and then sharply down across her nose, both ending on her right cheek. The scars were difficult to look at...almost monstrous...an intimidating and embarrassing example of his professional ability, he thought as he nervously sat down at the table.

He could feel his heart racing and an empty feeling, wanting to deny it all. His gut instinct...to just blame it all on someone else.

He took another look, not making eye contact with Hileman, before quickly looking away.

He felt anxious sitting this close to someone who had such a visceral dislike of him. Someone who had for the last two years been destroying his life…slowly…one little piece at a time.

Felt pissed about all the lies she had made up about him too. And pissed that she just hadn't had the scars repaired yet…that she was more interested in making him look bad than she was in making herself look good.

Her two attorneys sat on either side of her…One of them, John Turzak, was well known in the city with all his TV commercials and from all the astronomical awards that he had gotten for his celebrity clients.

Turzak had taken his contentious deposition a year earlier. Weed remembered what a nightmarish ordeal that had been.

The judge stood off to the side of Hileman in his long, black robe, leaned in, talked to her and her attorneys in whispers, then backed away slightly, smiling and laughing as if someone had made a joke, but ignoring completely his and Morgan's presence.

That was when Weed first noticed the small, black dog Hileman had cradled in her lap. Somewhat shocking at first…the dog…remembering for the first time since the night of the accident that the dog had actually been with Hileman that night in the ER. The dog was some kind of a miniature bulldog breed, with its pushed-back nose and bulging eyes. An ugly dog, he thought.

He had completely forgotten about the dog being with Hileman that night. How could he have forgotten something so bizzare as a dog running loose in the ER? Especially since the damn dog was one of the reasons he had gotten into so much trouble.

That night of the accident, he recalled, the dog had been in the car with Hileman when she'd had the accident, and she insisted that she be allowed to take the dog with her in the ambulance. That she had wanted the dog checked by the doctors to make sure it hadn't been injured.

He remembered thinking that she was no run-of-the-mill Saturday-night drunk.

That dog had been one of the reasons he had been so pissed off that night, he recalled now. Not only did he have to deal with an obnoxious drunk, he had to deal with her obnoxious dog too. How could he have forgotten that mangy mutt, he asked himself as the dog suddenly made eye contact, as if he might suddenly have recognized him.

That night, the drunken Hileman had been obsessed with her dog. Talking to it like it was human and could understood everything word she was telling it…and that it might at any moment start conversing with her. Kept asking if the dog was okay and then demanding that the dog be x-rayed. He remembered telling her that there was no way that he was going to x-ray any damn mutt. That had really pissed her off, he remembered now. And then he thought he remembered telling the orderly to get rid of the dirty mutt.

There were dog hairs on the surgical instruments, the bandages around Hileman's head, everything. He now remembered how he'd had to pick a ton of tiny black hairs out of Hileman's lacerations.

Like a bad dream, he thought, all of them together…again.

He remembered fighting with Hileman about the dog, too, and that he had made some derogatory comments about how disgusting and ridiculous she was acting…And then he recalled making some kind of joke about the dog. Something like, "Which one of you is the bigger loud mouth or pain in the ass?" But he couldn't really remember what he had said as he watched Hileman in the conference room rubbing the dog's head, occasionally looking down and explaining to the dog what was going on for everyone to hear.

"Gentlemen," the judge said, finally acknowledging their presence with a disgusted look while moving toward the head of the table.

"I think we all know each other," he said but introduced everyone before sitting down.

"I spent most of the last three nights reviewing this case: looking over all the interrogatories, depositions, expert witness statements, offers and counteroffers, and the demands that you've made over the last six months," the judge said, spreading out some papers in front of him. "So I think I'm pretty much up to speed on the case," he added, before pushing his glasses up on his forehead.

"And my job here today, if you don't already know, is to attempt to work out an agreement with both parties. This meeting is, of course, a sort of last-ditch effort to settle the case before going forward with a long and expensive trial," he continued. "And it's important to remember that we're not here to try the case; we're here to try and get both parties to agree on some loose framework for a settlement...to try to find a middle ground," he said and then paused, looking for something in one of the piles of papers in front of him.

"Actually," he said, taking his glasses off the top of his head and laying them in front of him on the table, "I'm not really sure why we're here, because a settlement at this time would seem highly unlikely...considering how far apart the sides are. But, according to state law, we have to go through the motions, regardless. But I can give you my opinion, and that opinion is...I believe the plaintiff's demand of seven million dollars to settle is very reasonable. Hell, an award for just the pain and suffering should be, in my estimation, near seven million dollars...and maybe more.

"But as required, I've looked at similar malpractice cases and the monetary damages they were awarded and then listed them all on the Damages Disclosure Form. The damages are listed on the right side of the form, and to the left, an estimation of the value for that particular injury," the judge said as he handed them all the papers.

It looked like a menu, Weed thought, with the injuries listed down the left side of the paper and the amounts awarded down the right. The total bill came to 6.9 million dollars. The judge

had given her almost one million dollars just for punitive damages: money she would receive for his bad behavior that night in
the ER...Money she would get for his insensitive and insincere
behavior, and for all the nasty comments that he had apparently
made that had bruised her psyche. Two million dollars were ear-
marked for the scars, one million—each—for the neck and back
injuries, and another million for pain and suffering. The remaining monetary awards were for all the other bogus injuries that she
had claimed in her lawsuit—including depression, Weed noted
incredulously.

This was ridiculous, Weed thought, staring at the paper as the
judge gave a detailed explanation of the settlement proposal, which
lasted almost thirty minutes.

"I already discussed it with the plaintiff's attorneys for about
an hour before you arrived, and they're agreeable to the terms I've
outlined," the judge said looking sternly at Morgan. "So, I guess
the only thing left to do is for the defendant to determine if he is
willing to accept them, too. I do understand that the defendant
has a one-million-dollar cap on his insurance policy, but there's
nothing I can do about that. That was his decision to buy such an
insufficient policy. And to tell you the truth, I believe this is the
best deal that you're likely to get," the judge said, looking squarely
at Weed. "If this goes to trial, who knows what might happen? Six
point nine million might look like a real bargain," he added. "I'm
talking about an award that could easily be in the range of fifteen
million dollars."

"I'll give you all about a half hour or so to talk it over," the judge
said as he stood and looked at his watch. "We can meet back here
at four to discuss it," he added before telling Morgan and Weed
that they could use the conference room across the hall to make up
their minds.

"A lot of help he was. More than half a million for punitive damages? Half a million just because I pissed her off that night...now

that's draconian," Weed said under his breath as they entered the other conference room.

"Yeah, well, I'll just tell the judge we're not interested. That we'll take our chances with a jury trial," Morgan said, wiping the sweat from his forehead. "There's no way a jury's going to give her seven million. At least I don't think they would. Scars do look bad though...worse than I thought they would," Morgan added as Weed stood silently at the window, staring down at the festival below. "Could have a big influence on a jury, I suppose. Those ugly scars sort of take your mind off everything else. Jury might not hear a thing I tell them."

"She's making them look a lot worse than they are. Anyway, she should have had them repaired a long time ago. You can tell a jury that! And Hileman looks like she's been drinking."

"Yeah, I thought the same thing," Morgan agreed.

"You know that damn smelly dog was in the ER with Hileman the night of the accident? Forgot all about it until now," Weed said. "That stupid dog was running around wild through the ER—contaminating everything with its little black dog hairs. They were everywhere—including my surgical field—probably spent half an hour picking those hairs out of her lacerations, so they wouldn't get infected. You can tell the jury about that, too. Tell the jury that's a big reason the scars look so bad...that she contaminated her lacerations with all the damn dog hairs!"

"Yeah, that's crazy," Morgan said, shaking his head. "Did you ever hear that Hileman was an actress? Was in a couple of movies, I guess, a long time ago?" Morgan asked after a long pause.

"No. I never heard anything like that."

"Yeah, twenty or thirty years ago. I overheard Turzak talking to someone about it. Heard him say that she was a movie star for a while, and he thought he might bring that up at trial. Like maybe how the scars would ruin her acting career...ha!" Morgan said, shaking his head in disbelief. "I mean, she is a pretty good actor,

I guess. "Anyway…I'm going out for a smoke," he muttered before getting up and leaving the room.

Weed stood at the window in the conference room for a while longer and looked out at the festival below, at all the workers and the vendors as they filled their tents with their art.

Now it was certain. He was going to have to deal with a long and embarrassing trial. A trial that was likely to draw even more attention to himself than he had already encountered. More degrading revelations and accusations of how incompetent and uncaring a person he was…for everyone to hear about, he thought. He picked out a person moving through the festival, carrying an armful of paintings…looked like Helen's husband, Frank, Weed thought, just as his cell phone started to vibrate.

Mordy's name came up on the screen. Finally, after waiting all day long, the bastard finally decided to call him back. He didn't need to talk to him now, Weed thought as he put his phone back in his pocket. Then he stood at the window and watched Morgan standing far below, smoking and talking to a small group of men that looked like attorneys.

From the courthouse window he could look out across the festival grounds to the river. He could see all the way to the west end of the city, to one small corner of the apartment building where Candy lived. He would have to call her again later, or maybe just stop by and see her, he thought as he watched the festival activity. Finally, Morgan came back into the room.

"You okay?" Morgan asked as they walked back across to the empty conference room, where they waited until well past four thirty before the judge finally returned.

"Well, what do you think?" the judge asked, looking first at Morgan and then at Weed.

"Well, we feel that the agreement is considerably higher than what we're willing to go for at this time, and we're going to have to decline for now. Our actuary feels that the case is worth—at a maximum—only between two and three million," Morgan stated matter-of-factly.

"That's fine. Didn't think we would come to any kind of settlement today anyway. I thought that this meeting would be, pretty much, a waste of time. But, like I said before, you should seriously consider this offer because they have a strong case, and it could be pretty rough going for you...from what I can see," the judge added as he closed the folder he had in front of him. "I'll tell Hileman's attorneys about your decision. And then I guess I'll see you both Monday morning at nine a.m. in courtroom three. So be prepared for pretrial motions and then opening statements, if we have time. And I don't want this trial to take forever, so keep the objections and motions to a minimum," Judge Wisensee said, pausing for a moment to give Morgan a schedule for the trial, before leaving the room.

"Don't like that bastard," Weed said as they started down the steps of the courthouse. "Supposed to be impartial, but he didn't seem very impartial to me...the way he was cavorting with Hileman and her attorneys."

"Yeah, well, who is impartial in this town? But he's who we're stuck with," Morgan said, stopping at the bottom of the steps. "So review your deposition, get all your answers straight, and I'll see you back here Monday," Morgan said before giving him a slight wave and then walking off down the street.

CHAPTER SEVEN

Friday, May 7
4:52 p.m.

Expected as much, Weed thought as he drove away from the courthouse and toward the Vegas bar to meet Liz.

And, as if his day hadn't been miserable enough, now he had to spend most of the evening acting interested and happy with someone who had lately become very annoying, he thought disgustedly as he continued to wade through the heavy traffic.

He was just going to have a couple drinks with her, eat dinner, and then make up some excuse as to why he had to leave. Wasn't going to fool around and spend the whole night with her, he told himself. After all, it wasn't his fault that their pathetic relationship had evolved into something more serious to her. And he certainly didn't need another pain-in-the-ass relationship to deal with now. Already had two of those.

Their relationship had been a mistake from the start, and it had been dying a slow death since he had started seeing Candy. And he had been trying to find a way to end it without her becoming too emotional…a plan where he could move away from her slowly—one inch at a time, instead of all at once—and then just hope that she didn't get too emotional when she realized that it was over. But, he knew that possibility was remote. At some point he was just going to have to end it, regardless of how badly it hurt her. What made matters worse was that Liz had come up with the crazy idea that he was going to leave Sandy someday and marry her.

Their relationship had just become too burdensome with everything else that was going on in his life.

And anyway, it was getting way too risky to try and hide two relationships from Sandy instead of just one, he thought as he pulled the bottle of bourbon from under his seat and took a drink.

But he certainly didn't need a messy break up to deal with now. He would just have to let it smolder a little while longer until the air cleared, he thought. But when the trial was over and things calmed down, Liz was going to have to be the first item jettisoned, he reassured himself as he pushed open the door to the bar. He looked around for a moment to make sure there was no one there that might recognize him, before moving back to a relatively secluded booth at the back of the bar where Liz was seated.

He gave her a quick kiss on the cheek and then slid into the booth across from her.

"What a day," he said, picking up the drink that she had ordered for him and drinking the whole thing before looking for a waitress to order another. Liz reached across the table and gave his forearm a squeeze.

"No settlement?"

"She doesn't want to settle, I told you. Money doesn't mean anything to her. She just wants to see me suffer and to slowly destroy my life—for some reason. She wants to see me homeless—out in the street like some destitute bum—I guess. And now, I'm not so sure even that would make her happy, or even why she feels she has to crucify me. I mean, so what? So I was a pain in the ass and offended her that night…big deal! I took care of her, didn't I? She could have died! And she's just upset over some petty scars? I don't think so! I think she's crazy! She's some kind of serial psychopath who's made me her cause célèbre…her mortal enemy. Some deep-seated psychological hang-up that she has to resolve, using me as her voodoo doll. That's the only thing that makes any sense. She's a psychotic head case that needs to be locked up in a psych ward. But then, I told you all that a long time ago.

"I think the alcohol has gotten to her brain. You know what she did the whole time we were discussing the case?" he asked rhetorically. "She sat there talking to her mangy mutt. You think that isn't the definition of crazy? Even her attorneys looked at her like she's crazy. And you think they would let me bring a dog into the courthouse? Security would have thrown me in jail," he said, thinking about telling Liz about Hileman having her dog in the ER the night of the accident, but he didn't. He already felt tired of that story.

"I guess I'm responsible for everything bad that has ever happened to her in her miserable life…just like in my miserable life. If the case gets any worse, I'm liable to end up on death row, he added sarcastically, thinking that Liz might laugh, but she didn't.

"I've thought about suing her for defamation or harassment or something for all the money she's caused me to lose…see how she likes it…But Mordy with his great wisdom tells me that that's not possible."

"Yeah, you told me."

"And it's not bad enough that I'll have to be with her every day next week at the courthouse, but then I'll have to be around her at this damn banquet at the country club next Saturday," he added as he looked at the menu. "And I'm sure that the lawsuit will be the main topic of conversation, with Hileman sitting there in her wheelchair at the head table—in front of everyone—with all her scars for everyone to see. Should be fun," he said as the waitress put another drink in front of him.

"And then with all the rumors flying around about how I'm going to lose everything. So I'm sure we'll be the entertainment of the evening. You know how people love dirt like that...a real-life soap opera. People love to revel in the misery of others. Makes them feel good to see someone else suffering. Makes them all feel happy that it isn't them," he continued after they ordered their meals.

"I get the feeling that everyone—including my friends—are actually rooting for Hileman to win. That a lot of my so-called friends want me to lose. That it's all just a source of entertainment for them. A tragic comedy that they can't wait to see play out," he added as Liz shook her head in a gesture of disbelief.

"And I don't think I'm being paranoid," he added as he sipped at his drink. "Mordy's happy, always talking to me about how I should be prepared in case I lose the case. Telling me I should take all my money out of the bank—which there is none left—and all of the valuable items out of my house—which Sandy has already done—so that I will at least have something left when I lose everything. Always telling me about people he knew who this has already happened to, and how bad it was—how destitute they had become. Yeah, a lot of people are anxious to see me lose...to watch me get humiliated and embarrassed, and then lose everything on top of that. It's something innate. I mean, how much more entertainment could there be than to watch someone you know lose everything?" he asked rhetorically.

Liz just sat there and smiled and listened and twirled her straw in her drink.

"And I'll just have to stand there at the banquet and take it all with a big, fake smile on my face and act like I'm happy and that everything is just fine," he added, taking another drink. "I should just dress up like a bum. See what the people's reaction would be then," he said as Liz smiled. "You really learn who your real friends are when something like this happens. I'm betting that most people at the banquet will try to avoid me like the plague…They won't even want to be seen with me—for fear that my misfortune might rub off."

"You can always start over," Liz said after he had stopped talking for a while, but Weed found the words annoying. "You're not happy anyway. This might be your opportunity to start a new life," she told him, but he knew the new life that she was talking about was her being married to him. Knew it wouldn't be long before she got around to his relationship with Sandy. Took her less than twenty minutes, he realized looking at his watch, as they sat in silence for a while and ate.

"Yeah, my life is really coming unraveled," he told her, finishing his drink and holding it up for the waitress to bring him another.

"But I'm tired of talking about it," he added.

When the conversation started back up again, they talked about other things. Mostly about Liz and how well she was doing at some inane course she was taking at the community college to improve her communication skills at work. Weed nodded his head and smiled like he was interested, and at one point tried to determine the number of drinks he'd had, and the relationship drinking might have had on his surgical ability the night of Hileman's accident, as Liz continued on with a story that didn't seem to be going anywhere. He half listened to her for the next thirty minutes, nodding his head and smiling, and half listened to a newscast on the TV behind Liz, before finally telling her about his fictitious early morning case at the hospital.

"We need to get together more often," she said in a somewhat sultry tone and reached across the table to gently squeeze his arm as the waitress brought back Weed's receipt and credit card. "Once this is all behind us, things will be a lot better and we can get our lives back together," she said as she gathered up her sweater and purse.

It was when he was sliding out of the booth to leave that the news being reported on the TV behind him caught his attention. The newscaster had just mentioned something about a shooting in a troubled night spot where one person was in critical condition. Weed caught that much, just as a picture of Tatter's Bar flashed up on the TV screen. The newscaster paused for a long time, as if she had lost her place, before smiling apologetically into the screen and telling everyone that she would be back with the full story after a commercial break.

The words stopped him in his tracks. He knew that the shooting wouldn't go away that easily. Not with his luck.

"Fuck," he mumbled as he jerked Liz's arm and abruptly pulled her back toward the table. "Hold it a minute. I want to see this," he said, sliding back into the booth and turning slightly so he could look directly at the TV screen.

"What?" Liz asked confused, setting her purse back on the table.

"Want to hear what they're saying on the news," he said irritated, trying to come up with a reason why, all of a sudden, he was interested in news about a shooting.

"About that shooting that she was just talking about?"

"Yeah," he repeated, already annoyed with her questioning.

"That's the strip club over on the south side you always hear about in the news, where they're always having trouble," she told him. After a pause she asked him, "Why the interest?"

He mumbled something in her general direction about a patient, who had been shot, being brought to the hospital. He wasn't exactly sure what he had just told her, because he was more irritated that her annoying comments were interfering with his concentration.

He tried to change the topic of conversation and act calm while he waited for the newscast to return, but it seemed awkward and incriminating.

"The owner of Tatter's Bar, Jerome Tatter, was shot last night sometime around eleven p.m. and was admitted to Devine

Providence Hospital in critical condition," Weed listened as the newscaster read from a teleprompter. "The police at this time are unsure of the motive and the police have no leads or witnesses at this time." That's all the information that he could process as he listened nervously. The newscaster's other words seemed foreign and jumbled. "The investigation is still ongoing and the police are urging anyone with any information to contact them at the number on the screen," she announced as a picture of the bar and a phone number appeared behind her.

"Two months ago, I think, the police raided that bar for drugs," Liz said as they both started to leave the booth again.

She was wrong about that, Weed knew. It was because one of the dancers had gotten caught soliciting, he remembered as he tried to calm down and assimilate what he had just heard.

"I remember when the police were trying to close that bar. A church, actually the church I go to sometimes, was upset about all the commotion at the bar, and then there were a bunch of condoms lying outside the church one Sunday morning," she continued as they left the bar to silence and the cool night air.

Her endless prattle about some damn church…made it so that he couldn't concentrate on the story, he thought.

"You're acting so strange tonight," she added as they stood in the parking lot. "You act upset!"

He shook his head that he wasn't; instead, he told her that he was just tired.

"Is it about last week…that you're upset again?" she asked, pausing as they continued through the parking lot. "I mean, things like that happen to everyone. You know that…You even told me. And I'm not worried about it," she said. "Yeah, I know it's frustrating, but you've just been under a lot of stress lately."

How the conversation had transitioned from the shooting at the bar to his inability to perform sexually two weeks earlier, he didn't know, but he was getting even more irritated and pissed at her.

"I don't know why you would bring that up now!"

"I just thought that you still might be upset about it."

"I'm fine! It's fine! Everything works fine! It's just the stress of this whole trial thing. I thought we already resolved that issue," he told her. Then he thought about telling her that maybe she was the reason he hadn't been able to get an erection. That maybe she was responsible. That she didn't excite him anymore; and how could you get an erection with someone you weren't interested in having sex with? But he didn't. He didn't want to talk about an episode of impotency over two weeks ago when he had other more important things to think about.

"Sorry, just forget that I brought it up. It was stupid. Sex really isn't that important in a strong relationship anyway," she added.

How many times had they had good sex, he thought, and she never complained about the one time—two times, actually—that he couldn't perform. And she reasons that he had become some kind of sexual invalid...that he couldn't cut the mustard anymore, he thought as he kissed her on the forehead and then stood on his toes to see where he had parked his car. He was tired of making up excuses for her.

He felt lightheaded thinking about the shooting, and almost stumbled as he walked toward her car.

"You sure you don't want me to drive you home?" she repeated as he opened her car door for her. He gave her a kiss and told her he loved her, before he started back to where his car was parked.

"I could drop you off down the street from your house, or call a cab," she called out to him as he moved away. "You could get your car tomorrow."

"I'll be fine," he said as he searched for his keys.

"You hurt your leg?" she asked as she watched him limping toward his car.

"Just a cramp," he told her as he took a quick look back in her direction.

"Call me," she yelled as he got into his car.

"Give you a call tomorrow," he said smiling. But he wasn't going to call the bitch tomorrow—or ever, as far as he was concerned. She pissed him off. He should just tell her that she was the reason he couldn't get a damn erection that night. See how she liked that. That would surely end their relationship, he imagined as he pulled away slowly, still aggravated at the news he had just heard.

Impotency…a shooting…just add it all to his list.

CHAPTER EIGHT

Friday, May 7
7:34 p.m.

This is bullshit, he thought as he pulled his car into traffic. How could the cops not know what happened? He took out his cell phone and called Candy. There had to have been over twenty people in the bar when the shooting occurred, he knew as he pulled under a streetlight at the side of the road and waited for her to answer.

Now there was still a chance that he might get drawn into some complicated police investigation, he thought, just as Candy answered the phone.

"Ben, I've been trying to get you," she answered.

"What the hell happened last night?"

"At the bar?"

"Yes, at the bar!"

"I guess Tatter got shot."

"I know, but how come the police don't know what happened?" he said, slightly exasperated. "There had to have been almost twenty people in the bar."

"I don't know. I mean, what's the big deal?"

"Didn't Pickles shoot Tatter? I mean, isn't that what happened?" Weed asked.

"Yeah, that's what everyone is saying, but I don't know for sure, because I was backstage getting ready to dance and didn't see a thing. But they didn't arrest him...I do know that...because I just saw Pickles a little while ago riding around on his motorcycle. But that's what everyone's saying happened," she repeated.

"I can't believe the police didn't arrest him. There had to have been plenty of witnesses."

"Well, yeah, but no one's going to say anything to the police, because everyone's afraid of what Pickles might do them. I told you he's crazy, didn't I? I mean, he just got out of jail for shooting someone else, so no one's going to tell the police anything. He would shoot them just like he shot Tatter." He could hear her lighting up a cigarette and then taking a long drag. "Didn't you see anything?" she asked.

"No, I was in the bathroom when it happened. But there were still tons of people in the bar."

"Not when the police got there. Only Pickles and Tatter were still in the bar. At least that's what I heard."

"Someone should just tell the police that it was Pickles. They could arrest him and that would be the end of it. What's the big frikin' deal?"

"Well, then maybe you should."

"I can't get involved. I don't want the police to know I was there. It would look crazy, a surgeon being in a place like that, especially with my trial coming up. I'm supposed to be giving the impression that I'm a clean-living Christian, not a sex pervert at some strip club. People find out about something like this, I'm going to be the laughing stock of the city."

"Yeah, you told me that before," she said, sounding depressed.

"Just make sure that you don't say anything about me being there. If the police start asking you questions, and they might since you work there, don't say a word about me."

"I know. I know. I'm not stupid. You tell me that all the time," she said, now angry. "Makes me feel bad, that's all, that you don't want anyone to know about me. It makes me feel dirty, like I'm just some kind of cheap whore."

"That's not true! You know that's not what I mean. I told you that. It's just that the bar has such a bad reputation. It has nothing to do with you. I love you, and I know you're not a whore. I just don't need anyone knowing about us right now, and I don't need any more problems. Would just be bad timing. Just wouldn't look good for a person in my position to be in a bar like that, right now. When this case is over, then it won't matter. I won't care who knows about us. You know I love you. We have plans together, I told you."

"I know, but it's just the way I feel," she said sulkily.

"With this trial I have to put up a good front and a good image for the public to see, but after the trial it won't matter that much. No one will care then. And that's my best defense in this case: that everyone…especially the jury…thinks that I'm a decent person… that I'm a respected surgeon," he said. "I might lose anyway…But there's no way I can win the case if they find out about something like this."

"I'm no whore."

"I know you're no whore. Did I ever say that you were a whore? I understand your position. I understand about your dancing…that it's an art. And I know that it's been rough for you…more rough on you than it has been on me," he told her, trying to console her as best he could, but thinking that she doeth already protested too much.

"I'm the one that should be worrying now. I don't have a place to dance, and I need the money, and I don't even have any idea when the bar will open up again," she said, pausing halfway to take a deep drag off her cigarette.

"I understand."

"I can't even get my costumes, including that one you like to see me dressed in when we're at my apartment. And how am I supposed to work if I can't get my costumes?" she added without waiting for an answer. "So I'm going to have to find somewhere else to dance, and that's not easy in this perverted town. At least not anywhere I can make this kind of money."

"Yeah, I understand. And don't worry about the money. I can get you some money. That's no problem. You know that. I told you that before. You need money—I can help you out," he said. "You hear anything about how Tatter is doing?" Weed added after a short silence.

"Nikki told me he was just shot once…in the ass. That he turned away when he saw the gun and Pickles shot him in the ass, so I don't think he could be too bad. One of the other dancers saw him in the ambulance, sort of sitting up sideways, and she said he looked okay."

"Who told you that?"

"Nikki."

"Why didn't she tell the police what happened? She was there. And why didn't Tatter say something?"

"I already told you. Everyone's scared shitless, and Pickles already told Nikki to keep her mouth shut and to tell everyone else to keep their mouths shut too. No one's going to say anything, Ben. Everyone's too scared of what he'll do if they say anything. I mean, when he isn't in prison he's in some psych ward somewhere. Even the police are afraid of him."

Damn, he knew something like this was going to happen, he thought before ending the call with Candy.

At least it didn't sound like Tatter was hurt that badly. The shooting wasn't likely to turn into some kind of complicated murder investigation, he imagined hopefully.

Police had to know what happened, though. How could they not? Maybe they were just waiting until they had more evidence to arrest Pickles, he thought. He punched in Mordy's number on his cell phone as he sat in his car at the end of his driveway.

"He's been up in the bathroom...seems like since last fall, Ben," Mordy's wife said when she answered the phone. "A least an hour. Thinks he got some bad food at that new Mexican place down the street...threatening to sue them all. But, I'll have him call you as soon as he gets out. And tell Sandy that I sprayed all the dirt off those lawn chairs that she wanted to borrow for your anniversary party."

"That's great. I'll tell her," he said before he ended the call.

As he walked up the driveway toward his house, he could see Frank and Helen moving around on the back deck, both holding drinks, but neither seemed to notice him as he entered the house.

He had half hoped they would be gone by the time he got home. He didn't want to have to deal with those two idiots, especially after what he had just learned, he thought.

"How'd it go?" Sandy said, coming into the house when she saw him through the window.

"What I expected would happen," he said as Sandy took a drink of her wine. She already looked drunk, he thought. "But I really don't want to talk about it. I've had enough of it for one day," Weed said after Sandy started to ask questions. He finished off the drink Sandy had made for him before he stepped out onto the deck. He tried to act as excited as he could about seeing Helen and Frank, shaking both their hands, smiling, and asking them both how they were doing.

"We've just been talking about the party," Helen said. "I think it's going to be wonderful, and with all the food and decorations, it's going to be the talk of the town."

"The party of the season," Frank added, trying to be amusing, Weed thought.

"Oh, that reminds me. The caterer called, and they told me they're going to be setting up everything on Friday evening," Sandy said while he took a bite of the steak she had made for him. "And the weather's supposed to be warm enough for everyone to swim. This is the menu," Sandy added, handing him a sheet of blue paper. "I ordered extra shrimp and a few more things. If everyone shows up, there should be well over two hundred people, so I want to make sure I have enough food. Did you remember to call the pool man?" Sandy asked as Weed looked at the menu.

"Yeah, they're supposed to be coming out sometime early next week," he lied...He had forgotten all about calling. Would call in the morning, he thought.

"I had to run the hose for almost three hours yesterday to fill it back up. I'm afraid that if the leak gets any worse, we won't be able to keep it filled...And I don't want an ugly hose running across the yard during our anniversary party."

"Wouldn't fit in with the Hawaiian décor," Frank said, making a weak attempt at humor.

"They're going to put the artificial palm trees—like this— around the pool," Helen said, showing Weed the drawing that Sandy had already shown him ad nauseam...and that they'd already had two fights about.

"Yeah, Sandy already showed me." Was excessive and going to cost a bundle, he knew. Twenty thousand dollars for an anniversary party when the marriage was already on the rocks. He didn't have that kind of money to spend—even in good times.

"We've decided to add a limbo contest too," Sandy said.

"And give out gag prizes," Helen said with a laugh. "It was really Frank's idea."

"I didn't think the limbo was a Hawaiian dance," Weed said as he picked a sliced carrot off a tray of vegetables.

"Yeah, it is...I'm almost sure. Might have started somewhere else, but they did it in Hawaii all the time when we were there three years ago. Will be a lot of fun," Frank said but seemed unsure.

"Yeah, we had that discussion already, and I think Frank's right," Sandy insisted. "Helen's going to think up some gag prizes," she continued.

"Yeah, we used to do the limbo when I was in high school. I was pretty good before I injured my back," Frank added.

"We need to let our hair down and let our worries just melt away," Sandy said, bringing him some potato salad on a paper plate as she sort of danced toward him. Now he was certain she was drunk.

"You didn't tell him about the surprise," Helen said.

"Oh, yeah! Frank gave us one of his paintings for our anniversary, and it's beautiful," she said, going off into the house and returning moments later holding a large painting. "I thought we could hang it in the dining room, before the party, so everyone could see it."

Another painting of a cabin by a lake with pine trees, Weed thought, looking at the painting closely as if he was really interested. To Weed, it looked like all of Frank's other paintings. Nothing looked real and the colors were too bright.

"I'm going to hang it in the dining room," Sandy repeated.

"Originally, I painted a dog by the cabin, but I didn't like the way it looked, so I sort of brushed it out and turned it into a tree stump," Frank said, seeming proud of his ingenuity as he took a sip of his drink and pointed to the brown patch on the canvas. Weed thought it looked like a dog-shaped stump.

"You know, dogs aren't easy to paint."

Weed watched the lights and Frank and Helen's image danced in the surface of the pool. He tried to concentrate on what Frank was telling him about the arts festival and where his booth was located. But all he could think of was pushing them both into the pool to join their reflections for a swim.

"You have to bring a sample of your work to the arts committee, and they have to approve it before you can set up a booth at the festival to sell your art," Frank continued. "I don't like that. I think everyone should be able to show their work—no matter what," he continued as Helen moved over closer, since Sandy had gone back in the house. "I mean, art is in the eye of the beholder."

"I wanted to talk to you alone, Ben," Helen said, telling Frank to be quiet for a minute. "I don't know if you have thought about it, but I thought it would be nice if you got Sandy something special for your anniversary," she said. "I know that she's already got something really nice picked for you, and I think that it would help cement your relationship."

"Yeah, I planned to get her something," he said, but he really hadn't thought that much about it and didn't give one damn about what Helen thought. Before he could finish, Helen had gone into the description of a set of diamond-and-pearl earrings that Sandy had already hinted about wanting. Earrings that were way too expensive and that he had already decided he wasn't buying—even if he had the money. He knew the ones, as Helen began to describe them again, just as his cell phone started to vibrate and Sandy came back out of the house carrying more drinks. He passed her on his way back into the house, telling her that the call was from Mordy and taking the drink she had made him off the tray she was carrying.

Weed went into the study and closed the door. He listened to Mordy complain about Mexican food and all his other bowel problems disinterestedly for almost fifteen minutes as he scanned down the fifty-three new e-mails in his mailbox and then set up a time to meet with Mordy in the morning.

"You want to give me some idea what this is about?"

"Just a small personal problem. I'll tell you all about it tomorrow. Probably won't amount to anything."

"It's not about the alcohol issue again?"

"No, it has nothing to do with the trial. And anyway, I think that issue of me drinking the night of the accident is dead."

"Fine. I'll see you at Starbucks at nine, if I'm not dead by then," he said.

Wasn't even sure why he was going to talk to Mordy about the shooting, he thought. Was going to give him a watered-down version of what happened. Would tell him that he had just gone into the bar to meet a friend, and he wouldn't say a word about Candy. Had already, sort of, made up his mind about how he was going to handle the whole situation anyway. He was just going to lay low, keep his mouth shut, and hope that it all just blew over, because he really couldn't risk telling the police that he had been there when the shooting took place. No upside to that. Could only cause potential problems, he imagined…And he didn't actually know what did happen at the bar, or at least he didn't know much. He had seen Pickles and Tatter arguing and had heard the gun shot, but he hadn't actually seen any crime being committed. It was when he deleted a threatening message off his e-mail from Movies Plus about a movie that was six months overdue…that he couldn't find…that he thought about Hileman.

The message made him remember what Morgan had told him about Hileman being in a movie years before. He opened up an actor's website on the computer and typed in Gertrude Hileman's name. He waited a short time before a picture of a movie poster of *Silky's Revenge* came up on the screen: a black man with a huge afro standing on a yacht with a couple of girls dressed liked hippies. The movie had been made in 1978, and the director was Clifford Henry. A low-budget film, set in San Francisco, about a black cop fighting crime, racial injustice, and drug abuse in the late '70s, he read. Then a list of characters followed, including Gertrude Hileman's name. Beside her name, the character she played was listed as Hippy Two. That was funny, he thought. She played a hippy in a movie. Not even the first hippy. She was Hippy Two. Quite a career, he thought. The site also listed her as being in *Silky's Revenge Two.* Two movies listed under her credits. The first movie got one star out of five; the second movie, one star with a minus in front of it. All she had ever been was an unnamed character in a movie with a negative star.

Couldn't believe Hileman was the same person that was pictured on the movie poster. Wasn't a bad-looking woman then, he thought, before clicking on her name and opening another screen with her picture and biography.

So that was her fabulous acting career, he thought as he read the bio under her picture.

Gertrude S. Hileman. Hometown: Pittsburgh, PA. Birth date: January 22, 1952, he read. She had attended Carnegie Tech School of Fine Arts, but it didn't say whether she had graduated. Then beneath that, it was listed that she was the great granddaughter of Clifford D. Hileman, founder of Hileman's Mustards, noted worldwide for its fifty-six varieties of flavored mustards. She had been one of the Hilemans' Babies, with her picture appearing on over sixty million mustard jars, the bio stated.

That was hilarious, he thought. That's who he had been fighting with that night and for the last two years. A spaced-out hippy whose picture was on millions of jars of mustard, he thought, collapsing the screen. Would have to tell Morgan what he had learned, he thought as he went back out onto the deck, just as Frank and Helen were starting their dessert.

"You should see the dress that Sandy's going to wear to the Spring Fling. It's beautiful, and the shoes...are what really set it off," Helen said as they all continued to drink. "I just wish that I could be there."

"Yeah, should be a real spectacle," Weed said sarcastically.

"Sounds like it's really going to be a lot of fun, and Frank and I are thinking about applying for membership next year," Helen said with her mouth half filled with a forkful of salad.

"Frank thought that it might be a good idea to get some influential people interested in his artwork. Would be nice if he could get a show at the art center, and the only way you can do that is if you know someone. He's on their list, but the list is pretty long. Might be two years before he can show his paintings...and then only ten, max. I'm sure people would realize what a talent he is, if he could only break the ice," she said. "That's how Andy Warhol started...a few people liked his work, and I'm sure Frank is every bit as talented as Warhol. I mean, Brillo pads?"

He thought that she looked drunk too as she awkwardly cut into a cupcake with a knife that was too big, while he wondered how long they had all been drinking.

"I don't know about that," Frank said.

"Warhol was a fluke," Sandy said, laughing inappropriately before realizing that she might have offended Frank. "You know that Ben operated on one of his brothers?" she added, changing the subject.

"Yeah, you told me that once, I think," Frank said, stepping back to view what he had just painted.

Weed sat at the table and drank and listened to them talk about the country club and the Spring Fling and what they had been doing to get ready for the anniversary party as Frank explained some nonsense about his painting technique.

Wished it was that easy to change things in real life, Weed thought, amused...thinking about what he would paint out of his life...whom he would turn into a stump, he thought. Then he laughed unexpectedly, an inappropriate gesture to the others, who looked at him strangely.

For almost an hour they talked about the anniversary party they were having in two weeks, before they all picked up their dirty dishes and carried them back into the house. It was almost eleven o'clock before Helen and Frank decided to leave. They all stood around the pool holding hands with their heads bent as Frank said a long, painful prayer, ending with tears in his eyes. Weed watched them as they slowly walked down the driveway, with long shadows in front of them, got into their car, and waved though the front window as they drifted away into the night.

"They're one weird couple," he said when they were almost out of sight.

"You still pissed about that thing Helen said about you being emotionally empty? Because she didn't mean anything, and anyway, she apologized, so let it go," she answered, but he didn't say anything else. He was too tired to fight and had other problems on his mind. Besides, no one could talk him out of thinking that they were weird.

"You think that we're going to lose?" she said going up the steps behind him.

"Don't know."

"I guess it would be sort of funny, if it wasn't happening to us," she said, laughing almost hysterically.

She'd had too much to drink and she was obnoxious. She always got that way when she was drunk, Weed knew.

"That's what I wanted to tell you," Sandy said at the top of the steps. "Bob called and wanted me to remind you about the basketball game you have in the morning," she said as they both went into the bedroom. "I really don't understand why you have to play basketball when you have a ten-thousand-dollar set of golf clubs just sitting in the closet," she said as they changed. "Some kind of macho thing?" she asked, but Weed remained silent.

"We spent all that money at the country club on a membership, and you go to the YMCA," she said as she lay down beside him in bed. "We should just drop our membership."

"Yeah, probably," he said, not really concentrating on what she was saying. She continued to fret over where she could hang Frank's painting, so that the fewest number of people would see it, and at the same time, not offend Frank and Helen.

Maybe talking to Mordy was a bad idea, he thought. His advice was mostly useless, and he always ran the chance that Mordy would open his big, fat mouth and tell someone...even though he always made a big deal out of how all their conversations were confidential. And he didn't like the way Mordy seemed to actually enjoy his misery. And then there was Pickles...If he did go down and talk to the police, Pickles might find out about it and hunt him down... making the situation even worse than it already was.

Might just call off the meeting with Mordy, he thought as he shut his eyes and watched the room spin in his head. He thought about saying a prayer as he lay there in bed...even though he was never a strong believer. He wasn't even a very weak believer, but then, he didn't ignore any option that might help him get out of his complicated situation. Pretty difficult to trick the omnipotent—the omniscient—he imagined...a prayer to get you off the hook. But then again, there wasn't much of a down side...nothing to lose at this point, he figured.

Maybe all his problems were just payback from God, for all the bad things he had done in his life. That God had just been keeping a tab on him, and it was time to pay the bill. That's what his mother would tell him. That was, pretty much, her answer for everything bad that had happened in his life, he knew. That all his problems could be traced back to the fact that he just hadn't spent enough time in church, he thought as Sandy finally seemed to have finished her disjointed tirade.

"Did you know Gertrude Hileman was in two movies...years ago?" he asked Sandy after he had run out of other things to think about. "*Silky's Revenge,* and *Silky's Revenge Two,*" he said, laughing and then telling her that Hileman's attorneys were concerned that the scars might ruin her acting career. "What a bunch of bullshit. Hippy Two...didn't even have a name in the movie," he said to Sandy's back, but he could hear the deep rhythmic breathing of sleep...just before she suddenly rolled toward him and spoke, as if she had not heard a word he said but had known what he had been thinking about.

"Did you remember to get your mother flowers for Mother's Day?"

He hadn't thought about it once all day. "I'll get them tomorrow," he told her.

Maybe the worst day in his life, he thought. Of all the tens of thousands of days he had lived, this may have been the worst, he thought as he finally drifted off to sleep.

CHAPTER NINE

Saturday, May 8
7:37 a.m.

Weed picked up the phone and held it to his ear before he realized it was the alarm clock that was ringing.

"What's going on?" Sandy said, sitting up in bed.

"I don't know. Must have been dreaming," he said, trying to gather his bearings. He hung up the phone and then turned off the alarm.

"I have my game today?" he said, more as a question than a statement, as he tried to clear his mind of the dream he had just had, and to determine if he was right, that this day in his life was a Saturday.

"It's too early," Sandy said leaning forward, taking hold of the clock beside her bed and pulling it close to her face so she could see the time. "Bob said the game was at eleven o'clock, and it's only seven," she said setting the clock back down on the nightstand.

"Yeah, I know, but I want to get there early to warm up," he said as he watched her walk across the bedroom and into the bathroom. "It's the finals for the Over Fifty League. If we win today, we get to play next Saturday for the championship," he told her, but he wasn't really sure why. He knew she wouldn't be interested.

"Whoopee," he could hear her mumble sarcastically from inside the bathroom.

He stood in front of the mirror as he put on his basketball jersey and shorts and then stuffed a change of clothes into his gym bag before lacing up the tennis shoes. Sandy had gotten them as a replacement pair for the shoes she had thrown out three weeks earlier, telling him that it had just been an accident. She hadn't realized that they "meant that much" to him, she said—in her sarcastic tone—even though she did know. But it hadn't been an accident, he was certain of that. She had thrown them away on purpose, to get back at him for some reason, but for what he wasn't sure.

And he hadn't played well since. Somehow, the new shoes had thrown off his game. They made him feel like he was out of balance. It pissed him off thinking about it. He had even gone as far as searching a smelly dumpster—at three in the morning, for almost an hour—to try and find them. Funny thing was that he'd had a premonition that she might throw them out.

Sandy was that kind of person. He knew that was her nature: impulsive and revengeful, anything to make his life more miserable. And he was just as certain that—somehow—he was going to pay her back. He was going to do something to piss *her* off, as much as she had pissed *him* off. Then he could walk around acting like he didn't have a clue why she was so upset, like she did to him, and tell her he "didn't realize it meant so much" to her. See how she liked it! He just hadn't come up with any good ideas as to what he was going to do—yet.

"Don't forget, we have reservations at the Villa at seven," Sandy said as she climbed back into bed and rolled toward the wall, before adding that she needed the car and not to forget the flowers for his mother. "And you'd better just pick them up. They won't deliver them this late," she added.

"Yeah, I guess. Have too much on my mind to worry about getting flowers for my mother," he mumbled. "She won't appreciate them anyway. They'll just remind her of how disappointed she is that I'm her son," he said, still looking in the full-length mirror at his shoes and thinking how out of place they looked. "She'll probably think that I'm just rubbing it in. That I'm making fun of her for having such a shit son."

"Well, she doesn't like 'the whore that broke up your first marriage' either, but you'd better get her something, anyway. And I'll bet you—right now—that she finds some excuse for not coming to our anniversary party," Sandy mumbled, her speech trailing off as she adjusted her pillow.

"Just as well," Weed said as he headed downstairs and into the kitchen.

Weed scanned the morning newspaper quickly but couldn't locate any articles about either the shooting or his trial, so he looked through the paper a second time, just make sure.

Maybe the shooting was no big deal. Not even worthy enough to report, he thought as he made coffee. Then he took two Percodan for the pain in his knee and put two more in his pocket for later.

There were low-lying clouds and a chill in the air when he left the house. He drove through light Saturday traffic toward the downtown section of the city and the Starbucks where he was supposed to meet Mordy. He didn't really want to tell Mordy too much. Mordy knew Sandy too well and already knew too much about his personal life, he thought as he pulled into a parking space across from Starbucks. As Weed walked across the street to enter the café, he could see Mordy sitting at a table inside, reading the newspaper and drinking coffee.

"Could you make this quick, Ben? I've got a full day and I've got to run pretty quick," Mordy said as Weed sat down across from him at the table.

"Yeah, yeah, no big deal. Won't take a minute, but I thought that you handled things like this when you first started and thought maybe you could tell me what you think."

"Yeah, no problem," he said as he bit into his donut and then took another sip of coffee.

"Yeah, well you know how bad my luck has been lately. Everything I do turns to shit. I'm almost embarrassed to tell you..." Weed said, smiling and shaking his head in disbelief, trying to find the words. "But anyway, last week I went into this bar to meet a friend, almost out of the blue, almost a coincidence that I'm there, but while I'm in the bar it just so happens—and this is the crazy part—someone actually gets shot! Can you believe that?" Weed said, waiting for Mordy to say something. "Can you believe that? Like I don't have enough trouble. Scared the hell out of me. You know, I'm just sitting there, minding my own business—and bang—I hear this loud gunshot...could hardly hear anything after that, it was so loud."

Mordy shook his head as he listened, with maybe a slight smile on his face, Weed thought.

"But anyway, I jumped up and got the hell out of the bar as fast as I could. Just ran out the back door...didn't ask questions...just jumped in my car and left. Didn't actually know what really happened. Just knew I had to get the hell out of there. Scared the crap out of me," Weed said smiling nervously and taking a drink of coffee, blankly looking at a section of the newspaper as if he were not that concerned about what he had just told Mordy.

"That's really crazy!" Mordy finally said with a look of disbelief.

"So I was in my car driving home, still shaking like a leaf and not really knowing what the hell just happened, sort of disoriented about the whole incident, but thinking that maybe I should just pull over and call the police or something. Even picked up my cell phone and started to dial 911. But that's when I started to think that maybe calling the police wasn't such a good idea, you know? I have all this other stuff going on with the trial right now, and I don't need to make it worse by getting involved with some criminal investigation. Instead, I thought that maybe I should just keep driving, and try not to get involved. That if I get involved it might look really bad…you know, with everything else going on. That somehow it might find its way into the newspaper—that I was in the bar or I was a witness or something. You know, that somehow I might get drawn into some kind of complicated police investigation," Weed said as he looked at Mordy for his reaction. "But now I'm having second thoughts. Last night on the news they said that the police were looking for witnesses. So…I'm thinking that maybe it would be better to just contact the police and tell them I was there, but that I don't know anything…and then hope that will be the end of it."

"Yeah, that is pretty crazy. I mean, you could have been shot! And I see what you mean about getting involved with something like that now. Just wouldn't look good when you're trying to maintain an image with this trial coming up…and then too about that alcohol thing with the trial and you're in a bar…wouldn't look good, if you know what I mean. You don't need any distractions or any more controversy right now," he said and paused for a moment. "But yeah, I see what you're concerned about. Could be a problem, I imagine…" Mordy said, sitting back in his chair and looking off in the distance as if he were in deep thought. "Weren't there other witnesses in the bar that could talk to the police?" Mordy asked after a long pause.

"Yeah, there were, but by the time the police got there, they all did the same thing I did. They all just sort of panicked and left the bar."

"Yeah, that happens," Mordy said, shaking his head in agreement. "No one wants to get involved anymore—with anything—and anyway, with the guy still in the bar with a gun—it only makes sense to leave," Mordy said before asking Weed where the shooting occurred.

"Just some little dive over on the south side, which I probably shouldn't even have been near. Just bad luck…one night…and I had to pick that night to be there," Weed answered.

"South side," Mordy said as if the words had caused him to remember something, as he grabbed for the newspaper that was lying beside him. "Was that the shooting that happened over at that bar at the end of Carson Street…where they're always having trouble?" Mordy asked as he started looking through the newspaper. "Just read about a shooting over there. That's not the shooting you're talking about, is it?" Mordy asked but continued on before Weed could answer. "Yeah, here's the article…Tatter's Bar. That the name of the place?" Mordy asked, looking over at Weed.

"Yeah, that's the place," Weed answered somewhat reluctantly, trying to look over the edge of the newspaper Mordy was holding, pissed at himself for not seeing the article earlier.

"You have to be kidding? I just read all about that shooting before you got here. That's hilarious," Mordy said sort of laughing. "I mean, just being in that bar is bad enough, but the whole story sounds pretty crazy. Hell, whatever possessed you to go into that bar, anyway?" Mordy asked, still acting amused.

"Yeah, don't ask. Just bad luck, I guess," Weed said, somewhat upset that Mordy thought it was funny.

"But I see what you mean. That bar has the worst reputation in the city. Police are always in there arresting someone for drugs or prostitution or a fight or something else. Hell, I think there was a shooting in there last year. But I see why you're concerned. You can't have the public finding out about something like this when you have this trial going on. A story like this would destroy your reputation. They'd label you as some kind of sex pervert or a drug addict or something worse. Not to mention what it would do to your personal life. What the hell were you doing there, anyway?" Mordy asked again, but Weed didn't answer as he continued to try and read the article. "I mean, it probably doesn't really matter why you were there, since there is no good explanation," Mordy continued, still acting somewhat amused.

"Jesus, Mordy! Can you just stop for a minute? I can't concentrate," Weed said as he tried to take in what he was reading. "And I just went in to see someone. Is there a law against that?" Weed said. "It was just bad timing. Bad luck," he said, but couldn't concentrate at all, so he slid the newspaper aside. "And to tell you the truth, Mordy, it's nobody's damn business why I was there," Weed said disgustedly as he took a sip of coffee.

"There's no good explanation anyway, Ben. No one would believe you. You could have been in there on a religious retreat. You could have even been in there with Jesus and it wouldn't matter. Everyone's going to draw their own conclusions as to why you were in there...and basically...none of them will be good," Mordy said. "They'll all just naturally think you're some kind of pervert with a drug problem."

"Well, it's like this, Mordy, if it really matters. I went into the bar to see one of the girls that dances in there—nothing illegal. No drugs. No prostitution. She dances in there; she's not a prostitute. And yeah, we're friends, but it's mostly just that...not what you think. She was a patient of mine a while back, and she asked me to stop in some night...a long time ago. And that's it—nothing sinister. That a reasonable explanation?"

"Fine. Sounds about as reasonable as anything else."

"And like I told you...of all the nights, I had to pick that night to go into that bar. Not like I hang out there every night of the week. I just got unlucky."

"Yeah, I understand. But considering...It is a pretty ridiculous story. Especially with all this other stuff you've got going on...And then something like this happens to you? But you probably did the right thing—leaving before the police got there. You don't legally have to tell the police anything. And there's no law against leaving a crime scene if you're not involved. And if you do give a statement, it becomes part of the public record. So...I don't think I would talk to them now, either. There's just too much of a chance that some nosey reporter down at the police station might find out, take it, and run with it. When someone like *you* gets caught in a place like *that*, especially when you're already front-page news...that kind of story just screams to have a reporter find out about it. Something to add even more interest to this trial than there already is—if that's possible," he said looking at his watch and taking a sip of coffee. "No, I would keep my mouth shut and lay low. The police will eventually figure it out, and hopefully it will be before you have to get involved or long after the trial is over," he said impatiently and looked at his watch again. "I mean, your chances are pretty good that you won't have to get involved. After all, it is just another shooting. Shootings happen all the time in this city. No big deal. But, I would tell that girl that you went in to see to keep her mouth shut about you being there. Because if she starts talking, it won't be long before they come looking for you."

"Yeah, I already did that."

"Good. So just lay low and hope that it all blows over or that nothing comes of it. Easy. Simple. You know, it's just another shooting," he repeated as he continued to clean off the table. "But Ben, I can't guarantee anything. These kinds of things seem to have a life of their own, and you never know where they're headed. Police might already know that you were there, and you might have to get involved anyway. Couple more days go by with nothing—maybe then you'll be out of the woods. And one other thing, Ben," he said as he stopped what he was doing. You have to hope this guy doesn't die, because if he dies and it turns into a homicide investigation, then all bets are off. If that happens, the police will be all over the place asking questions...And according to the article, he doesn't sound all that great. Listen Ben, I know it's none of my business, but you have to consider the devastation this would wreak on your personal life. Ben, if people learned you were in that bar... Sandy's going to flip if she finds out. She's already on the edge with this trial. And with all this marriage counseling you two have been through...I imagine she'll leave and take everything with her—if she finds out. A judge would give her everything...at least everything Hileman's attorneys don't get," Mordy said, pausing to drink the last of his coffee. "And then, Ben, with you being in a bar when your drinking problem is already a big issue at the trial...that won't be good," he said shaking his head.

"I think that issue has been resolved."

"Was resolved," Mordy corrected him. "And you ever consider that the state might pull your license over something like this? They've been pretty strict lately...with all the problems they've had," he said. "But those are issues for another day, I guess, because I've gotta run," he said as he started toward the door. "Please don't do anything rash. Hopefully this will all blow over, eventually...And let me know," he said pointing his finger at Weed. "Call me if anything happens. I want to know about it," he said, moving away from the table but turning back toward Weed when he was halfway out the door.

"Which girl was it, anyway?" Mordy asked, turning back again as if he had just remembered something important. "The girl? Which one of the strippers was it who you went in to see?" he repeated when Weed didn't answer. "Wasn't that redhead with the big tits whose picture's always in the newspaper, was it?" he asked, realizing too late that Weed was pissed at the question and then continuing through the door without waiting for an answer.

Weed sat at the table after Mordy left and read the article again. This time, he read it more slowly. He was disturbed—somewhat—by the description that Pickles had apparently given the police of the person who—he said—robbed the place. Description could have been almost anyone, but it sounded like it could have been him too.

It pissed him off thinking about it—that maybe Pickles had given the police his description just to cover his own ass, Weed thought. Should just go down to the police station and tell them exactly what happened. Didn't care what happened—or what Pickles did. Would get a gun of his own if he had to, he thought, stuffing the newspaper into a trash can as he left.

CHAPTER TEN

Saturday, May 8
10:48 a.m.

He hadn't even thought about the possibility that he could be considered a suspect. Sort of alarming, he thought, that the police might actually think he could have something do to with the shooting. But he was probably just overreacting, since it didn't really make much sense. And the description that Pickles had given the police was pretty vague, he thought as he drove toward the YMCA. He wasn't going to worry about it now, he told himself, even though he was having trouble forcing it from his thoughts.

Mordicah's advice was never much help. Still wasn't sure why he even talked to Mordy. Didn't even really trust him all that much, and didn't like it that Mordy thought what happened to him was funny. He didn't like that he asked him about the stripper, either. Pissed him off...considering how long they had supposedly been friends...and how much free medical advice he had given him over the years…and all the money he had paid him for his crappy legal advice, he fumed as he drove.

At least the basketball game would take his mind off his problems for a while, he imagined. At least for the next couple hours he could do one of the few things left in his life that he still somewhat enjoyed…one of the few things from his youth that still got him excited…and that made him feel young again. He imagined himself being a young player…with beautiful cheerleaders cheering him on…screaming…fascinated, enamored with how well he played. Just a fantasy…But that's pretty much all he had left to go on now—fantasies…and the leftovers of his youth, he thought as he contemplated taking another Percodan. He held the pill, rolling it in his fingers a couple times before popping it in his mouth and washing it down with a sip of bourbon from the bottle underneath his seat.

His knee was throbbing badly, and as he pulled out into traffic, he noticed that the car radio was still playing…even though he had turned it off. Still stuck on the same staticky station from the day before…with the same newscaster…giving what sounded like the same news even after he had turned it off, but now with the news about the shooting at Tatter's. Scratching…fading in and out…annoying, he thought. Again, he tried unsuccessfully to turn the radio off. The crappy car had taken on a life of its own…Christine—the car from the Stephen King novel—he thought, somewhat amused at the possibility.

He turned down a narrow street that ran behind the YMCA, barely missing an ambulance going in the opposite direction with its lights flashing.

Inside the large brick building, someone had draped a banner across the entrance to the gym. It was torn and unreadable now… something about the YMCA's Over 50 Men's Basketball Tournament. Looked like someone had made it on a cheap, outdated home computer, with a printer that was about out of ink, Weed thought. He pushed the banner up and out of the way so he could enter the stairway to the gym.

There were players on both sides of the gym and just a few spectators in the bleachers. A small group of players were standing around a man rolled up in a fetal position in the middle of the court. The man was sort of rocking rhythmically back and forth, moaning and holding his leg, Weed could see as he entered the gym.

"You hurt your knee?" Bob Seymour asked, turning his head to a better angle of Weed's knee as he approached, before asking him if Sandy told him he had called.

"Yeah, hit it on the damn door a couple days ago," he told him, before asking him what was going on with the guy who was lying on the court.

"Guy always gets leg cramps...on the Green team. You know him...They call him Charlie Horse. Now they can't get him off the court."

"Yeah, I know who he is," Weed said, leaning back on the bleachers and retying the laces tighter. This time he hoped they would feel more like his old shoes.

"Could have used you a little while ago too. That guy, Jenkins—from the Blue Team we're probably going to play next week for the championship—broke his ankle...came down wrong...made a big, loud crack...And it looked like the bone might have come right out through the skin. Said they could hear it breaking clear downstairs. Made everyone about half sick. Ambulance just took him away," Bob said as Weed stood and started running in place, trying to loosen up his knee. "But at least it's good news for us, since he was the best player on their team...And I don't think they can win without him," he said as they both sat and watched the finish of the first game.

The players moved pathetically up and down the court like a heard of aged buffalo, he thought. He had become one of them, Weed realized, somewhat mesmerized and amazed that he had just now made that observation. His youth was slipping away while he had been napping.

Weed shot around with the other players on their team for almost an hour before their game started and then played for most of the game. He played a little better than the week before, but not that much better, he thought. He'd made a few good shots and hadn't made any really bad plays...But the game didn't seem to be as exciting as usual...and worse...He hadn't been able to take his mind off any of his other bullshit problems. Couldn't quit thinking about the shooting and what Mordy had said...or Hileman and the trial...or Sandy and the house and wondering what she might remove next and how shitty it had been that she had thrown his shoes away...or Liz and Candy...or even his mother and what she would think about her crap son being caught in a sleazy strip bar. It all seemed like a jumble of thoughts. Once he cleared one thought, another sprang forward. The only thing the game accomplished was to cause his knee to get twice as big and to hurt twice as much...with the damn shoes making it even worse, he thought.

When the game ended he was limping badly, and he had run out of Percodan. It took him twice as long to change. He half listened to his teammates and how excited they were about winning... patting each other on the back...telling players from the other team how well they played...saying that the only reason that their team won was because of luck and a couple of bad shots their team had taken...then laughing and talking about all the great plays they had made. It was hard to recognize the game they were describing as the one he had just played in, Weed thought. Just another great victory, he thought sarcastically, as he gingerly pulled his pants up and over his knee.

Afterward, the players on his team slowly spilled out of the building and moved down the street to a bar where they all normally celebrated with eating and drinking. Their real reward for winning...maybe their real reason for playing, he thought as he limped after them.

Weed sat and drank and thought more about his problems as the other players continued to talk about the game...almost ad nauseam: the mistakes, the good plays, the great plays, how bad the other team was, how they could improve for next week's game... until they ran the analysis of the game into complete nothingness. Was hard to believe that such a meaningless game could generate so much meaningless conversation...He felt like telling them but didn't. Instead, he wondered what Pickles would do if he did turn him in to the police.

There were more drinks and conversations about next week's game, and about the defense they were going to use, and about the player who had broken his ankle...But the more he had to drink, the more difficult it became to concentrate. The conversation turned to the game that was being shown on the three big-screen TVs in the bar as the waitress brought drinks, fish sandwiches, complimentary bowls of nuts and potato chips, and more drinks. But it all seemed pretty fuzzy with the alcohol and the residual effects of the Percodan.

It was almost an hour before the victory celebration seemed to come to an abrupt end...Apparently, no one could think of anything else to say. Their self-appointed captain stood and tapped on his beer glass with a plastic spoon to get everyone's attention. He announced that the team was going to have a special practice before next week's championship game, and that the team next week would be a lot more difficult to beat, even without the player who had broken his ankle...all bullshit, Weed knew. The captain reminded everyone to try and get to the gym a half hour early for warm ups, before they all got up and left the bar, going off in different directions.

"Trial Monday?" Bob Seymour asked as they walked down the street together.

"Yeah, it's driving me crazy...Half the time I don't even care what happens. Sometimes I think that I would just as soon lose the case. Get me out of this miserable life I'm living. If I lose, I have this idea that I might give up my practice...maybe just move back to the old neighborhood...with my mother, if I have to. Sandy will probably be long gone by that time, especially if the money's gone," Ben said half jokingly as they walked along the street toward his car. "You know, like it used to be, when we were growing up there...not a care in the world...everything fresh and exciting," he said as they stopped beside the car. "Even if I win, I might give it all up...It's just that, if I lose, then I'll have a legitimate reason for giving it all up."

"Yeah, I think you told me that before," Bob said.

"Could get a job with you at the Quick Fix...I mean, you always have your Help Wanted sign out."

"Yeah, well, I know what you're saying, but it's just as bad over here," Bob said, lighting up a cigarette. "My life's miserable too. Wife's never happy, always pissed off about something...me working at the Quick Fix when I'm fifty-four...not making enough money... tells me it's a job for a teenager just starting out...not a job for a grown man...and she's probably right. Have to deal with customers that clog toilets with half-eaten burritos...and no one will dig them out but me. You think that's such a great life?" he said, taking a deep drag off his cigarette. "You think I wouldn't bolt if I had the chance? Just pick up and leave if I could? You think I haven't thought about it? I think about it all the time, but it's not that easy...I figured that out a long time ago. Always some catch. Always something pulling you back in...just like that movie...every time I think I'm out... something keeps pulling me back in. There's always a catch, Ben," he repeated. "At least you had a life. I've been stuck at some lousy convenience store for the last fifteen years."

"*Had* a life's right...but not anymore...I was never meant to be someone relatively important with a relatively respectable occupation," Weed said after a long pause. "I was never smart enough to do anything complicated like that. I just worked harder than everyone else, that's all. All to prove to everyone that I wasn't just a plain old garden-variety loser...like most people thought...even though I was...and never realized it until now. If I was smart, I wouldn't be in this mess. Even morons can be successful...if they try hard enough," Weed added.

"Yeah, well, you'll be okay once this lawsuit thing is over," Bob said, glancing at his watch. "You just hit a rough patch. When this is over, you'll be fine...couple months, no one will remember anyway...You'll be back to your old self," he said as he started to move a little further down the street. "But I'd better get going before Kim sends out the police to find me."

"Sandy wanted me to ask you if you're comin' to the anniversary party."

"Yeah, we'll all be there. I'll be there after work, but Kim's going to come earlier with the kids. They want to swim. Kim says that we're all supposed to bring our suits and dress up like Hawaiians?"

"Yeah, Sandy's idea."

"Yeah, sounds like fun...kids will have fun...maybe take your mind off the trial." Then after a short pause, Bob asked Weed if he wanted to shoot around tomorrow afternoon, and that maybe they could get in on one of the games at the park.

"Yeah, maybe...if my knee loosens up. I'll stop by after church," Weed said, losing his balance and then catching himself on the car.

"You think you're okay to find your way home?"

"Which way?" Weed asked, trying to be funny by acting confused about which way he should go.

Weed sat in the car and watched out his front windshield as Bob slowly disappeared down the street, feeling somewhat envious of Bob's relatively uncomplicated life.

CHAPTER ELEVEN

Saturday, May 8
6:16 p.m.

Weed's vehicle bumped into the car in front of him—lightly—as he pulled his car into the street and started the short drive home—feeling pretty inebriated. He drove past Sally's Gift Shop before remembering what Sandy had said about getting flowers for his mother for Mother's Day. He circled back around and pulled into a parking spot in front of the store.

Would just get her a card and some flowers like he usually did… nothing fancy, he thought as he pushed open the front door of the store. He looked around at the few, meager flower arrangements they had left. After he found one that looked okay, he moved over to the greeting-card aisle. Wasn't much of a selection left to pick from—this late, he thought. All the funny cards, like he usually got for her, were gone or didn't have an envelope. "From Your Adoring Son," one card read in big red letters across the front. He didn't really like how it sounded, but it was the only one left with an envelope to fit, and it didn't sound totally unbelievable. And anyway, he wasn't going to drive all over town to find something better, he thought, standing at the checkout counter as the clerk rang him up.

"Those are beautiful," the clerk said as he paid. But he knew she was thinking about what a big jerk he was for buying flowers that had already started to wilt and some ridiculous-looking card.

He was putting the flowers in the backseat of the MG when he caught the reflection of a sign in his car window: Half-Priced Books and DVDs, it read. He stood there for a minute looking at the sign, trying to make up his mind if he even wanted to walk the length of the parking lot to see if they had the DVD of the movie Hileman had been in. He was almost certain that nobody in the store would have even heard of a movie called *Silky's Revenge*, he thought as he scanned the posters in the window while he walked toward the store.

He still had time to kill before he had to be home...and the later he was, the more pissed off Sandy would be...just a little more payback for his shoes, he thought. Didn't really want to go to dinner with the Petersons anyway and listen to Carl drone on about some nursing home insurance that he had been trying to sell them for the last six months. Peterson was probably the only human being in the town who—apparently—didn't realize that he didn't have any money to buy any goddamned nursing-home insurance, he thought as he walked toward the video store. And he wouldn't buy it even if he did have the money.

He could at least see if anyone in the store had heard of the movie. Might be interesting to watch. See what kind of career he had "potentially" destroyed, he thought. Might even be able to bring it up at the trial somehow...make some sarcastic comment about her pathetic acting career, he thought as he looked through the racks of old DVDs.

"You ever heard of a movie named *Silky's Revenge?*" Weed finally asked one of the clerks who was walking by, carrying a handful of DVDs.

"I think, maybe," she said to his surprise as she put down the discs she was holding and began shuffling through a rack of DVDs. "I think that's the movie with Gertrude Hileman in it...You know, the Hileman baby," she either asked him or told him, he wasn't sure. She stopped for a second and then started looking though another section of DVDs. "It's sort of a cult classic. You know, like *The Rocky Horror Picture Show* movie. But, if we don't have it, we might be able to order it in from another store," she said as she continued to look. "No, I don't think..." she said, and then paused before pulling a DVD from the rack and holding it out in front of her. "Huh, I was wrong... here it is! Well...It's not *Silky's Revenge*, this is *Silky's Revenge II*," she said, starting to put it back in the rack before he stopped her.

"No, that one will do," he said as he took the DVD and then followed her to the checkout line to pay.

"I've never actually watched it the whole way through, but they say it's better than *Silky I*," she said, handing it back to him in a bag after ringing him up.

Sandy was sitting in the living room, in a robe with her hair in curlers and her makeup half on, drinking a glass of wine and reading a magazine when he entered the house.

"Bastards cancelled...Can you believe it?" she said when she noticed him. "Said that Marge wasn't feeling good...After I spent half the afternoon getting ready. Pretty damn inconsiderate...He could have called earlier," she huffed. "He didn't even try to apologize. Planned it three weeks ago, and he calls two hours before and says she's got the flu," she told him as she took a drink of wine and turned the page in the magazine. "I think they just don't want to be seen with us—in public. And to think just a year ago we wouldn't have even considered having dinner with those losers," she added. "Last time I try to do something nice for a bunch of losers."

"He just wanted to sell us an insurance policy anyway," he said, setting the card and flowers on the table. "I guess news travels slow in the insurance business."

"What?" she asked, confused. She'd already had too much to drink, he could tell. She was mumbling unintelligible comments—like she did when she was drunk. He found another Percodan and popped it in his mouth.

"There's a pizza on the way," she continued as she finished her glass of wine and then emptied what was left of the bottle into her glass.

"Probably the worst game I ever played…thanks for asking," he mumbled but wasn't sure if she heard. The words seemed to dissolve in the air before they got to her.

"All day long about the shoes…the magic shoes…knew that it would be my fault," she said after a long pause. "To tell you the truth, I think that it's all in your head…about some old shoes making you play better. And I told you, they smelled," she said as the doorbell rang. "It's only a game, Ben, and you don't need to win every game. So what's the big deal?" she said as she opened the door to a man wearing a Friendly's Pizza hat and holding a pizza box.

"We've got all these problems. We're going to lose the house, and you're worried about some stupid baseball shoes that I accidently threw out." She snorted, handing the confused man a twenty-dollar bill and telling him to keep the change. "I told you, you were too old to play that game. Every time you have a game, I have to listen to you whine and moan about something you twisted or turned or bumped. Just like your damn knee now. You're too *old* to play that game anymore. That's for *young* people to play," she said as she set the pizza box on the table beside the flowers.

"Those the best they had?" she asked, looking at the flowers on the table and then taking a slice of pizza out of the box. "That's what happens when you wait until the last minute…You get what no one else wanted…or what someone brought back to the store."

"Yeah, well, that's the best they had," he told her as she picked up the DVD.

"*Silky's Revenge II.* What the hell is this?" she asked holding the DVD in front of her. "Don't think I ever heard of it."

"That's one of the movies Hileman was in that I told you about. One of the girls on the front cover is her...I think she's the one on the left, but I'm not sure," he said peering over her shoulder. "Thought I'd watch it...for laughs!" he said, taking a piece of pizza.

"Pizza and a movie...who could ask for more..." she said sarcastically, blowing on the pizza to cool it down. The card's funny too," she said, reading the card he'd gotten for his mother. "'From Your Adoring Son'...almost sounds like one of those gag cards. You know, like the ones that when you open them up, they say something funny, or have something that's going to pop out at you... like a hand with the middle finger extended," she said and then laughed at her own stupid joke.

"Yeah well, take hold of yourself...It's all they had left. You think you've had enough to drink yet?"

"You've had your share too," she replied in an angry tone.

"And like I told you, I don't really care what she thinks about the flowers."

After they ate the pizza and drank another bottle of wine in silence, Sandy finally said, "Helen said that she saw something about the trial on TV."

"Oh, that's just great news."

"On local PBS, I think. She said they're doing some kind of week-long special on medical malpractice...maybe because of your case. She said she recorded it for us to watch later."

"Yeah, that would be real nice to watch."

He had two more drinks before walking upstairs, leaving Sandy in the kitchen talking to herself. When he passed by her closet, he stopped and looked at all the fancy shoes she had lined up—nice and neat. He imagined how she would feel if he threw a pair of them away as he continued into his office.

"You call about the pool?" he heard her yell from downstairs.

"Yeah, I called about the pool…already told you I did," he said, but he hadn't called, again. He turned on the TV and watched part of the news for any stories about the trial or the shooting before putting the DVD into the player. He pressed the play button and then he lay down on the couch and watched as the credits slowly rolled by. Some kind of crazy theme song was playing and the movie was just getting started when he fell asleep.

He couldn't tell how long he had been sleeping when he woke up, but it seemed like a long time. He woke to the sounds of voices and gun shots…And when he opened his eyes, Gertrude Hileman (a much younger, but undeniable Hileman) was standing there looking back at him…yelling at him. "This way!" she hollered once and then waited before yelling it again. It was as if she was actually speaking to him, as if she might have been waiting for him to wake up…yelling at him…ready to shoot…and then looking around in both directions before running off. She wasn't bad-looking in the movie, but time hadn't been very kind to her either, he thought—even without the scars.

He watched the movie for another couple of minutes, somewhat mesmerized by the thought that he was in a real-life battle with this woman. Couldn't imagine why someone who had so much would attack someone who had so little…and so unmercifully. She didn't really seem like a person who would be that vicious, he thought as he pushed the pause button. He would watch the rest of the movie later, he thought, checking the time. Almost 1:00 a.m. Almost had a full night in. He listened for Sandy, thinking she must have gone to bed by now.

"You still awake?" he said as he entered the bedroom, but she didn't answer as she lay there in the bed reading a book.

He lay in bed with his eyes closed and tried to fall back to sleep, but he could only concentrate on his multitude of problems and the annoying sound Sandy made turning the pages of her book.

CHAPTER TWELVE

Sunday, May 9
8:15 a.m.

Weed showered, dressed, took his vitamins, and rubbed the lotion in his hair. Then he tried to work the stiffness out of his knee before he got dressed. Sandy slept soundly through it all.

Downstairs, he searched the Sunday paper for any articles about the shooting or the trial. There was nothing about the shooting that he could find, but there was a long article about the trial. An overall recap of pretty much everything that happened over the last two years, most of which had already been printed numerous times. All the sordid details...all the allegations...all the claims of his negligence, rehashed one last time before the trial was to start—to jog everyone's memory in case anyone might have forgotten, he thought sarcastically. There was even a paragraph detailing his inadequate malpractice insurance and how it could lead to his bankruptcy...all explained in detail...He couldn't really say how many times those facts had all been printed.

The article including a personal section about Hileman and her family, all their fortunes, and all the charitable work she had done and money she had donated to worthwhile causes over the years. And then details about the accident and the agonizing recovery that she'd had to endure over the last two years.

And then there was a small section about Dr. Weed's twenty-seven-year career as a local surgeon...the schools he had attended, the positions that he'd held at the hospital and at the university... and the fact that this was his third lawsuit.

At the very bottom of the article were two small photographs of each of them...side by side...when they were both much younger... and Hileman without scars. Difficult to read, the whole article reminded him of an obituary.

Nice to keep everyone up to speed with a rehash of all the sordid details, he thought as he pushed the paper aside. But clearly a hit piece...and undeniably biased...written by one of Hileman's newspaper hacks, he was sure.

"Great way to start off the day," he muttered to himself.

When he finished his coffee, he took two Percodan for the pain in his knee. Made him nervous to think about tomorrow, the first day of his trial...how he would be placed under the spotlight like a criminal in an old movie...how the attorneys would rake him over the coals, calling him negligent and uncaring and whatever else they could think up to call him. And then all the scathing articles that would likely appear in the newspaper the following day. Was embarrassing just to think about it.

He noticed that the flowers he had bought for his mother had started to wilt and turn brown, even more wilted than they had been the night before, he thought as he picked a brown petal off one of the flowers and then another that looked as if it were about ready to drop.

He took the card out of the envelope and read it again.

"From Your Adoring Son"—did sound pretty hokey, he knew, wondering if any son really ever felt that way about his mother, and then he read the message inside the card: "To a wonderful mother who has been my guide through all the good times and bad times. Wishing you a happy Mother's Day." Pretty bland and noncommitting, he thought as he wrote his own message inside the card: "Hope you have a nice Mother's Day. Love, Ben."

Didn't sound too bad, he decided. Wouldn't matter much what he wrote...He could never change how she felt about him anyway. He had always been a semifailure in her eyes...was never quite good enough no matter what he did, he thought as he loaded the flowers into the MG and started the drive toward his mother's house—the house that he had grown up in. Never understood the mother/son relationship thing...after fifty-four years, he still didn't feel comfortable being around her...like she was always watching him—critically...as if she was just waiting for him to do something wrong.

She had been upset about the trial...maybe even more than he had been. She was upset for a lot of reasons, but the main reason, at least as far as he could tell, was because she had to make excuses to the old farts at church as to why her son had been such a mean and uncaring doctor...or whatever. Wasn't even sure what she was telling them...maybe that he wasn't even her son, or maybe that he was adopted, he thought, somewhat amused. Was certain that she had the old women praying for him...praying for his transgressions... praying for his redemption. He was "just killing her," she had told him. According to her, he had been killing her all his life.

Didn't know how he would ever explain the mess at Tatter's Bar to his mother—if she ever learned about it. That might *really* kill her, especially if she found out that he was having an affair with a stripper named Candy who was half his age. He *could* always tell her that it was all just a vicious rumor, he imagined.

She never really knew him, and he never really knew her...But then, maybe it was best that way, he thought. Does anyone ever *really* know anyone else? he thought, but he felt sick at his inane, rhetorical question.

All that religion she had spoon-fed him over the years hadn't helped a bit, he realized as he mixed his McDonald's Coke with bourbon and sipped at it as he drove, finishing it off just as he reached the house.

"Just me," he called out, picking up the newspaper from the porch before pushing the front door open and entering the house. He put the card and flowers on the dining room table, leaned the card on the vase, and then removed the section of the newspaper that contained the article about the trial. He folded the paper and shoved it securely into his coat pocket. She might not even notice it was missing, but he doubted that. And if she did someone would tell her about it anyway, he knew.

Flowers didn't look half-bad, he thought, turning the vase to a slightly better angle.

He could hear his mother calling out from upstairs about him eating something she had made for him as he walked up the steps and into the familiar comfort of his old bedroom. It was like a worn-out security blanket: same furniture, same books, same framed team photograph of the 1971 Pirate World Series Champs still hanging on the wall. The last good team, he thought as he touched it to straighten it, even though it didn't really need to be straightened.

Except for an old sewing machine his mother had pushed into one corner, the room looked almost the same as it had forty years earlier. Just like he left it…with all its memories…when life was new and fresh, and everything seemed exciting. Everything was palpable, then. No expectations, no deadlines…everything in front of him…anything possible. He was happy then, he thought, touching a plastic model of a car sitting on top of his desk that he had put so carefully together so many years ago. All remembrances of his lost youth, he knew.

Wouldn't mind moving back home if he lost everything, he thought as he stood by the window and looked out at the street and houses below…not so much changed, he thought.

But, he still hadn't been able to find his car collection. That he had for some reason packed away for safekeeping in a box in the basement, he remembered...And he was starting to get concerned. Maybe a hundred small Matchbox cars that he had collected when he was young that were now worth tons of money... and that had now somehow disappeared in the sea of clutter in the basement. Lost for at least six months, he estimated as he descended the steps into the basement to give finding them another try.

He could still remember buying the first car...still had it...if he could find it...a 1967 Customized Cougar...Paid ninety-nine cents and now probably worth three hundred dollars...maybe more. And the crown jewel of his collection: the Matchbox Flying Circus set... a present for Christmas one year, still in mint condition, and still in the original box. He had never even seen another one like it for sale anywhere...irreplaceable and probably worth close to five thousand dollars...maybe more, he imagined. His prized possessions, he thought as he tried to think of any place in the basement that he hadn't already searched.

Cars had to be here somewhere, he thought, stopping for a minute on the last step, deciding on somewhere to start...and realizing that his mother was always moving things around in the basement...repacking...stacking...wrapping things differently. And worse, he was starting to wonder if she might not have accidentally or maybe even intentionally thrown them all out, he thought.

He opened one box and then another...and searched. Old pots and pans, cookbooks, clothes, women's hats from the '60s, a box of candles, his sister's Barbie dolls, some old glasses, and a box of lampshades...but no cars.

After about ten minutes he sat down at the bottom of the basement steps, caught his breath, and wiped the beads of sweat from his forehead, still uncertain why he wasn't able to find them. He would just have to look later, he thought, wondering how many hours he had already searched. Searching for his youth, he mused. Maybe futilely.

It wasn't that critical that he find them today. They had to be there somewhere, he imagined, trying to reassure himself of that thought instead.

"I can't understand why I can't find those cars I put down here. You sure you didn't move them or throw them out?" he asked crossly as his mother appeared at the top of the basement steps.

"I don't know. I told you, I don't even know what you're talking about, really. You probably just forgot were you put them…You think you forgot where you put them?" she asked after a long pause and then moved away from the steps, at the same time trying to balance her hat on her head.

"No, I know where I put them!" he answered, irritated at how obtuse and incriminating she always was. "You…had to have moved them somewhere…" he said, his statement trailing off as he kicked a box out of the way and then recited a string of obscenities under his breath.

Forty-five fuckin' years he'd had those cars. If she threw them out, he was going to be pissed. What made it worse was the thought that she could have done it intentionally…as some kind of juvenile payback for what he was putting her though with the trial, he imagined as he brushed the dust from his hands. Just like Sandy throwing his damned gym shoes away. His mother didn't like his car collection, just like Sandy didn't like his old, allegedly smelly shoes. She never had liked those cars…thought it was too childish for a grown man to be obsessed over a few childhood possessions… or playing basketball with a few of his old friends. She never did grasp the concept that the cars were just good memories. One good thing that hadn't turned to crap in his miserable life.

"I'll be up in a couple of minutes," he answered when she call back down the steps, and he looked at his image in the small, shadowy mirror above the sink in the basement. The image that he had a hard time recognizing anymore. It almost seemed like some stranger looking back at him…a confused stranger…maybe pissed at the mess he had gotten them both into. But then, nothing in his life seemed to add up and nothing much seemed familiar anymore. It all seemed distant, as if he had split into two strangely different people in two parallel universes…the good and the bad. And then again, maybe he was just getting a little wacky and too philosophical.

The dim light did make him look better than most of the other mirrors in the house, he'd noticed long ago…a friendly mirror that shaded out most of the details.

"You do know what I'm talking about, right?" he yelled back up the stairs as he stood in the bathroom urinating, but he knew she wouldn't hear him, nor would she even care. "The damn cars in the box with the red letters on the side?" he mumbled. He was just starting back up the stairs when his cell phone began to vibrate. Candy's number came up on the screen.

"Why I called was…I mean, other than to see how you're holding up and to tell you how much I love you…was that I was wondering if you could lend me a little money?" she asked. "Couldn't dance Friday *or* Saturday night because the police wouldn't let Pickles open the bar. So I made exactly zero dollars this weekend," she continued as he listened to the sound of her lighting a cigarette. You know Friday's my big tip night and Saturday's good too," she said and then asked him why the shooting couldn't have happened on a Monday or Tuesday night—instead of on the weekend—and then paused as if she expected him to give her an answer. "Just need a little money to tide me over until they open up the bar again or until I can find somewhere else to dance. And Mac…or whatever his name is…is bent out of shape again over last month's rent…says he'll kick in my door and throw me out the window if I'm late with the rent one more time," she said, finally pausing to exhale.

Didn't know how much money he had given her over the last year. Thousands, he was pretty sure. A prostitute probably would have been cheaper, he guessed as he listened.

"How much you going to need?" he asked, knowing that he was running out of money too.

"Maybe six or seven hundred...somewhere around there?"

"Shouldn't be a problem...can bring it by later," he told her but was annoyed at the amount she wanted and unsure if he even had that much to give her. But he was already thinking about her thin, lithe body and full breasts, imagining her in her cowboy outfit, and the possibility of being alone with her in her apartment and having sex when he dropped the money off at her apartment. Was more an opportunity than money that he would never see again. Just when he thought he was going to have a pretty miserable day...He now had the likely chance of having sex with a very beautiful and sexy young woman. He was already getting aroused thinking about it and listening to her talk.

"I'll bring the money by in a little while," he told her. "Have to run a few errands, but I'll give you a call when I'm about there," he said before ending the call.

He could drop off his mother at church and then slip out the back of the church like he normally would. Get the money from the ATM—if he wasn't already overdrawn—and then drive over to Candy's apartment. The church service would give him a good two hours to have sex—maybe even a little longer if the preacher got carried away—but plenty of time to have sex and get back to the church in time to pick up his mother, he figured. Would just tell his mother there was an emergency at the hospital, like he did most Sundays, he thought as he took the basement steps two at a time.

When he got to the top of the steps, his mother was standing in front of the dining room table opening the card and looking at the flowers he had brought for her.

"Happy Mother's Day," he told her, trying to curb his excitement.

"They're beautiful. I just love pink carnations. They're one of my favorite flowers," she said as she leaned over and smelled the flowers. She read the card out loud and then went back to trying to get her hair under her hat—or something. Weed wasn't really sure what she was doing with her damn hat, but it was starting to get annoying.

"You about ready?" he asked after a short time of impatiently waiting...and then told her about his emergency at the hospital. "Going to have to drop you off and then circle back to the hospital, but it shouldn't take long...most likely be back in plenty of time for the service," he said, hoping that would hurry her along...But she didn't seem to be interested in his emergency at the hospital.

When she was ready, he helped her down the front steps of the house and into his car, like he did every Sunday, and then drove the three blocks down the street to the church. He helped her get out of his car, up the steps and into the church, and then hopped back into the car before quickly driving off...watching the church disappear in his rearview mirror.

CHAPTER THIRTEEN

Sunday, May 9
9:37 a.m.

Weed breathed a sigh of relief when the ATM pushed out the small stack of bills. With the five hundred from the ATM, the money in his wallet, and the fifty dollars from the church's offering envelope, he would have the six hundred dollars, he calculated as he ripped open the church envelope and took out the cash.

He tapped lightly on Candy's apartment door and then again before she answered.

"You're a life saver," she said as she opened the door and then disappeared into the bathroom at the back of her apartment while she continued to talk to him about the shooting: that she'd heard Tatter was on a ventilator, and if he died they might never reopen the bar, and then she wouldn't have any place to dance.

But all he was thinking about was having sex, and he couldn't really concentrate on anything she was telling him…And worse, he was becoming anxious and impatient with her incessant chatter. He couldn't wait forever, he thought as he made the first move, pushing open the door to the bathroom and giving her a kiss on the neck as she stood in front of the mirror. He took her hand and led her back into the bedroom, telling her how much he loved and missed her.

He gave her a long, passionate kiss before he slid his hands under her top and gently caressed her breasts. She took off her top and then lay down on the bed in just her skimpy panties as he quickly undressed and lay down beside her...kissing her bare belly and then her breasts.

As they lay there making passionate love, he realized that although he was very aroused, he still didn't have an erection. Maybe he had half an erection, but surely not an erection hard enough to have sex with—and worse, it seemed like his half erection might actually be going away. Not again, he thought, disgusted. But even after five more minutes of sensuous foreplay, he had nothing...less than when he had started, he knew. The more he thought about it, the softer it seemed to get. And now he was preoccupied with worrying if Candy was wondering why it was taking him so long...and at the same time trying to hide the fact that he still didn't have an erection. The situation was already embarrassing...and now he had to come up with some excuse to tell her why he couldn't perform...why he couldn't do something as natural as having sex. Ten minutes of kissing and caressing a sexy young stripper and all he could manage was half an erection...nowhere near hard enough to have sex...couldn't use it for anything. Mr. Empty Pants couldn't fake it any longer. His sexual gyrations were just getting more absurd and Candy was getting tired of waiting, he was sure as he backed away from her, rolling to one side of the bed, disgusted and trying to think up some kind of manly excuse.

Would just have to tell her what he told Liz the last time, he thought. Candy lay there for a minute...as if she hadn't even realized that he had stopped trying.

"You okay?" she asked, leaning up on her elbows looking at him, before he was able to say anything.

"Just too much stress with this trial…and now this shooting. Too much shit on my mind," he told her and then repeated it with a little more detail.

"Yeah, I can understand that," she said, reaching over to the nightstand and taking a cigarette out of her pack. No big deal. Happens sometimes…no big deal," she said, pausing to light her cigarette before continuing as if she had forgotten something, "At least that's what I've heard on all those TV commercials," she said as she took a deep drag of her cigarette. "I wasn't really in the mood anyway, so maybe it was partly me too," she said. "I've been under a lot of stress too with this shooting thing and me not being able to dance," she added.

"Yeah, it's all driving me crazy. All I can think about," he lamented, but was still frustrated at his abysmal failure.

"You'll be okay next time," she said as she took another long drag off her cigarette. But he didn't want to think about the next time. He was already paranoid about the next time.

He lay there with her for another couple of minutes, caressing her back, hoping that things might change…that there might still be a chance he would get an erection…before she got up and put her shirt back on and walked into the bathroom. He watched as a breeze came through the window and blew the money he had brought her off the night stand and onto the floor.

Six times: three with Sandy, twice with Liz, and now this one. Was tired of it…embarrassing…especially with Candy. He could almost explain it with Sandy and Liz…they weren't nearly as young and sexy as Candy…and he had sort of gotten tired of having sex with both of them, anyway. But with Candy…If he couldn't get an erection with a hot young stripper, then who could he get an erection with, he thought as he listened to her moving around in the bathroom.

Six times…well it wasn't going to happen again. Would just have to pick up a bottle of Viagra or something. He'd take the whole bottle if he had to. He was becoming a head case. Even sex was becoming an issue in his disgusting life. Even his dick was turning on him, he thought as he lay there—disgusted with himself.

"Have to go pick up my mother, anyway," he told her when she came out of the bathroom fully dressed. He really couldn't come up with anything else to make conversation.

"Pickles came by yesterday and knocked on my door," she said off-handedly while lighting another cigarette and blowing the smoke out her opened window as she gathered up the money. "I saw his motorcycle in the street, but I didn't open the door. He yelled through the door anyway, saying if I was in here, I'd better keep my mouth shut and to tell everyone else to keep their mouths shut too. Sort of scared me."

"Police have to know what happened…Someone should just turn him in," he told her while taking a drag off of her cigarette but still thinking about his embarrassing failure.

He talked to her for another twenty minutes. He was tempted to give it another try, but thought that a second embarrassing failure would just be too risky. Once, when he was making love to Liz and couldn't get an erection, he imagined that it was Candy he was making love to. That had worked, but he knew the opposite wouldn't stand a chance.

He kissed Candy again and then went down the back steps, checking to make sure that Pickles was nowhere in sight before getting back in his car.

Six times in two weeks. Maybe a record, he thought as he drove back toward the church. Three times with Liz and three with Sandy—and now once with Candy. Seven times, he calculated. He was becoming a sexual cripple, he thought, dismayed. Wasn't that important with Liz or Sandy…He didn't really care all that much what they thought, even though it was sort of embarrassing…and he planned on dumping Liz anyway. But he didn't want Candy to think he was some old sexual cripple...an impotent. Impotence... always sounded like such a terrible disease...like something that might end up being fatal...still seemed that way, he thought as he pulled back into the church parking lot. Would buy a bottle of Viagra...wasn't going to put himself through this again, he thought as he ascended the steps and entered the church.

Just in time for the offering (that he now didn't have), he thought as he took an empty offering envelope from the holder on the back of the pew, scribbled a fictitious name on it, smiled, and dropped it into the collection plate—empty.

When the service was over, he waited for his mother at the back of the church and then stood with her in line, waiting to shake hands with the pastor.

When they reached the pastor, he grabbed her hand with both of his hands, like he did every Sunday. The pastor came down close to his mother's eye level (like you would with a child) and said how good it was to see her. She liked it, Weed knew. It was what she lived for: to impress the minister every Sunday and to show him what a good Christian she was. If this pastor really knew her, he wouldn't think she was such a great Christian. How vindictive...how nasty she could be, Weed thought as he moved out of the church behind her.

"Ben!" the pastor yelled as they started to move away from the church. "Almost forgot...I want to talk to you about something when I'm done here," he said, and then he asked him to wait for a couple minutes while he finished greeting everyone.

"Ben," the pastor said coming toward him after a short wait. "Sorry, but I was hoping you could help me with something," he said and then paused, waiting for an answer.

"If I can, sure," Weed said. They stood there awkwardly as a few other stragglers moved by, one touching the minister on the shoulder as he passed and waved. The minister held up his index finger, motioning for Weed to wait as he stepped back and briefly talked with two other women.

"Sorry," he said as he came back to where Weed was standing. "I need one more member for a committee to represent the church at the Allegheny County Religious Symposium. I want to come up with ideas on how we can better serve the community...to discuss ways that we can improve the city's image, so we can lure people and businesses back into the city. You know, our attendance for the last couple of years has been dropping rather precipitously...been losing members right and left...and it hasn't been good for our finances, either. People are just afraid to come into the city because of all the crime," he added as Weed shook his head in agreement. "I guess our city finished way down on a list of cities where you would want to raise a family...and I thought you would make a good representative. A name that people will recognize, and at least give us a little bit of clout," he said and laughed as his long, black robe flapped in the breeze.

Weed listened intently as if he were really interested, shaking his head in agreement but thinking about the irony of it now. How would it look, being on some kind of religious committee...if they ever found out about his involvement with a stripper and a shooting in the city he was trying to clean up? Perfect timing actually, he thought. Why not? His mother, who was standing there listening (breathing down his neck with a fake smile on her face), would never forgive him if he turned down a request from the church.

"Yeah, I guess that would be fine," he said, trying to sound interested. He could always get out of it later with the trial as an excuse, he thought as the pastor continued to give him the details of the committee and when they were going to meet. Of all the members of the church he could have asked, Weed thought, smiling to himself.

He helped his mother into the car while he imagined the story that some reporter could write about that.

"I think that's nice," his mother said when he climbed into the driver's seat.

"Yeah, great!" he said, trying to hide his sarcasm as he drove the short distance back up the hill to her house, but knew his mother had already sensed his sarcasm.

After settling back into her house, he watched as his mother sliced the dry meat she had prepared, placed a piece on each of their plates, spooned out mashed potatoes for both of them, and poured gravy over all of it before putting the plates at either end of the small dining table.

They usually talked about the same things every Sunday: old times, the family, his dad, his sister. Mostly, it was a forced, uneasy conversation with long pauses...about his two children (her two grandchildren from his previous marriage), and what a shame it was that she didn't get to see them more often. Too many sensitive topics had developed between them over the years. He had learned, pretty much, to keep his mouth shut and to agree with whatever she said—regardless of how much it irritated him. It had always been that way. Not many topics that hadn't become sore points in their lives.

"Just try not to cause any more problems," she said out of the clear blue, when they had been talking about something else alto-gether. He knew she would eventually get around to the trial...She always did. "I'm old. I don't need any more stress like this in my life...I'd just like to die happy. So try not to say anything bad about Ms. Hileman. Just act like you're the best doctor in the world," she said looking like she might have tears in her eyes. "Please act like you care about people...that you care about her and that you're the best doctor—ever," she said, smiling weakly through wet eyes.

He had heard the same lamentation before...just two weeks ago. She had told him that he didn't seem to care about people any-more...that he had been a good doctor—once, and that she didn't know what had happened to change him so much.

"You don't know people the way I know people," he had told her. That she didn't have to deal with people—the public—every day like he had to. "They can be a real pain," he had said, but she hadn't wanted to hear it. She had come to the conclusion that he was becoming cold and heartless—and maybe he was, but he wasn't going to get into that argument with her again. He wasn't even sure he cared...was tired of caring what people thought of him, so he quickly changed the subject of their conversation.

"Wonder what it's all about?" he said, trying to act excited about serving on the committee.

"He told you," she answered as she finished clearing the dishes from the table. "Crime...But you wouldn't know how bad it really is around here because you live in that nice neighborhood now. It's really getting bad here, though. I'm half afraid to even go out on my front porch," she added. "You going to take a nap?" she asked as he dried the last dish and folded the towel across the chair.

"Yeah, I think. I'm sort of tired," he said and then grabbed the part of the paper that he hadn't read and walked upstairs to his room. He opened the window a crack to let in the old sounds and the fresh air, and stood there for a minute or two to look out at the tree-lined street below to the park and the swimming pool at the end of the next block. He could see the other streets and houses that he had passed for all these years. In the winter he could clearly see all the way through the stand of trees to the park and the swimming pool—now closed and in disrepair.

Would be easy to move back home, he thought. Even his mother made him feel comfortable now—for some reason.

He lay down on his bed as a cool breeze from the window blew across his face. He listened to the rustling leaves of the catalpa trees rubbing against the house outside the window and remembered something that he had long forgotten about: a plastic bag stuck in the tree, flapping in the wind for almost two years before the tree released its hold. Bob's Bargain's Store had been written across the yellow bag. How long it had held on? Seemed sad when it was gone…didn't know why he remembered things like that…obscure things about his youth…seemed strange. The sound of a train whistling in the distance…none now…but he could imagine that soothing sound…and the laughter of all the happy summer people at the pool at the end of the street.

Should have never let her get away, he thought as he shut his eyes and fought off sleep, thinking about the girl he had been in love with years ago: the girl that Candy reminded him of. The biggest disappointment in his life, that he had not married her. Had never really told her how he felt…how much he loved her. Should have…should have at least tried. His one big regret in life. If he had told her and she had fallen in love with him—even half as much as he was in love with her—his life would have turned out differently…would have changed his whole life…If only he had just seized the day. He would have been happy, he thought as he drifted off to sleep.

When he woke the sun's rays no longer flashed through the leaves and window and into his room. It was darker outside. He had slept for almost four hours, he realized looking at his watch. The best sleep that he had had in a long time.

On his way home, he stopped at the Quick Fix where Bob worked, but the clerk told him that Bob had gone home early… must have forgotten about their plans to meet, he thought as he got back in the car and drove around the neighborhood. He ended up at the basketball courts near his mother's house, and then he watched some teenagers finish up their game just as it started to get dark.

When they had all gone and he was the only one left, he ran up and down the court making pretend lay ups and jump shots, imagining he was young and playing in front of a large crowd of screaming fans…impressing the girls with his athletic ability…driving the court one last time…with time running out, dodging defenders, before spinning the ball behind his back and making the winning basket. Could have happened, but never did...he thought as he picked up his sweatshirt and walked back to the car. Weed stood there for a minute, looking back at the court...wondering where it had all gone...wondering where the years had all gone. Then he reluctantly got back into his car and drove home.

"She like the flowers?" Sandy asked when he came in the front door.

"Said she did."

"Your pastor called...that Dr. Grey guy or whatever his name is...said they changed the time...think it was seven thirty next Wednesday for pictures...I wrote it on the refrigerator...At first I thought it was a joke," she told him. "What's that about?" she asked, but she didn't really seem to listen to his answer when he told her that he wasn't really sure himself.

"That movie is something...that one you brought home with Hileman in it," she said, pausing to light a cigarette. "Pretty violent. I only watched about half of it, and I think she shot six or seven people...and they all died. Seemed like that was the main plot... to see how many people they could shoot and how many buildings they could blow up before the movie ended. She's the one with the blond afro and the yellow platform shoes," she said, handing him the cover to the DVD and pointing to one of the people pictured it. "Story has no plot...can't really understand what they're supposed to be doing actually, but she's a good shot," she added.

"Yeah, that's the one I thought she was," he said looking at the cover. Then told her about waking up halfway through the movie to her looking back at him from the TV screen, "Directly at me... was the weirdest thing...looked like she was actually watching what I was doing."

"I laid out a nice suit and tie for you for the morning. And re-member: stay calm, compassionate, and caring, like Helen said. The three Cs...says if you do that, you can't lose."

114

Another ridiculous revelation from Helen, he knew.

"Won't be easy with all the lies they're going to be telling," he said setting his alarm and then lying back in the bed. Sandy continued to ramble on about what their lives would be like if they lost everything, and if everyone—not just him—could be a little more conscientious, the world would be a better place. But he wasn't listening...He had heard it all before, so he closed his eyes and tried to sleep.

CHAPTER FOURTEEN

Monday, May 10
8:17 a.m.

Was awake most of the night tossing and turning thinking about the trial. He shaved and showered and then dressed in the suit Sandy had laid out for him.

Felt a little shaky...like he already needed a drink.

Nothing about the shooting today, he realized as he looked through the front section of the newspaper. At least that was a good sign, he imagined. The longer the shooting went unnoticed, the better chance he had of not getting involved, he reasoned, pouring himself a cup of coffee and then sitting down at the kitchen table. Four days and counting.

"You look nice," Sandy said coming into the kitchen unexpectedly, giving him a kiss on the head and adjusting his tie. "You feeling okay?" she asked sitting down at the table across from him. "You look a little piqued."

"I'm fine, I guess. Just stressed out about all the people and all the cameras…and reporters…that are likely to be there today. And then all the bad publicity that's likely…like a public flogging," he said getting up from the table.

"I'll have something for us when you get home, so don't stop anywhere to eat. I have it all planned. One of your favorites…a surprise," she told him as she sipped at her coffee. "I thought it might lift your spirits."

"Sounds good," he said reflexively but really didn't care. Needed something to calm him down, he thought as he waited for Sandy to get up and leave the kitchen before getting a fresh bottle of bourbon from under the cupboard and three of Sandy's Valium pills. Would drink the whole bottle if that's what he needed to calm him down, he thought, taking one of the Valium and putting the other two in his shirt pocket. Would take another before the trial started, he thought as he yelled up the stairs to Sandy that he was leaving. He could hear her muffled voice coming from the bathroom but couldn't make out what she said.

Agony was about to begin, he thought, mixing half the bottle of bourbon with half his Coke and then taking a drink…and then a couple more. Didn't want to drink so much that it would affect his mental ability…just enough to settle his nerves. And with the Valium, it would make his morning go a whole lot easier, he knew.

Could have avoided this whole mess, he thought as he drove. If only he hadn't lost control of himself…and his emotions. Now that relatively meaningless encounter almost two years ago was threatening to destroy him…was destroying him…coming back to haunt him. If he would have just kept his damn mouth shut. A human flaw…his volatile temper…his impatience…had it all his life…and had never been able to control it very well…was now surfacing to destroy him.

"You're the cause of your own problems," Sandy had told him… many people had told him over the years—and they were right. A character flaw that he was already aware of, he thought as he took another sip of the bourbon and Coke.

Seemed strange that he could lose everything so quickly…so easily…in the blink of an eye…all because of one bad night. The volatility of life: one day you're driving along fine, and the next thing you know you're off the road and in a ditch. Well, he was in the ditch now, he told himself.

And as if losing everything financially wasn't already enough, he would also be humiliated and destroyed personally in the process, he thought as he turned down the street to the courthouse.

He pulled into the lot directly across the street from the courthouse, a shady spot where he could look out his front window and see both the courthouse and the festival in the park. Then he tried to relax and at the same time get up enough nerve to face the day… felt like he was waiting to be led off to the gallows.

He watched people coming and going from the courthouse… mostly lawyers in nice suits and well-dressed secretaries. In the park he could see the vendors opening their tents, hanging out paintings and painted pots…And he could even see Frank (or a man that looked like Frank) working in front of one of the tents toward the back of the festival grounds.

He saw a TV van pull up in front of the courthouse and watched as it spent the next ten minutes trying to maneuver into a tight space, before the driver got out and began to set up his video equipment.

Morgan was the first to come down the street, dressed in a brown suit that looked exactly like the suit he had been wearing on Friday.

Then a sheriff's van pulled in. Two police officers got out of the front seats and led a man in handcuffs from the backseat up the steps and into the courthouse for a murder trial Weed had read about in the newspaper. A man who had been accused of shooting his wife and her boyfriend...He had claimed it was some self-defense thing, even though neither of them had a weapon, Weed remembered. Then he watched a bunch of clowns coming down the street in large, floppy shoes and turning into the park...instead of going into the courthouse...slightly amused at the irony.

Then Turzak, Hileman's attorney, dressed in an expensive-looking suit, carrying a briefcase, and sipping a coffee, talked to someone who was probably another attorney, before going into the courthouse.

He took a deep breath and tried to relax, taking his second Valium. Maybe the three Valiums wouldn't be enough. He still had a Percodan for his knee pain, which surprisingly wasn't hurting much today, he thought as he finished his drink and saw a long Mercedes limo pull up and stop in a no-parking zone in front of the courthouse. When the driver removed a wheelchair from the trunk, he knew that it had to be Hileman's car. The driver stood there for a minute talking to a police officer before helping Hileman into the wheelchair and wheeling her down the street to the edge of the park. Then the driver got back in the limo and drove off—only to appear a couple minutes later, walking quickly back through the park and carrying Hileman's mangy mutt. He placed the dog on Hileman's lap. Hileman kissed the dog a couple of times and gave it a hug before putting it down on the sidewalk beside her. Then for the next fifteen minutes, Weed watched as the driver and Hileman talked and smoked cigarettes at the corner of the park and the dog pushed an empty popcorn box around the sidewalk with its nose.

When they were finished smoking, the driver wheeled Hileman up a ramp and into the courthouse. In the doorway, Weed could see Hileman holding the dog up in front of her one last time, talking to it for a few minutes (as if she were giving it instructions), and giving it another kiss before handing it back to the driver.

What a nut case, Weed thought.

Already felt more relaxed now that the Valium had kicked in, he realized as he got out of his car and walked across the street to the courthouse.

"Just like at the airport, people," the security guard said as Weed got in line and waited. "Shoes and belts off, and everything out of your pockets. Laptops off and out of their cases, cell phones and keys in the baskets," the security guard said and then repeated it like a broken record as he handed Weed a plastic tray. "And keep it moving."

When Weed had his shoes on and everything put back in his pocket, he walked through the large rotunda and into courtroom 3, feeling more like a common criminal than a surgeon.

The courtroom looked like a set out of an old movie from the '40s: everything colored in sepia tones, dark wooden benches and railings ornately carved, and windows that ran from the wooden wainscoting almost to the ceiling. Oil paintings of long-dead judges in their long, black robes hung in streams of light coming through the long windows.

Courtroom was already about half filled, Weed thought as he made his way down the aisle to where Morgan was sitting at the table to the left of the judge's bench. More spectators than he had hoped for. Hileman, still sitting in her wheelchair on the other side of the room, was talking to Turzak as he shuffled some papers. And even in the dim light he could plainly see the scars...the shadows of the scars seemed to crawl across her face. And Hileman was sitting almost directly in front of the jury box...where all the jurors would be able to clearly see her scars...and her cervical collar...and her wheelchair. The best view in the house, Weed surmised.

Morgan nodded as Weed sat down beside him.

"The first couple of days will probably be the worst," Morgan said as he shuffled some papers. Then he sort of mumbled that the Hileman's attorneys would be presenting their case first, and after they finished it would be their turn. He reminded Weed not to take any of it personally, and to sit there passively without showing any emotion. "But especially no sarcasm—that's the worst thing you could do. Jurors don't like sarcasm. Compassion and understanding—yes…anger and aggression—no."

Weed nodded in agreement, but he was tired of hearing it.

"And I'm not going to raise many objections unless it's absolutely necessary," Morgan continued. Weed wasn't sure if he was actually talking to him or talking to himself…He seemed preoccupied with his thoughts, Weed noticed. "It might just draw attention to the very thing that I'm trying to hide," he said, and for an instant Weed thought that he might have smelled alcohol on Morgan's breath. "And anyway, the jurors might forget most of what Hileman's attorneys say by next week if we don't make a big deal out of it," he said. "Jurors have short memories. People have short memories. So don't get too excited if I just sit there and do nothing when he starts attacking you. We'll get our turn to tell the jury our side of the story later," he added.

"Want them to know how she acted that night…and how most of this is just lies and exaggerations," he told Morgan—even though he had told Morgan this same thing many times before.

Weed watched as people continued to fill the courtroom. A group of old Red Hats waddled in, in single file and agonizingly slow, like a child's wooden pull toy being pulled erratically by a child. Then a group of high school students entered—all dressed in suits…Future Lawyers of America, he imagined. And then a few more reporters filed in, moving into the section marked "Reserved for the Press"— eight already. An older reporter (whom Weed recognized from one of the TV stations but wasn't sure which one) sat with his glasses on top of his bald head, looking as though he were working a crossword puzzle, and another reporter (a young woman from Court TV, he was sure) talked expressively to someone on her cell phone.

From where he sat he could look out two of the high windows past some large oak trees into the park and see parts of the arts festival: some multicolored tents with colorful objects that were hard to make out and a couple of food booths. Looked like a silent movie being played out in front of him. Might serve as some distraction to take his mind off the trial, he thought.

"And not to complicate your day," Morgan said, "but the judge just gave me two names that Turzak gave him as potential witnesses. Didn't tell me who they were or what it was about, but I might have to take their depositions." Morgan handed Weed a paper with two names written on it. "Don't want them throwing a monkey wrench into the works," he added as Weed looked at the names. "You recognize those names?" Morgan asked as he searched for something in his briefcase.

Weed studied the two names on the paper. Wasn't sure, but feared that maybe one of the names on the paper, Edward Victor, was one of the bartenders at the Venus Lounge where he had been the night of the accident.

This was what he had been worrying about: that Hileman's attorneys might find out somehow that he had been drinking at the Venus the night of the accident. Wouldn't have been that difficult to discover...He went there often and people knew him. But it was unlikely that anyone would remember who was at a bar... almost two years earlier...on any given night...unless they had discovered a credit card receipt through a computer or something. Couldn't go anywhere these days without someone knowing about it, he thought, pissed at himself that he had paid by credit card that night. A record of what he had eaten, how many drinks he had consumed, and the time and date: all on the receipt.

And if they found out that Liz was the person he had been with that night, it would be a total disaster. Liz would never cover for him. She was too damn puritanical...religious...would never tell a lie to cover him, he knew.

Could maybe just have Candy cover for him...tell the judge that she was who he was with that night, and that she had been the person drinking. Maybe, he thought. Might just create more of a mess…using a stripper as a witness…and then…shit…Sandy might find out and want an explanation of why he had been in the Venus Lounge with a stripper. Hardly a solution to a problem, he thought. Sounded more like a bigger problem. And if the shooting thing became public, it would complicate it even more. Using a stripper as a witness didn't seem practical, he knew…at least not now. Maybe he could think it over later, when his problems settled a little more. He could work out the details or come up with a better solution all together…later, he thought.

"Don't have any idea who they are," Weed said, handing the paper back to Morgan.

"I just hope it's nothing big. We have enough problems already," Morgan said as he dropped the paper back in his briefcase.

Couldn't worry about it now, Weed thought. Had enough on his plate.

A little after 9:00 a.m., the courtroom was almost filled to capacity. The bailiff told everyone to rise for the honorable Judge James J. Wisensee. One of the doors along the back wall opened and the judge appeared. He slowly walked across the room in front of everyone and up the three steps to his judge's bench. He sat high above them, reading and shuffling papers and grumbling to himself, before finally turning to the bailiff and handing him some papers.

"This is our schedule," he said. "We have two weeks to complete the trial…which should be plenty of time…So I don't want anyone wandering off into the woods on some contorted tangent. So, keep the rhetoric and pontification to a minimum. No objections just because you don't like what you've heard…because it will be denied, and no long dissertations, redundancies, or grandstanding. I don't want a question rephrased ten different ways because it's not the answer that you wanted. I want this done well before the two-week time limit," he said, pushing his glasses to his forehead and then continuing on for another ten minutes—complaining, really—before telling the bailiff to bring in the jurors.

The bailiff led the eight jurors (whom the attorneys had chosen two weeks earlier) into the courtroom, single file: six middle-aged women and two older men, all staring straight ahead like zombies.

When they were all seated, the judge thanked them for taking time out of their busy schedules and then made a few poor attempts at humor to put them at ease. He spent the next hour explaining the case to them: what malpractice meant, what negligence meant, what punitive damages were, and what factors were needed to prove their case. The judge stopped frequently to ask the jurors if any of them had any questions. And then he read the entire lawsuit to everyone...all twenty-seven accusations...all twenty pages...agonizingly slow, emphatically stopping frequently to explain concepts and terms to the jurors, and to ask them again if they had any questions.

Twenty-seven times the judge read his name, and each time it was followed by a litany of his negligent behavior. All the things he had failed to diagnose, and all the things he had done wrong—medically—were followed by all of Hileman's injuries, which were a result of all the things that he had done wrong: all the pain and suffering, a neck injury that had caused permanent nerve damage, numbness, pain and weakness in both arms, a back injury (that he had failed to diagnose and treat properly) that left her in a wheelchair with intractable pain, a concussion (that he had completely missed) that left her cognitive ability impaired, headaches, memory loss, depression, insomnia, and scars that were painful and unsightly, had worsened her depression, and had somehow affected her eyesight. And the list went on and on until he arrived at the twenty-seventh accusation: Dr. Benjamin Weed made cruel and threatening comments that had caused Ms. Hileman emotional distress.

The longer the judge spoke, the more anxious Weed felt. Wisensee continued explaining the concept of punitive damages to the jury: damages rendered for any outrageous or egregious behavior that the doctor demonstrated while treating the patient. "Sort of a punishment for an individual's bad behavior," Wisensee told them.

He felt like standing up and telling everyone that it was all a bunch of lies...and that Hileman was an obnoxious drunk—but he didn't. He just sat there as emotionless as possible...accepting it as well as he could without showing emotion.

Another Valium or drink would help, he thought as he looked out the window at the festival. He suddenly remembered something he hadn't thought about in years: his mother had brought him to the festival the first year it opened...almost forty-five years ago. The only thing he could really remember about that day was how uncomfortable he had been in the pair of wool pants he had worn— that she'd insisted he wear—and how all he wanted to do was leave. He couldn't remember anything fun that had happened that day. Strange that he would remember that, he thought, just like he remembered the bag stuck in the tree outside his window.

The judge rambled on for over another hour before he finished and then warned the jurors not to discuss the case, or to read any newspaper, radio, or television accounts of the trial...that it might affect their judgment and be grounds for a mistrial.

"It's a little after twelve now," Wisensee said looking at his watch. "We can meet back here at one thirty for the afternoon session... and begin with the plaintiff's opening remarks," he added and then told the bailiff to remove the jury, before striking his gavel to adjourn the morning session of the trial.

Weed talked to Morgan for a couple minutes to give the courtroom a chance to clear...didn't need everyone staring at him like a criminal as he left, he thought as he finally stood and walked back through the courtroom and out into the rotunda, where he disappeared into a large lunchtime crowd. Just another face now... incognito...but he felt like a scolded schoolboy sneaking away as he walked down the courthouse steps toward his car.

"Dr. Weed," a voice called out from behind him as he was about halfway down the street. "Would you mind giving us a statement?" a reporter asked, holding a microphone and recorder as she followed him down the street, but he ignored her and just continued to walk away. Already being harassed, he thought.

"No specifics. Nothing about the trial," she said. "Just a personal interest story is all. How you feel. How it's affecting your personal life, your family. How you feel about the fact that you could lose everything."

"Not now, but sounds like it would be a lot of fun," he said sarcastically after taking a few more steps down the street. But when he finally turned and looked, she was already quickly walking away, back toward the courthouse in the direction of Hileman and her wheelchair and her dog.

When he was in his car and sure no one was near, he took the bottle of bourbon out and poured some into his empty Coke cup and sipped at it until it was almost gone. He took another Percodan and then watched as the reporters—like vultures—continued to gather around Hileman.

CHAPTER FIFTEEN

Monday, May 10
12:37 p.m.

The trial was as he expected it to be—almost. No great surprises—yet. And he was glad that, at last, the circus had finally
begun after a nearly two-year wait. At least this part of his misery
and aggravation would soon be over, he thought. And then maybe
he could get his life back in order—whatever that meant.

Would help if the damn shooting disappeared. Already had
enough with this mess…didn't need that mess too, he thought as
he drank the last of his bourbon and Coke and waited in the car
for a short time before walking across the street to a small sandwich
shop at the other end of the park. He was trying to avoid Frank as
he moved through the tents and food stands. He had too much on
his mind to have to deal with an annoying person like him today,
he thought as he sat near a window in the restaurant and ate while
watching the people in the park.

He would call Candy later and find out if she had heard anything more about the shooting. He was thinking that he might still have to use her as a "Liz Substitute" for the night of Hileman's accident. She would cover for him and would probably tell the judge whatever he wanted her to—if it came to that. If they had, in fact, found a copy of his credit card receipt, he would just have Candy tell the judge that she had been the one drinking that night, not him. Was the only solution that he could come up with so far, he thought as he took his last Valium before walking back through the park to the courthouse.

And if Sandy found out about Candy testifying for him, he could just tell Sandy that she had just been a former patient whom he had—coincidentally—run into at the bar that night...or something like that. He really wasn't sure what he would tell Sandy. He still hadn't worked out all those details, he thought as he moved through the crowded courtroom to his seat beside Morgan.

Was another thirty minutes before Turzak stood in front of the jurors and began telling them about Hileman's accident and her injuries: her concussion, her spinal injuries, her facial lacerations, and how Dr. Weed had mismanaged each one of them. He was, again, explaining all twenty-seven of the complaints of malpractice listed in the lawsuit—one at a time. And then he started telling the jurors how close Ms. Hileman had come to dying, as he cast incriminating glances in his direction. But he failed to explain how someone so critically injured could be up, walking around drunk in the ER, smoking cigarettes, and shouting derogatory comments at everyone as she chased her mangy mutt through the ER. *That* part of the story didn't seem to matter, Weed thought. He wished he could tell Turzak to explain *that* part of it to the jurors, too.

The truth was, Hileman hadn't been hurt all that bad, Weed knew. Mostly, she only had minor cuts and bruises. The worst of her injuries were her facial lacerations—but even they weren't all that bad. And as far as he had determined, she hadn't suffered one major injury and he certainly hadn't made any of the injuries any worse by what he had done—or hadn't done.

That was the real truth, Weed knew. He, possibly, could have done a better job at repairing her lacerations, but in the end, it wouldn't have mattered much. The lacerations would have had to have been revised and repaired later anyway. And that was it. Surely didn't add up to seven million dollars. And she had never been in critical condition...and never in any risk of dying...all just a bunch of exaggerations and fabrications to make it all sound more serious than it ever was...more dramatic than it had been...to add some meat to an already very weak lawsuit...to add credibility and validity to a case that had none. And besides, most of Hileman's complaints were exaggerations—bogus complaints—a product of her malingering, Weed knew.

No, the only real accusation with any substance and any legitimacy at all were her scars. Yeah, he could have taken more time that night and done a better job at repairing them, but that wouldn't have mattered, either. They still would have to have been revised by a plastic surgeon later.

But, like he had already realized, even if he didn't win the entire case outright, a small award for Hileman would be just about as good. It would look like a win for him. If her side wanted seven million, and the jury gave her anything less than one million, it would look like a victory for him—not Hileman. And how much could a couple of scars (that needed repair anyway) be worth, he thought as he continued to listen to Turzak. Maybe a couple hundred thousand at most. And if Morgan and their expert witness could convince the jury that all the other complaints were just "nuisance complaints," then he might fare pretty well.

If they wanted seven million and got less than a million, it would be a victory, he thought. His professional reputation would be preserved, maybe even enhanced a little, he told himself. And Hileman and her attorneys would be left with egg on their faces with an award so much smaller than they had demanded. He could still win…if you could consider a small loss as a "win," he reassured himself. He still had a way out—sort of…a way to save face…to save his reputation. And he might not lose a dime, either, since the insurance company had to pay the first million.

Of course there might be punitive damages…the damages for a few derogatory comments…for a few misplaced words that night, but they couldn't amount to very much. Big deal, he thought. He was either going to have to deny most of that anyway or claim that he had to be firm with his comments in order to shock her into listening to him, so as to prevent her from any further injury. That he was just looking out for the patient. And besides, it might be his opportunity to tell the jurors just how obnoxious and drunk she had been that night. At any rate, punitive damages couldn't be worth all that much. Maybe another hundred thousand—max, he thought.

Could potentially come out smelling like a rose, he imagined, unless the shooting at Tatter's screwed things up. That was still the big unknown. It had been almost five days, and he still hadn't had to get involved. Maybe Mordy was right and the shooting might just blow over, he hoped.

And then the other caveat was this alcohol thing, he thought as he continued to half listen to Turzak's opening statement…his opening salvo. Didn't know which way that would swing. Still a long shot, but it could affect the whole trial if it was discovered that he had been drinking that night. A drunken doctor taking care of a patient was just about as bad as a drunken pilot flying a plane. If that happened, then all bets were off. Wouldn't be a small settlement of less than a million then, he knew. No, it would be, more likely, the full seven million…if not more, he thought. It would destroy him professionally, too. Who would ever want to have surgery by someone who might be drunk? The state would probably pull his license anyway, if they found out he had been drinking, he knew. And then, if it was discovered that he had been in a bar like

Tatter's…would just add fuel to the fire…would confirm all doubts about the alcohol issue.

He would just have to cross his fingers and hope that the judge believed Candy…If he did have to have her testify. And then hope that the shooting just evaporated and didn't become an issue too, he thought while Turzak continued to talk.

It had taken Turzak almost three hours to explain the twenty-seven claims of malpractice brought against him in the lawsuit, before finishing up with Hileman's facial-scars issue.

"You can see how bad the scars really are," Turzak continued, moving over to where Hileman was seated and pointing to the scars on her face…sort of tracing the torturous outline of them with his finger. "You don't even need an expert to tell you how bad these scars are…how painful and unsightly they are…You can see that for yourself!" Turzak said now, with more intensity in his voice. "Devastating scars…marking her for life…unable to venture out into public without the fear…the *realization*…that everyone will be looking at her, offended and appalled at the sight of these unsightly scars. They are terrible, horrendous, life-changing scars. She is embarrassed, ashamed, and afraid to go out in public. She has nightmares and is constantly depressed because of these scars. A beautiful woman having her beauty taken away from her—needlessly—by a careless, uncaring physician. I want you all to remember these facial scars…to look at them every day while you're sitting here, and imagine what it would be like for her to have to live with these scars. And all because of some callous, uncaring treatment by a physician who feels he is above reproach," he said, pausing for a short time, seeming somewhat reluctant, before telling the judge he had finished his opening statement.

Turzak had droned on for almost three hours, Weed realized as the judge adjourned the trial, telling the jurors that they had heard enough for one day and then telling them that tomorrow the defense would present their opening statements.

Hadn't been as bad as he thought. Most of it was just a repeat of what had already appeared countless times in the newspapers. Maybe a few minor revelations about some of the care he had given and the derogatory comments he had made to Hileman that night, but nothing earth-shattering.

Nothing earth-shattering the whole day, he realized, but the constant attack on his character had been tiring and difficult for Weed to listen to at times. Wasn't near as bad as he thought it would be, and he was somewhat relieved as the courtroom started to clear.

And he would have his day in court, too. He would have his chance to debunk all the half-truths and lies that Turzak had told the jurors. To tell the jurors how drunk and obnoxious Hileman had been that night. How she insisted on smoking, and how she had shouted out obscenities at everyone as she recklessly chased her dog through the ER. Time to tell the jury how bogus all her injuries were; that they were fabrications of a malingerer. See how Hileman liked that. *His* turn to spin the truth, to tell *his* lies and half-truths, he thought.

But it was all just more of the same. Spin. Spin the facts to meet your own needs. Was what everyone did today anyway. Why did he expect anything different? Just make up the story that best serves your needs. Truth had nothing to do with anything anymore, Weed thought. He lied too, so why did he expect anyone else to be different? Lying almost seemed like the truth these days. It was all about who could tell the best lies. The truth be damned. That was life: who could lie the best.

But he felt strange as he rinsed his flushed face with cool water in the restroom outside the courtroom. A sort of melancholy feeling…as if it was all surreal…not really happening to him. Plus, he guessed he didn't really care all that much what happened. He was getting too old to deal with things like this anymore. The thought of giving it all up and moving back home sprung into his head again as he crossed the street and sat in his car for a minute, gathering his senses and breathing in some fresh air. He was thankful that at least the first day of the trial was now history.

CHAPTER SIXTEEN

Monday, May 10
5:24 p.m.

He tried to call Candy as he drove toward home, but there was no answer.

When he saw Frank and Helen's car parked in his driveway, he slowed the MG just slightly before accelerating and moving quickly past the house. Well, that was an easy decision, he thought. Wasn't going to deal with those two again tonight, he thought driving around aimlessly for the next half hour before stopping at a liquor store for a fresh bottle of bourbon.

He sipped at his drink as he slowly drove past Tatter's Bar once and then back again, trying to get a good look inside, but the bar seemed abandoned...dark, except for one fluorescent beer light flickering chaotically somewhere deep in the bar. Pickles's bike was parked at the side of the building, but luckily Pickles was nowhere in sight.

And when he drove past Candy's apartment, her windows were dark, and there was no answer when he dialed her number. He hadn't gotten around to buying any Viagra anyway, he thought as he drove on aimlessly until it was almost dark, mostly thinking about the trial...and not answering Sandy's calls on his cell.

He parked the MG down the street from his house when he saw Helen's car still parked in the driveway...far enough away that no one would see him but close enough to watch for Helen and Frank to leave.

He sat there for almost an hour before Frank finally came out of the house carrying an easel, with Helen trailing after him. He watched as they stood in the driveway and talked to Sandy for a couple of minutes longer before getting into their car and driving off.

"Where the hell have you been, and why didn't you answer your damn phone?" Sandy asked him at the door...drunk and holding an empty wine glass in her hand. "That was pretty ignorant to just drive by the house without stopping. Yeah, we all heard your rickety piece of junk go clanking by...slowing down and then just zooming on past. Only car in town that makes that kind of a racket," she said, following him into the living room. "And Frank was standing right by the window looking out when you went by...He saw the car...said that it looked like your car.

Embarrassing...And we all knew why you did it. Helen telling me that you probably were tired of seeing them...and then I had to make up some stupid excuse that it wasn't you...that it was probably someone else," she said as she poured another glass of wine. "And then I had to act like I was talking to you on the phone that you wouldn't answer...so that I could tell them you were at the hospital for some kind of lame-brain emergency," she ranted.

He really didn't feel like fighting, and she had had way too much to drink...enough fighting for one day.

"*Which* they didn't believe but acted like they did...*which* just made it all that much more awkward and embarrassing! *And* after

I spent all afternoon cooking...trying to be nice," she mumbled, shaking her head.

"How could you possibly invite those two annoying people over twice in one week after what I had to put up with today? We run out of friends?"

"You're just pissed off that she said something that made you mad. That for once someone actually told you the truth. And yeah, we *have* run out of friends...thanks to you. They're the only two people left, but at least they have stood by us through this whole damn mess," Sandy said, pausing to take a drink of wine. "And Helen has really helped me get through this mess, and without *her* we wouldn't even be having an anniversary party...And Frank has been nothing but supportive of you. Always telling me how great you are, and how proud he is to be your friend...and how great a surgeon you are, even after all this shit in the newspaper. You *know* he brought all his paint stuff over here just to help you take your mind off the trial...And then you go zooming by in your damn rickety heap of junk. How callous! Frank looked like a wet puppy. If we lose *them,* we won't have *any* friends all," she said as she finished off another glass of wine. "But sometimes I think it's the truth what she told you and that's why you don't like her. That you're empty inside! No emotions. No love. You don't care about anyone but *yourself*...and that's just what caused this mess," she said, finally falling silent.

"Not what she said, exactly...And it has nothing to do with what Helen said. I don't *care* what Helen says. And don't worry, I have plenty of emotions. *You* just don't know people like *I* know people. How they tear you apart a little piece at a time. You don't understand because you don't have to deal with them every day...You don't understand their true nature," he said as she drifted off into the kitchen when her drink was empty.

He let her cool down for the next half hour as he sat in the bathroom and read an article about some drug-abusing football player who was trying to make a comeback. But he couldn't concentrate hearing Sandy's intermittent rants.

"Frank said he saw you go through the park today and told me to have you stop by tomorrow," she said after he finally came out of the bathroom…much calmer now as she lay in bed. "So at least stop by and see him, and tell him that you were at the hospital like I told them you were, so we can at least get our stories straight. Don't want them to think I'm a liar too," she said as she lay in bed reading a magazine. "I might go down to the festival myself. Helen was there, and she said there's some pretty interesting stuff. And Frank told me to tell you he's in tent number seventeen…near the front…and that he already sold two of his paintings. I know that you don't really give a damn, but I just want to make sure that he knows I told you.

"I mean, I know you had a bad day…I can understand that," she added, laying the magazine aside and now somewhat teary-eyed. "But it's a lot of stress for me too. Not just you. I have to suffer the consequences of your lawsuit, too…listening to all the comments… reading all the nasty things they're saying about you in the newspaper…and that there's no way we're not going to lose everything," she said and then began to cry. "I had a bad dream that our house had been turned into one big garage sale with all our friends there… laughing and taking stuff without even paying…And Mordy dragging one of our expensive sofas down the street," she said, wiping the tears from her eyes. "You just shouldn't have pissed her off," she said, starting again on the speech he had heard so many times before. "You should have just kept your mouth shut that night and not ever said a word to her. That's why she's suing you…not because of those scars. And she has all these influential friends…And people seem to like her even if she is a drunk. And she owns half this damn town…employs half the people in the city, one way or another… And now they're all our enemies. We're just lucky they don't want to tar and feather both of us. That's why we're in this damn mess. You had to get smart and open your mouth to the wrong person," she said as she started to sob. "Didn't I tell you that was going to happen one of these days? That you couldn't control your temper, your emotions...just like Helen said?"

Deep sobs...hurtful sobs...But for some reason, he didn't feel bad for her. She seemed more concerned about the money than anything. He felt as if maybe she deserved what she had gotten, too.

"You never have been sensitive about my feelings," Sandy said, somewhat more composed now.

"I'm just as sensitive as anyone," he said, tired of it all. "But who cares about my feelings? Who cares about me? Who's sensitive about my feelings?" he said as rolled to the wall and pulled his pillow over his head to drown out her crying. "Twenty-five fuckin' years of taking care of abusive ingrates. You think anyone cares about my feelings?" he asked, but there was no answer...only silence.

CHAPTER SEVENTEEN

Tuesday, May 11
7:34 a.m.

The story about the trial was on the front page. One long column continuing on page two with three more half columns, he could see as he sat down at the kitchen table for day number two. Was like walking through a mine field reading the article... every line painful, a potential embarrassment...all the derogatory comments and harsh details—there, for the whole world to read. But then, not too much more than what had already been written about. Maybe people would eventually get tired of reading about it, he thought as he put a bottle of bourbon in his coat pocket just before Sandy entered the kitchen.

But nothing in the newspaper about the shooting at Tatter's, he thought, mildly relieved.

"Don't know if I can stand being in the same room with Hileman this Saturday," Weed said as he pushed the newspaper aside. "Our luck, we'll all be seated at the same table," he added.

"No chance of that...Hileman will be way up front at the awards table, like she always is. They're giving her another award this year... something about her donating fifty thousand dollars for the new Substance Abuse Wing at the hospital," Sandy said as she stirred some sugar into her coffee.

"Right up front to show off all her scars. To let everyone know just how bad a surgeon I am."

"Yeah, maybe, but I figure the lighting's always bad up there. And with all the shadows the scars probably won't look so bad."

"You think the hospital would ever give me an award...for all the money that I've made for them over the years?" he asked rhetorically but not sure why. "Maybe 'Schmuck of the Year.' Twenty-five years of my life...what's that worth? They abandon you like rats on a sinking ship," he said but hadn't even noticed that Sandy had left the kitchen. "No chance," Weed murmured to himself as he watched Sandy come back into the kitchen, unsure if she had even heard what he had said.

"We're already the main topic of conversation these days. People that I thought were our friends are just as bad as our enemies... spreading rumors," Sandy said. "Like you said...It's all a big soap opera to them...just entertainment."

"Yeah well, didn't I tell you? You don't know people like I do. You don't know how vicious people can be...with all the lies and rumors...just like the trial yesterday...was nothing but a bunch of lies and half-truths. And people just love to see you screw up."

"Misery loves company," Sandy added as she sipped at her coffee. "Didn't even know what those words meant—until now, I think. Anything in the newspaper?" she added.

"Small article. Old news...mainly."

"Mordy says that we should have a contingency plan—just in case," she said when he walked back over to the table. "Says that the police could take the house almost immediately...get an injunction or something, and that we should think about someplace else to stay—just in case. Mordy said, with how vindictive Hileman's attorney are, that they could go after all our assets right away—including the house."

"Yeah well, Mordy's a schmuck. He gives us a bunch of crappy advice and then charges us twice as much as any other attorney would charge. Why? Because we're his friends? He likes to see people suffer...You know that. And we haven't lost yet. Still might only be a small jury award...And like I told you...a small settlement is as good as a win, anyway. So we still might come out looking okay."

"Don't know...too much to even think about now," she said. "I'm excited about the banquet anyway...no matter how bad Hileman looks," she said after a long pause. "I'm not going to worry about what people think from now on...Helen told me that. I'm just going to have a good time...act like there's not a thing in the world bothering me. Dance and live it up and act like I'm happy and not worry about what people are saying or what Hileman looks like. I don't even care if she looks like Frankenstein. And you should too. Just make them all think that we don't care...that everything's fine with us."

"You hear anything back from the garage?" he asked her after a long silence...as he picked up the keys to the MG and started toward the door.

"Not a word."

"Well, I can't get the radio to turn off in the damn car now. Driving me crazy," he said. "I have to listen to the same newscaster and shit hillbilly music every day. Like that movie...what's its name... *Groundhog Day* or something...I'm being punished. Like the damn car is pissed at me too."

"That reminds me," Sandy said just before he got out the door. "A couple of men were looking at your car the other day," she said and paused. "I think it was Sunday. Scared me at first. I thought that maybe you had hit someone or something, and they might be the police. But then I figured out that it was probably just someone interested in buying your car…But by the time I got out there to see—they were gone," she said. "Maybe someone's finally interested in it. At least that's a little bit of good news for you," she added.

"Yeah," he said shrugging his shoulders, but a wave of fear shot though him, and the thought that it could very well have been the police. That someone had seen the car at the bar and told the police about it. The car stuck out like a sore thumb. Never considered that the car could undermine his attempts at avoiding trouble with the police. Car was turning on him, taking on a life of its own, he thought.

"Someone might finally take it off our hands," she said, giving him a kiss at the door. "And then you can get a more dependable car," she added as she followed him down the driveway. "And I'm sorry about last night…It was sort of thoughtless to let them come over," she said, but he could tell that her words were forced and difficult. "But what could I tell them?"

Was going to have to call Mordy again maybe, he thought as he backed the car down the driveway. He took a Valium and a drink of bourbon as he drove toward the courthouse. The bar shooting was getting a little too uncomfortable, he thought. Maybe it would be better to just talk to the police and be done with it, especially if they already knew about him being there. Just when he was thinking that problem might be behind him…that it might all just disappear…it might spring to life.

But what Sandy had told him still could be nothing, he imagined as he waited in traffic. People were always stopping to look at the damn car. Shouldn't have even been driving that car the night of the shooting anyway, he thought. If Sandy hadn't wrecked her car, he wouldn't have been forced to use that rust bucket. And the car could end up being the only reason that the cops knew he was there, he thought, angry at what Sandy had done as he continued his drive. Almost seemed as if it could have been intentional.

He pulled into the lot across from the courthouse and waited. A group of reporters were already gathered around two TV vans

parked in front of the courthouse...more reporters than yesterday...one or one hundred reporters—probably didn't matter much.

There were more people and more vendors in the park too. In
the distance, behind the tents, he could see the top of a Ferris wheel
spinning and some other rides still under construction. Frank's tent
had the flaps down, but Frank was nowhere in sight, he could see as
he sipped at his drink.

But when the ice shifted in the cup, he spilled the last few drops
of the bourbon and Coke on his tie. The smell of bourbon on his
tie...that's all he needed, he thought as he tried to blot it off. That
would look good too, he realized as he rubbed at the dark spots:
to come to court smelling like a distillery. Great, he thought. And
Sandy wouldn't like it if she smelled alcohol on his tie, and she could
smell everything a mile away, he thought, noticing how ridiculous
his life had become.

"Out damn spot," he said out loud as he rubbed at it, laughing
lightly about how funny it was but realizing that it really wasn't...
And then feeling somewhat annoyed at himself for taking the alcohol issue so lightly. He could lose everything and he was making a
joke out of it. Nice, he thought.

He left the car and walked across the street, avoiding the reporters who hadn't seemed to notice his approach yet, before quickly
entering the courthouse.

"They all for us?" he asked Morgan, nodding toward the reporters section of the courtroom and sitting down next to him.

"Who else? They're turning us all into celebrities," Morgan replied, shuffling some papers in his briefcase. Then he added, "Cut
my finger getting the tags off my suit this morning," holding up
his bandaged finger for Weed to see. "Had a hell of a time getting it stopped," he said as he pulled at the bandage to check for
blood. "But I think we did okay yesterday. Turzak didn't present a
very convincing case, and his explanations all seemed pretty weak.
Maybe the jury will see right through it all. You know, maybe if they

complain so much about so many things, no one will believe any of it in the end. At least that's what I'm hoping. I guess we still have a small chance of coming out of this with only a few bruises. And it does seem like a lot of the case is personal…like the injuries are less important than the way you acted," Morgan said. "But then, you never know how a jury will see it. That's the big unknown…Juries can do strange things sometimes…give people millions for nothing. Prepare for the worst and expect the best, I guess…" he added as his voice trailed off. "Oh, and I found out that the names on the paper I showed you, the one that Turzak gave to the judge, are actually people that work at a place called the Vegas bar…a bartender and a waiter, I think. Turzak wants them to testify that they saw you there drinking the night of Hileman's accident. Unusual, but the judge wants to take their deposition. You remember anything about being there that night?"

"Yeah, I was probably there. I mean, I go there a lot, but I wasn't drinking that night because I never drink when I'm on call—and I was on call. And I could probably get a witness who will testify that I wasn't drinking. And I thought that issue had been settled," he added but thought that his explanation sounded too well-thought-out and fabricated.

"Well, not quite yet. He threw out the nurse's testimony, the one who said she'd smelled alcohol on your breath that night, because of previous personal problems you two had, so maybe he'll throw this out too…especially if you can find a witness to refute it. Judge is in a big hurry to get this thing over with…He has some kind of big vacation planned or something…so he won't be happy adding names to the witness list. But if he does let them testify, we're in trouble," he added as he took an anatomical model of the cervical spine from his briefcase and looked at it closely before running his finger across some of the labels he had dangling from a couple of the vertebra, whispering to himself some complicated medical term.

"Just Hileman's hacks trying to make me look bad...They know their case is weak," Weed added.

"Well, if you have a witness, that would be really helpful. You know, 'he said/she said,'" he added after a long pause, staring up at the ceiling as if he was trying to remember something about the plastic model in front of him. "Always had a fear of speaking in front of crowds," Morgan admitted, for some reason, before going back to studying the model.

"Welcome," the judge said after the bailiff led the jurors into the courtroom. "Already too hot in here...We're probably going to have to finish up early today," he added when they were all seated and then turned to Morgan and told him to proceed with his opening statement.

Morgan stood, thanked the judge and the jurors, and then spent the first hour refuting most of the accusations Turzak had made in his opening statement: explaining to the jury that the injuries were the result of the accident and not the result of the treatment. That fact was the most important thing to realize, he stressed. That, along with the fact that none of the injuries she was claiming to have suffered were the result of anything Dr. Weed had done improperly or hadn't done at all.

The outcome of Hileman's injuries would have remained unchanged, regardless of the medical treatment, and everything had been done properly, he added. Then he showed the jurors the plastic model of the spine and demonstrated how removing the collar would have had no untoward effect on Hileman's neck injury. That it wouldn't cause her paralysis, or headaches, or depression, or cause her to be confined to a wheelchair, Morgan told them.

And then Morgan told the jurors how initial repair of any laceration often needed to be revised—especially facial lacerations—and that it is standard practice to do the secondary revision much later, after the lacerations had healed. Then Morgan showed the jurors blown-up "before and after" pictures of patients who'd had their unsightly scars revised.

"You can see the dramatic difference," Morgan instructed, running a pointer across the facial scars on one of the "before" photographs. "As you can see, this patient's scars—not much different than Ms. Hileman's scars—were revised by a plastic surgeon, and now as you can see, they are almost unnoticeable," he said as he showed them the "after" photo. "That's exactly what Dr. Weed had planned to do. To do a secondary repair later, under better surgical conditions...or to have a plastic surgeon revise the scars—which still can be done. And I assume that Ms. Hileman will have them revised. But contrary to what Attorney Turzak stated, Dr. Weed did spend an appropriate amount of time repairing the lacerations... And he did use a more-than-adequate number of sutures in order to repair this laceration—primarily," he said emphatically.

Short and sweet...and the truth. Wasn't bad. Wasn't quite as dynamic as Turzak, but maybe more convincing, Weed thought as he watched Morgan move in front of the jury. Yesterday, Turzak had seemed more tentative and unsure of himself, and he had lost his place a couple of times, going back over material he had already covered. And Turzak seemed unsure about his explanation of a concussion. But today, Morgan seemed to be confident about most everything he said to the jurors.

But Morgan looked different toward the end of his remarks, Weed thought. Like someone had beaten him up and he was coming apart at the seams. His shirt was misaligned, and part of it was sticking out over his belt and another part was sticking to his sweaty body. Like a big, overstuffed chair with the stuffing coming out, Weed thought. Huffing and puffing, not lifting his feet any higher than he had to, scraping his shoes across the courtroom floor...He even seemed shorter and fatter now too...like the insides of his body had settled some. Maybe he had actually evolved into a more sympathetic figure at the end, or maybe it was just Weed's imagination.

The jurors listened and seemed interested. But what had been irritating, what had been most disturbing to Weed the entire time, was that Morgan had not made even one derogatory statement about Hileman's behavior that night. Morgan finally came to the end of his opening statement…nearly two hours…And he had not made even one minor attack on her character, on her behavior that night. Maybe the only thing about Morgan's opening statement that Weed hadn't liked, hadn't agreed with.

"I think that's enough for now," the judge said, barely waiting long enough for Morgan to get back to his seat.

"We can return at 2:00 p.m., and the plaintiff will begin his case against Dr. Weed, but we're not going to go very long. We'll hear the first witness and that's probably it…keeps getting hotter in here every day—every hour," he stated disgustedly as he dismissed the jurors and then brought down the gavel.

Weed stood on the courthouse steps for a minute and stretched, gazing out at the street, the parking lot, and the festival before noticing two police officers walking toward his car. Weed froze for an instant—in fear—recalling what Sandy told him earlier about the two men who had been looking at his car. But the two cops just passed by his car uninterested.

He was getting paranoid, he thought as he continued down the steps and across the street. He sat in his car for a few minutes, scanning the horizon to make sure no one was looking before taking a drink of bourbon and watching a clown ride a unicycle precariously down the sidewalk.

CHAPTER EIGHTEEN

Tuesday, May 11
1:48 p.m.

Still had a good bit of time before the trial would resume, Weed thought as he ate lunch at a small diner next to the courthouse. Through the window he watched as Hileman's driver came down the street carrying Hileman's dog.

"For customers only!" the owner said to the driver as he carried the dog inside the shop and past where Weed was sitting.

"I am a customer," he said. "Dog's a customer too," he said, sort of laughing as he entered the restroom at the back of the shop. When he came out of the restroom he sat at the counter, two chairs down from where Weed was sitting, still holding the dog under his arm but now talking on his cell phone and glancing at a menu.

"Bitch is wacky, I tell you. Drivin' me crazy," he said into the phone, and then there was a long pause. Had to be talking about Hileman, Weed thought as the driver transferred the dog to his

other arm without turning the dog, so that now the dog was looking directly back at Weed.

"Yeah well, I don't care. I'm no fuckin' nursemaid. She has me
giving this damn thing some kind of medicine every two hours.
Some little green pill, but the dog doesn't look sick," he said and
then paused to listen.

"I understand," Weed could hear a female voice say on the other
end of the line but couldn't make out anything else she was saying.

"That's bullshit, babe," he said whining and then laughed at
something she said. After another pause he said, "Some kind of
bowel problem...colitis or some irritable bowel something. Have
to give her two pills every two hours...doesn't that colitis have
something to do with your bowels?" he asked, and then paused for
a short time, and then started laughing. "I hope she doesn't start
shittin' either," he said, laughing after another pause. He talked
for another couple of minutes and then closed his phone before
looking back around at Weed and nodding in his direction when
he realized that he had been watching...just as the dog let out a
bark.

"You can't have that dog in here," the owner said, coming over
and standing in front of him, waiting for him to respond. "It's a
health-code violation," he said with a heavy Italian accent. "State
will shut me down. You're going to get dog hairs all over the pies. I
told you the same thing yesterday," he said angrily, moving the pie
display further down the counter. "You see the sign?"

"Yeah well, just give me whatever you got back there. The special, I guess," the driver said throwing down money on the counter
as he stood and started toward the door.

"I'll bring it out," the owner said, taking the money off the counter as the driver carried the dog outside the shop. The driver leaned
up against the frame of the window of the restaurant and smoked a
cigarette and made two more phone calls as the dog sniffed around
at the sidewalk. When the store owner brought out his food, he

stood there and ate, tossing small pieces of his sandwich onto the sidewalk for the dog.

When Weed had finished eating, he walked past the driver and the dog…smiling…as he moved away from the barking dog. Should have kicked the damn mutt, he thought as he walked back to his car. Could have made it look like an accident, he imagined. At least get a little retribution…and the dog had been part of the problem anyway, he thought.

When he got back into his car he took a few sips of his bourbon and Coke, making sure that none of the reporters were anywhere near to see him. And he sipped more carefully this time, so that he didn't spill any more on his tie. He called Candy. While he waited for her to answer, he thought about his embarrassing sexual experience with her and wondered what she must have thought. An old man who couldn't cut the mustard anymore…probably…maybe she even laughed about it later with her friends. He had seen her make fun of other customers with her friends many times.

Wasn't going to let it happen again, he told himself…as he listened to the phone ringing. Would pick up some Viagra and take it an hour or so before he got there…or whatever the instructions were…and make sure that he was ready. Didn't give a damn about the side effects…If you couldn't have sex, wouldn't matter if you did go deaf…or blind…or whatever else, he thought as he listened to the call go unanswered.

Would worry about that problem later, he told himself as he walked back to the courtroom.

For the next hour and a half, he listened to Turzak and Morgan examine and then cross-examine the ER doctor who had been working the night of the accident. His testimony was not much different than his deposition: that the collar had been removed inappropriately, and that the laceration (at least in his expert opinion) had not been repaired properly. The ER doctor also added that the laceration had not been cleansed or debrided properly, and the actual repair had been done incorrectly. He testified that a laceration that severe should have been repaired in layers with finely placed, well-approximated sutures, instead of in one layer with just a few sutures. "Actually, she probably should have been taken to the OR and had her laceration repaired by a plastic surgeon," he had concluded after Turzak's questioning. But he couldn't really state what—if any—damage had occurred from removing the collar, since no factures had actually been observed, and that a secondary repair is often necessary for facial laceration.

"Not too bad," Morgan said after Wisensee adjourned the trial for the day. "Nothing devastating...no real damage...would probably call it a draw...But we've still got a long way to go," he said as he stood and gathered up his papers.

"Oh yeah," Morgan stated out of the blue, as they sat there and waited for the courtroom to clear. "We take the depositions from those two people from the bar, in the morning. Judge wants to talk to both of them tomorrow morning, before the trail begins...So I'll need the name of that witness you told me about," he said stopping to take out his pen and paper. "Judge said if she's credible, he's going to make it a 'nonissue.' You know, like I told you...a 'he said/she said' sort of situation. Who do you believe...I mean, how credible can a fifty-two-year-old bartender be—who's probably an alcoholic, too? How could he remember who was or wasn't drinking at his bar two years ago?"

"Yeah," Weed said pausing for a moment, thinking before writing Candy's name on the paper Morgan had given him. "Have to get her phone number, but here's her name," he said handing the paper back to Morgan and hoping that the name he had written down was her actual name, which he always had doubts about. Not every stripper could be named Candy, he reasoned, even though she had adamantly claimed that it was her real name.

"'Cause we might just need her. I just hope she looks and speaks like Mother Teresa," Morgan said, laughing.

Didn't even know if she would testify, and he had already given Morgan her name—if it was her real name...and she definitely didn't look like Mother Teresa, he thought as he left the courtroom and entered the rotunda. Might just open up a whole new can of worms, he thought. Was all getting too complicated...His life was unraveling. This witness...that witness...this problem...that problem. He could hardly keep it all straight himself. Seemed to be all blending...all his problems bleeding together. The bar shooting... Candy...his trial...and Ms. Hileman were all becoming one big family. Using a stripper as a witness in a malpractice case? If they found out, that would make him look pretty ridiculous, he imagined. Especially if they found out about the bar shooting too. But then, it was all so ridiculous anyway...couldn't really get that much worse. He stopped at the top of the courthouse steps and took in a deep breath of fresh air. Didn't like it...could be risky...She could be a loose cannon answering questions...and she could say some pretty inappropriate things sometimes...using some pretty colorful language, he knew. Wasn't sure if he could pull it off, but then again, he didn't have much choice. If they could prove that he had been drinking that night, then the State would almost certainly pull his license...And without a license, he would be finished. And to make matters worse, someone might recognize Candy from all her stripper pictures that had been published in the newspaper over the last couple of years. But at this point, she was his only option; the only person that he could depend on to lie for him. Couldn't even ask his best friend to do something like that, he thought as he watched two reporters aim their cameras in his direction. He started down the steps, ignoring their questions as he hurried off in a different direction. He moved away as quickly as possible, trying to blend into the festival crowd, until he was sure he had lost them. Then he backtracked across the street to his car.

Would have to set up a meeting with Candy but tell her about testifying later, he thought as he listened to her phone ring. Didn't have the strength to go into it now. When she finally answered, he listened to her drone on about all her problems: that she still needed money, that Tatter had taken a turn for the worse, that Pickles scared her, that he was still threatening people who had been in the bar that night to keep their mouths shut, that what was more important was that she couldn't find anywhere else to dance, that the police wouldn't let her get her costumes out of Tatter's Bar—blah, blah, blah. For over a half hour he sat in the parking lot and just listened, until she finally paused to light a cigarette.

"Think I might need a big favor..." he said before telling her that he would explain later.

He sat at the bar near the YMCA, drank for a while, and looked out at his car in the dim light of the parking lot. He was trying to convince himself that it wasn't the police who had looked at the car. If it had been, he would have known by now. Sandy was probably right...It was just someone who was interested in buying the pile of junk.

Life After the Fall...after he lost it all, he thought as he drove toward the Quick Fix. Reservations for a spot beneath the Ninth Street Bridge...with the rest of the bums...that was his contingency plan...the one Sandy and Mordy wanted him to make. Wondered what they would think...if he told them what he had come up with? Could hold up a beat-up piece of cardboard...by the side of a road...WILL DO SURGERY FOR FOOD written on it—if he didn't end up losing his license—which seemed more and more likely. He thought about how absurd his situation had become. Could maybe drive the Senior Center bus for bingo night...or work at the Quick Fix with Bob...some easy job without any stress...couldn't be any worse than what he had been doing for the last thirty years, he imagined as he pulled into the Quick Fix.

"How is the Mustard Queen, anyway?" Bob asked him when he entered the store.

He helped Bob restock a soft-drink cooler and a grocery shelf as they talked about basketball and the trial, feeling somewhat relaxed by the simplicity of the mundane tasks he was performing.

The Mustard Queen. Never heard that one before, he thought as he left the store and started his drive home. Was sort of funny.

When he got home, Sandy was gone. One less problem for him to deal with, he thought as he poured himself a drink, lay down on the sofa, and turned on the TV—tired and exhausted.

Was a terrible day, he thought, closing his eyes and falling into a deep sleep almost immediately and dreaming about the past...a recurrent dream that he had had many times...a good dream about when he was young and the star on the high school basketball team. Making winning shots, impressing everyone and listening to all his friends cheering him on. But it had never happened...never was a star anywhere or at anything...and when he woke he felt empty. Unfulfilled dreams...his nightmare in reverse...when the good dreams end and reality returns, he thought as he listened to Sandy pulling her car into the garage.

He didn't need any more misery today, he thought as he hurried up the steps to bed and then just lay there in the dark.

"You sleepin'?" she asked when she came into the room and turned on the lights. But he didn't answer her. He could tell she was angry about something.

"Quite an article...can't believe the things you said. Well...I can," she continued after a short, dramatic pause, "since you call almost everyone an obnoxious bitch," she said and then began throwing things around and slamming things down, just to make sure he was awake. "After all she has done for this community and all the money she's donated. You're a real gem," she added. He could tell that she had been drinking heavily.

"That was a lie," he said mumbling into the pillow, pissed that she was turning on him too. "What I actually called her was a 'drunken, obnoxious bitch.'"

"Yeah, real funny. That's just the attitude that got you into this mess in the first place...that and your sarcasm that you think is so cute and funny...But that makes everyone sick...Even Helen can't stand your attitude," she added before slamming the door and leaving the room.

CHAPTER NINETEEN

Wednesday, May 12
8:12 a.m.

"Might bring a book to read...trial's getting pretty boring," Weed said, trying to break the ice as Sandy came into the kitchen. But Sandy just sat there, ignoring him...reading the newspaper and drinking her coffee. Probably still pissed off about last night, he thought as he poured more coffee. "Don't even know why I have to be there," he said, laughing lightly. "Bob called her the 'Mustard Queen'...never heard that one before, but it's sort of funny," he said. Then, he added stupidly after a long pause, "Her dog has irritable bowel syndrome...Can you believe that? Saw her driver talking to someone on the phone about the dog. Never heard of a dog with irritable bowel syndrome," he continued speaking into the dead silence.

"Yeah, now *that's* really interesting," she said sarcastically. "And the reason you think it's so boring is because you're in *denial...*

The trial is just so overwhelming that you can't *accept* it…" she said, sounding disgusted.

"Was just trying to make a joke…thought it would be funny," he said, pissed that he had to deal with her attitude this early in the morning.

"Newspapers and TV stations don't think it's so boring. They're all saying that she's really sick—bedridden…in a wheelchair—paralyzed. They say she could be confined to a wheelchair for the rest of her life…that she has intractable pain…and is on high doses of pain medication. They also say that this case could be one of the largest in the State…*the* largest, actually…that the award could be up to twenty million dollars, since she's some kind of CEO with the company and she makes over ten million a year…not including bonuses," she said, moving the paper toward him. "You see why I'm so paranoid? As soon as our party's over, I'm loading everything that's left in the house into a truck and taking it over to my mother's storage locker. I *might* even have Ronnie take down some of the curtains and remove some of those expensive fixtures in the bathroom."

"What's left?"

"Yeah, what's left! Well, if it wasn't for our anniversary party, it would be empty by now…And Mordy agrees…hide as much as you can."

He really didn't want to argue and especially didn't want to bring Mordy into the conversation—again. He had done enough arguing and listening to the same old spiel. Enough, he thought as he read the paper, including the two articles about the trial. But there wasn't anything there that he and probably everyone else wasn't already aware of.

"You know what they have those girls doing, down at the ice cream store?" he finally asked as she continued to sit at the table—like a mummy—drinking her coffee. "They're having the waitresses dance when they're waiting on you; singing some kind of little kid's song. And then at the end, they all stomp their feet like they're happy," he said. "I guess it depends on what you order, but I don't think I've ever seen anything so ridiculous. Even the two-year-olds think it's ridiculous, I think."

"Yeah, I saw them last time I was there. They're doing it to bring in customers, and I think it's cute. Same thing as they do at that other restaurant right across the street. Must be a new wave."

"Yeah, well, pretty soon we'll all be dancing," he said. "I'll be dancing, too...dancing while I'm taking care of my patients...to distract them...so they won't realize how bad the ice cream really tastes. They all act like they're so happy. That's the strange thing... dancing and singing and wearing funny hats...like they actually like what they're doing," he added. "It's sort of fascinating—making people try to act happy. It's all part of the job..." he went on with his one-sided conversation as she went into the bathroom.

"Just like life," he said as he looked for any mention of the shooting in the paper. He let his mind wander about when Candy might answer her phone...would have to call her at lunch again, he thought.

"I sort of like it," Sandy finally said as she came back into the kitchen. Dr. Scott told me that I shouldn't watch or read anything about the trial, that it's making me too depressed. Says my affect is getting flat, whatever that means. So that's what I'm going to try to do—starting today," she said.

"Get to suffer all by myself. Just stick your head in the sand and ignore it. Wish I could do that."

"Don't worry, I suffer enough without reading the newspaper... putting up with all the snubs and all the stares. People saying behind my back, 'There goes Dr. Weed's wife; she's the one who's married to that doctor in the newspaper.' Dr. Jim thinks that I'm getting a little paranoid so he gave me a new medication that he said should help, but I'm not paranoid...It's real."

"Every time you go in to see him he gives you another pill?"

"Not every time," she answered, irritated.

He continued to half listen to Sandy while she rambled on about not wanting to act too interested, and he scanned the newspaper once before finding an article about a bank robber who had gotten away with his crime—even though the bank had been warned that they were going to get robbed. He couldn't be so lucky, he thought.

And there it was...He knew it would be. He could see it as he perused another section of the newspaper. Fortunately not on the front page, but there it was, a few pages back: Hileman in her collar and wheelchair, pictured in front of the courthouse talking to a group of reporters. Right there below the picture was a detailed account of Tuesday's testimony.

Seemed harder to read about it today than it had been to listen to yesterday in court, he thought.

And then beneath that was a small article about the shooting at Tatter's Bar...He had hit the trifecta, he thought as he quickly scanned the piece. Little progress had been made in the investigation...Tatter was still in critical condition...Anyone with any information was asked to contact the city police department...But the article didn't mention anything about the police looking for any cars.

Good news, he thought sarcastically, taking a Valium before finishing his coffee and leaving the house with a fresh bottle of bourbon.

He sipped at his drink as he sat in front of the courthouse and watched Morgan come down the street, then Turzak, and then Hileman's Mercedes pulled up and let her out. Same routine: smoking a cigarette, giving the dog a kiss, the driver pushing her into the courthouse, and then coming back out with the dog before disappearing into the park.

Morgan was sitting with his head bent, studying some papers when Weed sat down beside him.

"This is the problem," Morgan said, sliding a slip of paper toward him. "Turzak has a copy of your bar bill the night of the accident.

There were six mixed drinks ordered and paid for, before you left just after one-thirty. The witnesses were crap, but this bar bill is a real problem, so we're definitely going to have to talk to that witness you told me about," he said as he searched his briefcase. "You have her number? I'll give her a call and set something up, because this could cause the bottom to drop out for our case," he said as he took out his pen and waited for the number.

"Yeah, no problem," Weed replied, acting as if he was looking up the number on his cell phone. But after a couple minutes, he told Morgan he didn't have it and would have to give it to him later.

"Yeah, okay, that's fine," he said but sounded reluctant. "But get it soon, because I'm going to need to talk to her before she gives any statement. See what she's going to say," he said, putting the paper back into his briefcase. "Need her address, phone number, where she works, what toothpaste she uses, the whole nine yards," he added.

"Yeah, I'll get all that for you. I'll give her a call when I get her number from home. Give her a heads-up."

"And I need it as soon as possible," he said, pausing for a short time before looking back at him. "She okay?" he said and waited for an answer, but Weed just looked at him inquisitively. "You seem tentative. You know what I mean? Six drinks? I don't want some flaming alcoholic stumbling into the courthouse—drunk—giving a statement to the judge…If you know what I mean," he said as the bailiff led the jurors back into the courtroom. "Well, maybe I do want that," he added, talking to himself.

"She's fine…great girl…no problems," Weed said but didn't know if he sounded very convincing. Shit! He was going to have to talk Candy into testifying, Weed thought as he waited for the jurors to file past. Would have to come up with some kind of cover story for her. Certainly something other than working as a stripper at a bar…and praying they didn't dig too deeply into her past…Hell…

he didn't even know that much about her past, himself...She could be wanted in three states for all he knew.

For the rest of the morning he only half-listened to Turzak's expert witness, a neurosurgeon, tell the jurors (in no uncertain terms) that the neurological damage in her arms and legs was the direct result of Dr. Weed removing the cervical collar that had been supporting all her vertebra. The loss of this support had compressed all the nerves coming out of her neck. Graphically, he showed them all what he was talking about with scans, x-rays, and a plastic model. But Weed couldn't concentrate, and he didn't really care...thinking more about what he was going to do about Candy...trying to work out the details for coming up with a fail-safe plan...and trying to figure out how to pass off a stripper as a reliable witness.

"Cost them ten thousand," Morgan said, after the judge ended the morning session for the lunch break.

"What?" Weed asked, somewhat confused about what Morgan was telling him.

"That's what they had to pay that expert witness, that neurosurgeon, to say all those ridiculous things. Ten thousand...plus expenses," Morgan said, shaking his head. "That's what you should do: go around and testify in malpractice cases. Tell a jury whatever the lawyers want you to tell them; doesn't matter if it's true...just tell them whatever helps your case. You'd make a million dollars if you did that. And I never heard such a theory as that," he said with a laugh as he gathered up his papers, but Weed wasn't sure what theory Morgan was talking about.

When he got back to the car, he called Candy. "I need you to do that big favor for me that I told you about," he said when she answered. "What I need is to have someone cover for me that one night at the bar I told you about. I need someone to tell the judge that they were with me that night of Hileman's accident...and that they were the one that ordered the drinks...and that they were the person that drank the bourbon and Cokes, and that I didn't have anything to drink at all."

"Yeah..." she said, pausing for a long time before answering. "I been reading about it in the newspaper..." she went on hesitantly. "But I don't know, though...My brother did something like that and got thirty days in jail...made a big deal out of it...was in the paper and everything. Judge was just going to give him a fine, but then he said something nasty and they sent him to jail instead," she said as he listened to her light a cigarette. "I think they called it 'perjury' or something like that."

All of a sudden she had turned into an attorney, he thought. "Isn't really perjury...I mean, I'm not even sure you would be under oath or anything. And anyway, if I hadn't told you about that night, you would never have known that you weren't there. As far as you would have known, you could have been there that night. Right?"

"I don't know, Ben...I really like you, you know that...But I don't know...I don't like to get involved with legal things like this," she said. Then he told her that he could give her money, and that it really wasn't perjury when you didn't know for sure, and there was absolutely no way they could ever find out any differently. But she told him that she still wanted to think about it first.

"Need to know soon. To tell you the truth...if you don't go and talk to the judge, I'm probably going to lose the case. And if they think I was drinking, I could lose my license...couldn't even practice medicine then," he said in the most pathetic tone he could muster.

"Well, maybe...and I could use a little more money, since I can't find anywhere to dance...I mean, I've got bills coming out of my ears," she said. She told him she had to "vamoose" because she was going for another interview...but that she would call him later and they could talk then. And if she couldn't do it, maybe she could find someone else who would.

Great...maybe get another stripper to testify, he thought, although he did feel somewhat relieved that she hadn't just outright refused, he thought as he left the courthouse and headed for his car.

CHAPTER TWENTY

Wednesday, May 12
12:31 p.m.

What luck, he thought, the second day in a row that he had run into Hileman's driver. This time at a taco shop a half a block away from the first restaurant. After he had finished eating and was walking down a long, graffiti-covered hallway to use the bathroom, he could hear the muffled sound of a dog barking. When he opened the door to the men's room, Hileman's driver was standing there, leaning up against one of the sinks smoking a cigarette, and Hileman's dog was sniffing around one of the stalls.

The dog let out a bark when it looked up and saw Weed. The driver waved away a plume of thick, blue smoke circling his head and nodded at Weed. "Sorry 'bout the smoke," he said apologetically. Then he asked Weed if it was still raining outside as Weed stood at one of the urinals.

"Still coming down pretty hard," Weed answered off-handedly.

"Better watch, she's pretty unpredictable," the driver said when Weed was finished and leaned down to pet the dog. The driver pulled up his sleeve and showed Weed a small, fiery-red area over his right forearm.

"Little shit bit me there three days ago—for no damn good reason…other than she's a pain in the ass. Just decides to up and bite me. Have one on my leg, looks just like it. Hurts like a son-of-a-bitch too…and she isn't even my dog," he said. "She was my dog…she would be down at the pound a long time ago. Wouldn't think a little bite like that would hurt so bad," he said, talking to himself as he took a closer look at the bite.

"Yeah," Weed answered with a nod as he stood at the sink, looking in the mirror at the driver's arm.

"Not even my dog…" he repeated. "Belongs to some lady named Gertrude Hileman. You ever heard of her?" the driver asked, taking another drag off his cigarette.

Weed shook his head that he hadn't but then told him that maybe he had heard of her somewhere, but he wasn't sure where.

"Yeah, I never heard of her either until I got this job. She has more money than God…owns Hileman's Mustard. And I don't even like that shit, either. Sixty-seven flavors, or something like that, and I never found one that I liked," he said, taking another drag off his cigarette. "My wife likes the spicy hot jalapeno," he said, and then asked Weed if he minded if he smoked but kept talking without waiting for an answer.

"She hired me as her executive secretary six months ago…thinking I was supposed to be wearing a suit and sitting in some nice, plush office downtown. Instead, she's got me running a damn kennel. If I would have known I was going to be babysitting a dog, I never would have taken the damn job…'course, the money is pretty good."

Weed smiled and nodded as someone else hurried past them and into one of the stalls.

"Pain in the ass," he said, waving the smoke away again as Weed washed his hands. "She's over at the courthouse right now. You probably been reading about it in the paper...It's that story about her suing some poor bastard for all he's worth...over some scars on her face. And since they don't let dogs into the courthouse—I guess unless they're Seeing Eye dogs, I have to watch the mutt. Have to keep the damn thing close, so Hileman can see her whenever she comes out of the courthouse. She can't be away from the damn dog for any more than five minutes."

"Yeah, I know what you mean," Weed told him but felt strange standing so close to Hileman's driver and her dog...without him having a clue who he was. Sort of intriguing, he thought.

"Have to give it two of these pills every two hours," he continued, but Weed wasn't sure if he was just talking to himself now, setting his cigarette on the edge of the sink and then taking a bottle of pills from his shirt pocket. "She tells me the dog will die if it doesn't get these pills every two hours. I think they're some kind of pain pill, and the dog acts like she's addicted—the way she jumps all around until I give her one," he said as he tried to fish a small pill from the bottle.

"See how she acts?" he asked as the dog started jumping up and down as he held the pill down toward her and then took it away. "You ever see anything like that?" he said before flipping the pill up into the air. Weed watched as the dog jumped up and twisted around awkwardly, attempting to catch the pill in midair and then chasing it as it rolled across the floor.

"You ever see anything like that?" the driver asked again, looking over at Weed. "I'm half tempted to try one myself—if they're that good," he said and then laughed. "You ever hear of a dog that had a spastic colon?" he asked as Weed started toward the door.

"Not that I can remember," Weed said sort of laughing.

"I think they're both crazy," the driver said as Weed bent down in front of the dog and gave her a pat on the head before leaving.

Seemed eerily strange, almost bizarre, petting Hileman's dog and talking to her driver without her knowing about it and without the driver knowing who he was talking to. Wondered what Hileman would say if she knew he had been this close to her precious little dog, he thought as he walked back to his car.

He sat in the car for another couple minutes and took one last drink before walking back to the courthouse. Courtroom was warmer. Too hot to concentrate on anything for too long, Weed thought as he sat down beside Morgan. And the jurors all looked torpid, struggling to keep their eyes open.

Another long, tedious afternoon, Weed thought as he listened to Turzak's next expert witness tell the jurors about head injuries and concussions...droning on and on, for over two hours. More of the same...that Hileman had suffered irreversible *brain* damage this time, instead of the irreversible *neck* damage the other specialist had told them about. And that the brain damage had left her with an array of complications: migraines, depression, anxiety, post-traumatic stress disorder...demonstrated again on more plastic anatomical models. All leading to the same conclusion: Dr. Weed had been grossly negligent and responsible for all her problems.

Another afternoon of getting raked over the coals. Maybe not quite as bad as the morning session, and the witness seemed more dramatic...which made what he told the jurors seem all that much more unbelievable...And to tell the truth, it was almost too hot for anyone to really care, Weed thought.

When Turzak finished, Morgan stood and presented their side of the case. Again, trying to discredit most of what the expert had just told the jury. Same circumstances but a completely opposite conclusion. Didn't even sound like they were talking about the same case. Could have all been said in five minutes too—instead, it had taken them all afternoon. Almost appeared that at the end of the day the trial ended up back where they had all started—with nothing resolved.

It was almost 5:00 p.m. when the judge finally adjourned the trial for the day, but it seemed like it had taken a lot longer, Weed thought when Morgan reminded him that he would be on the witness stand testifying tomorrow.

"Make sure that you go over your deposition and all the questions that we worked on," Morgan said as they both left the courtroom. "And don't forget about that phone number," he added as an after-thought before he moved off in a different direction. Weed stood in front of the mirror in the men's room and rinsed his face. Looked tired, felt tired, and was exhausted. Three days closer to ending this misery, he thought as he left the courthouse.

He drove home and tried to sleep for an hour, but Sandy kept interrupting his sleep by either asking him or telling him about party arrangements and the leaking pool before he gave up on any hopes of sleep. He changed into some basketball shorts and left the house, relieved to get away from her annoying, incessant chatter.

CHAPTER TWENTY-ONE

Wednesday, May 12
6:48 p.m.

W hen he got to the basketball court, Bob was waiting for
him. They played two games against some younger guys
who were already there, but they lost both games. Then they sat on
top of a picnic bench and talked for a while as it started to get dark
and cold.

"Took me two days to recover from that last game," Bob said,
standing down from the picnic table as Weed put on his jacket. "I
think this might be my last year playing."

"Yeah, does seem like the luster has worn off. Not as exciting
as it used to be," Weed said, sitting down on the other end of the
table just as his phone started to vibrate with Candy's number on
the screen.

"Just be a minute," he said, but Bob waved and jumped off the
table, jogging a short distance away from the courts toward his

house before slowing to a walk. Weed watched as he disappeared into the rising darkness.

"Sorry, things have been crazy," Candy said after he answered. "The bar is probably going to close and I'm going to be out of a job, and Pickles has been acting crazy. He's threatening everyone to keep quiet about the shooting. Says he's not going back to prison no matter what happens. He's acting the same way he did before they took him to that psych hospital…hearing voices and things like that. I don't like even being near him. Told me to tell you to keep your mouth shut, too…only he wasn't very nice about how he said it," she added.

"He knows me?"

"He knows a lot more than you think he does, but then, you've been in the bar a lot lately. He's crazy, but he's not stupid. He know you're a doctor. Wanted me to give him your phone number, but I told him I didn't have it…And then he wanted your address, and I told him I didn't have that either. He said some nasty things about how I couldn't possibly *not* have your phone number, when…well, you know…when we're having a sexual relationship together and all. But…he didn't say it quite that way."

"Don't tell him anything…I don't want that lunatic showing up at my front door."

"I didn't…so far," she said but didn't sound very convincing, he thought. "But if he gets crazy…I don't know what…" she started to say but didn't finish her sentence.

"If he gets violent, just call the police," he said, but he wasn't sure if he wanted her to do that either.

"Oh yeah, that'd calm him down," she said sarcastically.

"Just tell him that I don't know anything…that I didn't see a thing. And besides, why don't the police just arrest him?"

"I don't know, probably because everyone's still too scared to say anything," she said, pausing for a short time before adding, "He said he would call your wife if you did anything. You know...probably to tell her about us."

"Jesus, how's he know I'm even married? I mean, I never met the guy...never even talked to him once...And he acts like we're best friends."

"Yeah, well, I told you he was crazy...and all crazy people are like that...They know everything."

"It's just that this is exactly what I didn't need right now. A crazed, unpredictable lunatic that might come looking for me," he said, still somewhat shaken by what she was telling him. "Just tell him that you can guarantee one hundred percent that I won't say a word to the police about *anything*...so he doesn't have to worry."

"I'm *not* going near him again."

He listened to her talk for a while about her costumes and an interview for a new job, but he couldn't really concentrate, thinking about the implications of what she had just told him.

"But I could use a little more money...until I can find a place to dance," she said.

"Yeah, I can give you some money...But did you think about that other thing we talked about?" he asked. Then he explained all of it to her again: about having her testify, how critical it was for her to just talk to the judge, and how there was no chance she could get in trouble.

"I guess...I don't like it...But I guess, if it means that much to you...I don't want you to lose your license or anything," she said, pausing to light another cigarette. "So...you want me to just tell the judge that I was with you that night and I had a bunch of drinks, and you didn't have anything to drink?" she said. But it already sounded like a lie, Weed thought.

"Yeah, but it has to be more natural...like you were there and remembered other things about that night...like what you had to eat—things like that. Because he might try to trick you up with some questions...like, tell him we both had linguine...that's one of your favorites, and you remember it because I told you later about the accident and the important person I had taken care of that night."

"Yeah, I guess I could...But that's what I said...I don't like it and it's complicated. It's not easy to lie truthfully," she added.

"And the other thing is...you can't tell the judge you're a stripper. If he asks you what you do for a living, tell him something else...like, maybe some other job that you had in the past...like, the best job you ever had."

"This is the best job I ever had! The worst job was when I had to wear tight shorts and a bikini top and skate around waiting on people at Ken's hotdog shop for two-dollar tips...if I was lucky."

"Great...well...that's *much* better," he said somewhat sarcastically but thought maybe she believed him. "I'll try to think of something else you can tell him," he said.

"And another thing is, it would be good for you to sort of dress down...Wear something conservative...like a dress or a skirt...something to make you look more...serious...give you more credibility."

"So that I don't look like a whore," she said with an angry tone.

"I didn't say that. Just something to make you look more...I don't know, presentable...like you work in an office or department store or something."

"I don't know...I'll see what I can find," she said, still sounding disgusted.

Knew that somehow something like this would happen. Wasn't like his life was moving along smoothly, but it was too late to worry about how his plan would turn out. He had painted himself into a corner, and when it came right down to it—she was the only option that he could come up with.

His whole life was disgusting...Using a stripper as a witness... And now a psychotic shooter was on the loose—looking for him, he thought as he listened to Candy tell him again why she didn't think it was a good idea for her to testify. Didn't even know why he was putting himself through all this. What was he fighting for, anyway? To get his miserable life back to the way it was before the lawsuit started and the shooting? Was that what he was hoping for? Losing might not be any worse than winning, he thought as he walked back down the hill to his car, Bob now long out of sight. That was the thing. His life was all coming apart at the seams...unraveling like a big ball of yarn.

He drove back home...wondering how his planned, relaxing, peaceful evening playing basketball had turned into such a nightmare.

Sandy was in the back yard annoyingly messing with some of the decorations that she had already put up for the party...But at least Helen wasn't at the house.

"What do you think?" Sandy asked him as she stepped back away from colored, fruit-shaped lights she had just strung.

"Nice," he said, looking and smiling.

"How'd it go today?"

"Wonderful...the same...who knows...I don't know...all seems like one big circus...may as well be having the trial in the park with all the other clowns...You can't tell the difference. They paid some neurosurgeon ten thousand to testify against me...ten thousand! He was on the stand less than two hours telling the jury it was all my fault: the scars, the wheelchair. But no facts—just conjecture. One person's word against another. That's all the trial is, really. Has nothing to do with what actually happened," he said, "just their distorted account of what they want the jury to believe, followed by our distorted view of what we want the jury to believe. Half-truths and half-lies—mostly, and I'm not even sure that the jury understands most of it," he said as he entered the house, made himself a drink, and went upstairs, leaving Sandy outside by herself.

He lay on the bed thinking about his conversation with Candy. Not only was his life in shambles, but now there was the distinct possibility that his life was in danger...that Pickles might be looking for him…and he wasn't even sure why. If Pickles was as crazy as everyone said, then he might do just about anything. Another wave of fear washed over him at the thought.

Could call the police on him…But that would accomplish exactly what he didn't want to happen—getting involved. And if Pickles found out that he had talked to the police…he would be in even more trouble. That could jeopardize his well-being even more than it was now. "Jeopardize his well-being"—that phrase didn't even sound close to what could happen.

And Candy was a real long shot…for giving an official statement…unless he could come up with some fantastic reason why strippers were reliable and trustworthy witnesses, he thought.

"You ever feel as if maybe you've stayed at the party too long?" he said when Sandy finally came into the bedroom. He had been tossing and turning for over an hour, unable to sleep. "That it's all boring, and you're not interested anymore, and people wish you would just go home? That you have become annoying…and you don't even care?"

"I don't really even know what you're talking about," she said.

"Well, that's sort of the way I feel: like the party's over. I don't even know if I really care that much about *what* happens anymore. It's not worth it," he said. "What does it all mean, anyway? Nothing! Just all a big waste of time…practicing medicine all these years. Sacrificing so much…just to end up like this. I actually feel like I might be disappearing…like I'm just slowly fading away. That I'm becoming irrelevant."

"You always get philosophical when you've had too much to drink…and that doesn't make any sense, anyway…" she said, her voice trailing off.

"I guess maybe that's how everyone ends up, eventually: a failure," he told her as she changed, thinking that he hadn't had too much to drink, either. "Worked all my life to end up here…almost seems pointless…almost seems ludicrous. Probably could've gotten to this point in my life a lot faster and a lot easier. I mean, I had to do all this, just to end up here? A loser?"

"You'll feel better in the morning," she said, annoyed that he was still talking to her.

"Could work at the Quick Fix," he said, and Sandy let out a small laugh. "That's all I'm really suited to do. Maybe I could do a good job at that...But I doubt it."

"You're too hard on yourself...You'll feel better in the morning," she told him, and for a few minutes he felt bad about all the terrible things he had done to her over the years. She had put up with him for a long time...And she might have actually loved him...at one time.

"Never should have been a surgeon. Never had the ability, the intelligence, whatever it takes to be a surgeon. Don't even know what it takes myself," he confessed as he watched Sandy's reflection in the bathroom mirror. "I just worked harder than everyone. That's the only reason I was able to become a doctor. It's not because I'm smart, it's because I worked harder than the rest of those retards. I'm actually pretty fuckin' stupid, and I guess it's just getting harder to hide it," he told her. "My real self...finally coming through...always does...eventually. Never wanted to be a physician. I told you that. I don't even like people. Dislike them even more now than when I started...And I didn't like them very much then."

"You keep saying that. How can you keep saying that you don't like people? That's ridiculous! It's almost macabre that a doctor says something like that."

"It's true. I just know them too well...know their nature. You wouldn't like them either if you knew what they were really like...if you had to deal with them every day."

"Not all people. Maybe it's just a reflection of yourself? That you don't like other people because of who you are. Or, I don't know, maybe you could be going crazy."

"Yeah, maybe...that's probably it," he answered, somewhat pissed at her response. "Actually, I wanted to be a writer," he said after a long pause. "That's what I wanted to do years ago...before I got sidetracked. How crazy is that? But I couldn't do that either. Thought it would be sexy, or mysterious, or some bullshit like that. Having my picture on the back cover of some great American novel...impressing everyone...You know, some bullshit intellectual... since I couldn't make it as a jock," he told her. "You know how you think when you're young, when you don't know any better? One of my teachers in college—creative writing, I remember...well, she said my stories were like a broken-down time machine. I'll never forget it. She said when you got into a time machine you expected something new and exciting to be waiting for you when got out...in the future...you know? But with my stories, she told me, when you got out of *my* time machine nothing had happened...everything was still the same. Everyone was still just standing around...looking stupefied at things the same as they did when they got into the machine...like, what the fuck happened? I guess that was her way of telling me that everything I wrote was boring...or confusing... just not good enough," he said poignantly, but when he looked over at Sandy, she was turned away and he could hear the slow rhythmic breathing of her sleep. He thought about waking her up and telling her that there might be some homicidal maniac coming over to the house later...just to see if that might be any more interesting to her, but he didn't. "Teacher gave me a B minus for the class. That was good for her...good for me too," he said, laughing lightly to himself.

Aspirations...dust to dust...dust on a dust cover...that's all it was, he thought in the twilight of his sleep.

CHAPTER TWENTY-TWO

Thursday, May 13
6:43 a.m.

He hadn't slept well and had awakened once during the night in a cold sweat, dreaming about Candy and Pickles and the shooting; a bizarre dream that didn't make any sense but had left him feeling like he was in danger.

"That pastor from your mother's church called yesterday to re-mind you about some meeting, I think, but I forgot to tell you," Sandy told him just as he was about to leave the bedroom. "Said that that group of whoever that he talked to you about is supposed to meet at the First United Church of Christ today at six o'clock, I think…for some kind of meeting or pictures or whatever…couldn't really tell what he was trying to tell me," she said before rolling over and going back to sleep.

Just what he needed to make an almost guaranteed shitty day much better—a church meeting, he thought as he sat at the kitchen table looking through the newspaper. There was, as he expected, another long article about the trial with all the details of the previous day's testimony and then a letter to the editor from a woman complaining about the poor treatment she also had received at the hospital three weeks earlier. But surprisingly, the woman was complaining about some other doctor and not him.

At least there was nothing in the newspaper that he could find about the shooting at Tatter's Bar, but he checked the newspaper a second time just to make sure he hadn't missed something.

As he drank his coffee, he looked over a copy of his deposition, reading over the answers to the questions the lawyers had asked him, like Morgan wanted him to do before he testified today. He mostly reviewed the important parts of the deposition, the parts he had underlined three and in some places four times. The best answers he could come up with to make it appear that he had done nothing wrong that night. The fabricated answers he had given to Turzak while he was under oath. Couldn't really tell Turzak the truth, that he had been pissed off that he had to sew up some obnoxious, intoxicated bitch at 3:00 a.m. on a Friday night when he had to be up early for a Saturday morning basketball game—even though that was the truth. Had to remember what he had told him in the deposition because lies were always harder to remember.

Then he studied some anatomical diagrams of the face and neck. He wanted to make sure he didn't look stupid by not knowing the answer to some simple medical question, like he had done once or twice when Turzak had taken his deposition. He certainly didn't want to screw up any answers to basic medical questions in front of the jury, he thought.

He took one Valium, and then another, and then finished off his bourbon and Coke as he drove to the courthouse.

"You have that number?" Morgan asked when he sat down beside him inside the courtroom. "They're being a pain in the ass about it. They want to talk to your witness first thing Monday morning, before the trial resumes," he added.

"Yeah, yeah…I already talked to her…She's okay with it," he told Morgan as he wrote down Candy's number on a slip of paper for Morgan.

"Yeah, I guess that's fine, but just make sure she shows…because it's important. If she's believable—convincing—we might not have to worry," he reassured. "Otherwise, it could tie up the trial at least another week with legal maneuvers, trying to block their witnesses' testimony. And if we can't block Turzak's witnesses…that bartender and whoever…from testifying, then our chances of winning are going to be pretty slim…Especially if the jury *suspects* that you might have been drinking that night—so make sure she's there," Morgan added as the jurors filed past them.

For the next two hours, Turzak questioned Dr. Wilpret, the chief of the Plastic Surgical Department at the university, about Hileman's facial lacerations. Wilpret came quickly to the basic conclusion that Dr. Weed wasn't near qualified to repair such complex lacerations. Then, using a large diagram, Wilpret showed the jurors how the lacerations should have been repaired and how they would have looked if they had been repaired properly.

At one point, Wilpret came out of the witness stand to demonstrate to the jurors what he was trying to describe, moving Hileman directly in front of them so that they could see the scars more clearly. By shining the light from a small flashlight across her face at different angles, he demonstrated how the light made the scars look worse and how the muscle structures in the face had been irreparably damaged. Then he asked the jurors if they could see what he was talking about, as if they were his colleagues or old friends… if they could see the way the scars were all bunched up in certain places and pulling at the skin on her face.

But it was all just a big show—more dramatics, Weed knew, as Turzak pushed Hileman's wheelchair back to where she had been originally seated.

As Weed sat there and listened, he thought mostly about the alcohol issue, what it meant, and what he was going to do about Candy testifying...and how he was going to make her sound believable and look respectable.

Was almost two hours before Turzak finished questioning Wilpret. And then for the next hour Morgan questioned Wilpret, trying to undo most of what Turzak had tried to prove and to emphasize to the jury that the scars were only temporary disfigurements and how easily the scars could be repaired.

Still not many new facts presented...no new revelations...no new dirt for the newspapers...nothing that everyone didn't already know, Weed thought as he left the courthouse.

Weed sat at a corner window of Stan's Restaurant and ate Stan's tasteless special, and for some reason felt strangely disappointed that he hadn't run into Hileman's driver or her dog.

He would have to drive clear across town to the church later for the damn meeting, he thought as he left the restaurant. And then drive clear back across town when he was finished there to meet the team for their final practice. They had been pretty sloppy the last couple games, and he didn't think that one practice was going to change that. Winning the championship...wasn't even sure that he cared anymore, he thought as he jogged back to his car in a light rain.

Would meet with Candy later and tell her about the meeting with the judge and then just hope that she agreed. Still had until Monday to work out all the details with her, he figured as he sat in the car, sipped his drink, and looked over his deposition one last time before he crossed the street and entered the courthouse.

He combed his hair back into place and checked to make sure his tie was straight and unstained in the mirror inside the courthouse, catching his eyes as they stared back at him. The eyes of a stranger...wondered who that person really was...where that person had come from…He was almost mesmerized by his stare before he finally looked away.

Weed could feel his heart racing as Turzak called him to the stand…and felt he might have lost his balance for a moment as he walked toward the witness stand, but he didn't think anyone had noticed…And it seemed as if his thoughts were a bit jumbled…as if he might be taking the wrong route as he walked past the jurors.

The jurors seemed more intimidating up close…that being this close to them might expose the truth or something about him that he was trying to hide, he thought as he raised his right hand and took the oath.

Turzak slowly moved in front of him—like a vulture, Weed imagined—before he started asking questions. The first few questions were benign about his professional career, before switching to questions, over Morgan's heated objections, about two other embarrassing lawsuits that had been filed against him years earlier. The first was a case where he had accidentally left an instrument inside a patient, and the second a case where he had operated on the wrong patient.

No good answers, Weed knew…answers were going to make him look incompetent no matter how he answered them.

"Responsible, yes…I take full blame…But to be honest, I'm really not responsible for the instrument count. I have to rely on others to determine if all the instruments are accounted for…and to deliver the right patient to the right operating room." Nice and simple, he thought as Turzak moved on after intimating that negligence might be the rule instead of the exception.

"Why did you remove the collar so soon after Ms. Hileman arrived and without taking x-rays first?" Turzak asked abruptly. "In your deposition you stated…" Turzak said as he picked up a paper off his desk, "that you 'couldn't repair the lacerations adequately without removing the collar.' That it was getting in your way," he said but didn't wait for an answer before continuing. "But that's not really true, is it?"

"Yes, it was difficult to repair the lacerations with her head in the position the collar was holding it in…It was much easier to repair the laceration with her head turned slightly to the right… which was impossible to do with the collar still in place," Weed answered, just like he had answered in his deposition.

"But you didn't even examine her neck before you removed the collar?"

"I did examine her neck, and there was no evidence that she had any significant injury," he answered—a lie. He had never examined her neck, but there was no definite proof to the contrary… And her neck was fine anyway, he knew.

"Well, the nurses didn't see you examine her at all…said that you unsnapped the Velcro holding the collar in place and actually pulled the collar rather briskly from her neck…causing her head to fall back quickly to the exam table…that her head actually made a loud sound when it hit the stretcher, causing her to scream out in terrible pain."

"Well, that's not exactly the way I remember it. I did examine her neck. There was no significant pain…no indication of an injury, so I removed the collar using ACEP protocols…wasn't brisk… and I never put her well-being at any risk. And I don't recall that she had any significant pain when I removed the collar or that her head struck the table. And I don't believe that she actually suffered any significant neck injury," he said. But for some reason his words didn't seem like his own. They seemed hollow…like someone else was giving the answers.

"You heard our expert…what he said," Turzak said and then read to the jurors what the expert had told them about Hileman's neck injury, "That 'the cause of Ms. Hileman's weakness and paralysis and continued pain in her neck and arms was due to the increased swelling caused by Dr. Weed's inappropriate and premature removal of her cervical collar.'"

Then Turzak stopped speaking, slowly taking off his glasses before giving him a sarcastic, disgusted look. He then shook his head in disbelief and moved on to questions about Hileman's facial lacerations.

"Our expert and the ER doctor who works with you at the hospital both stated that the lacerations should have first been cleaned, irrigated, x-rayed, and explored before they were repaired, but according to the records and the testimony of at least two nurses, you didn't do any of those procedures. Isn't that true?"

"I examined them...made sure that they were clean. It didn't need debrided or irrigated, and x-rays wouldn't have made a difference, since there were no foreign bodies or evident fractures present," Weed answered.

"So you're saying that you didn't do any of those things that our experts and the American College of Surgeons state were 'routine and recommended standards of care' prior to performing the surgery?"

"I told you, I did what was necessary...It's not necessary to x-ray or to debride every laceration."

And then more questions from Turzak about her concussions... and back injury...and pain and suffering...and mental distress. But his answers seemed flat, even to him. Didn't seem to sound solid or real, as if they were stiff and overly prepared and maybe sounding unbelievable, Weed thought. That maybe he had given the answer so often that the explanations had worn out, or that his answers had exceeded the boundaries of believability. Hard to make anything sound believable when your actions seemed to demonstrate just the opposite, he knew. He had never been a good liar anyway, he thought, even though he had had plenty of experience.

"Were you in a hurry?"

"No," Weed said emphatically. Another unprovable lie, he knew.

"Nurses said you were in a hurry…sounded like you were in a hurry too," Turzak said as Morgan objected…

"Speculation and hearsay!"

"Did you say you weren't 'going to spend all night taking care of this obnoxious bitch'?"

"I don't remember ever saying anything like that."

"Did you make any derogatory comments about Ms. Hileman's demeanor or behavior?"

"I may have been terse, but it was for a reason. I was concerned about Ms. Hileman's well-being. She was not listening. She appeared intoxicated and insisted on smoking around the oxygen tanks, and she insisted on having her pet dog with her at all times, potentially contaminating the entire emergency room and running the risk of a serious infection," he said, seizing on the opportunity to tell the jurors how Hileman had actually acted that night—to get a little retribution—before he was cut off with another question by Turzak. But he felt satisfied that he had at least gotten one good punch in, before Turzak was finished with him.

"You're just lying about it all to cover the truth. Isn't that the truth, Dr. Weed? Isn't everything you said here today, more or less, a lie to cover your incompetence?" Turzak asked in closing. Morgan objected and then Turzak finally ended his examination dramatically by telling the judge tersely that he had, "No further questions."

Weed felt his cell phone vibrating for the third time just as Morgan started his cross-examination, but this time he took a quick look at the phone to see that it was Candy who had been calling. Would have to call her later, he thought before answering the first question Morgan asked—giving the answer that they had gone over many times.

For the next hour he answered all Morgan's questions with preconceived answers they had devised to deny any wrongdoing and to shift any blame for Hileman's injuries away from him and back to the accident, explaining that the accident had been the direct cause of all her injuries; that nothing Dr. Weed had done or hadn't done had caused any further injury; and that with the lacerations, a secondary repair was actually the recommend treatment—which he had ultimately planned to do or have a plastic surgeon do for him later.

But while he was watching Morgan and Turzak argue about some legal point, for some reason an image sprang into his mind: an image of Hileman dancing somewhat expressively at last year's Spring Fling. He could see her in his mind now: bouncing around awkwardly as she danced...drunk...laughing hysterically...uninhibited on the dance floor...But surprisingly, it was only *now* that he remembered it. And that had occurred well after the accident... and well *before* she had started her big act with the neck injuries and the brace and the wheelchair, he realized. How could she have danced at the Spring Fling a year after the accident if she had been so severely injured the night of the accident?

Would be nice if he had a picture or two of her that night to show the jurors, he thought as he continued to listen to Morgan and Turzak argue. Might afford a golden opportunity...if he could get incriminating pictures of Hileman dancing semiwildly after the accident...especially now that she claimed she was in so much pain and paralyzed, he thought, losing track of the question Morgan had just ask him...and Morgan repeating the question.

Thought more about it when he was finally off the witness stand. Maybe he could get some pictures of her at this year's Spring Fling... out on the dance floor...but doubted that she would be so stupid as to do anything like that this year. That possibility was probably a long shot now that everyone was watching—but not impossible. When Hileman got drunk, she got crazy—got impulsive. He witnessed that firsthand in the ER the night of the accident...And she might just let her guard down again, long enough to "slip up," he thought. Could maybe even hunt down some old photographs of last year's Spring Fling. Could ask Mordy...He was there and he was always taking pictures, he knew. And even if Hileman didn't do something like dancing, maybe she would do something equally as stupid. It was a possibility. He thought excitedly about the prospect as the judge finally adjourned the trial for the day.

"Well, we knew it was going to be a rough week," Morgan said as they walked together down the steps of the courthouse. "But not bad with what we had to work with," he added as they stop for a few seconds to talk. "Tomorrow, Hileman testifies and then Turzak will be finished presenting his case. And then next week we get our turn," Morgan said as he started off in a different direction before stopping and turning back toward Weed. "And don't forget we need your witness here early Monday morning before the trial resumes. And I want to talk to her first to make sure she doesn't say something she shouldn't. Have her meet me at eight thirty in that conference room we met in before...number three," Morgan said before waving and walking off.

Candy testifying...Just another fly in the ointment, Weed thought as he sat in his car and drank the last of the bourbon before driving off.

CHAPTER TWENTY-THREE

Thursday, May 13
4:58 p.m.

A light rain and chilly wind with dark clouds settled in just as they finished the church meeting, and the photographer lined them all up in front of the church for their group photo. What a big joke it could become if they found out about his other life with murderers and prostitutes in some seedy strip club, he mused. Could leave all the pains-in-the-asses in the picture with egg on their faces, he thought as he waved at those who still remained of the group, before driving off to meet Candy.

He waited for almost an hour before Candy arrived. She leaned across the table and gave him a kiss as she sat down across from him in the booth. After they ordered, Weed told her about the meeting at the church and almost told her how funny it would be if all the ministers found out that he had been hanging out at a strip club, before realizing that it might offend her. He quickly changed the subject to the trial and how he had talked to Hileman's driver about her sick dog, and about how he had learned that Hileman had been in the movies years before, and that he would give her the DVD to watch sometime…and then told her about his idea to try and get some incriminating pictures of Hileman at the Spring Fling on Saturday.

But the whole time, he was trying to slowly lead up to the subject of her testimony. He didn't want to scare her off, he thought as he smiled and listened to her talk about Tatter, and Pickles, and her costumes—again, and then about her still not being able to find another place to dance.

"I'm thinking of just picking up and leaving…moving to Florida. My girlfriend got a great job dancing down there. Makes *twice* as much as *I* do, and *she's not even a very good dancer,*" she said as she took a long drag off her cigarette. "I just want to get away from all of this. I don't like it here, anyway," she said. "You should come with me. You're always telling me you want to leave and do something different. You could be a doctor in Florida," she added as she swirled a straw in her drink.

"They set a time for that meeting I told you about," he finally told her when they seemed to have run out of other things to talk about. "We're supposed to be there at eight-thirty on Monday," he said. "Shouldn't be much, though…thought that maybe you should just tell them that you are a waitress at that restaurant you used to work at…But maybe leave out the parts about the skating and what they made you wear."

Her eyes were cast downward and she had a concerned look on her face when she replied, "I'm not ashamed of what I do. I mean, I'm not afraid to tell anyone what I do for a living—that I'm an exotic dancer. I *could* tell them that…That doesn't sound that bad," she added somewhat emphatically.

"Yeah I know, it's just how it looks…you know? It doesn't matter to me, and you're good at what you do. There's no shame in that… It's just that…well, you know the misconception people have about some exotic dancers...some people think all *that* kind of dancing is the same. We talked about that...how this town is too religious about things like that."

"I don't know, Ben," she said after a long pause. "It scares me. There're things in the past that you don't know about—nothing really bad, but if I did something like this, it might cause me even more trouble. I mean, I didn't do anything bad—nothing like robbing a bank or killing someone—nothing like that. It's just some small stuff...crazy stuff you do when you're young and don't know any better...that you don't want people to find out about, you know? I don't want them digging stuff up that happened ten years ago... like they did with you that time. I've changed anyway—straightened out my life, and I want to move forward—not backward. And you know, perjury can be a pretty bad crime," she said and then told him about her brother again.

"I know, but I really think it's all okay. And I'm sort of already committed. I told them that you were the person who was with me the night of Hileman's accident. I already gave them your name and everything, so I can't change my story now, or I could lose my license. And all you really have to do is just tell them that you were with me and that I didn't have a thing to drink. That's all you have to say—that you were the only one drinking that night...and you remembered it because of Hileman being so well known and me telling you all about it afterward. They'll never know any different," he said. Then he tried to coach her through a mock encounter, asking her questions like he thought the judge might ask, which she reluctantly answered. But he thought she might be right—she didn't sound very convincing.

"Oh, I don't know. I'll have to think about it," she said. "I already have all this other stuff on my mind—Pickles, and trying to find a job...and no money," she said as if she was about ready to cry.

More drama, he thought as he kissed her and told her everything was going to be fine, before taking out his wallet and giving her all the money that he had left and then telling her that he would give her more on Monday when he picked her up to take her to the courthouse.

As they stood in front of the diner, he told her to call him if she heard anything more about the shooting. She was upset and unpredictable, he thought as he got into his car. There really wasn't much he could do about it now, except hope she was there Monday morning when he went to pick her up, he concluded as he drove toward the basketball courts.

Bob was sitting at one of the picnic tables in the park drinking a can of pop when Weed drove up. Didn't feel much like practicing basketball, he thought as he got out of the car and carried his shoes over to where Bob was waiting.

"Court's too wet to play. Puddles are all over the place. Feels like winter's returning," Bob said as Weed approached.

"Where's everyone else?"

"You're it, and it's late. Everyone else left after they got here. They all agreed it was too cold to practice," he said, standing and then dribbling the ball across the wet grass toward the court. "Oh yeah, and Stan has the flu, and the doctor had to put three screws in that guy's ankle last week...pretty scary. Told him if he came down on it hard again it could all just come apart like a cheap wrist watch. You ever hear anything like that?" he asked but didn't wait for the answer. "If that happened to me and I couldn't work—Kim would kill me!"

"Yeah, I know what you mean," Weed said, lacing up his shoes and then taking a long shot at the hoop from the edge of the grass.

"They don't have shit without that guy with the broken ankle, anyway. Should beat them by twenty points, at least. That's the other reason everyone took off...No one thinks we even need the practice now," Bob said, grabbing the rebound and putting up another shot.

They shot and talked until their hands were too cold and numb to feel the ball, before quitting and walking down to the Quick Fix for a few minutes as Bob finished up some paperwork he had forgotten to do earlier. Then they walked across the street to a small bar.

"We can practice drinking instead of practicing basketball. We're good at that," Weed said and laughed as they entered the bar.

They ate wings and drank and watched a meaningless baseball game on a big-screen TV.

"They're just trying to make me look like some incompetent physician who doesn't care about any of his patients," Weed finally said after a long silence where it seemed as if they had run out of conversation. "They're trying to make it like I turned a princess into a hideous, crippled monster...another Quasimodo like I defaced an icon. Can you believe that's what the newspaper said? Those scars make *me* look a lot worse than they do *her*."

"Yeah, that's what my wife said. That the newspapers are saying some pretty nasty things about you...and even the TV. You're sort of like becoming a real celebrity in reverse," he joked.

"Yeah, like an anticelebrity. Funny thing is that I'm not sure I even care...sort of numb from all of it, and I'm tired of all the bullshit, anyway. The office, the hospital, the lunatic patients, the politics, the lawsuits, my life—tired of it all. Would be a relief to get rid of everything and start over with a clean slate, you know? Just consider what's happening to me now as nothing more than a golden opportunity, a chance to start again. You know, when one door closes, another door opens? Give up the practice and just move back to Catalpa Street with my mother and live like a carefree king—like it used to be."

"Yeah, you told me all about your plans," Bob said. "Was pretty nice back then."

"Would be nice to have it back like it used to be...those golden days."

"Your mom wouldn't care?"

"I don't know. She'd probably get pissed like she always does, but she'd get over it. She'll moan and bitch for a while, give me a lecture every so often about how immoral I've become, or some shit like that, but so what? No different than it used to be. Would at least be free from all this," he said and laughed.

"Yeah, it all sounds good, but it's never that easy. There's always a catch," Bob said.

"I know...You told me that too. But if I lose everything, then it won't make much difference what I do, and there's no way I'm going to start over. I don't have the strength. I'd just be paying off Hileman for the rest of my life, anyway. And Sandy will leave me the minute she realizes the money's gone. That's the only reason she's still around, I imagine. Just waiting around to see if there're any bones left to pick when Hileman gets finished with me. Never really loved me...I don't think...was always just about the money and the prestige," he said. "Maybe she did love me at one time," he added after a long pause. "I don't know...because according to Helen, I'm not even sure what that is—love. She thinks there's something missing inside of me that I need in order to understand what love is...something that I never had...So I don't understand it," he said, but Bob didn't seem very interested in what he was telling him. "But then, Helen's crazy. I mean, do you know what love is?" Weed asked trying to sound serious, even though he was already feeling too drunk to really concentrate on anything for very long. And the question sounded sort of gay, he thought. "In my opinion, love is ninety percent lust—and sex—and maybe ten percent something else I can't explain. And once you get tired of the sex, all you have left of love is ten percent of some innocuous thing...that Helen says I don't have. And ten percent isn't much today," Weed said but wasn't sure why—or if he was even making any sense. "Physical attraction and sex melt away like a spring snow," he added. "That's my definition of love."

"Yeah, probably," Bob said as he tried to fish a hair from the side of his glass.

"The bad thing is, I don't think I really care that much what happens," Weed said, wondering if he might be repeating himself. "Half the time, I think it would be easier if I lost the case and everything I owned. I do have a plan if that happens, but not much of a plan if I win. Seems strange...but it's true. If I lose, I'm just going to walk away from it all. If I win, I'll just..." he said and paused. "Maybe just walk away from it all, too," he said and laughed again.

He felt really drunk now, but he had another drink anyway before telling Bob about the bar shooting. Wasn't sure why, maybe just to get it off his chest. Wasn't going to tell him much about it...just the high spots, he thought as he continued talking over the din of the bar.

"You're crazy to ever go in that place," Bob said halfway through the story.

"Just to see one of the dancers, I told you," he said, misunderstanding Bob's statement until after he had answered, and then he was upset with himself for telling Bob why he had been in the bar, so he took another drink. "And now I'm worried that the police might find out that I was there, and then it could get into the newspapers and screw up the trial even more than it already is—not to mention everything else. You see what I mean?" he asked Bob as if he might have some answers.

"Yeah, I see what you mean." But Bob had no answers.

"Could all become one big, confusing mess...especially with the trial...especially now that the spotlight is already on me. You see what I mean?" Then he told him about the church meeting and standing between two priests, and how ridiculous it would be if they found out he was involved with the exact thing that the committee was trying to prevent...But it didn't really seem all that amusing now.

"Might not even notice," Bob said sort of sarcastically.

"What?" he asked but couldn't really understand the context of Bob's response. "And then, there's this lunatic called Pickles...that's the guy who actually did the shooting. Some crazy lunatic who's been in a psych hospital a bunch of times and in prison for shooting some other guy, I guess. He's all pissed off, running around with a gun, telling everyone—including me—to keep their mouths shut. And the police are just sitting around with their thumbs up their asses doing nothing. Guy could go psycho and start shootin' people any time, for all I know. Been thinking maybe I should go down to the police station and tell the police exactly what I know... what really happened...get the asshole off the streets," he said, taking another long drink. "And I would, if I was sure the police could get to him before he gets to me. Makes me paranoid thinking about it...always looking over my shoulder to make sure he's not anywhere in sight."

"I can't believe it! You have all this stuff going on, and you go into a bar like that?" Bob said incredulously. "Every drug addict and pervert in the city hangs out at that bar...and transvestites, too! At least that's what I heard about the place...big article in the paper a couple months ago," he added.

"See? Can you believe it? Can you believe my luck? But I never heard anything about transvestites...I mean, that's news to me," he added as if it made a difference. Wasn't sure why he had said anything to Bob in the first place. Bob looked pretty drunk and probably wouldn't remember anything anyway, Weed hoped.

Bob told him that he was lucky he hadn't gotten shot, before he checked his watch...and then told Weed Kim was going to be mad that he was late and had been drinking instead of practicing basketball. That he had "spent all his lunch money on booze," he quipped. Then he flagged a waitress and ordered a bucket of wings for his wife.

"Might not bitch so much if I bring her something to eat," he said, laughing. "And I wouldn't worry about it. Nothing's going to happen. I mean, it's been a week since the shooting—like you told me. Nothing happens after a week. Police in this town can't find anyone anyway. Everyone knows that. And so what? The hell with what people think. You didn't do anything wrong," Bob said as he stood, losing his balance for a moment. As drunk as Weed was, he could tell that Bob was trying to make him feel better about the whole situation.

"Time's going by so fast," Weed said as they started toward the door, after the waitress brought Bob his wings. "I wrote a check the other day. Wrote 2012 for the year," Weed said as they were leaving the bar, "and for a second I had to stop and think…What year is this? Couldn't believe it. Where did '13 and '14 go?" he said as they walked back down the street to his car.

"You sure you're okay to drive?" Bob asked when Weed got behind the wheel of his car. "We've had a little bit more than usual."

"I'm fine. I'm used to it," he said, laughing and waving him off.

"Yeah, well, be careful. Roads might be slick with the rain," he said. "And I wouldn't worry about all those other things. Everything will work out for you—eventually," Bob said through the car's open window as Weed slowly pulled away.

CHAPTER TWENTY-FOUR

Thursday, May 13
9:35 p.m.

That asshole's driving too damn close, Weed thought as the headlights blinded him from the reflection in his rearview mirror.

He reflexively held his middle finger up for whoever was driving behind him to see.

Should just slam on his brakes and let the asshole slam into the back of his car, Weed thought before he touched the brakes lightly for an instant and drove on. And then two more times before the driver behind him slowed and moved further back. But the damn car continued to follow him, Weed could see.

Left onto the boulevard, right onto Causewell Street, then two more right turns...and the frickin' car was still behind him, Weed saw. Car has to be following him, he realized as he took two more quick turns before turning into his driveway. Probably had pissed him off, Weed thought, hoping the car would pass by. Really didn't need this now. Didn't need a case of road rage tonight, he thought as he turned off his headlights and crouched down low in the front seat.

But instead, the car slowed, stopping near the end of his drive-way. Couldn't decide if he should make a dash for the house or just keep his doors locked and stay in the car. He watched in his rear-view mirror as two good-sized men wearing suits slowly got out of the car and started up the driveway toward him. One of them was holding a clipboard.

Looked more like two detectives than some pissed-off driver, he thought as he watched their approach. Probably a couple of cops pulling him over for driving erratically, he thought as he opened his car door and got out. Was just going to have to get his act to-gether and act sober, he thought as he stood there, waiting. Only two mixed drinks...That's all he was going to admit to, he thought, nodding his head and smiling as they arrived.

If they thought he was drunk, they would probably arrest him and all his efforts in court to deny his alcohol use would be wasted, he thought as he moved forward to shake the their hands and intro-duce himself. He took a little misstep backward as he moved away from them, losing his balance just for a second, but he didn't think that either of them noticed.

"Dr. Benjamin Weed, glad to meet you," one of the men said be-fore taking a step back. "I'm Detective Clark and this is Lieutenant Grayson, he said tersely before explaining that they were city detec-tives working on a case. "Yeah, we stopped by a couple of days ago. Saw your car parked out front and felt that it was maybe the car we had been looking for," the officer continued.

Shit, he was busted, he thought, trying to act as sober as he could and still stay focused on the conversation. Seemed like the driveway was steeper than he remembered...His left leg was numb from just getting out of the car, and he felt like he might fall forward and lose his equilibrium while trying to concentrate. He moved from one foot to the other. As long as he moved some, he seemed to be okay, he thought while nodding his head like he knew exactly what they were saying. At least they didn't seem to notice that he had been drinking yet, he thought.

"Yeah, that's my car: a seventy-five-thousand-dollar piece of junk. Can't get the radio off now...makes it hard to drive when you can't hear anything," he said, hoping that would explain his erratic driving. "Keeps playing some lousy news station in my ear...Can't even concentrate," he said with a laugh, hoping they might think he was sober if he could make a joke.

"Yeah, been looking for this fancy, little red car all week. You remember where you were last Thursday evening?" one of the officers asked.

Knew it would be the damn car that did him in, he thought. Now they knew he had been at the bar. What luck, he thought. At least they weren't going to arrest him for drinking...At least not yet, he thought as he continued to listen and tried to act sober.

"Don't even remember where I was an hour ago," Weed said with a laugh while trying to come up with some believable story he could tell them about why he had been in the bar that wouldn't get him into more trouble. All this time to think about the shooting... and he still hadn't come up with exactly what he was going to tell the police if they found out that he had been there.

"You ever been to Tatter's Bar over on the south side?"

"Tatter's?" Weed said and laughed. "I was, but I'm not sure when. I go in there every so often to see a few friends...have a few drinks. Don't really like the place, myself," he told them before Clark cut him off.

"You hear about what happened down there last Thursday night?"

"What's that?" Weed answered, trying to act confused.

"Bar was held up and the owner shot. And for the last week we've been trying to locate any witnesses who might know anything about what actually happened. And it just so happened that someone thought they saw a car like yours parked outside the bar around the time of the shooting. And I mean, it is a pretty unusual car."

"Yeah, I guess I could have been there last Thursday," Weed said shaking his head, acting like he was trying to remember.

"So you don't know anything about any shooting there that night? 'Cause if you were there...you would surely remember."

"Not that I can recall...And I definitely would have remembered something like that," he added after a long pause, feigning a weak laugh. "Always a lot of confusion in that bar...You never know what's going on in there. You can be in one corner of the bar and not know what's going on in the other corner. I don't even like going in there," Weed said and laughed nervously, but it already sounded as if he was trying to hide something, he thought.

"Yeah, it *is* pretty difficult not to notice someone getting *shot*," Clark laughed sarcastically. "But that's pretty much what we thought. We thought that if a person like yourself knew anything, you probably would have given us a call," the officer said as he wrote something down. "Maybe you were gone by the time it all took place?" Clark added.

"Yeah, that might be what happened. I know it probably seems strange that someone like me would go into a place like that, but I've got a couple of friends I've been meeting there for a while...I actually started going into that place before it got such a bad reputation...if you can believe that," Weed told them.

"Understood," Clark said. "So...you *were* probably there about the time of the shooting, but you didn't see *anything*. That about right?"

"That's right, I suppose." Officers seemed to be buying his story and looked as if they were getting about ready to leave, Weed thought. And they still hadn't seemed to notice that he had been drinking.

"That's pretty much all the information that we need right now," the other officer said just as Sandy stuck her head out the front door and called to him. He thought she might have said, "Are you okay?" but he wasn't sure.

"Fine, honey," he answered, turning slightly toward the house. "Just a couple people interested in the car. I'll be up in a minute."

Sandy stood there for a moment, watching, before finally going back into the house.

"My ball and chain," Weed said quietly as the officers laughed gratuitously. "Don't want her to know about me being in a bar like that, if you know what I mean. She'd be pissed," he said and laughed again.

"Yeah, we know what you mean. And I don't want to keep you any longer, but we're going to need you to come down to the station sometime and give us an official statement," he added.

"This statement's not enough?" Weed asked, somewhat confused as to why they would need an official statement when he had just told them he didn't know anything about the shooting. But then they might know more than he assumed they knew, he imagined.

"No, not really. We always need an official statement in cases like this. And anyway, it will give you a little time to think about that night. Maybe you'll remember something important that you forgot to tell us...like maybe who you saw in the bar that night, or if you noticed anything out of the ordinary," the other officer added. "You know, things like that...because we've been having a lot of trouble piecing it all together. This witness says this, and that witness says something else. We think they're all trying to cover up what really happened."

"Maybe you can do better and shed some light on the whole mess," Clark added. "Maybe we can finally talk to someone we can actually believe. You know the kind of riff-raff we have to deal with in a place like that."

"Don't often run into a professional like yourself in a place like that," the other detective said, laughing.

"We should just arrest the whole bunch of them," Clark said as he closed the cover on his clipboard.

"Yeah, I could do that, I guess," Weed told them. "But I'm still not sure that I can be of much help."

"Yeah, well, whatever. We never know what we're going to turn up," Clark said. "Tomorrow morning okay with you?"

"Well…I have this trial thing going on tomorrow…and probably most of next week," he explained before the officers reluctantly agreed to a meeting Saturday morning.

"You have a few drinks tonight?" Clark asked just before they started back down the driveway.

"Yeah, just a couple of mixed drinks," Weed answered sheepishly.

"Yeah, looks like a little more than a couple, and you shouldn't be driving in your condition," Clark said. "Puts us in a bad spot, seeing you driving like that…the way you smell and the way you look…and then giving us the finger back there," he said, a little angry now.

"Don't know…" he said, trying to act confused about what Clark was talking about. "Oh, that…No, I was just adjusting my rearview mirror so the light wouldn't hit me in the eyes."

"Yeah, well it looked like you gave us the finger. And I'm just giving you some words of advice. According to the book, I should put you in handcuffs and take you downtown for a Breathalyzer. But I'm going to be nice and just give you a warning."

"I appreciate that, but I really haven't had all that much."

The other police officer waved him off, smiling as if he didn't believe him before they both got back into their car. "Remember… Saturday morning, nine a.m."

"Absolutely, I'll be there," Weed said as Clark handed him a business card with his name on it. Weed watched as the two officers drove off and then just stood there—stunned—until the taillights of their car disappeared around the corner.

"Shit! Damn! What luck," he softly said out loud to himself as he stood there under the streetlight, trying to analyze what had just happened. He'd just barely dodged one bullet, only to be hit by another. Getting arrested for DUI when it was already an issue… wouldn't matter what Candy told the judge then. Christ, he was going to have to start being more careful when he drank.

And worse, now he was going to have to deal with the shooting, he thought as he walked up the driveway. Knew that it was eventually going to rear its ugly head…was inevitable with his luck. Should have gone to the police first…should have been proactive. Probably would have, if it hadn't been for Mordy's stupid advice…And he didn't like the sounds of giving an official statement. That's exactly what he *didn't* want to do. And he was pissed at Sandy for being the reason he had been driving the MG that night in the first place. It was all Sandy's fault, he thought—pissed—as he passed by the pariah. He kicked at the car's front tire, but he missed and struck the tip of the fender with his shin instead, shooting pain up his leg and causing him to buckle for an instant, before limping the rest of the way up the driveway.

Now he risked everyone finding out about the bar shooting and his relationship with Candy. That would be great—just great. That should make the trial much more interesting, he thought sarcastically. Like it hadn't been embarrassing enough…it needed more. The cake needed some icing.

He wasn't going to tell the officers much more than he had just told them now, anyway. He might give them a few vague descriptions of people, but no names. Wasn't going to even acknowledge that he knew anyone named Pickles. He would probably have to tell them about Candy…that they were just friends…because he would have to have some legitimate reason for being there. But he wasn't telling them anything else, he thought as he pushed open the front door. Might still be able to prevent it from going public, he imagined—if he played his cards right.

"Forty thousand dollars. Can you believe it? They wanted to give me forty thousand for a car I bought for seventy-five thousand," he told his wife before she had a chance to start asking questions. "Guys wanted to buy the car...fix it up to make a quick buck, but I told them nothing less than fifty."

"Should have sold it...And why'd you park way down there?"

"Better light," he answered, pleased with the ingenuity of his answer.

"I think they might have been the guys from the other day, but for a minute, I thought they were cops stopping you because you had been drinking," she said with relief.

"No...no, just wanted to know about the car, and I only had a couple with Bob."

"Every time you play basketball you 'just have a couple' and then come home drunk. It's becoming a routine," she said.

"Bob's been having problems, I told you. I had to sit and listen to him bitch and moan about this and that," he told her. "I sort of feel bad for him, though, being stuck at the Quick Fix for the last fifteen years," he said, trying to change the topic. "You know he's had a lot of money problems," he said before starting up the steps.

"Yeah, I know money problems," she said, acting disgusted as she followed him. "Well, how did it go?"

"Shit, like always, but maybe not as bad as some of the other days. Morgan gave me all those papers to go over, about all the nerves and muscles that he wanted me to know, and Turzak didn't ask me one question about any of it," he told her as he sat on the edge of the bed and turned on the television. "Thought you weren't going to worry about the trial anymore?" he asked.

"I'm trying...but it's not easy. The story's everywhere. Can't turn on the TV without hearing about it. Can't read the newspapers. Can't stand my friends...They all act like I'm some kind of crippled leper they don't want to be around anymore...laughing behind my back. We're just a big joke. Look," she said, handing him part of the newspaper. "I caught a couple of my friends laughing at this comic in the newspaper. Some kind of editorial," she added. "Ignorant bitch...standing there, right in front of me. Embarrassing...but what could I do?"

Weed looked at the black-and-white cartoon drawing. Frankenstein on a stretcher, wearing a blond wig like Hileman's, drawn to make it resemble her. And a doctor who was supposed to be him, standing over her with surgical instruments in his hand, dressed up like a farmer in bib overalls and boots, standing in what looked like cow shit. He was bald, except for a few strands of straw as hair. The drawing did sort of look like him, Weed thought. "The state of the city's current health care," it said directly beneath the cartoon. And below the cartoon was a long editorial about health care in the city, but he didn't see his or Hileman's name mentioned anywhere.

"Yeah, well, what did I tell you? People love this kind of stuff. They love to see other people getting destroyed...makes for good drama...makes them feel good," he said, pushing the paper aside.

"You know, I was thinking," he said after he had lain down on the bed with his clothes still on. "I thought about it today when I was sitting in the courtroom, looking at Hileman and thinking about the banquet last year..."

"What are you talking about?"

"You remember how she was always out on the dance floor last year? Well, not always, but she was out there a lot...dancing," he said as he unbuttoned his shirt and tossed it over to where a chair had once been and then watching as it fell to the floor. "She was in the conga line. You remember...Her dress went way up and you could see her girdle...and we were laughing about how disgustingly funny it was?"

"Yeah, I remember something like that."

"Doing the twist at the end of the banquet...She was so drunk. Well, she didn't look like she was very injured last year. No wheelchair. No collar."

"Yeah, I think I remember…So what's the point?"

"Wouldn't it be something if she did the same thing this year? If she got drunk and started dancing around doing the conga? What if I got some pictures of her dancing and had Morgan show them to the judge and the jury…and everyone else in the courtroom… including all the reporters? It would ruin her whole case. It would prove what I've been saying all along—that there's nothing physically wrong with her…that it's all just a big act to destroy me," he said, pausing to finishing undressing. "We would win the case, just like that. Show the judge and everyone that it was all a big act," he said excitedly. "Unmask her charade with the wheelchair, and all the other bullshit that she's claiming was my fault."

"She's probably not going to do that this year, but it *would* be something. Would turn the tide and make her look bad…would make you look like the victim then. I think it's a great idea, but I don't know…It's probably not going to happen. Her lawyer's probably already warned her about doing anything as foolish as that."

"I don't know. She gets a little drunk, she just might do anything. Wouldn't the papers like to get a story like that? And they would *have* to print something like that. I'm going to take my phone…and then just wait. Follow her around if I have to. If she slips up even one time, even if it's just getting out of her wheelchair, I'm going to be there to get a picture…but just sort of clandestinely. Make it look like I'm taking a picture of something else…No one would even know, and personally, I wouldn't care if they did," he added.

"Might be worth a try," Sandy said as she lay down beside him. "At this point I'd do just about anything to win…can't imagine what it will be like if we don't," she said. "Maybe you could get someone from last year's banquet to testify, or find some photos of her from last year," she added.

"Yeah, that's an idea," he said as he lay in bed, mulling over the possibilities for a while before thinking about his encounter with the police. He was still pissed off at Sandy about the car as she continued to babble, now about Helen and Frank and how nice it was that they offered the use of their spare bedroom in their basement if they lost the case and the house. But he was only half listening. He was thinking more about what he was going to tell the police on Saturday morning; trying to figure out what they might ask him and what they might already know, and trying to convince himself that is was all just routine and nothing bad was likely to happen.

He would just go down to the station, talk to them for a couple of minutes, tell them that he really didn't know anything, and that would be the end of it. And then hope that they were smart enough to figure out what really happened without any help from him. That it was Pickles and arrest him. Take him off the street before he came looking for him...before he did something irrational, he thought as he lay there in bed for most of the night, tossing and turning, unable to sleep.

CHAPTER TWENTY-FIVE

Friday, May 14
8:16 a.m.

Those are the shoes Sandy is going to wear to the Spring Fling tomorrow, Weed figured as he looked down at all the shoes lined up at the bottom of Sandy's closet. Those have to be the ones, he concluded as he looked over his shoulder to make sure Sandy was still sleeping, before picking them up and quietly carrying them out of the room. Seemed childish what he was doing, he thought, but he was still aggravated about her throwing his best tennis shoes away, as well as the damn car thing. Would serve her right...let her hunt for her damn shoes, just like he had to hunt for his for over an hour in that smelly dumpster.

Was unlikely she would discover that they were even missing until right before the banquet, he thought as he carried the shoes down the stairs and out to the garage before deciding to hide the shoes under the seat of his MG. That would be a safe place where Sandy wouldn't likely find them, he knew. Could tell her that he didn't have any idea what had happened to her shoes…didn't have any idea where she had put them, he thought as he went back into the house. See how she felt when she didn't have the shoes she wanted to wear…see how mature she acted…see if losing her shoes was a big deal to her, he thought, somewhat gleeful. But he wasn't quite sure about the rationale behind what he had just done. Was actually pretty juvenile to take someone's shoes for revenge, and also pretty obvious after she had just done the same thing…And she was likely to quickly figure it out, he thought as he sat down at the table, drank his coffee, and opened the newspaper. Should probably just take the damn shoes back upstairs and put them back in her closet. What was he thinking? Would have to be a little more subtle than that, he imagined. Could think of some better way to get even with her, anyway, he thought just as he heard the stairs start to squeak. Would just have to put them away later. But it would have been good payback, he thought. Didn't look like any of the other shoes were even close to matching the dress she was going to wear…And she was always so obsessed with her shoes. Would ruin her whole evening, having to walk around at the banquet in shoes that didn't *exactly* match her dress, he knew as Sandy came into the kitchen and poured herself a cup of coffee.

"Mustard Queen supposed to testify today?" she asked, sitting down across from him at the table, sipping at her coffee, and taking a section of the paper to read.

He nodded his head, but for some reason it didn't sound so funny today…seemed more annoying than anything.

"Jury might get some idea of what I had to put up with," he said, putting the newspaper aside. "Acts like she's drunk most of the time: slurs her speech, moves real slow like alcoholics do sometimes, and Turzak had to shake her two days ago to wake her up when the judge asked her a question. With her sunglasses on, you can't tell if she's awake or asleep, or whether her eyes are open or closed, or even who she's looking at. Maybe I'll get lucky and she'll make a fool of herself on the stand today. Fall asleep or slur her words or get confused and forget where she's at," Weed said. "I just really hope Morgan tells the jury about all the bullshit I had to put up with that night: about her damn dog, and about her smoking, and how drunk she was, and all her cussing and abusing me and the staff," he said, taking a sip of his coffee. "Morgan doesn't want to say anything...But I'm going to talk to him again. Make *her* look like an asshole, for a change—instead of *me*...It's *her* turn," he told Sandy as he started leafing through a stack of mail that had been lying on the table.

"Did you see that Mordy sent a bill?" she asked. "Thought we had him almost paid off, but it's still about two thousand dollars," she said as he looked at the bill. "Seems like it should be less."

"Some discount," Weed said as he scanned the charges...until he came to a charge for the meeting he'd just had with Mordy on Saturday. Mordy had listed the meeting on the bill as "a one-hour consultation for the Tatter problem." And Sandy had seen it...and now he was going to have to come up with some explanation. Just tell her it was a mistake, he thought somewhat panicky. Nothing else he could tell her...if she asked...and he knew she would.

Couldn't believe Mordy would do something so stupid! Send a bill to the house for a confidential problem...even after he had sworn no one would *ever* find out about it. Sending it right to the house—for Sandy to see. Was surprised Sandy wasn't already grilling him about it.

"I told you before he was too damn expensive. I'll call him," he said, sticking the bill in his pocket. "Still don't know why we have him as our personal attorney," Weed added disgustedly. He had told Mordy *emphatically* that it was all confidential, and then Mordy puts it right there—in the bill—and sends it to the house! How fuckin' stupid could he be? Probably intentional, too...Mordy would just love to have Sandy find out about that, he imagined.

"I'll talk to him today. Get the damn thing straightened out," he said, starting to think that maybe luck was with him and Sandy hadn't noticed.

Weed called Mordy's office as he drove toward the courthouse.

"Ben, what's up?" Mordy asked when his secretary finally got him on the phone.

"Jesus, Mordy, you're killing me! You sent a fuckin' bill to the house—about the shooting I told you about! How could you be so fucking stupid? Sometimes I think you would like to see me fail... that you do things like this on purpose."

"Just calm down, you're overreacting," Mordy told him. "I've got your bill up on the screen, right in front of me," he said, pausing for a moment before adding, "That was a mistake. That was a clerical error...and it's probably the new girl. I'll change it right now and send out another bill to make it look like it was an error," he said and then fell silent. Weed could hear him typing on his computer.

"Personally, I think it might have been intentional."

"That's crazy. Why would I do anything like that, Ben?"

"I don't know. You tell me...some Freudian slip or something?"

"Nothing more than a mistake. I think you're getting a little paranoid about things, Ben," Mordy said. "I'm always looking out for my clients. And really, why would I do something like that? It's already been removed from your bill, completely. And I'm not going to charge you for it now," he said somewhat to himself. "I'll send out an amended bill today."

"Don't bother. Just draw more attention to it."

Weed could hear him rustling some papers in the background. "I always tell the girls not to put any specifics about anything we discuss, but we're human too, Ben. I mean, you should know about that—people making mistakes," he said. "And what did Sandy say?"

"What's that supposed to mean, exactly? And luckily, I don't think she saw it."

"So you're making a big deal out of nothing."

"Isn't there some kind of a law against doing shit like this? Attorney–client confidentiality?"

"I get it, Ben. I'll take care of it. I'll shoot the secretary and then hang myself...Is that draconian enough for you?"

"And that was real good advice you gave me last week about the shooting: 'Don't say anything to the police...just wait until it all blows over.' Well, it didn't all blow over. The police stopped me last night. Someone saw my damn MG at Tatter's that night, and now the damn cops want to talk to me. I told them that I didn't know anything, and they still want to talk to me. What would that be about?"

"Oh, so now it's my fault you were in a strip club with a stripper? And how should I know what the police want to talk to you about? Probably the shooting."

"I'm just one step closer to having this whole mess blow up in my face. I can see the headlines now: 'Local Doctor Witness to Strip Club Shooting: Friends with Twenty-Five-Year-Old Stripper,' and my attorney can't even tell me why the police want to talk to me again, when I told them I didn't know anything."

"I don't know. Could be a million reasons, I suppose."

"Said they want me to tell them who I saw in the bar, but that's not going to happen. That crazy guy finds out I've been talking to the police, I'll end up like Tatter—with a bullet in my ass."

"That where he shot him?" Mordy asked, laughing lightly, but Ben didn't answer. He was already disgusted with Mordy and the whole mess. "Well, how's this Pickles, or whatever his name is, going to find out you talked to the police?"

"I don't know. Maybe because he seems to know more about my life than I do. And I'm getting a little tired of looking over my shoulder to see if he's standing there. He's psychotic...hears voices...sees things...shoots people. If he hears that I talked to the police, he's liable to come looking for me, and I'm sure he'll find me long before the police find him. And to make matters worse, Candy thinks he might be looking for me already."

"Yeah, well, shit happens…And who the hell's Candy?" Mordy asked. But again, Weed didn't answer.

"You should maybe come with me…might be good to have an attorney with me when I get arrested."

Mordy laughed. "Not me…I definitely don't want to get involved with something this bizarre, and I don't do criminal law anymore. And besides, my whole week is booked solid…and you're not going to get arrested," he said before Weed abruptly ended the call.

What a schmuck, he thought as he continued his drive to the courthouse, taking another Valium and washing it down with his bourbon and Coke. Might just call Mordy after he talked to the damn police, tell him that he had been arrested, was in jail, and needed someone to bail him out. Mordy would probably like to see that; to have it all brought out in the open for everyone to find out about. That bastard, he thought as he took a deep breath, pushed open the car door, and walked across the street to the courthouse.

The bailiff pushed Hileman to the witness stand in complete silence, except for the rhythmic sound of the squeaky wheelchair moving across the hard wooden floor. She gave a grimace of pain and a groan as she tried to push herself up and out of the wheel-chair—twice…dramatically, falling back into the wheelchair both times before making it to her feet. She stood there for a short time, as if to right herself, before finally taking the last couple steps past the jurors to the witness stand. And for added effect, Turzak held her arm the entire time, Weed thought. Hileman shuffled along in slow, halting steps, stiff, as if in great pain, and seemed to have a difficult time maintaining her balance. She moved like a drunk-en robot, pivoting awkwardly, stumbling up the step, and finally plopping down—hard—in the witness seat. Quite a transformation from just twenty minutes ago when he had seen her smoking in the park and holding her dog high in the air to give it a kiss. Could see why she had only been in two low-budget films…She wasn't such a great actor, he thought.

But worse, it seemed as if she had doctored up her scars to make them look even more hideous than they had looked the day before.

Would make her "big act" even more obvious, if he could get the pictures of her at the Spring Fling, he thought as he listened to Hileman answer Turzak's first question by telling the jury how much pain she had been in the night of the accident. How it had gotten noticeably worse, and how her legs had become numb and difficult to move after Dr. Weed had improperly removed her collar. There were more scathing questions about Hileman's lacerations, more accusations about Dr. Weed not using enough Novocain, and then Turzak told the jury how much suffering and verbal abuse she had to endure.

"So in your opinion, Dr. Weed was very impatient and made numerous derogatory and abusive comments directed at your behavior on the night in question even after you were confused from the concussion that you had suffered?" Turzak asked Hileman.

"I believe. I was in so much pain it was difficult to follow his instructions…And I was confused because of the concussion I had suffered…yes."

"She was up and walking around, smoking a cigarette…couldn't have been in too much pain," Weed whispered to Morgan, who continued to sit there, stoically, ignoring him.

"Had you been drinking that night?"

"Absolutely not! I don't drink when I drive. And actually, I very seldom drink…maybe just socially. I think the reason I was acting abnormally was totally because of my concussion," she added.

"And the police didn't charge you with driving under the influence, did they?" Turzak continued before she answered, "Absolutely not."

It was all a lie. She was drunk, Weed knew as he continued to listen to Turzak question Hileman. Questions about pain and suffering and how she had to depend on powerful narcotics, and about her nightmares, memory loss, headaches, and depression. And then questions about the horrid scars and how she was embarrassed to be seen in public.

"The scars, they have ruined my life. Every day that I wake up, it's a struggle. Looking at myself in the mirror, I just cry. It's difficult for me to live this way," she said sniffling, pulling out a tissue and wiping her eyes. It all seemed so phony, Weed thought.

Turzak continued for almost two hours, stopping twice; once to painstakingly slowly remove Hileman from the witness stand and wheel her out of the courtroom past the jurors so that she could rest and take her medications...and then to have her neck brace adjusted by a doctor who had accompanied her to the trial. Then another five minutes just to get her back into the witness stand. Just another finely choreographed exhibition to make him look bad in front of everyone in the courtroom, Weed knew. And what made matters worse was that Morgan just sat there quietly even though there were plenty of opportunities for him to object to Turzak's leading questions and Hileman's fabricated lies.

When Turzak finished, Morgan stood and paced as he questioned Hileman. But the questions seemed weak, passive, and non-threatening, Weed realized. And not one word from Morgan to the jury about how drunk and obnoxious Hileman had been that night, Weed thought with disgust and frustration.

"You should have said something," Weed told Morgan after the judge adjourned for the day.

"How could I? Turzak would have just told the jury that it was all because of her concussion...a concussion that they're claiming you missed diagnosing. No, we don't need to draw any more attention to that...We need to move away from that as quickly as possible.I told you that before...It's part of our strategy...so let it slide. By next week, most of the jurors won't remember much of what was said here today... Trust me...I *know*," he said as they both walked toward the exit. "I told you, our strategy is simple...You *know*...We talked about it. We tell the jury that the injuries were the result of the accident, not anything you did or didn't do…and that the scars just need to be revised. That's our plan—plain and simple. That's our defense—our best chance of winning this thing. Nothing vindictive that looks like we're uncaring and insensitive. Our strategy isn't to fight about whether someone is, or isn't, an obnoxious drunk," he said with irritation.

"Yeah, well, I'm telling *you*—there's nothing wrong with her. It's all an act."

"Yeah, and that might be the truth, but what am I supposed to do? I can't pull the wheelchair out from under her," he said as they started down the steps of the courthouse.

"Sometimes I think you're more concerned about your own career than you are about mine," Weed said as they reached the bottom of the steps.

"You said that before and I didn't say anything," Morgan said, stopping and turning toward Weed. "You want to know the problem, Ben? You want to know the real problem why this trial isn't going the way you want it to go? It's because you didn't leave me anything to work with. The whole case stinks. Everything you did and said that night looks crude and unprofessional. And no matter what I tell the jury, it just draws more attention to that fact. So don't blame *me*. I'm doing the best I can, with what *little* I have to work with. If you want a magician, then go find Houdini—I'm no Houdini," he added, turning as if he might walk away, before turning back. "You think *your* career is on the rocks? Well, *I'm* a lot worse off than *you*. *You* can go back to practicing medicine or whatever you plan to do…But what law firm is ever going to hire an attorney who pissed off Gertrude Hileman? She *owns* this city. *You* read the newspapers. They're making *me* look just as bad as *you*. I'm committing suicide. And *I've* already started to pack," Morgan said before shaking his head, turning, and continuing off down the street.

When Weed turned to walk back to his car, a reporter was standing behind him, taking fervent notes. He had a fleeting desire to push the reporter out of his way but didn't.

Weed stood in a stream of sunlight coming through the trees and took a deep breath of fresh air before continuing on toward his car. His life…his miserable life had all turned sour, he thought as he reached under his seat, pushing Sandy's shoes out of the way to get to the bourbon. Didn't give a damn who saw him today, he thought as he took a long drink, straight from the bottle in broad view.

Was still early, he thought as he sat there. Too early to go home. Didn't want to have to get involved with putting up decorations for the party, or watching Sandy move furniture out of the house, or listening to her sob story about what was going to happen to them.

Could call Candy and talk to her, he thought as he dialed her number. Maybe see if he could talk her into dressing down to look more respectable, and remind her not to wear too much make-up… and to make sure that she covered the red-and-black tattoo of a baby devil on her right breast. Make her look different than her stripper picture that appeared every Sunday in the newspaper, so that no one recognized her. Would be like rearranging the deck chairs on the *Titanic*, he imagined as his call went unanswered.

CHAPTER TWENTY-SIX

Friday, May 14
2:15 p.m.

He tried to relax as he drove aimlessly around for a while. First, he passed his mother's house but decided he didn't really want to deal with her now, so he drove off in another direction. He slowed down as he passed the Quick Fix, but inside, Bob looked busy with customers, and he didn't really feel much like talking, anyway.

Had to remember to put Sandy's shoes back before the banquet, he thought as he pushed them further beneath the seat to make room for the fresh bottle of bourbon he'd just picked up at the liquor store.

Could drive out and see Candy, he imagined, but he hadn't picked up any Viagra yet, and he was too exhausted for sex.

He instead drove to a small, out-of-the-way bar where he could drink alone and undisturbed. But as he sat there drinking, all he could think about was how messed up his life had become. He sat there for almost two hours feeling sorry for himself, he knew, before driving across town to the basketball courts where he had played when he was young. He took off his tie and jacket and just stood there in the night air before taking a few long shots with a worn-out basketball that someone had given up on. He imagined being young again, when life was all in front of him…running up and down the court gracefully in the cool night air in front of an imaginary crowd that was cheering him on wildly…before making the final shot…to win the game…to become the hero—and to impress Kathy Marks, the one girl that he had been in love with so long ago.

But those days were gone, he realized with regret as he watched his last shot twirl around the rim once, hanging there for what seemed like a long time…undecided…before falling harmlessly to the cold wet ground…and reality.

When he got home, Sandy was forlornly looking out the back window.

"They tore up the whole back yard, and they still didn't get the damn pool fixed," she said, impatiently pulling aside the curtain so that he could see into the back yard. "I told them we were having a party next Saturday and not to make a mess, but they still tore up the back yard," she said as he stared out the window at a muddy trench that ran the length of the yard from the house to the pool.

"Next thing I knew, they had this big hole dug and mud everywhere. They've been out there for almost four hours and they still haven't found the leak. And if it rains, it's going to be an even bigger mess for the party," she whined.

"Looks like it's going to cost me a fortune," Weed said looking out the window over Sandy's shoulder at the workers. "They give you an estimate?" he asked, but she seemed to ignore his question.

"The weather is supposed to be nice next Saturday. We're supposed to get rain all this weekend, and then nice weather all next week," she continued as if he had never spoken. "Lucky I called them, because they told me they didn't know anything about the pool leaking. You sure you remembered to call?"

"I called…They just didn't remember or didn't want to be bothered…as usual," he answered, although he had long forgotten to call.

"How'd it go today?" she said, letting the curtain drop as she turned toward him.

"Hileman put on a big show, as usual," he said, getting some ice from the freezer to make himself a drink. "Just sits there and acts like she's near death. My guess is that she's not having any pain at all. Had to stop the trial—twice—so she could rest and take her medication, and have her collar adjusted…or some crazy bullshit like that. It pissed me off. Right in the middle of her testimony, a doctor came up and took her blood pressure and then gave her some kind of medicine. Unreal!

"And that's the other thing I remembered…You couldn't even notice her scars at the banquet last year…you remember? Now she has herself looking like some kind of monster, sitting up there in front of everybody. All just a big act to impress the jury," he said, pausing to look out at the back yard again. "But I'm going to say something next week…tell them that Hileman's nothing more than a malingering alcoholic. Morgan might get pissed, but I don't give a damn."

"You should be careful about what you say. You don't want to screw things up any more than they all ready are. Don't want to lose the case because of something stupid that you said."

One of the workers waved when he saw them standing at the window and then started walking toward the house.

"I didn't tell Morgan about my plans to get pictures of Hileman tomorrow. If she gets plastered like last year—and makes one false move—I'm going to be there. If she takes her collar off, or gets out of her wheelchair for just one second—I'm going to get a picture of it," he said, watching the muddy worker as he moved closer. "And

I'll bet you'll hardly be able to see her scars tomorrow. I'm excited. And if I get pictures, I'm going to make damn sure that the jury sees them, too...don't care what Morgan says about that...might not even tell him...just hold them up for everyone to see."

"I don't know. Sounds too easy...And she's probably too smart to do anything that stupid...especially with a bunch of people around."

"I don't know. She's pretty stupid. She's one of those people who lose control when they have too much to drink."

"And you just can't hold up pictures for people to see during a trial. They have to be submitted as evidence...even I know that. You could really get in trouble for that."

"Yeah, I know. I was being sort of sarcastic, anyway. "But alcohol makes people do crazy things, and if you would have seen her that night in the ER, you would know what I'm talking about. She was wild...cussing, stomping around. Not like she is now, in court...all calm and collected," he said as the worker finally arrived on the patio. "Yeah, I drink some, but if I ever get that way—shoot me," he added.

"Looks like the outlet valve to the filter is leaking. Probably take us the better part of two days to get it all put back together," the worker said.

"You remember about my party?"

"Yeah, sure. Should be done in plenty of time. Get this hole all filled back in and tamped down, put the grass back in place," he said. "It'll look just like new for your party."

"How much are we talking about?" Weed asked as the worker turned to leave.

"Don't know for sure. You're a doctor...You know about things like this. Depends on what we find when we do the operation," he said, trying to make a joke, but Weed could only muster a tight smile. "If we can slip in a gasket, maybe three thousand...If we need to rebuild the whole inside of the pump, then would probably be somewhere around five thousand—give or take a little. But re-gardless, we should be out of here by Tuesday, if everything goes as planned—if we don't run into any snags. Decorations look nice," he said, pointing to the streamers as he continued off in the direction of the pool. "Hawaiian...nice," he added as he looked around and smiled at the decorations.

"Yeah," Sandy answered, excited that someone had noticed.

"Shouldn't even be able to notice that we've been here at all," the worker repeated in a mumble as he started to gather up his tools.

"Now we're going to have a muddy back yard. I don't care what he says," Sandy said when the worker was far enough away that he couldn't hear. "They should have never started digging. If I had known they were going to do all this, I would have stopped them and put the hose in to fill it up the night before the party," she added sourly.

"Looks like a wake," Weed said after a long pause as he sipped his drink and looked out the window.

"Looks like a what?"

"The back yard. It looks like we're having a wake...like at a cem-etery, with the hole dug for the body, and the big white party tent for everyone to sit under. Like they're just about ready to bury some-one...with all the chairs lined up, waiting for everyone to arrive. How ironic..."

Offended, she insisted that it didn't look like a wake, and that really wasn't what a wake was anyway, and that she couldn't imagine how he could ever come up with a party looking like a funeral... that he just had a bizarre sense of humor. "How about all the party lights and decorations, what do you think about that?" she asked defensively.

Did look like a tent set up for a funeral, he thought to himself as he walked behind her into the living room and sat down in front of the TV. Prophetic…Why couldn't she see the irony? Maybe it really was a wake. Maybe it was a wake—for him.

"Frank wants you to buy some of his holiday calendars. You know, the ones that feature a different one of his paintings for each month of the year. Like those Thomas Kinkade calendars they have at the mall. Said you could give them out at the office…to your patients."

"That's just great."

"Yeah, I guess he spent a bunch of money and hasn't sold too many yet."

"I'm not passing them out at the office. Patients are already pissed off at me," he said, but she didn't get the joke or didn't think it was very funny. "And tell him it's May…Nobody buys calendars in May."

He surfed through the channels, quickly going past Court TV and the news stations in fear that there might be another scathing story about the trial before settling in to a rerun of the *The Jeffersons*. Probably wouldn't be anything about his trial on *The Jeffersons*, he surmised, lying back on the bed and watching.

"You have your game tomorrow?" Sandy asked, leafing through a magazine as she waited for his answer that never came. "And re-member, we need to get to the banquet a little early," she added. "I have to set up for the raffle, and I want to leave here by six. They're giving away a trip for two to Hawaii, but all the other prizes are just crap…a free dental exam and a tooth brush," she added, laughing heartily. "Can you believe that's what one of the dentists donated?" she added before making a few disparaging comments about him playing basketball in his best suit as she brushed off the suit coat and hung it back in the closet.

"Yeah, I'll be back in time. Game should be over by two," he said, remembering about her shoes he had taken. Would have to bring them back in the morning when she was sleeping, he thought, but he was having a hard time remembering where he had hid them now.

"And don't drink after the game. We'll have plenty to drink at the banquet, and I don't want you to be drunk before we even get there," she said laying her magazine face down on the coffee table. "I don't want you doing something embarrassing, because everyone will be watching us tomorrow night…And I'm already embarrassed enough with everyone talking about us…about how we might lose everything. Seems almost foreboding…like a premonition that something bad is going to happen, no matter what anyone does," she said, shaking her head in dismay and then adding that he was right about some people, and that she could already sense people treating her like an outcast.

"That's the way people are, I told you…human nature. People love to see other people suffer. Especially your friends…They really like to see you suffer. And we're the entertainment—the real-life drama. And you watch…They're all…including our friends…going to treat us like pariahs."

"Like what?"

"Like someone no one likes," he answered. "Won't be anyone there who wants to be seen with us, especially if Hileman's in the room. Too dangerous…She might ruin their lives too, if they get too close to us…guilt by association."

"Well, I'm not even going to worry about it now…I'm just going to try and have a good time," she said, coming out of the bathroom with a few oddly placed curlers in her hair. She was still holding her drink, and she danced around strangely in front of the mirror, as if she were suddenly carefree and happy…all side effects of her new medication, Weed imagined.

"I think that we should both act happy—even if we're not. Make everyone think that there's nothing wrong…that everything is just fine with us," she repeated like a mantra.

"To tell you the truth, at this point, I don't give a damn what any-one thinks. All I know is that I'm going to get a picture of Hileman doing something stupid, even if I have to pull her out onto the dance floor by her hair and dance with her myself," he said.

"Wig," Sandy corrected. "It's a wig she wears…But that's what I'm saying. I don't want you to go and do something stupid like that. So don't drink after the game."

It was still early, just getting dark, but he was dead tired. The week had been exhausting, and he would have another big day to-morrow—with the police interview, and the game, and then the banquet. He could hardly wait.

The day would get a lot better after he was finished with his interview with the police. To get that out of the way would be a big relief…just hoped that the interview would go smoothly, that the police would believe his story, and that there were no surprises, he thought.

Weed lay in bed for a long time anxiously thinking about the police interview and what he was going to tell them and what they might already know, hoping that there were no big surprises as he watched Weezie and George fight over some mundane problem with the big English guy. Wasn't funny then and it isn't funny now, he thought as he switched off the TV, closed his eyes, and spent the rest of the night in a fitful sleep.

CHAPTER TWENTY-SEVEN

Saturday, May 15
7:43 a.m.

"You're inside out," Sandy said as Weed moved around the bedroom, gathering up the things that he would need for his game: his uniform, shoes, a towel, and socks, shoving them all into the bottom of his gym bag.

"Your shirt…it's inside out," she said when he looked back at her with confusion on his face.

He had slept well for a while but then awakened early and couldn't go back to sleep, thinking about his meeting with the police. He was anxious to get it out of the way and had almost convinced himself that everything was going to be okay, that he was obsessing over something that wouldn't amount to much at all, and that no one was likely to find out about anyway. But rationalization could be a dangerous thing, he knew. And for some reason, he still couldn't remember where he had hidden Sandy's shoes. Maybe it was some Freudian thing, he thought.

"Remember, we need to get to the country club by six thirty," Sandy said, sitting up in bed and turning on the nightstand light. "It's going to take some time for you to put on your tux, so make sure you're home on time," she said as he turned his shirt right side out. "And remember, *nothing* to drink at your game and three drinks *max* at the banquet. Scares me when you drink...And I don't want you doing something stupid to make the situation even more ridiculous."

"Yeah, yeah, I'll remember," Weed said irritated.

"I just don't want things getting out of control. I think that it's important for us to keep a low profile tonight...Act happy, but keep a low profile. There's going to be a lot of important people there, and I don't want you to cause any kind of a scene. Just want to take it slow and easy...Act like everything is fine with us, and maybe we can get through this thing without any problems," she said and then continued to repeat the same things she had just told him. He didn't need a lecture but didn't want to fight either, he thought as he let her babble on.

"Try to get a table close to the dance floor to make it easier for me to get pictures...because I'm convinced Hileman's going to do something stupid," Weed said as he finally got everything that he needed into his bag.

"Tables have already been assigned," she said and then asked him why he was leaving so early for the gym.

"Going to practice with the team," he told her, waving back to her as he left the room, but she had already turned off the light and pulled the covers up over her shoulders.

Shouldn't take too long to give his official statement, he thought, picking up the newspaper from the front porch and tossing it back inside the house. Didn't even care what they printed anymore. He reviewed in his mind one last time what he was going to tell the detectives as he sipped at his coffee and drove, taking two Valiums to calm his nerves. Didn't want to act nervous around the police and make them think he had something to hide.

He parked a block from the station and pulled his baseball cap down over his eyes as he walked quickly down the street, giving no indication where he was going before turning sharply up the steps and into the police station. Didn't need anyone seeing him going into a police station, he thought.

He waited in a small room with blurred images of people moving around behind thick frosted glass; people talking and laughing about something, but he couldn't make out what they were saying.

A man sat sleeping at one end of the room, snoring while leaning awkwardly against the wall with his head nestled in his arm. Another woman sat filling out some kind of form on a small coffee table in front of her. There was a faint, nauseating odor coming from one of them, Weed realized as he picked up a magazine, but he was unable to concentrate on what he was reading. He waited for almost thirty minutes before one of the officers, the one whom he had talked to on Thursday but couldn't remember his name, came out from behind one of the doors and shook his hand, thanked him for coming, and then directed him down a long corridor. They made small talk about the heavy rain they were having as they walked.

"Yeah, that's what they said…supposed to rain all day and then get a lot worse this evening," the nameless officer said, showing Weed into one of the small offices at the end of corridor. "Some kind of tropical depression, I guess."

He hoped he didn't seem too nervous, but he was. His palms felt cold and sweaty as he sat down in one of the chairs that was placed in front of a large metal desk. A nameplate on the desk read: *Lieutenant Michael Clark.*

"Yeah, there's really supposed to be a downpour later," he said as Clark came into the room and shook his hand. Two women dressed in police uniforms walked by and looked into the room somewhat inquisitively, as if they had walked by just to see him, Weed thought. One looked familiar. He could see them standing behind the opaque Plexiglas room divider as if they were listening to what was being said.

For the first couple minutes, Weed repeated the same rationale for his presence at the bar that night—just as he had told them the night they'd stopped him. Basically, he said that he had not seen or heard anything that would indicate a shooting. And although he had recognized familiar faces, the only people he could definitively say were there that night were Candy and Tatter. They seemed satisfied, Weed thought as Clark continued to write. Then Clark paused for a long time, before leaning forward and turning on a computer screen in front of him.

"We want you to watch this and tell us what you think," Clark told him.

"We put this surveillance camera in about a year ago, when we found out about all the drugs and prostitution that were moving through Tatter's Bar," he added as the fuzzy white screen went dark and then sprang to life, showing what Weed immediately recognized as Tatter's Bar. The screen had a rolling time-bar at the bottom, with the date and time. He could see his car in the parking lot along with a few others but said nothing as he watched.

The video remained unchanged for about a minute before a few people came running from inside the bar. First, three people struggled to get out the front door—all at the same time—and they scattered in different directions to their respective cars in the parking lot. One person nearly fell, but then two more people came running out the back door, which opened directly into the parking lot. It looked vaguely like a silent Charlie Chaplin film, Weed thought apprehensively. And then about ten seconds later, he could see himself coming out of the bar, fumbling with his belt buckle and his cell phone and looking around apprehensively as he quickly walked to his car. The screen showed him looking around one last time before getting into his car and driving off—without turning on his headlights.

"You see what I mean? This is why we're having trouble believing your explanation of what happened. I mean, that is you coming out of the bar and getting into your MG, isn't it?" Clark asked.

"That's me...I guess. It's a little fuzzy, but very well could be me," Weed answered, trying to search for some alternative explanation that could support the one he had already told them.

"But you see what I'm talking about? All these people running *out* of the bar, like something just happened *inside* the bar, like maybe someone had just gotten *shot* and they were trying to get away from the situation. And then you come out after them, looking around like you were trying to get away without being seen, too. You see? That's what bothered us, right from the start...because it appears as if that was exactly the time Tatter was shot, *and* it looks like you were trying to flee the scene of the crime," Clark said as Weed listened, still trying to come up with something—anything—to get him out of this mess. "Yeah, it looks to us like you were trying to flee the scene...without anyone noticing. But what really bothered us," he continued after a long pause, "is that it looks like you're trying to stuff something under your belt," he said, pausing again and looking at Weed. "Something that suspiciously looks like a small handgun of some sort."

"What? No...no! That's not a gun...That's my cell phone," Weed answered, leaving out a sickly nervous laugh, shocked at the accusation but realizing his story had just come completely unraveled. "It came loose when I left the men's room and I was shoving it back into my pocket," he told them, showing them the cell phone he had attached to his belt. And I don't even own a gun."

"Yeah, we know you don't own a gun, but your girlfriend does... And she has no idea where that gun is right now," he said, pausing to wait for Weed's reaction.

"This is crazy! I didn't shoot anyone. Why would I do something crazy like that?" he said, still reeling from the accusation and trying to regain his composure.

"Could be for just about anything in a place like that, I imagine...drugs, money, girl problems...?" the officer added, looking up at Weed. Weed took a deep breath and resolved to end this crazy speculation. "But whatever the reason, we think that you got pissed at Tatter, started arguing, and then got to a point where you just ended up shooting him. Happens all the time...Things get out of control."

"Whoa...let me backtrack...maybe clear things up some," Weed said, finally getting their attention as he let out a long sigh. He took in a deep breath and then wiped the sweat from his forehead. "What I told you about that night is *mostly* the truth, and I didn't actually *see* anything because I was in the men's room at the time, but...I did *hear* what I thought sounded like a gunshot. And that's when I sort of panicked and ran out of the bar acting that way," he told them. Then he explained, again, how his cell phone had come loose and he was just trying to put it back in the holder. "*Not* because I had anything to do with any shooting. Like I told you, I didn't actually *see* what happened," he said, pausing to take another deep breath as they listened. "What I *did* see, but what I *didn't* tell you, was that Pickles and Tatter were fighting—just before I heard what, I guess, was the gunshot," he said, taking another deep breath before continuing. "They had been arguing for almost a half hour, I think, right before the shot, so I just assumed that it was one of them who had been shot. That's when I panicked. I ran out of the men's room and out of the bar, but I definitely didn't have *anything* to do with that shooting," Weed said, letting out a long sigh as both of the detectives looked closer at the computer screen. "That's when my damn cell phone came loose...and that's what I'm doing—right there—putting my phone in my pocket," he told them, pointing at the screen. He held up the phone for them to see, in a way that mimicked what was on the computer screen, but both officers seemed more interested in watching the surveillance tape than to listening to what he was saying now.

"Actually, I figured it was Pickles who shot his father. That made the most sense, and I didn't want to be anywhere near the place… knowing that he had a gun." Clark ran the tape backward and then forward a couple more times, stopping it each time it showed Weed holding his phone, as Weed continued to try and explain away their accusations. He seemed somewhat bolstered by their interest in what he had just told him—about it being his cell phone instead of a gun—as if maybe they were no longer sure that it was a gun. "And also, I was concerned about how something like this would look, you know? A doctor in a place like that…getting drawn up into a police investigation, when I'm already headline news over this stupid trial thing. Didn't need any more problems, you know what I mean? And I thought it might even cause me to lose my case," Weed said, wiping the sweat from his forehead. "That's the real reason I didn't come down here and talk to you sooner."

"Yeah, I can understand that, I guess," Clark mumbled as they all continued to watch the tape. Clark finally said he still wasn't sure that it was not a gun that Weed was holding. "Doesn't really look like a cell phone either," he said, rewinding the tape again.

"I think it's a cell phone," the other officer finally said as he backed away from the screen, shaking his head. "Didn't I tell you that we should have locked Pickles up when we had him down here questioning him?" he added, looking at Clark for a response.

"Yeah, well, we had two witnesses who said he wasn't there… And with this tape, what were we supposed to do? We couldn't hold him, anyway. And I'm still not a hundred percent sure that's a cell phone," Clark added.

"It's not a gun. I can guarantee you that," Weed repeated, somewhat relieved that at least one officer now agreed with him that it wasn't a gun. And then Weed told them about the threats Pickles had been making.

"To tell you the truth, I'm really concerned about being here right now."

"Makes sense what he says, I guess," the other officer told Clark, as if they hadn't heard anything Weed had just told them. "It makes as much sense as Pickles not being in the bar that night."

"Yeah, I guess, but we have witnesses who say Pickles wasn't anywhere near the bar that night. And anyway, Tat told us what happened," Clark added.

"Yeah, but Tat was all doped up on pain meds and hooked to a ventilator when we talked to him. To tell you the truth, I'm not really sure what he was trying to tell us," the other officer told Clark. "And in fairness," he said, "the other two witnesses are worthless."

"Yeah, probably," Clark said reluctantly.

"Didn't I tell you I thought it was Pickles the whole time? Only thing that made any sense."

"And then he gets one of those whore dancers who works down there to come in and tell us he was with her the whole night—way across town. Should have locked him up when we had him."

"Yeah, because we might not get another opportunity."

The officers discussed it all for a while, finally loosely coming to the decision that what they had thought was a gun, was more likely a cell phone. Then they concluded that it probably was Pickles who shot his father, as Weed listened somewhat relieved. When they were finally finished, they had Weed give another official statement.

"You sure this version's the correct one?" Clark asked when Weed had finished, still acting pissed.

"Absolutely," Weed answered and then tried to make a feeble attempt at an apology for the trouble he had caused them.

"Well, we're going to check it all out again, anyway. So, if you could tell your girlfriend to try and think a little bit harder about where she left the gun, it might help," he added, shaking his head in a gesture of disbelief. And then after a long silence, he told Weed that as far as he was concerned he was free to go, but he still sounded reluctant and pissed.

"You should have told us what the hell happened the first time. Now we have a lunatic roaming the streets, so anything he does now—is on *you*," Clark said acting happy, as if he had absolved himself of the whole mess. "And if I was you, I would keep looking over my shoulder," he added, before calling a uniformed officer into his office.

"You need to go out and pick up Gerome Tatter's son, Pickles, over on the south side," he told the uniformed officer while handing him a paper with Pickles's address. "Could be armed, so don't take any chances. He's got a long psych history…And he snaps pretty easily."

"Yeah, I know where the asshole lives," the officer answered, reluctantly taking the paper.

Well, I guess you're free to go," Clark repeated. "But stay in touch because, technically, you're still a suspect until we get this mess all straightened out," he added, as Weed tried to apologize again.

Weed started toward the door, but he needed to ask one more question. "I know you can't say anything for certain, but what're the chances of something like this getting into the newspaper anytime soon?" he asked Clark.

"Don't know," Clark answered, acting somewhat annoyed at the question. "We have no control over shit like that. If Pickles comes quietly when we try to arrest him, then no one might notice…So then, probably nothing—just a routine arrest. But if he resists, puts up a big fuss and starts shooting—which, I assume, he might—then we'll all know about it," he said.

Shit! It couldn't have gone much worse, Weed thought as he walked toward his car, somewhat dazed by it all. The only consolation was that they hadn't actually arrested him—at least not yet—but he was still a suspect. He couldn't believe that.

Well, it was over…out of his hands now. Whatever happened—happened, he thought somewhat relieved, but more disgusted at himself. Just exactly what he hadn't wanted to happen: to get involved with a police investigation and to rat out some homicidal lunatic, he thought while taking a sip of his bourbon as he sat in his car. Creating even more of a chance of exposing this entire, sordid side of his life. He would just have to make up a story for Sandy—if she found out. For everyone, for that matter. Would have to tell her that he had just been a victim of circumstance; he had just gone into the bar to meet a friend…or that he had actually gone into the bar to help the shooting victim. Didn't know what would stick…and maybe he was just digging his grave a little deeper. What was the difference which excuse he used at this point in his life? He was in so much shit; wouldn't make a damn bit of difference what he told anyone now. No one would believe him anyway, he thought. Just couldn't get his mind around all of it.

He had created the perfect storm for himself, he thought as he took two more large swallows of bourbon before placing the bottle under his seat, and at the same time realizing where he had hidden Sandy's shoes.

CHAPTER TWENTY-EIGHT

Saturday, May 15
11:05 a.m.

Drove to the Y, upset and nervous, thinking about the police interview…about his bad luck…about Mordy's bad advice…about Sandy, for screwing up his already screwed-up life. His life… Pickles…all a jumble of twisted thoughts. He was trying to calm down, not really believing what had just happened to him.

There was no answer when he called Mordy. Wasn't sure why he was even calling. Maybe just to tell him how pissed he was at his bad advice.

No answer when he called Candy either. Had to tell her what happened…to get their stories straight, and then to tell her to find her damn gun.

He changed in the locker room and walked up the stairs to the gym, but it seemed different than most other Saturdays. Too much activity and too many people in the gym for a Saturday morning, he realized as he watched a sea of small children moving chaotically around the gym, all dressed alike in blue shorts and white T-shirts with the YMCA logo across the back. They all seemed to be receiving instructions on how to play basketball, he guessed as he watched for a minute. Those kids shouldn't be there now, with the men's game about ready to start. Weed watched the children running up and down the court in every direction, trying to bounce basketballs, flopping around on the floor, screaming, chasing errant basketballs. All seemed like mass chaos—mass confusion. Mothers were everywhere, sitting in the bleachers, standing around the edges of the court, and chasing after the kids. Must be getting ready to leave, he hoped as he checked his watch again before pushing open the door to the gym.

His team was standing, huddled in one corner of the gym.

"Can you believe this?" Bob said coming up to meet him. "That asshole, Walt, double-booked the gym…scheduled some kind of a basketball camp for all these little bastards…at the same time we're supposed to be playing our game. How fuckin' stupid can he be?"

"They want us to play in the basement gym, so all these little shits can use the gym up here."

"That's bullshit. Walt knows you can't play down there," Weed said as a woman, who was standing behind them, scolded them for using vulgar language around the children.

"There's no way you can play down there with the warped floors," Weed said sitting down to tie his shoe—again, but tighter this time.

"Tell Walt to move the kids downstairs," Weed said to Bob as they navigated around the children.

"We did. Jack's down there right now, talking to him."

"Let the kids play down there. Won't matter where they play. Look at them. They don't know the difference between a basketball and a Frisbee."

"I told him, but he says that it's some big deal basketball camp for preschoolers, and there's nothing he can do about it now," Jack said when he returned to his teammates.

"Let's go talk to Walt...tell him we're not moving," Weed said to Bob as he started toward the exit.

This is just what he needed...the only good thing about his day—destroyed, he thought as he walked down a flight of stairs to the director's office. "He's known about our game for months," Weed said, pushing open the door to Walt's office.

Walt was sitting behind his desk with the phone wedged between his shoulder and head. He held up a finger and then talked for another couple of minutes as they stood there and waited.

"I can't do anything," he said as he hung up the phone, before they had a chance to speak. "I just talked to the big cheese and he says that he wants you guys downstairs."

"Bullshit. We should have priority, and the kids won't know any different, anyway," Weed said.

"Yeah, but their mothers will," he answered. "And what would it look like if I sent a bunch of little kids with their mothers down there? We're trying to improve our image—not destroy it—and money's tight. It makes us look bad if we move them down there, when we're trying to get them to buy memberships. We send them down there—we could lose a ton of money."

"That's bullshit, Walt. We had the gym first...for over a year."

"You going to bust my balls over this one little game?" Walt said. "I knew that this was going to happen. The court down there's not that bad. We did some work on it a couple of years ago...fixed all the leaks we could find...And anyway, there's nothing I can do about it now."

"Oh, for Christ's sake, Walt! The whole floor sags at one corner, and there are loose floorboards all over the place. You can't even dribble the ball three feet without hitting a dead spot...And this is an important game," Weed said. "We spent all winter working our butts off, and you want to send us to the dungeon for the most important game of the season."

"They're all important, Doc, but these mothers think their kids are important too. Everything's important. Everyone's special. But you can't all play upstairs, so just do me this one big favor, Ben, because I can't move all those kids down to the basement. That's out of the question. I mean, it would look really bad, and frankly, I'm afraid that a couple of them might get hurt down there," he said with as much sincerity as he could muster. "And besides, we have a membership drive going on now, and all these families are here for their free one-month membership. That's why the lemonade and cookies are in the lobby. It's about the young kids. They're our future. Not about some old farts like us, Ben. It would look bad if we moved them downstairs," he said as he stood and looked through one of his desk drawers until he found a key.

"We only sponsor the Over Fifty basketball program as a courtesy to you guys, anyway; to make a little money and to fill in the dead space on the schedule. Board doesn't even like you guys in here, and I had to put my ass on the line last time they brought it up. I told you before that having you guys play here is a wash for the Y, because we don't make a dime with what the insurance company charges us. They're pushing our liability insurance right through the roof—with all the medical claims we've been turning in. You know what happened last week…guy breaks his ankle in three places. Now, that's going to cost us a bundle. That's the sixth broken bone we've had this year, and five of them were people over the age of fifty. You guys are killing us," he said with mock desperation in his voice. "To tell you the truth, and I don't want you to get pissed, but we can't really afford you guys around here anymore. It's a liability nightmare, to have fifty- and sixty-year-olds running up and down the court, acting like a bunch of punch-drunk teenagers," he said as he searched through some papers on top of his desk. "Half you guys look like a team from a nursing home…Those aren't my words, that's what someone else told me, and I'm trying to be kind," he added, pulling out one of the papers from the stack of papers he had been looking though.

"Jesus, you see right here…this bill?" he said, holding up the paper in front of them. "I just got this from our insurance company… wrist fracture…four thousand dollars. And how much d'you think that guy's broken ankle's going to cost us? I mean, you're a good bunch of guys, but you got to understand where I'm coming from."

"Just throwing this out, but what I'm trying to say is that we're probably not going to sponsor the Over Fifty League next year. Doesn't mean that you can't use the gym. I mean, legally we can't just throw you out," he added. "We just don't want to encourage you…that's all."

"It's the principle, Walt. We've been playing here for years."

He shrugged his shoulders. "We have just over a hundred families signed up for this basketball clinic. That's—potentially—one hundred new memberships at two hundred fifty dollars—each. Well, you do the math. There's no way that I'm going to send them downstairs. So just do me this one favor…because I'm not moving the kids," he said. "I'll make it up to you someday…buy you all a six-pack or something," he said jokingly. "You're all big boys. You'll manage."

"Forty years I've been coming here and now we're getting tossed out like a bag of dirty laundry."

"The gym's not that bad," he said, holding a key out in their direction before tossing the key to Weed. "And there are some boxes off to one corner that you're going to have to move, but be careful; don't want you breaking anything that's inside. And when you're finished, I'd appreciate it if you would move them back to where they were."

"Bastard won't budge," Weed said when he got back to the team, before they all started down the steps to the court. "We should all just drop our memberships," someone grumbled.

Weed pushed open the door to the gym and turned on the lights. It was worse than he remembered. It was dark and damp and musty-smelling, and it was at least ten degrees warmer than the upstairs gym. Suffocating, like hell might be, Weed thought. The condition of this gym was ridiculous…like his life…full of defects and uncertainty, he thought as they all waited for the referee to call a start to the game.

And just like Weed knew it would be, the game was difficult to play, with the ball bouncing erratically most of the time, or sometimes not at all. The game was a genetic variant more like a retarded cousin of the standard game of basketball: distorted, aberrant, a different game. A game fallen apart; barely recognizable…And in the end—a joke.

Pissed him off that the championship game had turned out like this; something that should have been serious and important had become meaningless, he thought disgustedly. Most of the other players were now just standing on the court, talking and laughing. The referee, long standing at the fountain, was disinterested, apparently, in what little play was still taking place.

Such a waste of time, Weed thought. The game was finally put out of its misery when one of the rims broke off of the backboard under the weight of one player from the other team. The fragile appendage was barely hanging on to the backboard, dangling precariously for a few moments before giving up its hold and crashing loudly to the floor, with a tinny, empty cry that almost sounded human, Weed thought.

"Game over…" someone said and laughed, and for some reason Weed suddenly felt much older…unable or unwilling to see the humor in any of it, but the words somehow seeming prophetic to him.

"Call it a draw," he heard someone else say with a laugh.

"We were up by eight when you pulled the damn rim down… you asshole," Weed said, but he wasn't really sure why. "You guys should forfeit…since you're the ones who pulled down the rim." But everyone who hadn't already left just sort of looked at him— strangely, as if he were some kind of jackass for making such a big deal out of nothing.

"They knew they were going to lose, so they broke the rim," Weed said as he walked back up the steps with Bob.

"Yeah probably, but what difference does it make? It's just a game...And it was crazy, anyway," Bob said as they walked up to the locker room and changed.

"Yeah, just a game," he said. "Maybe our last, though."

"Maybe it's for the best, anyway."

"Heard you guys trashed the place," Walt said as Weed threw the key back to him. "Should call the police," he mumbled as the door closed behind them.

"Twice in one day," Weed mumbled out loud, somewhat amused at the thought.

"What's that?" Bob asked.

"Almost got arrested—twice in one day," he said, and when Bob looked at him confusedly, Weed told him he would explain later as most of their team started down the street toward the bar.

"Well, at least we didn't lose," one of the other players said as he pulled a chair out for Weed to sit at the table. They all ordered drinks, and they talked and drank for a while before ordering food.

The team sat around, drank and ate pizza, and talked for a couple hours about the game and how bad the gym was. But mostly, they talked about how they were all going to cancel their memberships, until it occurred to someone that that was exactly what the YMCA board and Walt wanted them to do, so they all changed their minds.

Weed was feeling pretty drunk by the time he started talking about the trial. Wasn't even sure why he had brought it up...just felt like it, he guessed, even though he knew that the judge had warned everyone against talking about anything related to the trial. He didn't care...just wanted to tell everyone how ridiculous it had become. Get it off his chest, maybe. But he tried to make the whole story sound as funny as possible. He told them about how he was going to have to live in a tent, and how Sandy had taken all the furniture out of the house, so he almost sat on the floor before he realized that she had taken his chair to her mother's house... which wasn't really true, but he thought it would be funny. And he told them about Hileman's clown make-up, and called her the Mustard Queen, but no one seemed to think that was very funny either, he realized...except for one time when they all sort of laughed at something he said, but he wasn't really sure what. At one point, he almost started to tell them about the shooting...trying to think up something funny about it, but at the last minute he thought better of the idea...and really couldn't think of anything that funny, anyway. He thought maybe the waitress had come over to tell them to keep it down because they were bothering other customers, but he wasn't sure.

So for the rest of the afternoon, he sat and drank, getting more intoxicated...And every time he looked up, it seemed as if someone else had just disappeared into thin air, until it was only Bob and himself who remained. At that point, he finally told Bob about his police interview, and how they had all thought that he had been involved, and how he had almost gotten arrested.

"They had a tape of me leaving the bar. Showed it to me a bunch of times. Looked like I was carrying a gun. They had this crazy idea that I was, maybe, some kind of drug addict—or something—and got pissed off and shot Tatter," he said as they finished another drink. "Thought that my cell phone was a gun. Would have probably arrested me if I hadn't told them what really happened. And who knows what that lunatic Pickles will do now...if he finds out what I said to the cops," he told Bob, who just smiled and shook his head.

He talked to Bob for a long time after the others had left, ignoring the calls Sandy was making to his cell phone, and lost track of the time...and how much he had to drink. But it was more than usual, he knew. When he checked the time, he realized he had been sitting at the bar for almost four hours. Late already, he thought.

"You feel okay to drive?" Bob asked him when they got back to his car, just as it started to rain. "You had a shitload to drink. A lot more than me...more than usual...and I don't know if you should be driving."

"I'll be fine," he said with a laugh, trying to brush it off as he got into the MG. "Remember, I'm used to it."

"You know, my life is coming unraveled," he said to Bob through the open window as the heavy rain started to come down. "Not one thing in the last year has gone right for me. Even this damn game... the one thing I look forward to all week, and it gets destroyed."

"Maybe things will change. Maybe your luck will change," Bob said, moving away from the car as the heavy rain began to fall. "Luck's a funny thing..."

"Fuck luck...I don't think it even matters now. I'm finished—one way or the other. If the trial doesn't finish me off, this shooting will. And if the shooting doesn't get me, Sandy will," he said, trying to act somewhat cavalier as he watched Bob back away from the window, pulling his jersey up over his head to get out of the rain. "That's if I survive long enough to see it...If Pickles doesn't find me first," he said as he pulled away from the curb and into the street, looking at Bob in the rearview mirror as he slowly drove down the street. Only real friend that he had left, he imagined. Fifty-four years old and one friend, he thought...fucking amazing.

A sudden wave of depression spread over him, thinking about all that had happened lately. With nothing to look forward to, he drove toward his house, becoming maudlin—almost teary-eyed—as the clouds open up and it started to pour...heavy, thick rain, like molten lead. What had happened to him? Where had it all gone... How had he gotten to this point in his life? How did all the steps of his whole pathetic life end up bringing him here to this spot on this dreadful night...to this miserable point in his life?

"It's me, and I'm on my way home," he told Sandy when she picked up his call on her cell. He was trying to act sober and come up with an excuse for why he was going to be late, but he could hardly see the road in front of him from the torrential rain.

"Where the hell were you? I've been trying to get you all afternoon."

"I don't know. I tried to call you too," he said. "Car's on the fritz...Had to call Triple A to get it fixed...Took them all afternoon," he told her.

"Well, I couldn't wait any longer, so you'll just have to meet me at the country club, if you can find it. You know what time it is?"

"I told you—the car...had to get it fixed before I could get it back on the road. I mean, don't blame me, you're the reason that I'm driving this piece of shit to begin with," he said. "Not my responsibility," he added, pleased at how quickly he had come up with a reasonable explanation.

"How much did you have to drink while they were fixing your car?" she asked sarcastically.

"A couple, maybe, but that's it."

"I told you not to drink," she said, clearly upset. "I can hardly understand what you're mumbling about now. So, just put on your tux and get over here as soon as possible. I knew this was going to happen," she said. "And what did you do with my shoes?"

Had completely forgotten about the shoes. "What?" he said, trying to sound confused.

"My shoes...the ones I was going to wear to the banquet. The ones I told you about. I couldn't find them," she said, pausing for him to answer. "And I don't even know why I asked...because I know you took them."

"I don't even know what you're even talking about. You probably just forgot where you put them. But that's fine; just blame me, because I'm pretty much responsible for everything bad that happens in this world."

"Can't believe you would do something quite that low...I think that's some kind of a record for you," she said, hanging up the phone abruptly. Just then, he heard a loud thump come from some-where under his car. The thump and vibration of the car running over something small...maybe like a small animal, but in his rear-view mirror he couldn't see anything lying in the street behind him.

He poured himself another drink when he got home. Probably wouldn't have if Sandy hadn't made such a big deal over how much he'd already had to drink. Didn't need her help to count how many drinks he consumed, he thought as he went upstairs to his bed-room. And anyway, she sounded like she may have already had a few too many as well, he thought.

His tux, shirt, pants, and tie were all laid out on the bed, just like he was supposed to wear them, like an invisible man in a cof-fin, as if he might not know what went where...with a note pinned over the crotch of his pants. But when he looked at the note, he only saw that it was much too long and involved for him to even at-tempt to read, and he probably already knew what it said anyway, so he crumpled the note and threw it in the direction of the trash can. A bitch note—about him taking her shoes, and drinking, and being late. He could almost guarantee what it said, he thought as he dressed. Didn't need to read it to know that. He checked his ap-pearance in the hall mirror, thinking that maybe he still looked a little disheveled. Probably wouldn't even go, if he didn't need to get some pictures of Hileman doing something stupid.

"What a shitty day," he muttered out loud as he finished dress-ing, still hearing the rain pounding against the side of the house, before taking another swig of his drink and sitting down on the bed for a minute to catch his breath. He felt lightheaded as he straight-ened his jacket in front of the hall mirror and then buttoned one button to hold the coat shut, double checking to make sure that he had gotten it in the right hole before leaving the house.

He drove off toward the country club, making one wrong turn and then another...in rain falling harder than he had ever seen before.

CHAPTER TWENTY-NINE

Saturday, May 15
6:47 p.m.

He felt a sudden uneasiness as he drove, and he thought maybe he heard the approach of a motorcycle somewhere behind him. But there was nothing in his rearview mirror, and it was raining too hard for anyone to be riding a motorcycle, he thought. Just his imagination and the alcohol.

He searched the parking lot at the country club for a parking space, driving down one row and up another before almost hitting a man who had suddenly appeared in his windshield—like a specter out of the night fog. A man wearing a yellow parka, directing traffic with a red flashlight, motioned for him to roll down his window just as it began to rain even harder.

"You're gonna have to park around back, bud. This lot is filled," the old man in the parka told him as he walked beside his car, directing him down a narrow dirt road that led to a large field at the back of the country club. "Just pull'er up onto that grassy area over there by the other cars," the man said, leaning in close to the window. "And watch, it's pretty damn muddy back there."

Weed drove to the muddy field that he knew led to the golf course, finally finding a tight space between two cars before nudging one of the club's ornamental cement lions with the bumper of his car...sending it face-first into the mud. He stepped out of the car and into the downpour and then navigated through the sloppy mess of mud and slippery grass across the field, almost falling— once, before getting out of the rain and under the portico of the country club. His black shoes and the cuffs of his pants were a mess of light brown speckles of mud, he noticed as he moved under a light.

The front doors of the country club opened up into a large vestibule of fluted pillars decorated with spring flowers and straw hats and colorful streamers. The doors of the vestibule opened into a large banquet hall, and inside the banquet hall were rows of round tables with vases of flowers on each of them. Large, ornate crystal chandeliers hung from the ceiling and gilded mirrors hung on all the walls. The whole thing was nauseatingly gaudy, Weed thought.

A greeter shook Weed's hand as he entered the vestibule, smiling and handing him a nametag, as well as a ticket for the raffle drawing for the trip to Hawaii and all the other door prizes. Weed shook hands with a few other physicians and two hospital administrators who were all standing in the vestibule, before he entered the ballroom. He stood at the entrance for a few moments and scanned the crowd for Sandy. When he couldn't see her anywhere, he looked for Hileman.

He was walking around shaking hands, talking to people he barely knew, trying to act sober and happy at the same time, when he saw Victor Ledig, the psychiatrist at the hospital, taking pictures off to one side of the room. Ledig always had a camera hanging around his neck and was always taking pictures. If anyone had pictures of last year's Spring Fling, it would be him, Weed thought as he made his way over to where Ledig was standing. Didn't want to tell him his real motive for wanting the pictures...would only tell him that he had lost his own pictures and that Sandy had been pissed about it.

"Yeah, I have plenty...will send them to you...can probably do it right now," he said, taking out his phone and working with it a couple of minutes before telling Weed he had just sent them to him in an e-mail.

Worth a shot...might find something good he could use, he thought, excited at the possibilities. He thanked him and then moved on, shaking more hands, before noticing Hileman sitting in her wheelchair, wearing her collar, and talking to a small crowd of people who had gathered around her. Everyone doting over her... The scars didn't look quite as bad as they had during the trial...at least not from this distance, he thought. And that in itself might be worth a photograph, he realized as he quickly took out his cell phone and took her photo as inconspicuously as possible...trying to act like he was making a call. He moved on, continuing his search for Sandy...finally seeing her off in one corner of the room, taking to Mordy. When she saw him waving vigorously at her, she abruptly moved away from Mordy and stormed across the banquet hall to meet him—still obviously angry as she took his hand and led him off to another corner of the room.

"Where were you? I told you to be home no later than six," she said and then stood back to take a look at how he was dressed. "You're a mess, and you're buttoned up all wrong. I thought you looked like you were buttoned up wrong...when you walked in. Don't even know why I care," she said as she rebuttoned his coat. "And you've already had enough to drink." She tried, unsuccessfully, to take his glass of bourbon away from him as she brushed off his lapel and then stood back and looked at his appearance, shaking her head again in disbelief.

"Didn't you get any of my messages?" she asked.

"None," he said.

"You drink too much; that's the problem. You drink so much that you don't even know when your phone's ringing...And how much did you have to drink?"

"I don't know. I don't keep score. Three or four, probably...No more than that."

"Well, it sure looks like you drank more than that...And you walked right past me half an hour ago. Didn't you even notice me standing there, yelling at you?" she asked. "Because everyone else did."

"How can you hear anything in here with all this damnedable racket? The floors are shaking."

"Floors are not shaking, so back off the booze. And try not to make a fool out of us...We're in enough trouble," she added. "And I don't want you to cause a spectacle. I don't want people talking about us any more than they already are. And how many times have I told you that I don't want you walking around acting drunk when everyone can see you...when you know that it might already be an issue at the trial. Now, go find table number thirty-three and sit down and just wait—and no more booze!"

Could get downright nasty when she was drunk. In his opinion, she was just about as drunk as he was. And he didn't need her attitude either, he thought as he started off, walking somewhat aimlessly in the general direction she had just pointed to.

"Hey, wait! First, you have to go clean the mud off your shoes, and don't smear it around. Looks like you just walked through a cow pasture," she added, coming up behind him again, now strangely holding his drink.

"Made me park in the damn field behind the building," he said looking down at his shoes, but noticing Sandy's shoes instead. Didn't match her dress...even he could see that...and they sort of stuck out, he thought, somewhat pleased with himself.

"And they squeezed six of us around one table. Every other table only has four, but they put six at our table...like we were an afterthought," she said. "I think they put all the people no one wanted to sit with at our table...the Bakers and the Paulsons."

"And us too," Weed said.

"Yeah, us too," she said sarcastically. "We were supposed to be sitting with Mordy, but somehow we got moved...and the table's almost in the frickin' parking lot!"

He just shrugged his shoulders as he walked away, trying to locate the door that led to the restrooms. All the weird people at one table. Didn't really care where he sat, he thought as he got another drink.

For a minute, he had to reorient himself from where he was standing in the room to where the restrooms were actually located. With all the decorations and streamers and tables and loud noise, he wasn't exactly sure where he was standing. When he thought he had it all figured out, he headed off in that general direction... finally finding the door that opened to the downstairs, and the corridor that led to the long hallway to the restrooms. He had to steady himself as he made his way slowly down the steps...before noticing Hileman's driver standing at the bottom of the steps, talking to a waitress and holding Hileman's dog under his arm. The dog gave out a few, feeble barks as he approached. The driver nodded to him as he went into the restroom but didn't seem to recognize him from their other chance encounters. He had forgotten for a moment why he had even come into the restroom, but he reflexively ended up standing in front of one of the urinals before realizing that, for once, he didn't actually have to urinate, that he was there to clean the mud off his shoes. He reached out for one of the stalls to regain his balance as he took off his shoes, setting them both on the sink before wiping off the mud with a wet paper towel. "Doesn't look too bad," he mumbled aloud, holding up one of his shoes, in front of his face. "Looks like new," he mumbled as he dropped the shoe to the floor.

"How's it going?" Hileman's driver asked, his image suddenly reflecting in the mirror behind Weed. Weed watched as the driver combed his hair and flipped his lit cigarette into one of the urinals. Hadn't even noticed him coming into the restroom, Weed thought and then wondered if he had heard him talking to himself about his shoes.

"Same thing happened to me...ruined a brand new pair of shoes," the driver added as he lifted the dog onto the baby changer before giving it a pill as he explained it all to Weed again.

"Yeah, a real mess out there," Weed said as he left the restroom, feeling somewhat disgusted at another chance encounter with Hileman's driver...He had seen him and her damn dog enough already.

When he got back upstairs he wandered around aimlessly through the crowd, only stopping when he had to, to shake a hand or to make polite small talk. He smiled and walked past most of the people he knew because he really didn't feel like being sociable...wishing that he was with Candy in her apartment instead of in this stuffy ballroom. He finally found his way back to the bar and then—drink in hand—headed off in the general direction to where he thought table number thirty-three might be located. Making his way slowly across the crowded ballroom, he caught a glimpse of Hileman again, off in the distance, still sitting in her wheelchair at the same table but with a larger crowd of people around her now; laughing, talking, drinking. She was still in her neck collar, but she was acting pretty inebriated, he thought...maybe getting closer to screwing up and doing something stupid.

He put down his drink on table number seventeen, sat down, and took out his phone. He held it under the table so no one could see him pressing the zoom button until he was sure he had it on the closest setting. Bringing it up to his eye and finding Hileman in the sights, he clicked off another picture. Number two…just in case, he thought as he put his cell phone back in his pocket. Not a great shot, but it would be okay for starters. How would that look to the jurors…seeing how happy she was acting and how the scars miraculously seemed to appear so much better, he thought, turning in his seat. Only then did he realize that someone else was sitting at the table with him. He nodded and smiled as he stood and walked away with his drink.

"You're headed in the wrong direction, Ace. We're this way," Sandy said, her voice coming out of nowhere and sounding almost as if it were coming over the loudspeaker. She took him by the arm and led him off in the opposite direction from where he had been headed.

"Remember, don't make a scene."

"I think I got a pretty good shot of Hileman," he said, realizing after a sip that he must have picked up the other person's drink sitting at table seventeen, and then telling Sandy to flag down a waiter to get him another. "I think I got a good one of Hileman," he repeated, taking his phone out and placing it on the table.

"Can you tell me later? People are going to hear you," she said, turning directly toward him in her seat so that no one at the table could hear her. "And put that damn thing away. Why don't you just climb up on the stage and tell everyone what you're doing," she said sarcastically.

He sat at the crowded table with the two other couples and tried to act sober and interested. But almost everything that he said came out as forced, obtuse conversation that was hard to follow, especially with all the noise. They all listened to a stream of boring speakers talk about how great the hospital was, how well things were going, how much money the hospital was making, how many awards the hospital had received, and how the hospital was rated as one of the top ten hospitals in the region, the last speaker said as everyone applauded politely.

Big fuckin' deal…all bullshit…all bastards, Weed thought as the waitress finally brought more drinks to the table.

"So, we should all be proud of the jobs we all have done this year," the CEO said and then encouraged everyone to give themselves another round of applause while he started clapping along with everyone else. It was all just an endless stream of drivel that Weed couldn't listen to—or understand—as he picked at a piece of stuffed chicken that had magically materialized in front of him. He listened to his tablemates talk, smiling and nodding in approval when it seemed appropriate, but he had difficulty concentrating on anything anyone was saying, with the music, and all the noise, and everything else he had on his mind. He was preoccupied with possible angles and potential places in the room where he could stand to get good photographs of Hileman.

He was trying to listen and nod his head along with the conversation. Apparently, he hadn't noticed that someone asked him a question once, because he sat there—dumbfounded as the whole table stared at him—waiting, evidently, for him to answer. Finally, Sandy nudged him and repeated some obscure question about some new surgical procedure that he had never heard of or didn't care a damn thing about, before giving a vague bullshit answer as seriously as he could. Guy wouldn't stop with the questions, he thought after the same asshole asked him a couple more follow-up questions.

For the next half hour, Weed listened to the hospital administrators give out awards. Each of the awardees gave a short, generic speech and thanked the hospital. Volunteers, Years of Service, Community Activity…it was all a huge jumble of boredom. He decided that he was going to leave—as soon as he got the pictures he wanted of Hileman—while a waiter placed a little dish of what looked like crème brûlée in front of each of them.

"She seems to get an award every year," the CEO finally said toward the end of the presentations, turning and smiling at Hileman and then helping her to the stage. She was moving slowly, but not nearly as slowly as she had been moving in the courtroom. And then, when she finally reached the podium, she began her speech.

She looked drunk, Weed thought. Her speech was slow and somewhat slurred, even more than usual, as she continued some rambling, self-aggrandizing prattle.

Strive for this...strive for that...and other hackneyed clichés praising the hospital, and maybe some obtuse references about her own, unfortunate situation...her unfortunate care at the hospital the night of the accident. Weed thought he heard her say that, but surprisingly, he wasn't really sure...wasn't sure if he just might be imagining it all. People laughed when they thought she was trying to be funny, and applauded when they thought she expected applause—even though nothing she said seemed particularly funny or applaudable, Weed thought.

She talked on...But the scars made it hard for him to concentrate on what she was saying. He could only focus on what the people might be thinking about *him*...seeing *her* standing there; how terrible she looked; how bad of a surgeon he was. She was a shining example of Dr. Benjamin Weed's medical ability, and he was the loser doctor sitting at table thirty-three with all the other losers. He did this. He was the negligent doctor who had destroyed her life... who had defaced the city's icon. She might as well have pointed right at him, so that everyone would know whom she was talking about, he thought...even though he knew she hadn't actually said any of it.

When she was finally finished with her speech, the CEO got back up and wished her well and thanked her for all the money she had raised for the hospital dialysis center's two new wheelchair vans.

"Well, that was pretty boring," Weed said loud enough for everyone at the table to hear, and laughing lightly...But Sandy was the only one to respond with a dirty look.

He moved around the room, waiting and watching Hileman, as the music started and people began to dance. But after nearly an hour, Hileman hadn't budged…hadn't gotten off of her fat ass. She hadn't even gotten up to go to the bathroom, he thought as he sat back down at his table. After another half hour, the bitch still hadn't moved an inch—even though she had had plenty to drink.

"She's not that stupid," Sandy said when he came back to the table for the third time. "She's not going to go dance or do anything stupid."

Was probably a pipe dream…But maybe Ledig had gotten some pictures of her dancing last year that he could use. Night might not have been a complete waste, he thought, disgusted at his failed plan.

"And some of these people are being real pains in the ass," Sandy said. "Just like I told you, no one wants us around anymore. We've become persona non grata…no better than a damn leper. May as well go home," she lamented. "And after all that I've done for some of these people. I'm finished with all of them." She reached out and stopped the waiter for another drink.

"You got any ideas how I can get this bitch to do something stupid?" he asked after she had settled down. "Because if she doesn't get up soon, I'm going to piss my pants."

"You *could* ask her to dance, I guess," she said and then started laughing at her own joke as the band stopped playing.

"Yeah, funny…" he said as the CEO came back on stage and told everyone to take out their raffle tickets for the big drawing. Then he reminded all of them about the grand prize of a goddamn one-week time-share in Hawaii that some lucky bastard was about to win. But Weed couldn't find his raffle ticket.

"I'm going home…I've had enough," Weed said. Sandy had her chair pushed back away from the table with her head under the table cloth like an ostrich, and for a second, Weed though it looked pretty funny and was some type of prank.

"I think I lost my damn earring," she said, coming up from under the table. "It felt like it just fell off and went somewhere under the table," she said as she touched her ear to check, again, if it was missing. "Ooh, I've had it...now I've lost my diamond earring," she said before telling him to help her look. He pulled back the edge of the tablecloth and leaned back, away from the table, taking a quick peruse underneath it.

"Can't see anything," he said. He had more important things to worry about than her damn earrings. Plus, he really had to piss now, remembering the opportunity he had wasted and not knowing how much longer he could hold it.

"Thanks, Sherlock. You're a real help," she said grunting as she put her head even further under the table.

He had never seen her quite this drunk, or acting quite this strange, he thought as he started toward the men's room. Suddenly, he felt like turning and telling her just how much trouble she had gotten him into because of her shitty driving...and how the police had tracked him down, all because she didn't know what "yield" meant...and now there was a good likelihood that she had set loose a lunatic with a gun, who was probably at this very moment looking for him...and that—ultimately—she was the reason he was about to lose everything. Served her right, he thought, as he moved away from the table.

Felt happier about her shoes too. That was one thing that had worked out okay over the last two weeks, he thought as he felt for the wall a couple of times to steady himself. It seemed like all the noise and the alcohol were uncontrollably gliding him across the bouncing floor. With all the people moving around, it was difficult to get his bearings...like the room was spinning...like the people were still dancing, even though they were all just standing still. It was almost as if he could still hear music in his head... as if the band had never stopped playing and the people continued to dance, he realized as he finally found the door that led to the men's room. He pushed open the door and started down the narrow stairwell as the door slammed solidly shut behind him, offering silence...except for the muffled sound of the CEO announcing the first raffle number.

CHAPTER THIRTY

Saturday, May 15
11:49 p.m.

The glow of the lights made halos and reflections along the glass-paneled stairwell. They blinded Weed as he descended the stairs. He held the railing for support and guidance because he was way too drunk to attempt it unaided, he knew.

Down the empty staircase he maneuvered in a haze. In front of him was only the empty hallway—and Hileman's dog, but this time the dog was sitting alone with the driver nowhere in sight... the dog's leash loosely secured over the doorknob to the restroom. The dog watched him as he moved forward down the hallway. Just Hileman's dog and himself alone together...and at the very end of the hallway...a door with a bright-red exit sign above it.

It was just then that he thought about it...The plan popped into his mind like a lightning bolt out of the blue. Everything was lining up, like the combination to a lock. The dog—abandoned...the driver—off to win a trip to Hawaii...and the escape door—at the end of the hallway. He was almost certain that it opened very near to where he parked the MG. All lined up like the stars. It all seemed too good to be true, he thought, amused at a plan that had just sprung so suddenly to life.

The plan seemed to be perfect...and so simple that it was difficult not to at least consider it, he thought. He continued moving toward the restroom and the dog. He could slip the leash off the doorknob, pick the dog up, and just walk away through the exit door. No one would ever know. Her favorite dog...the dog she couldn't live without. The dog she had to take everywhere she went—gone. He could even leave the exit door open a crack to make everyone think that the dog had just run off through the door that someone had inadvertently left open. Then he could keep the mangy mutt for maybe a day or two...long enough to scare her...or maybe a little longer...to make sure Hileman suffered for a while. At least long enough to extract his pound of flesh. Long enough to make her worry and fret over her lost dog...to agonize, like she had made him agonize. Make her just as miserable as she had made him. Then in a couple days—poof! He could just let the dog go somewhere. Simple...a plan almost too good to pass up, he thought excited at his creative ingenuity.

Would serve Hileman right...give her a little taste of her own medicine—poetic justice for what she had put him through over the last two years. She deserved at least that much, he thought, stopping for a moment to look at the dog and to reassess his plan. Would be great to get even with the bitch. Take the dog and scare the hell out of her for a while, he mused and then looked back over his shoulder to make sure the door to the banquet hall was shut tight.

This was his night—finally, a stroke of good luck. Maybe he hadn't gotten the pictures of Hileman that he wanted, but this was better. Maybe his bad luck was finally changing, he thought. If he could just get into the restroom and piss before anyone else came down the stairs, then he could probably pull it off. What a fait accompli it would be, he thought as he pushed open the door to the restroom and entered. He doubted anyone would come down the steps to the restroom now that they were all preoccupied with the CEO drawing tickets for the raffle, he thought as he tried to empty his bladder as fast as he could. But his stream was slow and weak, and at one point came to a complete stop. Would be here all night at this pace, if he didn't cut it off somewhere, he knew. Didn't need an enlarged prostate to ruin his plan…needed to get this underway before it dissolved, he thought as he stopped urinating and impatiently pulled up his zipper.

This plan might be even better than winning the lawsuit, he thought as he left the restroom. Taking something that meant so much to her…something that would cut her to the core. It would be easy, too. He could just lift the leash off the doorknob, pick up the dog, and carry it off through the exit at the end of the hallway… an exit door that he was almost certain opened to the back of the country club where he had parked his car…Yes, his luck had finally changed.

No time to assess any theoretical risks…was a good plan, he assured himself as he stood in the hallway with his back against the wall for a moment to check that he was still alone. The dog and the exit to his right…The steps and the closed door to the ballroom to his left…and no one—not a single person—in sight…and the dog just sitting there quietly looking up at him.

He could get away with this. Wouldn't be anything, he thought as he took a deep breath and pushed off the wall. He could feel his heart racing and his hands shaking ever so slightly as he looked from the dog to the exit door and then listened to the muffled sound of the CEO announcing another raffle number. Yes, he could get away with this, he thought as he slipped the leash over the doorknob, picked up the dog, and petted her lightly once on her head before carrying her quickly down the hall and through the back door. It was all completed in one seamless movement. Like a ballet move. A veritable coup de grace, he thought as he stood motionless for a second in the pouring rain, before glancing back to make sure he had left the door open, just wide enough for a small dog to get through. A nice touch, he thought…to make everyone think that the damn thing had just run off through a door that had been mistakenly left open.

And so what? He had taken her dog. No big deal, he thought as he made his way through the muddy field in search of his car. The pounding rain drowned out the dog's feeble bark. What harm was there in taking her dog for a couple of days? He wasn't going to hurt the damn thing, he thought as the dog squirmed almost uncontrollably under his arm, finally biting him on his right hand once, and then twice, before he could pull away. Two sharp pains radiated up his arm, but he couldn't worry about a small bite now, he knew as he tried to get a safer hold on the dog.

After a couple of minutes of sloshing around in the mud and rain, and almost falling on top of the dog, he still hadn't found his damn car. He couldn't find his car but everyone else could, he thought, pissed as he searched awhile longer before tripping over the stone lion that he had knocked over earlier with his bumper.

Luck again, he thought as he got into the car and pushed the growling dog away from him and onto the passenger seat, just as she nearly bit him again.

"Just relax," he shouted, pointing a finger at the dog, before looking back to check the door he had just escaped through. It was still the way he had left it—slightly open, and no one had seen him leaving with the dog, he was sure. No one was standing near the door…and no one was running after him, yelling for him to bring back the dog.

He had done it. He had gotten away with taking Hileman's dog, he thought with a satisfying sigh…almost elated. Hileman would be devastated when she found out that her dog was missing, he knew, feeling excited and amused about what he had just accomplished.

How creative! How intelligent! How successful he had been to come up with, and carry out, such an ingenious plan that would give him so much satisfaction.

Too late for anyone to catch him now. If there wasn't someone at the door by now, then he was home free, he thought, imagining how hysterical Hileman would be when the driver told her that he couldn't find her dog. Poor bastard...sort of liked the guy too, he snickered.

He sat in the car for a few seconds—nervous—his hands shaking, taking deep breaths, and the dog beside him, acting a little more settled now. He wasn't sure if he could even start the car, he was so excited. But the door to the country club remained undisturbed as if nothing had happened. Just one long, thin stream of light spread out from the door across the muddy field in front of him.

He was gleeful, and all he had gotten out of it was a couple of small bites, he thought as he started the car and then held his hand up in front of him in the dim light to see the bites. Not bad...just two small rows of teeth marks between his thumb and index finger...superficial, but they were already throbbing painfully. Small price to pay for what he had just accomplished, he thought as he drove slowly down the road away from the country club. The dog barked a few times, but not nearly as vigorously as it had before... muffled barks lessened by the pounding rain. The dog stood up with her front paws against the side window, forlornly watching the lights from the front of the country club go by. A group of men in tuxedos stood under the portico, smoking, but they didn't even look in his direction as he drove away. And the toothless security guard, who had shown him where to park, still stood in his parka like the grim reaper—disinterested as Weed quickly drove past him.

He couldn't believe how easy it had been. He could only imagine what would happen when Hileman discovered that her dog was missing...lost in the dark, rainy night...not to be found...no matter how hard they looked for it. Thinking that maybe it was already dead...hit by a car as it tried to run across the busy road in front of the country club. Maybe lost forever. Give Hileman a little bit of her own medicine. Give her something to think about other than making his life miserable. Let everyone at the banquet see just what kind of an obnoxious bitch she could be, he thought as he drove.

It was turning out to be a great night, he thought; one of the best nights he had had in a long time. Yeah, maybe he hadn't gotten any good pictures of Hileman, but what he had just accomplished was much better...And maybe Ledig had some pictures from last year that he could use too.

How good could it get, he thought as he pulled the MG out onto the highway and started his drive home. Felt good, that for once he had a little control over the situation...over Hileman. Let her frantically search through the muddy field. Let her think that something bad had happened to her dog. He had her dog...and he could decide when she would get it back. He could decide when she had suffered enough, and he could clandestinely watch it all play out during the trial. Just sit there in the courtroom and watch her misery...and know that he was the person responsible for that misery.

Maybe the alcohol was partly responsible for what he had just done...wasn't sure, he thought for just an instant as he drove away from the lights of the country club. The dog seemed fairly settled now, he thought as he held up his hand to check the bites in better light. The two small rows of teeth marks between his thumb and index finger were already turning black and blue and swelling...looking and hurting a lot worse than they had just a few minutes earlier.

"You just sit there," Weed said somewhat startled and pissed as the dog jumped into the backseat. "You'll be okay...not the end of the world," he told her as he looked over his shoulder at the dog, her paws up against the back window. "Won't be any worse being with me than it was being with that bitch, anyway," he told the dog as she jumped back into the front seat, looking over and growling before sitting down on the seat beside him and letting out an occasional bark.

"Will only be a couple of days, so you may as well get used to it," he added as he opened and closed his hand a couple times to see how much pain he was going to have when he used it. Wasn't too bad, at least he could still make a fist, he thought as he tried to collect his thoughts.

It was the second half of the plan that he didn't seem to have a firm grasp on...that he wasn't so sure of, he thought. Now he had a dilemma, he realized for the first time since the heat of the moment. What was he going to do with a damn mangy mutt for a couple of days, he asked himself as he slowed the car and wondered about what he had just done. Didn't seem quite as funny or quite as good a plan now as it had only minutes earlier, he thought. Didn't seem quite as rational or as ingenious now, for some reason. A fifty-four-year-old doctor doing something as bizarre as stealing someone's dog. Just when he thought that he couldn't top the messes he had already created, he had come up with something even more depraved. And worse—where was he going to keep a dog where no one would find out about it? Where was he supposed to store a dog for a couple of days? Why hadn't he thought of that problem earlier? Why hadn't he seen that little fly in the ointment? Now slightly disgusted with himself, he drove slower and somewhat aimlessly in the general direction of his house as he tried to clear his mind. Finding a place to keep a dog didn't really seem like that much of a problem. There had to be a lot of places he could hide a dog for a couple of days, where no one would find out about it. Just for a couple of days—tops, he assured himself. He couldn't keep it at his house. That was certain, he knew. There were no places in his house that Sandy wouldn't eventually find a barking dog... And it was too risky to try and bring Sandy into such a bizarre plan, anyway. She would likely call the police and have him arrested, he imagined, so he didn't know why he was driving in the direction of his house. He pulled the car into the parking lot of a darkened strip mall and tried to come up with a solution.

In the distance he could still see the lights of the country club, and for an instant, he thought about just returning the dog. Maybe he'd just drive back to the club and push the dog back through the door and then slam it shut…But that solution would probably be too risky now.

"Not such a great idea now, Ace," he scolded himself out loud. Just more trouble that he didn't need. Wasn't a plan…was a dilemma. No more than fifteen minutes had gone by and already he had come to the realization that taking Hileman's dog was probably going to end up being a huge mistake. He considered the possibility of just releasing the dog to fend for itself, but that would be too cruel…even for him to do…plus he couldn't be assured that the dog wouldn't get hit by a passing car…didn't want the dog to get hurt. And the fight wasn't between him and the damn dog, anyway. Dog had never done anything to him—other than the bites, but those really weren't the dog's fault. Dog was just an innocent victim…in the wrong place at the wrong time—the intermediary. Now, if it were Hileman instead of the dog sitting beside him, he wouldn't hesitate to let her out by the side of a busy highway in the dark and pouring rain…with a chance of her getting hit by a car— no problem. But her dog…that was different. Didn't want the dog to get hurt…just wanted Hileman to suffer, he knew, still confused about what he was going to do.

Maybe Bob could keep the dog. He could tell Bob the whole story without worrying about him telling anyone else. He could leave the dog there for a day or two and then just drop the dog off at a shelter, or somewhere safe, where someone could find it, he thought, feeling bolstered by his plan. He turned his car around and headed back in the direction of the country club and Bob's house. Bob probably wouldn't mind if he left the dog at his place, he reasoned. They had been friends a long time and he would understand what a great plan it was…just like all the other crazy stuff they had done together when they were young.

The dog had settled down in the seat now, just lying there beside him, wide-eyed and moving her eyes from side to side, actually listening to every word that Weed was mumbling to himself, as if she understood what he was saying.

"Don't worry. I'll get you back home soon," he told her and then explained his plans to her all over again.

He could sneak another quick look at the country club when he passed by, just to see if anyone had discovered what he had done. But now, he was even more pissed at himself for getting involved with something that was probably just going to complicate his life even more. An innocent prank turned sour, he thought, slowing the car as he passed by the club. It already looked like there was some commotion in the field behind the building. Long lights and shadows were spreading out across the golf course, as if someone might already be looking for the dog. There was no way he was going to be able to return the dog to the country club now, he realized as he drove on toward Bob's house, stopping only once to finish urinating. He stood at the side of the road, in the pouring rain, trying to piss and act like he was checking his tires all at once…since almost every car slowed as it passed by. The dog watched him, annoyingly, through the side window of the car.

The trial, the shooting, Pickles…and now he'd stolen Hileman's dog, he thought as he pulled up his zipper and got back in the car. His life had just gotten a whole lot more ridiculous.

CHAPTER THIRTY-ONE

Saturday, May 15
11:54 p.m.

The rain had almost stopped by the time he had reached Bob's house. He got out of his car, slamming the door quickly behind him to prevent the dog from escaping. When he checked his watch it was almost midnight, and for an instant, he wasn't sure if he should knock on Bob's door. At this hour, he was almost certain they were all asleep, but he knocked lightly anyway. When there was no answer, he knocked a little louder...hopefully just loud enough to wake Bob and no one else, he thought as he looked back through the foggy window at Hileman's dog standing with its paws against the steering wheel, looking as if she might drive away. If she could reach the pedals, she probably would, he thought. He knocked once more, this time even louder, and then turned to leave but noticed the reflection of a light going on somewhere in the house. An instant later, Bob's face appeared in the small window cut into the front door.

"It's Ben," he could hear Bob saying quietly as he watched Bob look back over his shoulder, unlock the door, and push it open.

"Everything okay?" his wife asked, appearing over Bob's shoulder.

"Yeah, everything's fine. Just was in the neighborhood and wanted to talk to Bob about something. Sorry about the hour," he said, sounding as apologetic as possible, but he thought she made some kind of disparaging remark to Bob about alcohol as she disappeared back into the darkness of the house.

"Was on the way home from the country club and wanted to show you something. Thought that you might still be awake and might get a kick out of it," Weed said as he motioned for Bob to follow him.

"Past midnight...better be good...have to open the Quick Fix at six a.m.," he said as he followed in his underwear and bare feet through the wet yard.

"What the hell's going on, Ben?" he asked halfway across the yard.

"See?" Weed said, stopping a short distance from the car and pointing to the dog that was looking out at them from the side window. "D'you see the dog in there?"

"Yeah, great! You got a dog. Nice," he said sarcastically.

"Yeah, but not just *any* dog," he said, pausing. "Guess whose dog it is?" he asked, trying not to laugh.

"Jesus, Ben, it's midnight and I have to be up at five, and you have me playing a guessing game? To tell you the truth, I don't really give a damn whose dog it is," he said. "Uh, yours?"

"You won't believe it," he said somewhat disappointed and concerned at Bob's lack of enthusiasm. "Actually, it's Gertrude Hileman's dog," he said and then waited for Bob's reaction. "Can you believe it? I've got that bitch's dog!" Weed told him.

"Whose dog?"

"Gertrude Hileman. You know, the lady from the trial...the one who's been suing me for the last two years. You know, the Mustard Queen?"

"What the hell are you talking about?" he asked as he looked through the foggy window at the barking dog. "What the hell are *you* doing with *her* dog?" he asked, still acting somewhat groggy as he looked back at Weed.

"For all the shit she put me through…that's why I got her dog…I took her dog."

"You took her dog?"

"Yeah…was just sitting there, so I took it. Just for some payback. She loves that dog so much she won't go anywhere without it…I told you about it…and now, I have it. She takes the damn dog to the courthouse every damn day…had it at the hospital the night she wrecked her car…and at the banquet tonight…And now that I have it, she can't take it anywhere."

"You're crazy," Bob said, backing away from the car. "Tell me that you're just making all this up."

"Why would I make it up? You tell me it's not a good idea."

"It's not a good idea," he said, turning and starting back toward the porch.

"I mean, who's going to know? And anyway, I'm not going to hurt the damn mutt…just going to keep her for a day or two and then give her back. Just to shake Hileman up a little. To make her suffer like she's made me suffer for the last two years. Not even sure that it's against the law to take someone's dog," Weed added.

"It is—I can assure you. It's call theft. And no rational person would do something like this," he said, turning back toward Weed for an instant. "Especially you. You have enough problems with her already, and then you take her dog? And now you've told me, and I don't want to have anything to do with it. I have enough problems myself. I do *not* want to get involved. I saw nothing."

"They don't even know I took it. I made it look like she just ran off," he said as he followed Bob through the yard and the light rain back to the porch.

"If it was me, I would get rid of it. Drop her off down the street somewhere before someone finds out what you did."

"I'm going to, as soon as I make Hileman suffer a little, like she's making *me* suffer. Destroy *her* life like she's destroying *mine*...just a little payback...And she deserves it," he said as he waited on the porch for Bob to go inside for his cigarettes.

When Bob came out, he was shaking his head and smiling. "Yeah, it is sort of funny...would be a nice way to get even, but it's crazy! And you could get into big trouble...more than you're already in," he said, lighting a cigarette and then sitting down on the top step of the porch. "You ever hear about jury tampering or something like that?" Something Weed hadn't thought about at all. "How'd you pull that off, anyway?" he asked sarcastically.

"Dog was just sitting there by the back door of the country club, all alone. And then, I don't know, I just picked her up and took off. Didn't even really think that much about it. Just seemed like such a great plan, that I couldn't do anything else...that I couldn't pass up something so...good," he said. "It was like an exorable force was pushing me to take the damn thing."

"Like a what?"

"Like a force that I couldn't see...that was just pushing me along. That there was nothing else that I could do...like destiny."

"Was it maybe Jack Daniels that was pushing you along... *exorable?*"

"Uh, maybe a little. Damn thing bit me too," he said, holding up his hand.

"Looks nasty," Bob said, looking closely at Weed's hand as Weed held it up to the light coming from the house.

"Nah, it's not that bad..." he said, even thought it was throbbing with pain. "But that's why I came by," he said, "I was hoping you could help me out...that maybe you could keep the dog around here somewhere...just for a day or two."

"You have to be kidding. You know I would do just about anything...But I just told you, I can't risk getting involved with something like this. No way! It's just too damn risky...And I don't even live that far from the country club. And anyway, our dog would pick that little thing up by the fur and throw her into the neighbor's yard. And if Hileman likes this dog as much as you say she does, then the police might come looking for it. You ever think of that? And I don't need that. I got a crappy wife and two crappy kids and a crappy job to consider," he said, taking a long drag off his cigarette. "Not much, but I can't afford to lose it all right now," he added.

"You think that it's crazy?" Weed asked.

"Yes, I think it's crazy and I think you've had way too much to drink," he said and took another long drag. "And did you ever stop to think that maybe you could be the prime suspect?"

"I don't think so. That was the genius of the plan, I told you, I left the door open just wide enough to make them think that the dog ran off. That's the way I made it look. They'll think that its leash came loose and the dog just ran off through a back door that someone carelessly left open. And anyway, no one saw me. They won't have any idea that I had anything to do with it," he said, hoping that he might change Bob's mind and hoping that his foggy logic was sound.

"Yeah, probably, but you never know. Just like that shooting. Look how that turned out. You thought that it was nothing...and now look. Besides, it's just too big of a risk to leave the dog here. The next thing I know, the cops will be knocking at my door wanting to know what Hileman's dog is doing in my back yard. I just can't risk it. I mean, you can understand that?"

"It's just that I, sort of, factored you into the equation."

"Take her up to your dad's old cabin. Leave the dog up there."

"We sold that over five years ago."

"Then just take the dog back," he said. "That looks really sore," he said, taking a puff off of his cigarette and looking at Weed's hand. "You really should get on some antibiotics."

"Does ache a little."

"How about Liz? And Mordy has that big farm...out someplace. You could leave the dog out there."

"You have to be kidding. Mordy would have me arrested...And Liz, I don't know...don't know if I can trust her either."

"Then how about that girl at the bar...What's her name?"

"She's already too involved with things...And the police are all over that place, talking to people and looking for Pickles. They would find the dog and then I would have even more questions to answer," he said, sitting down beside Bob. "You think it's crazy?" he asked and paused for an answer. When there was none, he added, "Thought that you might."

"I don't know. I see where you're coming from...sounds like a good idea, but it's just too dangerous. I mean, Hileman is probably a billionaire...She knows everyone and everyone knows her... and probably her dog...and everyone will find out about it and then go looking for the damn thing. You know...just for the recognition...to get in good with someone influential. And she'll probably offer a big reward," he said, pausing for another puff. "Going to be hard to get away with something like that. My suggestion is that you just get rid of the dog...maybe take it back...might not be too late...because if you don't, she's going to be really pissed and come looking."

"I don't know. It's been almost a half hour," he said and then told him about the lights he had seen in the field. They have to know by now."

"Yeah, well, then I don't have any other suggestions...And I would like to help you, but you see where I'm coming from," Bob said as he got up from the porch.

"Yeah, probably was pretty stupid, now that I think about it. Just more of the same: my miserable life...my miserable bad luck... bad timing. Hileman...Candy...Pickles...the shooting—everything. And now I have a dog to deal with. Always at the wrong place at the wrong time. The gods must really hate me and I'm not even sure why," he said.

"I mean, your plan's not that bad. I see where you're coming from," Bob repeated. "If it works, if you get away with it...would be great. Because if what you say is true and she is a real pain in the ass, then she probably deserves it. It's really going to piss her off. But it's too damn risky...and the aggravation. And like I told you, if it was me, I would get rid of that hot dog as soon as possible," he said and then realized that what he'd just said was sort of funny. "A hot dog, get it? Get rid of the hotdog," he said, looking over at Weed to see if he'd gotten the meaning of his joke.

"Yeah, I get it," he said but was even more disgusted at Bob's lack of seriousness.

Bob stood and told Weed that he had to get some sleep, that he was still hung over from the drinking they had done earlier after the game, and that he didn't want to be a pain in the ass, but he was going to deny everything. That if the police came, he was going to tell them he didn't know anything about a missing dog, and that he hoped he understood.

"Give me a call in the morning. I want to know how things turn out," Bob said as he stood and started toward the front door. "And if you really get in a pinch, call. I'll help you work something out. Like drive you to the police station. But, I'll think about it. Maybe I can come up with something good," he said as he flicked his lit cigarette off into the night air, which gave off sparks like a Roman candle. "A hot dog..." he said softly, shaking his head and smiling as he entered the house.

Yeah, great...nice friend...glad someone was having a good time, Weed thought as he walked back to the car. But maybe Bob was right. Maybe he should unload the dog as soon as possible. Less than a half hour and he was already screwed, he thought, pushing the dog back away from the door with his coat wrapped protectively around his hand. The dog suddenly turned at a strange angle, barked once, and then tried to bite him again.

"You take another bite out of me and I'm going to send you flying," Weed told the dog.

He silently drove back toward the country club as the light rain turned back into a downpour. Dog was going to finish him off before morning, he thought. "Should just throw you out the window," he mumbled as the dog jumped into the backseat again.

From the road, he could look down the hill to the country club. There were already a couple of red flashing lights. It looked like they had probably already called the cops, he thought. Jesus…for a goddamn missing mangy mutt they called the cops. Thirty minutes and it already looked like a major crime scene as he inched past the club. They wouldn't do this much if he had been a mass murder. Two police cars sat behind the building, in front of the door that he had left open. Lights were skimming across the field, with people dressed in their tuxes and gowns manning flashlights. He could see it all, but he couldn't believe it. Couldn't believe how stupid he had been and now how crazy everyone else was acting.

Well, that option is caput, he thought. He stopped along the road, when he was far enough past the country club, to collect his thoughts and to urinate again. He looked back at the dog, framed like a picture in the car window. The dog looked back at him like he was some kind of an idiot.

He could leave the dog with Liz, he supposed. Of all the options he could think of, that seemed to be the most logical. She lived alone way out in the country…at least twenty miles from the city. She didn't have kids or pets. And no one would think to look way out there, he thought.

He would have to make up some kind of story to tell her…maybe that he found the dog roaming around the side of the road and didn't know what to do with it. Could tell her that he was in the area…but unlikely at this hour…or that maybe he was coming out to see her…that he felt lonely and needed someone to talk to, or that he hadn't seen her in a while, or some bullshit like that. But he definitely didn't want to overdo it. Didn't want to undo the progress he had already made in making the break while encouraging her to believe that he was still interested, he thought. He didn't need to re-kindle that annoying relationship, he confidently reassured himself as he turned onto the freeway and started the drive to Liz's house, feeling a little more lucid and a little less drunk…unfortunately.

CHAPTER THIRTY-TWO

Sunday, May 16
1:12 a.m.

O f all the options that his foggy mind could conjure up as to what he could do with the dog, leaving it with Liz seemed liked the most logical. He could tell her that he was driving around trying to unwind after a long day, was near her house, not realizing how late it was, and thought he would just stop by to see how she was doing. Then he could tell her about how he had found the dog at the end of her driveway, just wandering around lost...and that he was afraid if he didn't do something, it might run into traffic and get hit, so he picked her up and put her in the car. Then he could tell her that he thought maybe someone had just dropped off the dog at the side of the road to get rid of it because they probably didn't want it any longer. Story didn't sound too bad. At least sounded reasonably believable, he thought. That was the most innocuous explanation he could come up with, he thought as he continued the drive toward her house. Plain and simple...something that she was likely to believe. And if he told her that he'd found the dog at the end of her own driveway, then she would almost be obligated to at least take partial responsibility for the dog's care. At least she might be more willing to keep the dog for a while. He could tell her that if she kept the dog at her house for a couple of days and no one claimed it, then he would come back and take it to the Humane Society or to a shelter in town. Whole story sounded very plausible, and it would be unlikely that Liz would find out anything about what had actually happened...or that anyone would think to look for the dog this far away from the country club, he surmised. And the police probably wouldn't give a damn about a lost dog...like Bob had warned...even if it was Hileman's dog, he tried to assure himself. Police wouldn't find anything, anyway. If they couldn't find a lunatic riding around all over town on a motorcycle, how the hell were they ever going to find a small dog way out here?

What he didn't like was the idea that he might be rekindling their flagging relationship...didn't need that...had already invested enough time and effort trying to end it...didn't want to backtrack now...didn't want to give Liz even the slightest bit of false hope. But given the circumstances, there wasn't much else he could do. And what were a couple more miserable days added to a miserable two-year relationship? He was just lucky that he hadn't already broken off their relationship completely. If he had done that, then he wouldn't have any place to leave the dog now.

Was sort of risky stealing someone's dog, even if it was for just a couple of days, he imagined. And he realized that technically it was a crime, but not that much of a crime. It would be difficult for the police to prove anything. Might look suspicious, but he could just tell the police the same story he was going to tell Liz. Only maybe that he had found the dog a little closer to the country club. Would be awkward...somewhat unbelievable, but what could they do? It was his word against theirs. Might even make him look good...stopping on a rainy, wet night to pick up a stray dog...all because he was concerned about its safety. He could tell the police that he didn't know it was Hileman's dog. All just a coincidence, he would tell them. The explanation eased his anxiety a bit as he continued the drive along the single-lane country road. He worked his hand a little now and then, so that it wouldn't get any stiffer. For a little dog, the two bites hurt like hell.

It was a good story. Maybe not perfect, he thought. In fact, the further he drove and the more sober he became, the more ludicrous his whole scheme seemed to be. Now he was just stuck with another problem that he didn't need.

He could only imagine how distraught Hileman would be by now, which was at least some consolation for his sore hand and the awkward situation he had created. She might even be running around like a maniac in that sloppy, wet field trying to find her dog herself. Now *that* would be the picture to get, he thought. Made him feel good...thinking that he was finally going to get some kind of revenge for all the nights he had tossed and turned, for all the embarrassment that he'd had to endure. Would serve her right, he mused. And he was almost sure that many of the other people at the banquet would be out in the muddy field trying to help Hileman find her dog. They couldn't pass up such a good opportunity to impress someone as important as Hileman. Doctors, lawyers, socialites, and their spouses...all sloshing around in the mud...hunting for the dog. Looking for something that wasn't there. He had gotten even with every last one of the pains in the ass. And most of them deserved it for the way they had been treating him lately. It was just an unforeseen benefit of his plan. And no one would dare refuse to do anything that Hileman wanted. They would all be falling all over themselves trying to find the damn dog. He would love to see that. He could even go back and help them search, after he dropped the dog off at Liz's...just to see the mess, he thought, forcing a laugh...would be a nice touch. He could drop the dog off at Liz's house and then go back to the country club and make it look like he had never left, and then just start looking for the dog with the rest of them…like he was really concerned. Would be hilarious, he thought.

And anyway, he was going to return the dog unharmed—no worse for wear—if everything went according to plan. He would just have to leave the dog someplace safe where someone responsible would find it…like a dog shelter or at the Humane Society. Tie her outside an animal shelter somewhere, when no one was around… then make an anonymous telephone call to tell someone where the dog was, he thought as he slowed the car and tried to find the driveway to Liz's house.

No one would ever find the dog way out here, he reassured himself as he turned into Liz's driveway.

A light was still on inside Liz's house, he could see as he drove up the long, wooded driveway. Maybe she was still awake, he hoped. He pushed the dog back away from the door as he got out and then walked up the small hill to her house. He tapped lightly on her door at first, and then a little harder, until he saw another light come on.

"Liz, it's me, Ben," he said softly, as the porch lights went on and she tentatively called out from behind the door.

"Ben," she said, just cracking the door slightly. "You scared me."

"Sorry. I know it's late, but I was in the area and thought that you might still be up. And well…I just thought I would stop by to see how you were doing…But if it's too late, I can come back some other time."

"No, no, it's fine," she said and then told him to come in. "Doesn't matter how late it is, I'm always happy to see you," she said as she moved away from the door, having him follow. She invited him to sit, but she quickly scooted into another room. When she returned a few minutes later, the curlers were gone from her hair, she had put on some makeup, and she had changed into a semisexy blue jumpsuit. She gave him a kiss and a hug and told him how happy she was to see him again before excusing herself, again, to go make coffee.

And then for the next ten minutes or so, he told her how miserable the trial had been, and how he always enjoyed talking to her…and how reassuring she could be, as she brought him coffee… but thinking that was enough. She told him how much she missed him when he wasn't around and how great their relationship had become. But to him, it was annoying listening to her disinteresting drivel while trying to act interested…and trying to smile appropriately and pretend he was happy to be there. While he was preoccupied the entire time with trying to pick an appropriate break to tell her about the dog and then to get the hell out of there.

Didn't want to spend all night here, he thought before acting as if all of the sudden he had remembered something. Getting up from the couch, he told her to follow him. They walked across the yard in the light rain and back to the car just as he had done with Bob, and he told her the story he'd made up about finding the dog.

"I found her at the end of your driveway," Weed repeated, standing by the window of his car and pointing at the dog that was looking out at them. "Was just wandering around down by your mailbox… almost hit her," he said as she came up closer to the window.

"It's so cute," she said.

"And I couldn't just leave it out there in the rain where she could have gotten hit," he said, trying to figure out how he was going to get the dog out of the car without getting bitten again.

"Seems like she's a little scared," Liz said before pulling the door open and sticking her head inside the car. "Hi there, little pup," she said as she petted the dog. "She's so cute," she repeated, and for the first time the dog seemed completely calm, Weed thought.

"I'd watch. You don't know what she might do," he warned, but by the time he finished warning her to be careful, Liz had the dog comfortably under her arm, rubbing its head as if they were old friends.

"You found her down at the end of my driveway?" Liz asked as she carried the dog back toward the house and just as the rain started up again.

"Yeah, down by the highway. My guess is that someone probably didn't want her anymore and just turned her loose…people do that all the time…with the economy the way it is, or…who knows? Maybe she just ran off," he said as they both ran to the house to take cover from another downpour.

"Well, she needs dried off. She's all wet and shaking. Don't want her to get sick. Did you look to see if she had a collar?" she asked, looking over at him as she left the room.

Jesus, how dumb could he be? Didn't think about a collar, he realized, shocked at his own carelessness.

"Doesn't look like a dog that someone would just want to get rid of, because I think she's probably a pretty expensive breed," Liz said, holding the dog out in front of her as she looked at the collar. "I'll bet she probably just ran off, but then…I can't remember ever seeing a dog like this anywhere in this neighborhood," she added. He waited in dreadful anticipation for her to tell him that the dog was Gertrude Hileman's…and for her to stop and look up at him, inquisitively, and ask him what he was doing with Gertrude Hileman's dog—but she didn't say anything. She just moved the collar around the dog's neck a couple of times before shaking her head.

"Hmm, nothing…I don't see a thing. Expensive collar, but there's no identification tag…Doesn't even have the dog's name written on it," she said to his relief, before mumbling something about a chip.

Liz seemed to be pretty comfortable with the dog, he thought, somewhat relieved as Liz and her new friend left the room for a few minutes before returning with the dog wrapped in a large, fluffy towel.

"Poor little guy," she said as she dried off the dog. "I have some leftovers in the fridge that I can give her later," she said, putting the dog down on the floor. Liz looked over at him and smiled, as if she had suddenly lost interest in the dog—and had suddenly regained interest in him.

"Probably going to have to take her to the Humane Society if no one claims her," Weed told her.

"Yeah, maybe...I mean, she is a nice dog, though. Probably someone had to pay a fortune to buy a dog like her, so maybe...I mean, I'm just sort of thinking out loud and I'm pretty sure it's not going to happen, but if no one claims her, then I might just keep her. I mean, I know it's unlikely and I'm sure that someone is going to come looking for her, but she's so cute. And if no one does claim her...you know...I might just keep her here at the house...of course after I did all the paperwork. I was thinking about getting a dog anyway, being alone and way out here in the country," she said as she smiled down at the dog.

"Yeah, well, I guess that would be okay...but I sort of agree with you. I think that someone will probably claim the dog soon," he said, pissed that Liz was already being a pain in the ass with her suggestion to keep the damn thing...always coming up with something to complicate the situation even more.

"Maybe I'll put a few signs around the neighborhood in the morning," she added. "I can understand why you became a doctor—stopping to pick up a dog on a night like this. That was really thoughtful and caring," she said smiling passionately as she grabbed his sore hand and gave it a squeeze. "That's one of the things I like about you so much; you care about things," she said. He sipped nervously at his coffee and tried to figure out a tactful way to disappear, now that he had accomplished what he had set out to do. She was already getting on his nerves and was acting like she might want to get intimate, before finally coming over to where he was sitting and giving him a long, passionate kiss.

He acted like he was enjoying it, but felt nothing. And he noticed that he wasn't getting sexually aroused even though they continued making love for the next couple of minutes. Strangely, he had now become preoccupied with thinking about this encounter becoming another one of his sexual failures—that this might become his eighth consecutive sexual encounter where he had been unable to perform. Eight times…He was pissed off with himself for even thinking about it, abruptly backing away from her while telling her about a big surgery he had scheduled for the morning. And then awkwardly adding to his excuse by saying that he had already caused her enough problems with the dog…But his words sounded phony and forced—even to him, he realized as he tried to act regretful for having to leave so soon, while stumbling over an explanation as to why he had to perform surgery so early on a Sunday morning.

"Thought you wanted to talk for a while," she said, sounding annoyed and doubtful of his explanation.

"I did, but I guess I didn't realize how late it was. And anyway, we can get together this week and talk. That's what I wanted to talk to you about…to set up a time when we could meet this week," he said squeezing her hand before moving a little further away from her and a little closer to the door. "Can spend all evening together—this week—when we're not so rushed," he promised, giving her another passionate kiss.

"Fine," she said, still acting perturbed at the situation he had created. Then she followed him to the door before giving him another kiss and telling him that she loved him.

"And don't worry about the dog, I'll take good care of her… You've got enough to worry about," she added as she followed him out to his car. And for the first time, he realized that he might have difficulty getting the dog back from Liz…when no one showed up to claim it. That she might not want to give the dog back—voluntarily—unless there was some good reason. And taking it to a dog pound did not sound like a particularly good reason, he thought as he got into his car. But he wasn't going to worry about that problem now. That was a problem way down the road of worries…plus, it seemed like a pretty simple problem to solve. And he hadn't done too much damage to his future attempt at ending their relationship. Maybe he had actually helped it come to a close, he thought. Was still going to dump her the first chance he got, he knew as he looked back at Liz standing in front of her picture window, holding the dog. He smiled and waved as he backed the car down the long driveway.

At least he had solved that problem, he thought as he drove toward the glow of the city lights in front of him. Again reveling in the image of what might be happening at the country club. He liked that mental picture: Hileman and all her cronies, all dirty, getting into their cars, getting the insides of their cars muddy, ruining thousands of dollars worth of clothing, searching for something that wasn't there. It was a gratifying thought; he hoped Mordy and his wife had to get out in the muddy field and search, too. He would have paid to see that.

As he approached town, he jerked—startled—almost falling asleep, imagining in a light dream that a motorcycle was passing him in the heavy rain, and that Pickles's face had appeared for just an instant in his side-view mirror. He could feel his heart racing, but there was nothing…not even another car in sight, he realized.

By the time he reached his house, the rain had stopped. A full moon had broken through the clouds to light the landscape and the path to his house. Upstairs, he found Sandy lying on her back, sound asleep, snoring angrily at the ceiling, and still wearing her party dress. Her muddy, nonmatching shoes were lying on the floor beside the bed, glowing in a beam of moonlight that was coming through the window—just like Cinderella, he thought. Maybe things would be better in the morning, he hoped as he lay down in bed and closed his eyes…spinning like a dancer on the dance floor, dancing to the music of the ten-piece orchestra still playing in his head.

CHAPTER THIRTY-THREE

Sunday, May 16
8:31 a.m.

He slept soundly...and could hear church bells ringing in the distance as he woke, and someone calling his name in the background, and a throbbing headache clouded his mind. He felt off-balance even lying still and flat on his back...like he might fall off the bed.

What had happened last night? he wondered. He couldn't actually remember coming home. Couldn't really remember much of anything that had happened. It all seemed like a mishmash of images flashing in his thoughts.

"You're going to be late if you don't quit pissing around," Sandy said, her voice seeming to come out of nowhere. "Didn't you hear me calling you a while ago?" she added as she dried her hair with a towel as if maybe she had just stepped out of the shower. The mirror in the bathroom was steamy, he could see, so he must have been right about that.

He sat on the edge of the bed for a while before most of it came back…one piece at a time. But even then it didn't seem real. Like most of last night had just been a dream.

Maybe he did take Hileman's dog like he thought he remembered doing. But he wasn't completely sure where he had left the dog…maybe at Liz's house. Unless something else had happened after that. Unless he had taken the dog somewhere else after he left Liz's house. Though he didn't think that he had.

"I got a shit headache," he told Sandy when she came back into the bedroom.

"I can see why, after last night," she said as she stood in front of the mirror putting on her make-up.

"Yeah, I guess it was pretty crazy."

"Where'd you get to, anyway?" Sandy asked as he moved tentatively toward the bathroom. "When I looked around you were gone," she added but he didn't answer. "You must have left just before all the excitement started," she said, taking a bottle of pills out of her purse and holding it up to see how many were left. "You missed all the excitement," she continued, laughing lightly.

Even though it was difficult, he tried to listen to what she was telling him. His vision was blurry and his head hurt when he moved his eyes and he was going to have to hurry if he was going to be on time to take his mother to church. She would be pissed if he was late again.

"You're not going to believe what happened," Sandy said, moving around him to look in the mirror to put on her make-up and then pausing for a few seconds, as if she might be trying to collect her thoughts. "You know that dog you told me about of Hileman's? That you said was with her all the time…in the ER the night she had her accident and at the trial?" she asked but didn't really wait for him to answer. "Well, I guess she had the dog with her last night at the banquet. I mean, I didn't actually see the dog…" she said, pausing as she searched through a container for more make-up.

"Yeah," Weed said trying to act interested.

"Yeah? Well, somehow…I guess, the damn dog got loose and ran off," she said, laughing slightly. "Maybe sometime around about when you left the party, I guess…But I'm not sure," she said, stopping to carefully apply her lipstick. "But everyone looked around for a while and couldn't find it…But when Hileman found out about it, she sort of went ballistic…got crazy like you told me she got that night at the hospital…yelling and cursing at everyone… And she was drunk, which made it that much more ridiculous… actually that much more hilarious," she said and paused again to blot her lipstick. "And then she got pissed off at some guy name Henry that was supposed to be watching the dog…And then she had someone call 911 and the police and then turned the whole thing into a big circus. 'Course, everyone stood around and tried to console her…'sorry, Gertrude this and sorry, Gertrude that,' acting like they really gave a shit about her damn mutt. Was all that I could do to not laugh right in her face and to tell her how happy I was that her damn dog was gone. But I just sat there and acted like I was really concerned…like the rest of the idiots. But the whole time I'm thinking 'good, just what she deserved' and praying that no one finds the damn thing…"

"You're kidding," he said, trying to act surprised at what she was telling him as he watched her in the mirror while he shaved.

"You should have taken some pictures then, because she didn't act like she was very debilitated then…She just got right up out of her wheelchair and ran around crazy like a wild woman. Didn't look like there was a thing wrong with her then…"

"Yeah, sorry I missed it…I should have stayed," he told her, trying to sound disappointed.

"Anyway, a bunch of people went outside into that muddy field behind the country club to look for the dog…and then a bunch more…all of them out there sloshing around in the muddy field… all in their gowns and tuxes and shoes…covered with mud…You should have seen it," she said, pausing again to check her appearance in the mirror. "You know, everyone just sort of got stuck in the mud until someone came along to help pull them out and then that person got stuck," she said, laughing again.

"And what a mess when they came back inside...mud everywhere. I tell you it was the funniest thing I've seen in a long time," she said, laughing again. "At least it was for me. But everyone was too scared to laugh. But I felt really good about the whole thing. Served her right for all the suffering she put us through. Turning all our friends against us. Trying to ruin our lives," she added.

It had worked out pretty much as he thought it might. And it didn't sound like anyone had realized that he had anything to do with it, Weed thought, feeling satisfied and somewhat elated as he finished shaving and turned on the shower.

"And that wasn't the best part of it," she said just as he stepped under the warm spray.

"The best part of it...and I mean I don't like to wish bad things on anyone...even my enemies...but given the circumstance," she said, pausing, "I think that she just might have had a heart attack... At least that's what it looked like, and what a couple of the other doctors were saying," she said but now acted a little more serious. "I mean, it's a shame that anyone gets sick...I know that...but I think she just got so excited when she realized the dog was gone that she probably had a heart attack," she repeated, looking at Weed for some kind of a response. "Can you believe that?" she asked, but he didn't answer. He just stood there, shocked and mortified at what she had just told him.

"I mean, I don't really like to wish a serious illness on anyone, and I am as religious as the next person," she said as she crossed herself, "but I can't help thinking that if she happened to die... or even if she just got really sick, it would really be...well, I don't know how to put it...but, you know, sort of fortunate for us. At least that's what I'm thinking," she added after a long pause. "I mean with the trial. If something bad did happen, then I figure the judge would have to do something...I don't know what...maybe a mistrial or something...I mean, you really can't have a trial with just one person...and then the whole trial would just maybe go away. I really think legally that if she actually dies, the trial would be over. I mean, I'm not wishing her to die...that's not what I'm saying. But that's why I'm sort of excited. To think that our nightmare might soon be over is pretty exciting."

"Yeah, I don't think...She's just a crazy hypochondriac...that's all it is," Weed finally told her, but he was still shocked at the possibility that he might have indirectly caused Hileman to suffer a fatal heart attack. "She's not going to die. She's a hypochondriac. I told you," he repeated, having a hard time getting the words out this time, and hoping that he was right...but all he could think about now was that stealing her dog could have indirectly caused her death. And somewhere in the back of his mind, he knew that doing something like that was considered some type of involuntary manslaughter...to cause the death of someone in the commission of a crime. What luck, he thought. The bitch had found a way to ruin his plans already, he thought. He could only half listen to what Sandy was telling him now as he tried to calculate all the possible consequences of what he had done.

"Probably won't amount to anything...She always thinks that she's sick," Weed repeated, unable to concentrate on what Sandy was telling him. "Just another act...just more of her histrionics," he told her, but the possibility of her dying disturbed him. And you never knew. She could have had a heart attack, he supposed as he finished dressing. He was going to have to call the hospital to find out what had actually happened.

"Didn't look like an act to me...and a couple of the doctors acted like it was pretty serious. Paramedics put two IVs in her arm and gave her a bunch of medicines before they took her away in the ambulance," she told him, still acting upset at his lack of enthusiasm.

"Seemed pretty serious to me. But anyway, I thought that you might be a little more excited...since something like this might end the trial and prevent us from losing everything we own and preserve what little respect we have left," she added sarcastically. "And people die...not our fault about that...just maybe a little bit of good luck for a change...a little bit of good fortune that could work to our benefit," she said, seeming more irritated now.

He would just deny it, he thought as he shook his head blindly in agreement with what Sandy had just said even though he hadn't heard one word. He would just tell the police the same story that he had told Liz. That he had just found the damn dog roaming around lost by the side of the road...but only this time at a location a lot closer to the country club. Tell them that he had found the dog running along the highway and didn't know anything about whose dog it was. And if they checked his story with Liz, he would just tell the police that Liz had apparently been confused about what he had told her. Could tell them he thought it was just a stray, and that he'd had a few drinks and really couldn't remember all the details himself. But the story might be a hard sell. It would be suspicious with the trial and with Hileman's driver possibly being able to identify him. Jesus, he just hoped that she didn't die, he thought as he finished tying his tie. Bitch was screwing him again...turning it all around and making him suffer instead of her, he thought.

He would call the hospital as soon as he left the house to see how Hileman was doing, he thought. And now he would have to get rid of the dog as soon as possible. Not in a couple of days...but *now*, he told himself. Was getting too dangerous to have anything to do with Hileman and her damn dog, he knew. He would just go out and get the dog from Liz as soon as he could and turn it loose somewhere, he thought as he finished dressing. That is if he could get Liz to return the dog. A simple prank turning into another major disaster. A disaster that rivaled and maybe even exceeded his preceding disasters.

"Police were pissed that they called them about losing some mangy mutt until they found out it was Hileman's mangy mutt," Sandy said after a long pause. "Then of course everything was just fine."

"You do something to your hand?" she asked when he absent-mindedly held his hand up in front of the bathroom mirror to see where all the pain was coming from…forgetting completely about the bites.

"Looks nasty," Sandy said, grabbing him by the arm of his suit jacket to look at it more closely. "What the hell happened?"

"It's nothing," he said, trying to pull it away. "Caught it on some briars last night."

"Where was that?" she asked, trying to look at it more closely. "I'll get some Betadine," she said, going back into the bathroom as she repeated her question.

"I think over at the country club when I was trying to find my damnable car. You know they made me park way around back by some rose bushes…couldn't see a damn thing," he said, looking at the two rows of teeth marks that didn't look much like scratches made by briars.

Weed grabbed the tube of Betadine from Sandy when she returned and quickly squeezed a large ribbon of ointment over the bites and smeared it around before she could get another good look…before she became any more suspicious. "Yeah, I think I caught it on one of those rose bushes at the back corner of the country club," he answered as she slowly moved away.

"You find your earring?" he quickly asked, hoping that changing the subject might help her forget about the bites.

"With the way you were drinking last night, I can see how something like that could happen…just glad you didn't do something really stupid," she continued as she left the room.

How prophetic, he thought, wondering if she would think stealing Hileman's dog was really stupid.

"You get any pictures?" she asked, finally standing completely dressed in front of the mirror.

"Don't know. Maybe one or two, but Ledig gave me a bunch of the pictures he took last year that I have to look at...Maybe there's a few of Hileman in them that I can use," he answered.

"Might not even need them now," she said, holding her crossed fingers.

But all he could think of was how he was going to get out of another mess that he had created needlessly. Just more shit to complicate his life. He was going to have to get rid of the dog as soon as possible.

"Yeah, I found my earring," she finally answered and then explained how she hadn't remembered to even put it in her ear. That she had put one in but had left the other in her purse.

"Yeah, I was in such a hurry, and then I couldn't get you on your cell, and then I couldn't find my shoes. I guess I just forgot," she said, laughing. "I must have been walking around all night with just one earring. But no one apparently noticed...And I'm sorry about the shoes, too. I figured you wouldn't do something like that. I think I might have actually returned them accidently to the store. I guess I was upset and just sort of lost my cool," she told him. But he was still preoccupied with Hileman. Trying to reassure himself that nothing bad had happened to her and that she was going to be okay.

"I guess someone left the door open," Sandy added as Weed started to leave the bedroom.

"What?"

"Someone left the door open...at the country club," she answered. "That's how the dog got away. Seemed strange that the dog just sort of vanished into thin air in such a short time, though. You see anything when you left?" she asked as he started toward the door.

"Not a thing," he answered as he left her behind in the bedroom.

CHAPTER THIRTY-FOUR

Sunday, May 16
9:45 a.m.

That Hileman had been admitted "in stable condition" was all the hospital nurse would tell him. Which was some relief, he imagined, and he was even more convinced that her so-called heart attack had been nothing more than an act.

But now there was the distinct possibility that the trial would be delayed, he supposed. Trial wasn't long enough already…He had to make it last even longer with some stupid prank, he thought, disgusted. Couldn't seem to win no matter what he did, he thought, as he drove toward his mother's house.

He was still feeling hungover, had a throbbing headache, sort of felt feverish, and the bite on his hand looked like it might be getting infected, he thought. And the Betadine bleeding through his clean white shirt was making him feel nauseated. Would have to start taking some antibiotics soon…before he died, he thought sarcastically but amused at that possible solution to all his problems.

Was just going to have to get the damn dog as far away from him as possible before the whole thing spun out of control. Couldn't afford making his life any more complicated now, and he didn't want to get blamed for something as embarrassing as stealing someone's dog, he thought, pissed at himself for doing something so stupid and irresponsible to complicate his life.

That was it; he remembered now what Hileman's driver had told him...The dog had spastic colon. That was great...to add to his misery, he had stolen a defective dog with bowel problems, he thought as he pulled his car up in front of his mother's house. If he was Hileman's dog, he would probably have spastic colon too, he imagined.

He walked up the steps and entered the house...The flowers he had given his mother for Mother's Day still wilting and neglected where he had left them last Sunday. Not moved an inch or watered a drop as far as he could tell. And his intuition had already detected his mother's foul mood...probably over what she had been reading in the newspapers about the trial.

"Shouldn't even go to church," she finally said as she stood in front of the hall mirror adjusting her hat with tears in her eyes. "Getting harder and harder to explain to everyone how you have turned into a heartless person that doesn't care about anyone or anything anymore," she added, giving him a disgusted look in the mirror and shaking her head.

Didn't need her attitude this morning, he thought. Had more important things to do than to listen to some whining old woman bitching at him, even if it was his mother. And he wasn't going to explain his side of the story to her again either, he thought as he sat at the table and looked at the photos Ledig had given him...searching for any shots of Hileman that he might be able to use in court.

"People used to always tell me how lucky I was to have a son like you...How you were such a great doctor...That everyone loved you...and wanted to be your patient...and patients coming from miles around just to see you…" she continued. "Used to give me all kinds of presents…used to leave baskets of fruit at my front door…because they liked you so much. But I guess that's over with, now…Can't even remember the last time someone said something nice about you."

"Yeah, well, times have changed," he said, opening the door for her to leave. "People don't do things like that anymore…People aren't like they used to be…so don't worry about it," he told her as he helped her down the steps and into the car. He drove down the hill to the church as she continued to complain…and as he continued to remain silent. Best rebuttal was to say nothing…just keep his mouth shut. He had learned that lesson many times before.

He helped his mother across the street and then up the steps and into the church…and away from him for at least a couple of hours, he thought as he sat in his car and called Bob on his cell.

"Going to have to get rid of the damn dog," he said when Bob answered the phone, and he told him about leaving the dog at Liz's house and then about Hileman's big act at the country club. "Made everyone think she was having a heart attack. So I'm going to get rid of the dog as soon as I can…drop it off at some animal shelter or something. Can't risk it anymore…Can't risk having anything to do with her anymore. She's poison. Someone finds out about what I did, then I'm in even more trouble."

"Didn't I tell you last night that it was crazy? Bob asked. "And she had a heart attack?"

"She didn't have a heart attack. That's what I'm trying to tell you. It was all just a big act like everything else she does. I checked on her this morning, and she's doing fine, but she's turning this into one big fuckin' mess. And now I'm not sure how I'm going to get the dog back from Liz. Liz is already acting like the dog belongs to her by default. That's what pisses me off about her…She's always doing something annoying to me. Just little things that eat at you slowly. That's why I've been trying to dump her. And now I have to figure out how I'm going to get the damn dog back from Liz to get it back to Hileman."

"You should have just let the dog out on the side of the road last night like I told you to do…But now you got someone else involved," he said. "I guess you could tell Liz the truth about what happened…"

"No chance. She would just call the police and have me arrested…She's got no common sense…I told you that last night. That's why I didn't want to leave the dog there in the first place. You can't trust her…"

"Well, to tell you the truth…I don't want to get involved either, or they'll accuse me of being your accomplice. And if Hileman dies, you could get blamed for that too. You ever think of that?"

"She's not going to die. She's just a crazy hypochondriac, that's all…I told you…It's all just an act. She didn't even have any heart attack."

"Well, then just go out and break into Liz's house and get the damn dog."

"Yeah, well, I might have to," he said, knowing that he had already considered that possibility. "I was thinking that I could get someone to go out and tell Liz that the dog was their dog. That makes the most sense. Have someone tell her it's their dog and then just have them take it. Just don't know who to ask."

"Yeah, well, doesn't make any sense to me. I mean how's anyone going to convince Liz that it's their dog? Especially if the dog bites them like it did you."

"Was okay with Liz. Didn't bite her."

"And what happens when they call the dog and it doesn't come? How they going to explain that? You know what Hileman even calls the mutt?"

"Not really…Some shit name. Might come when it knows you just called it," he told Bob but felt sort of stupid that he hadn't thought of that problem.

"And if Liz is the kind of person that you tell me she is, she's going to want three forms of identification before she's going to turn the dog over to anyone."

"Yeah, maybe. You know I knew it was a bad idea five minutes after I took the damn thing," Weed said. "Even sooner...When I was trying to find my car in that muddy mess...I even knew then it was a big mistake," he added. "I can't believe it. Some gift from the gods. Maybe I figured that it wouldn't really matter. That I was in so much trouble already that one more problem wouldn't matter... or maybe it was just some futile desperation," he said, pausing and then mumbling some platitude about the futility of life that didn't make much sense even to him.

"Shouldn't make decisions when you've been drinking. I told you that before. And all I know is that if it were me, I would get rid of the dog as soon as possible. Before the police start snooping around, or before Hileman decides to die...There's just too many bad things that could go wrong."

"Yeah, maybe, but I don't think the police have time to go around looking for lost dogs."

"Probably not, but its Hileman's dog. That changes things," Bob said before telling Weed that he had to end their conversation to go wait on a customer...and then reminding Weed that he wasn't trying to be cold or insensitive, but that he was going to deny he knew anything about what Weed had done.

He could ask Candy to go out and get the dog, he imagined as he sat in his car and watched people going up the steps and into the church. She was the only person that he could trust not to say anything, but she was already too involved with his other messes... and she probably couldn't pull it off anyway...She had a difficult time hiding the truth, he knew, and Bob was probably right that it wouldn't work anyway, he thought as he dialed her number and waited for her to answer while he searched through Ledig's photographs again.

No answer...voice mail...He just hoped that she would be around tomorrow for her meeting at the courthouse with the judge and attorneys, as he ended the call.

Almost a hundred photographs, but only two showed any promise, and they were just distant shots of people out on the dance floor. But one of the people did look a lot like Hileman...would have the photos blown up later, he thought as he walked back across the street to the church and then waited impatiently in the last pew for the service to end.

When they got back to the house, Weed sat across from his mother at the dining room table and ate...mostly in silence...as he read the newspaper and as she looked at recipes in a cookbook. Silence was better, he knew.

At one point as they ate, he had an ominous feeling that Hileman had just that very minute died...but then wrote it off to just an overactive imagination.

"Roast was a little tough," his mother mumbled as she left the table and slowly walked over and sat down in a chair by the phone.

She would sit there most of the afternoon talking to all her annoying cronies like she had done as long as he could remember, Weed knew.

"Might go upstairs and just rest for a while and then walk down to the Quick Fix...I think Bob's working," he told her, but she showed no interest as she tentatively dialed a number that she was having a difficult time reading off one of the pages of her black book of numbers.

He took the steps to the basement and then called the hospital...His premonition had been wrong...She hadn't died...She was still in stable condition. He looked through a few boxes...clothes, books, other junked up boxes mostly. Looked like the front of the Salvation Army on a Monday morning, he thought as he stood back looking at the whole mess. He dumped the contents of two more boxes out on the floor. But he was beginning to wonder if his search was futile and that maybe his mother had thrown all the Matchbox cars away as payback for the all the embarrassment and grief he had caused her with the trial.

Would maybe look later, he thought before walking up the stairs to his bedroom.

He lay in his bed looking up at the ceiling, thinking about how best to get the dog back to Hileman. That question seemed like his most important problem at the moment. He was probably going to just have to go out and somehow get the dog himself. Maybe when Liz wasn't around. Tell Liz that he had come out and when he opened the door the dog just ran away, or that maybe the owners were there waiting and he gave them back their dog. That would be a better story, he thought. Then she wouldn't go crazy looking for the damn thing.

Taking the dog was looking more and more like a really stupid idea. Had already backfired, he thought. He closed his eyes and tried to force sleep as a cool breeze blew through the window. Taking Hileman's dog was probably causing him a lot more grief than it was causing Hileman, he imagined. How had that happened? It had at least caused some of his so-called friends to ruin some pretty expensive clothes, he imagined. That had to be worth something.

He would figure something out...some way to get the dog away from Liz and back to Hileman without anyone finding out about it and before the whole thing exploded. And then that problem would be over. That's assuming that Hileman didn't die. If that happened...he didn't know what...didn't even want to think about that remote possibility, he told himself. Involuntary manslaughter for stealing someone's dog. Pretty embarrassing, he imagined, and it didn't make a lot of sense. Seemed almost draconian somehow, he thought as he slowly drifted off to sleep.

CHAPTER THIRTY-FIVE

Sunday, May 16
2:15 p.m.

It was warm and it was summer and he was young again, dreaming about knocking a bees' nest from under the eve of his mother's house and then running. He could feel the bees all over his body, ready to sting, before one bee stung him sharply on the back of his hand...And then he could hear a bell ringing, warning him that he only had a short time before the swarming bees caught him.

But when he woke it was the doorbell that was ringing, and the bee sting was not a sting at all, but the pain from where Hileman's dog had bitten him.

He lay there, still foggy, holding his swollen hand out in front of him to see how much worse it looked now.

He could hear his mother still talking on the phone, but either she hadn't heard the doorbell ring or more likely didn't want to be bothered, he thought as the doorbell rang a second time and then a third. He lay there wondering just how many times it would have to ring before she decided to get off the damn phone and answer, as the doorbell rang for the fourth time. And then wondered how many times whoever was ringing the doorbell was going to ring before they stopped...four times was more than enough, he thought, sitting on the edge of the bed. Didn't they get the memo?

"Answer the fuckin' door," he finally responded as he sat on the edge of the bed, but not loud enough for his mother to hear...but maybe loud enough for the pain in the ass ringing the bell to hear through his open bedroom window, he thought, finally standing and looking out the window to the street below.

He could see a group of young girls gathered in the street in front of the house doing something, but he couldn't tell what.

"I'll be down in a damn minute," he yelled out his window at whoever was standing on the porch still ringing the doorbell.

"Okay," a young girl's voice answered him.

He slipped his shoes back on and walked down the steps to the front door as he tried to work the stiffness out of his swollen hand.

A young girl dressed in a Girl Scout uniform was standing looking in at him through the screen door with a strained smile on her face. Cookies, he thought. She had woke him out of a deep sleep... the best sleep he had had in weeks...to buy some crappy-ass Girl Scout cookies, he thought as he pushed open the screen door.

But instead of cookies, the girl took a yellow paper from a stack of papers she was holding and held it out for him to take.

"Did you ever see a dog that look like this?" she asked, looking up at him as she struggled to not drop the other papers she was holding.

When he looked down at the paper Hileman's dog was looking back up at him, and for a second he thought that he might still be dreaming. It was unmistakably Hileman's dog, even though Hileman's name was nowhere on the flier. The black dog looked directly back at him in a stance as if at any moment she might jump off the paper at him...as if she might recognize him.

The words "Lost Dog" and "$500 reward" were written in large, red letters across the top of the flier. Beneath the dog's picture, its name was written in large, red letters: "Pepper." And in parentheses was "PupPup." The bottom of the flier was a vertical column of identical phone numbers cut like a hula skirt so that they could be easily torn from the flier.

The fliers were hanging everywhere in the street in front of the house.

"We're looking for this dog," the small girl told him as she pointed to the dog's picture.

He couldn't believe it. People acting like it was worse than the Lindbergh kidnapping, he thought, looking down at all the fliers in the street.

And the country club was almost three miles from the house and on the other side of town. How could anyone ever believe that a small dog could survive traveling that far and through all the heavy city traffic? And how many people did they expect were going to rip numbers from all the fliers? Pissed him off just thinking about it.

At least his picture wasn't on the flier as a suspect, he thought. And at least it appeared as if no one yet had expected any kind of foul play...by some drunk doctor...at least not yet, he thought, handing the flier back to the girl.

"It ran away last night right over there," the Girl Scout said, pointing back over her left shoulder but not in the direction of the country club, Weed knew. "If you see the dog, just pull one of these little numbers off the bottom and call that number," the little girl told him and then awkwardly demonstrated how he could rip one of the strips of paper off the bottom of the flier.

"No, sorry! I didn't see any dog like that," Weed said, amazed that he had actually watched her demonstration and annoyed at the absurdity of the whole situation. A grown man being questioned by a Girl Scout about a dog that he had stolen. Seemed like some kind of bizarre plot from *The Twilight Zone*, he thought. Even the Girl

Scouts were out to get him, he thought as he tried to give the flier back to the girl a second time.

"You can keep it. I have a whole bunch," she said showing him the pile of fliers she was holding. "We're supposed to give every-one we see one of them and then put the rest up on telephone poles...and then ask if they want any cookies," she added before pulling an order form from underneath the fliers. "We're selling cookies too."

"Yeah, that's cute. But I don't think that I need one. I'll remem-ber what the dog looks like," he said as one of the adults standing with the group of girls in the street started up the steps toward the house.

"Let me see," Weed's mother said, coming up from behind him at the door. "I want to see what the dog looks like. I heard about it at church this morning," she said, trying to see around Weed.

"*Now* you come to the door," he said, turning to give her a dirty look. "Didn't you hear the damn doorbell ringing?"

"I was on my way, and watch your language in front of children."

"On your way? It rang four times and I heard you talking right though it all. I was trying to get some sleep. Woke me out of a sound sleep."

"I was busy talking to Stella."

"Well, why aren't you busy talking to Stella now?"

"You tell them...?" the woman that was standing in the street said as she arrived on the front porch. "She sometimes forgets," the woman continued and then reminded the little girl not to forget to tell them about the dog being sick.

"Oh yeah, the dog needs medicine or it could die," the little girl told Weed and then turned and looked at her Scout leader for approval.

"That's right," the woman said, complimenting the girl. "The dog has some kind of a medical condition and needs medicine so it won't get sick, so it's important that we find it as soon as possible," the woman added. "They're saying it might only live a couple days without its medicine," she added.

"You're Dr. Weed," another woman from the group said, coming up on the porch behind the first and holding out her hand for Weed to shake. "You took my gallbladder out a couple of years ago," she said and then introduced herself, but he couldn't remember her. "I almost died."

"Before or after the surgery," he asked, but she didn't appear to get the joke.

"Poor little thing...it's a shame," Weed's mother said before going out on the porch and telling all the women that Hileman's lost dog had been the main topic of conversation at the morning service.

"She's giving the Girl Scouts a big donation to help find the dog," one of the mothers said as Weed went back inside the house and up the stairs. Didn't want to hear anymore...He had had enough of missing dogs, he thought as he picked up his cell phone and started back down the stairs.

There was a Speedy Foto shop near the Quick Fix. He could have Ledig's photos and the couple of photos he had taken enlarged, he thought.

When he started to leave the house his mother was still standing at the door, talking to the women and ordering cookies.

"Should I order an extra box of Tagalongs or an extra box of the Thin Mints?" she asked him as he tried to move around her.

"I don't care," he said, disgusted, and felt like saying that he didn't really give a shit what cookies she ordered.

"I told the girls that you could put a few more of their fliers up when you walked down to the Quick Fix," his mother told him, handing him a stack of fliers as he went by. "I guess you already heard about the dog?" she asked him, but he didn't answer.

"I guess someone accidentally left the door open last night at your party," she added louder now as he continued down the steps and into the street smiling at all the annoying women as he passed.

They surely wouldn't put up signs out where Liz lived he wondered as he walked toward the Quick Fix. Liz lived over twenty miles away, out in the country, but she might see them if she came into town, he thought. He was definitely going to have to get the dog back to Hileman soon, he knew. Didn't want the dog to die either. Probably just a hypochondriac like Hileman, he imagined as he continued his walk to the Quick Fix.

Maybe he could get the dog back from Liz tomorrow, he thought as he watched another group of Girl Scouts turn the corner and disappear down a side street.

Wasn't a chance in hell that he was going to put any more dog posters up, he thought. There were dogs tacked up everywhere… watching his every step. Wasn't any place to put up any more of the posters even if he wanted to. If it was like this all over town, he didn't stand a chance. And with a five-hundred-dollar reward, everyone in the county would be looking for the dog.

And Liz would almost certainly find out about it eventually, he thought as he looked around to make sure no one was watching before pulling one of the fliers off a telephone pole and then another, before adding them to the other posters and tossing them all into a trash can near the curb.

He would have to just stick with his basic story if they found out that he had something to do with the missing dog. He would just tell them that he had found the dog along the highway and he didn't have any idea whose dog it was, and so he'd just left it at Liz's place. As soon as he could get the damn thing back from Liz he was going to somehow get it back to Hileman, he thought.

"You see all the posters?" was the first thing Bob said when Weed entered the Quick Fix. "They're all the way up and down the street…as far as you can see. Didn't I tell you it was a hot dog," he said, laughing again before realizing Weed still wasn't amused. "I mean, I'm not trying to make fun of it, but you have to admit that's pretty funny," he said. "That it's a hot dog, a stolen dog, and then with all these mug shots of the dog," he said, awkwardly explaining his joke again as he tried to hold back his laughter.

"Yeah, that's hilarious. And a lot funnier now than the first six times you told me," Weed said sarcastically. "I could have killed three people last night and no one would have given a damn, but you take someone's smelly mutt and it becomes a federal case," he said as they left the store and walked toward the Speedy Foto.

"Yeah, well, most people like their dogs more than their friends anyway...and even their family sometimes," Bob said. "You get any good pictures of Hileman?" he added, looking over Weed's shoulder at the pictures he was scanning through on his phone.

"Don't know...Most of them are from last year's banquet and hard to see. Won't know until I get them enlarged, but I think there might be one or two I can use.

"I'm just going to go out and get the dog," Weed told him after they had walked another couple blocks toward the store. "Don't know what I'll tell Liz though. Thought that I could maybe go out sometime when she wasn't home...maybe while she's at work or something...and just take the dog. Make up some kind of excuse for being out there when she wasn't around. That would be the easiest. Tell her that the owners were there when I got there or something, and that I had to give them their dog," he added. "Maybe tomorrow or Tuesday. I don't think she works Mondays, so I might have to just wait until Tuesday," he said as they entered the store. "Will give me a little time to work out the details, but I'm going to do it soon. I don't need this with everything else I got going on right now, and it's getting too complicated," he said as they stood in line. "Police could arrest me, I suppose, if they found out. Make a big deal out of it. With all Hileman's influence, who knows what they might do to me...probably make a federal case out of it," he added sarcastically.

"Could be worse than the shooting. More embarrassing at least," Weed began after a long pause as they waited in line. "A stupid, juvenile idiotic prank that everyone would think I was insane for doing…I mean, dating a stripper's bad…but not juvenile. Makes the shooting at Tatter's almost seem like something respectable… something good that's happened to me," he said, talking quietly so no one in the line could hear what he was telling Bob.

"You could plead insanity," Bob said as a joke, but that wasn't such a stretch, Weed thought.

"Yeah, insanity…Might work," Weed agreed as he showed the clerk which photos he wanted enlarged and then emphasized how important is was that they not get lost.

"Hand looks nasty," Bob said as he watched Weed awkwardly trying to fill out the paperwork.

"May be getting a little worse," Weed said as he held his sausage-shaped fingers up in front of him.

"You're going to have to make sure no one sees it tomorrow. Might look suspicious," Bob said as the clerk handed Weed back a receipt. Something he hadn't even considered.

"Liz keeps a key under one of the flowerpots on her porch. I could just open the door and grab the dog and be done with it… At least I know its name now," he said. "Tell her that the owners were just waiting for the dog when I got there, and then hope that she doesn't find out what really happened," he said as they walked down the street and into one of the small bars along the street.

They sat at the bar and talked about his plans to get the dog back for almost an hour as they drank, before they returned to Speedy Foto for the pictures.

"Not bad, I guess," Weed said, taking a quick look at the photos. "See, she doesn't have her collar on in this one," he said as he handed one of the photographs to Bob. "And here she is out on the dance floor dancing, I think," he said, holding it up to get a closer look.

"That's her?" Bob asked, acting unsure as he held the picture close to his face. "Pretty hard to make out who it is," he said, finally handing the picture back to Weed.

"Yeah, that's her," Weed assured him. But he wasn't really sure himself…the photos were all pretty grainy, he thought disappointed as he put them back into the envelope. Pictures didn't seem half as good as he thought they might be, but he was going to show them to Morgan anyway. Might help his case…unless they found out about all the other shit that was going on in his life and then it probably wouldn't matter how many pictures he had…he would be screwed, he thought as he left Bob at the Quick Fix before walking back to his mother's house.

When he got there he sat down on the porch and called Candy.

"You okay with tomorrow?" he asked when she finally answered.

"I guess," she answered, sounding unsure.

"Remember, eight a.m. And you know where to go?" he asked.

"I know where to go. I've been there before," she assured him.

"And don't worry. Just stay calm and tell the judge what we talked about…Don't go into any details…just tell him it was you that had been drinking that night…not me…that I didn't have a drop… And if he asks you what you do for a living, just tell them that you work as a waitress somewhere."

"Yeah, yeah I know…Make sure that I don't let it slip that I'm some stupid two-dollar whore…I'll try to remember that," she said with anger and sarcasm.

"You know what I mean…" he said and then tried to explain again before telling her that he would make it all up to her later… that he would give her enough money to pay off all of her bills so she wouldn't have to worry about working for a while.

"You see Pickles lately?" he asked after a long pause in their strained conversation.

"Yeah, I saw him yesterday standing out in front of the bar. He waved for me to pull over when I drove by, but I just acted like I didn't see him. Was no way I was going to stop," she answered, confirming his assumptions that the police hadn't arrested him yet.

When he got home, Sandy was gone. He felt feverish and his hand looked like a balloon from Macy's parade, he thought as he took his temperature and inspected his hand more closely in the bathroom mirror. He took twice the recommended dose of two leftover medications that he had laying around that he was almost certain were antibiotics before lying down. Might be hard to hide his hand tomorrow with how red and swollen it was, especially if he had to put it on a bible to be sworn in…to tell the whole truth and nothing but the truth…he thought about how stupid that statement was…No one ever told the whole truth, he knew. He would just have to wear his largest suit coat and let the sleeve hang down over his hand as far as possible or people might start asking questions, he thought as he held his hand over his head in an attempt to lessen the throbbing pain.

It was late when Sandy got home, and he had been sleeping for what seemed like a long time.

"Well, she didn't die yet," she said turning on the bathroom light. "Nothing ever goes our way," she added as he watched her in the mirror while she removed her make-up and continued to chatter about how miserable her day had been and her life was…and as he realized just how drunk she was.

CHAPTER THIRTY-SIX

Monday, May 17
7:20 a.m.

He couldn't sleep because of all the pain in his hand.
So he lay in bed thinking about the trial and the dog and
Liz and Hileman, and when he got tired of thinking about all
those things, he thought about Candy and the bar, and Pickles and
Sandy, and even Mordy once, and then about everything else that
had gone wrong in his life…jumbled thoughts…and the whole time
mostly praying for morning to come to end it all. All night sleepless
before finally hearing the newspaper hitting the side of the house,
fluttering downward like a wounded bird to the porch, letting him
know that any attempt at sleep had ended and the long night was
finally over.

What would be written in the newspaper today about his miserable life? he thought as he sat on the edge of the bed for few minutes, looking out at the approach of the crimson morning.

He showered and dressed and moved around the bedroom quietly, hoping not to wake Sandy. He didn't want to have to talk to her. She would only complicate things, he knew as he made his way down the creaky steps unscathed.

Downstairs he retrieved the newspaper and then called Candy on his cell.

"Yes, Ben, I'm up...Jesus...I'll be there," she said emphatically and irritated when she answered...but hung up before he could say another word.

He drank the last of the orange juice straight from the bottle and ate a piece of toast as he peeled back the pages of the newspaper with his swollen hand, looking for any articles about his life... the lawsuit, the shooting, the missing dog, Hileman's demise...the whole paper would soon be nothing more than articles about his life...maybe they would start a new section just for him, he imagined, amused and disgusted at the same time as he scanned down the list of names in the obituaries...stopping, shocked for an instant when he came to a name that he thought was Gertrude Hileman's... before realizing that it wasn't.

Nothing about the shooting. And nothing about the trial...or any articles about any missing dogs. A good way to start the week, he imagined. Even his horoscope was encouraging. "Good days to follow," it read, but he doubted it.

The trial would be over by the end of the week unless it was delayed by Hileman's malingering, he imagined. And maybe the photographs of Hileman dancing would change things...wasn't going to let Morgan weasel out of using them at the trial if he could help it.

And then he just hoped that no one recognized Candy today at courthouse from all her stripper pictures that had appeared in the newspapers for the last year or so, he thought...as he backed his car down the driveway, only then noticing the two perfectly formed muddy paw prints at the top of the windshield. More incriminating evidence right out in the open for everyone to see. That was all he needed, for someone to see paw prints all over the inside of his car, he thought as he rubbed them painfully clean with his swollen hand.

When he got to the courthouse, he drank his Coke and bourbon and examined the pictures of Hileman at the banquet as he waited for Candy to come out of the courthouse. There was at least one good photograph of Hileman out on the dance floor with a big smile on her face, holding her hands up in the air like she was dancing. No collar, no wheelchair, no visible scars, and the picture taken over a year after her accident...over a year after he had repaired her laceration. No apparent problems with back pain that night...and he was almost certain that it was Hileman in the picture. That was the money shot...and it could really make a difference if the jury saw it, he knew. Might not lose a dime.

He waited for almost an hour before Candy finally appeared at the top of the courthouse steps. Dressed pretty provocative...but not bad, considering, he thought as he got out of his car and waved her over to where he was parked. He gave her a quick hug and kiss before they both got back into his car.

"Didn't know Pervert George was your judge," Candy said as she sat in the car beside him searching her purse for her cigarettes.

"What?" Weed asked, confused at what she had just told him.

"Pervert George...That's what they call him down at the bar...That's who your judge is," she said, lighting up a cigarette and taking a deep drag.

But he still wasn't sure what she was trying to tell him.

"Yeah, that's what I'm telling you...I know that man...your judge...He comes into the bar all the time...hangs out with that girl, Tracy...that one girl you can't take your eyes off..."

"What? You're telling me that Judge Wisensee comes into the bar and that they call him Pervert George?"

"That's exactly what I'm telling you," she answered, sounding somewhat irritated at his confusion.

"Name's not even George...You sure you don't have him mixed up with someone else?"

he said, now shocked thinking about what might have gone on at her deposition.

"I know exactly who he is...And that's just what they call him down there...I mean, I know they don't call him that in court...but that's the name he uses at the bar. Sort of like when you didn't want to tell me your real name when we first met...Remember you told me that your name was Frank or something...I think I called you Frankie for I don't know how long," she reminded him. "He's a real freaky guy. That's why I remember him. Has this thing for women's shoes or underwear or something...paid one of the girls to wear something strange, but I can't remember exactly what now...maybe a couple of things...something freaky like that."

He listened, still somewhat stunned and amused at the story she was telling him.

"I didn't like him, but I never knew he was a judge. But Tracy could tell you more about him...maybe she knew he was a judge," she said, looking over at Weed. "But he looks a lot different...You know how he's bald? Well, when he's in the bar, he has this crazy-lookin' wig thing that he wears...and these big glasses...But I could tell it was him right off."

"He recognize you?"

"Yeah, he knows me...but he didn't say anything...acted like he didn't know me and I didn't really act like I knew him either," she said, lighting her cigarette. "And you know him too...He sat right next to you the night those two gay guys had that big fight in the bathroom," she continued before taking another drag off her cigarette. "I think Tatter threw him out once when he got too grabby with one of the other girls," she added. "But he seemed okay today...only asked me my name, and then what I remembered about that night...and then said he believed me and told me that he didn't need to talk to me anymore," she said as she exhaled a long plume of blue smoke into the car. "That one guy acted pissed, but Pervert George just told him that there was nothing he could do...that he wasn't going to have anyone testify...that the trial was already getting crazy-long and that it was all hearsay evidence anyway, or something like that. Didn't really know what they were talking about."

"You're kidding. And Morgan and Turzak...the lawyers?"

"No, I didn't recognize either of them," she said.

"Yeah, but what did they say?"

"Nothin' much. Judge wouldn't let anyone else ask me any questions. And that was it. The one guy was pissed like I told you...said that it was some kind of travesty of justice or something like that."

"Maybe he didn't recognize you."

"Yeah, maybe, but I doubt it...He knows all the girls."

Didn't know if what he was hearing was good news or bad news... If the judge knew that he was using a stripper as a witness, might cause him problems, but then again it might open up an even bigger can of worms for the judge too...And it did seem like the judge might be trying to sweep the whole alcohol mess under the rug, Weed thought...And trying to get Candy out of the courthouse as quickly as possible.

What luck, he thought, somewhat relieved as he made her tell him again what happened at the deposition...and then asked her more questions before he told her how much he appreciated what she had just done, and how much he loved her, before giving her most of the money he had left in his wallet.

So as far as he could tell, the drinking issue might be off the table...If what she said was true, then it would be one big problem that he no longer had to deal with. One problem solved, he thought.

"You hear anything more about the shooting?" he asked after they had talked for a while longer.

"No...well, yeah, sort of. I heard that Tatter's out of the hospital, but that the police won't let him open the bar...and that they might not ever let him open the bar again," she said as she put on a fresh layer of lipstick.

"Thought Tatter was in critical condition."

"Yeah, well, Wendy said he looks fine…I mean, he was only shot once in the ass…I mean, what did you expect?" she asked, looking over at him as if she expected him to answer. "And Sue, that girl I told you about that used to dance at the bar with me…well, she's making good money dancing somewhere down in Florida," she added, looking out the window as if she were in deep thought. "She's making twice as much as I'm making up here…pisses me off. There's just no good dance jobs in this God-awful town. Too many old people, I guess…And it's warmer down there," she told him as she put on another layer of eyeliner. "More old people in this state than any other state in the country, someone told me once…other than Iowa or some state like that," she added. "And I'm seriously thinking about moving down there. Sue said I could stay with her until I get established and get a place of my own. And you should think about it too," she added as she turned the rearview mirror to check her make-up. "You could start a practice down there. Start over. A fresh start, like you always said that you wanted," she said as she pushed open the car door to get out. "Leave all this shit behind. Leave all your worries behind," she said and then laughed, giving him a kiss before getting out of the car. "Have things to do," she said, looking back at him. "Like picking up my outfits at Tatter's," she said in a sexy voice and then gave him a sexy smile as she started off down the street.

With the way things were going in his life, it only made sense that the judge would be some pervert that knew Candy…that the judge might even recognize him now…seeing her might have jogged his memory just enough to remember seeing him at the bar. But he didn't have any idea what it all meant. The whole thing was too complicated to even reason it out now. Just like everything else in his life…just another jumbled mess to worry about. But at least the alcohol problem was apparently off the table...which was a big relief. Now if everything else worked out just as well, he thought.

Should have asked Candy about helping him with the dog, he thought as he looked out the window to see if he could still see her. She had done such a good job with the judge, that maybe he could ask her to go out and try to get the dog...tell Liz it was her damn dog...and at least he knew the dog's name now, he thought as he watched Candy move through the park until she was completely out of sight. Maybe would call her later.

So the judge was some kind of weirdo too, he thought, amused, as he sat in the car and finished his drink, gathering up the pictures or Hileman before walking across the street to the courthouse.

"Got good news and bad news," Morgan said as Weed sat down beside him in an almost empty courtroom. "The good news is your witness was great...wasn't in there three minutes and the judge threw the whole issue out...So we dodged a bullet with that one. Pretty good looker too. Where'd you ever run into a girl like that?" he asked, but Weed didn't answer. "Judge said that it was all just hearsay and not admissible. So apparently, we won't have to worry about that issue any longer," he continued.

"The bad news is there's another problem," Morgan said turning toward Weed. "I guess you probably already heard about Hileman being admitted to the hospital Saturday night? Well, I guess her dog ran away and she got so upset that she had some sort of a mild heart attack or something...But it must not have been too bad because they tell me they're releasing her sometime this morning...So the trial's been delayed until tomorrow. But the judge wants to talk to us in his chambers," he said, gathering up his papers. "Says there's some kind of rumor going around that you might know something about what happened at the country club Saturday night...something crazy like that...that maybe you could have been the person that left the door open or something. Turzak's making a big deal out of it…said that you did it on purpose so that the dog would run off."

"Don't even know what they're talking about, but I guessed they would eventually get around to blaming me somehow…" Weed answered, shocked and alarmed at the revelation that he was now a suspect…but trying to act unconcerned. "I mean, I get blamed for everything else bad that's happened in her life…might as well get blamed for her damn dog running off," Weed told him, letting out a feeble laugh. Apparently, the dog issue was not going to go quietly into the night.

"Well then, just tell Wisensee that you don't know anything about her damn dog, so we can all get out of this loony bin of a sweat box and go home early for a change," Morgan said as Weed opened the manila folder and took out the pictures of Hileman.

"This is what I was telling you about…That's Hileman at last year's Spring Fling…out on the dance floor without a collar and without her wheelchair, and you can barely see the scars," he said. Morgan took the photo and looked at it closely as Weed tried to figure out just what he was going to tell the judge about Hileman's dog.

"Yeah, pretty interesting, but I don't know if you can absolutely say that's her for certain…I mean, it's hard to tell at that distance," he said as he looked a little closer at the photograph. "And anyway, he's probably not going to let any new evidence into the trial now…not after today with this drinking thing," he said, handing the photograph back to Weed as he picked up his briefcase. "Might be a Hail Mary pass, if we really get desperate…a last-ditch sort of thing…But we still have a good shot at surviving this mess relatively unscathed without it, I imagine…or at least we have a chance that the jury won't give her much money…And our chances just increased a hundred-fold after your friend gave her statement this morning. That's what I was really worried about. And I don't want to muddy the waters any more than they already are," he added as they walked back to Wisensee's chamber.

Weed took a closer look at Wisensee when he entered the room but still didn't recognize him as anyone he had seen at the bar... And luckily, Wisensee didn't seem to recognize him either...And if he did, he didn't seem to be acting like he did, Weed thought, relieved.

"Don't want to get into anything more...I've had enough of this trial already. So I'm just going to ask you one question, and I want the truth," Wisensee said, looking over at Weed even before they had a chance to sit. "You have any idea what happened to Hileman's damn dog Saturday night? And please say no."

"No, not a thing...wasn't even there when the dog ran away... But I heard about it."

"And you didn't leave the damn back door open...or whatever damn door they're talking about being open?"

"Don't think I left any door open at the country club that I can remember."

"Great...Now you can give Ms. Hileman our condolences," Wisensee said, addressing Turzak. "And you can assure Ms. Hileman that this trial had absolutely nothing to do with the unfortunate loss of her beloved pet...and unfortunately, people leave doors open all the time...wind could have blown it open...who knows...Doesn't mean a thing...Can't lock a man up for leaving a door open anyway...and that's the end of that issue. But I want to warn you all that you're pissing me off real quick," Wisensee continued, pointing at Weed. "And in case you didn't know...there's a trial going on here," Wisensee added as he looked at both attorneys. "So I'm done with all these outside bullshit distractions like dogs running away and doctors in bars. So any more motions or requests to enter new evidence into this trial will be denied... Two years is enough time to get your acts together...Is that understood?" he added, stopping to look around at everyone's reaction. "This trial is scheduled to end Friday, and come hell or high water, it will end Friday. So that's the end of this nonsense," he said and then told them all that they could leave, as he got up and left without saying another word.

"See what I told you...You should have thought of the photographs earlier," Morgan said as they left the judge's chambers.

Was going to have to undo this dog fiasco pretty damn quick, Weed thought as he left the courthouse, still reeling from the fact that he so quickly had become a suspect in Hileman's missing dog. No time to dick around, he thought as he walked down the courthouse steps in a half daze thinking about what had just happened... at what he had done. Lying to the judge...What was the penalty for lying to a judge? Wasn't really under oath though. He was just going to have to stick to his story...that he didn't know how the dog got out...and when he found the dog, he never made the connection that it was Hileman's dog. Would have a hard time convincing anyone to believe that explanation now, he imagined. Now he needed to come up with a foolproof plan to get the dog away from Liz and into an animal shelter as quick as possible...before anyone else found out about it...only thing that made any sense, he thought, feeling nauseated from the heat of the morning and the pain of his hand and maybe everything else.

CHAPTER THIRTY-SEVEN

Monday, May 17
10:23 a.m.

He left the courthouse under gray skies and an approaching storm, and people at the festival hurrying everywhere to get under shelter. In the distance, heat lightning and angry clouds. The silvery leaves flapping wildly in the wind above the festival tents as he watched a woman chasing three of her paintings of children down the street...skipping, jumping, running happily along as if they had suddenly come alive.

Had to get the dog back or it might get pretty ugly, he thought as the downpour started. Seemed like he was the only one that had been taken in by his foolish scheme...always the way it was, he knew as he took the bottle of bourbon from under his seat and took a long drink.

Would just go out and get the dog tomorrow while Liz was at work, he thought. And that would mean he would have to go out when the trial recessed for lunch. That was probably the only window of opportunity he would have, he thought as he sipped at his drink and reconsidered.

He could just take the dog from Liz's house and then keep it somewhere until the trial was over for the day, and then just drop it off at an animal shelter somewhere. Maybe after dark when the shelter was closed and no one around to see him, he thought. And then he would at least be finished with another one of his many messes.

He could tell Liz that he had come out to see her, but that she wasn't there…that he had forgot she worked Tuesdays, or something like that, and then maybe he could drop the dog off somewhere at the Quick Fix with Bob for the afternoon while he was in court. He would have to pass the Quick Fix on his way back to the courthouse from Liz's house anyway. Would be a good place to hide a dog for a couple of hours, he imagined. Then he could get the dog after the trial was over for the day.

Would have to run the plan by Bob, though. He didn't want to have a dog and nowhere to leave her when he was due back in court…couldn't bring the dog to court with him, he thought, imagining how ridiculous it all was as he drove toward the Quick Fix.

He would take the dog from Liz's house during the lunch recess, leave it at the Quick Fix with Bob somewhere, pick the dog back up after the trial was over, and then somehow drop the dog off at the animal shelter later. That plan made the some sense, he thought. Was at least logical…and it seemed doable.

He parked in front of the Quick Fix and then watched until all the customers had gone before walking across the street and entering the store.

"I need to get the dog back to Hileman, before it gets any more complicated," he told Bob. "Hileman's attorney already thinks I had something to do with it. He had the judge ask me what I knew about the whole mess."

"Yeah, well, didn't I tell you…I knew it was going to be trouble."

"But anyway, I came up with a plan," Weed said. "I just have to work out all the details. And then I think that it will all work out fine," Weed said as he got a Coke out of one of the coolers.

"What I was thinking about doing, was to go out during the lunch recess from the trial tomorrow and get the dog when Liz is at work. Only opportunity that I'll have when Liz isn't around, and I think that I would have plenty of time, if everything went smoothly. We usually get close to two hours for lunch…sometimes longer. I could get the dog and bring it back here somewhere and leave it for a couple of hours while I finished up at the courthouse…And then I could pick the dog up here and take the damn thing to an animal shelter after it got dark and there was no one around to see me."

"Here?" Bob asked quietly, looking up from a paper he was holding as a customer came in the store. "You mean here…here?"

"Yeah, just for a couple of hours. Maybe keep her in the empty shed out back until I can get back to take her to a shelter."

"Jesus, Ben. I told you I didn't want to get involved."

"That's why I stopped. I just need this one favor. I mean, I have most of it worked out. I think that it's pretty foolproof, but I need someplace to leave the dog for a couple hours while I'm in court…I have to go by the Quick Fix to get from Liz's place back to the courthouse anyway…And it would save me time if I could just drop her off here for a couple of hours," he said as Bob shook his head. "You keep the damn thing here for just a couple of hours, and I'll never ask you to do another thing."

"I don't know, Ben. Don't want to get mixed up in this mess…I mean…Hileman's an important person with all this influence in the city…hard to tell what she might do to me if she found out I was involved…And I could lose this great job," he added sarcastically.

"No one would have to know. I could just bring the dog back here and put her in that old shed in the back. You wouldn't even have to know about it…And then when the trial was over, I could come back and get the dog."

"Yeah, I get it."

"And that would be the end of it. You wouldn't even have to get involved at all. You could deny knowing about any of it…And if someone did find out…I would just deny that you knew anything."

"I don't know, Ben. I need to think about it," he said as another customer came into the store.

"It's just that I have a limited amount of time to pull it off. My only window of opportunity is tomorrow. I have to go out when she's at work and just take the dog. Come up with some kind of a reason for me being out there. Then maybe tell her that when I opened the door that the dog just ran off or that the owners just happened to be standing there and I gave them their dog. I just haven't worked out all the details."

"I don't know. They could consider me an accomplice."

"If anyone finds out, I'll just tell them that you didn't know a thing about it. That I left the dog here without your knowing. No one's going to find out about it anyway. It will be over before you know it."

"I'll have to think about it…Come by later…I'll be finished soon," he said as he moved away from Weed to wait on a customer.

He wouldn't have any room for error and wouldn't have much time to pull it off, he knew as he sat in his car. The noose was getting tighter, he thought, trying to work out the details in his mind. On the surface it didn't seem like a particularly difficult plan. He would have well over an hour. Probably closer to two hours if tomorrow was like all the other days. Would be plenty of time, he thought, trying to calculate the exact time it would take…Half hour out to Liz's house, ten minutes to get the dog, a half hour back, and then another ten to drop the dog off at the Quick Fix. Would still have some time left over if things went smoothly, he thought.

Would have to make up some kind of story to tell Liz about what happened to the dog too.

He would have to give her some legitimate-sounding reason why he had to go out to her house and didn't know exactly what excuse it would be. And then maybe tell her that the owners showed up when he was there...or better, that they were waiting when he got there...that would sound more believable...that they had seen one of the posters she had put up...and there they were and there was nothing he could do but to give them their dog. That sounded like a plausible explanation why the dog was gone, he thought.

Maybe call her when he was finished getting the dog...when he was still out there...and tell her what had happened. Tell her that there was nothing he could do. That they wanted their dog back. Maybe make up something about kids crying, all happy to have their dog back. She might buy that. Might sound more believable if he threw in some details like that. She might get suspicious if it didn't sound legitimate, he thought. Tell her how bad he felt since he knew how much she liked the dog.

Maybe he could tell her that he had lost his wallet Saturday night when he was out there and needed to look around the house to see if he could find it. That he had looked everywhere else and hadn't found it and that was the only place he hadn't looked yet... and he needed his wallet for his license or something...maybe for the trial. That would be excuse enough to explain why he had to go out to her house. Would have to call her first to make sure that she still kept the house key under the flowerpot. That could destroy the whole plan, if he couldn't get in the house when he got there, he knew.

And then when he got there, a man and his two small children were waiting, he would tell her. A small girl and a boy that looked like he was a little older then the girl. What were their names... would have to come up with some names. "Couldn't remember the girl's name, but the boy's name was maybe Jeremy or something," he could tell her. Make it all sound believable.

That had to be his plan, but it would have to go smoothly. The time was tight, he thought. Couldn't fool around chasing a dog all over the house. Had to get in and out of the house in less than ten minutes, max...that was the critical part. Should be doable, he thought...if the dog cooperated, which was a big unknown too. Then he could bring the dog back and leave it at the Quick Fix, call Liz and tell her what had happened, and then get back to court. That had to be the plan. Nothing too complicated. He could do it.

Then he could pick the dog up at the Quick Fix after court had been adjourned for the day and just drop the dog off at an animal shelter later when it was dark and no one was around the place to see him.

Should maybe make a trial run, he thought. Just to make sure he hadn't left something out. Didn't want any surprises. Make sure that he had enough time. Didn't want to be late getting back to the courthouse. Didn't want anyone to suspect anything, he thought.

Would be doable if everything went well, he tried to reassure himself. As long as there were no delays in the trial, and no traffic problems, and no problems with the dog, and he could get into Liz's house.

And Bob would probably agree to keep the dog at the store for a couple hours. He could drop it off at the Quick Fix on his way back to the courthouse and then pick the dog up after the trial ended. Then take the dog somewhere safe and wait until it was dark when he could drop it off safely at the animal shelter without anyone seeing him. Maybe take the dog out to the old reservoir. No one ever went out there anymore, he knew.

Would drive by the shelter on his way home tonight, he thought. Just to make sure the shelter still had cages placed outside the building for people to drop off stray animals when the shelter was closed.

The plan sounded reasonably simple. Something so Liz wouldn't get too suspicious. And then he would be done with at least one more of his pain-in-the-ass problems.

Should never have taken Hileman's dog. Was causing him way more grief than it would ever cause Hileman, he knew, as he watched all the people running for shelter when the rain started falling hard again.

He drove around for a while thinking about his plans before driving back to the Quick Fix and waiting for Bob to finish his shift.

"Listen," Bob said when he had finished waiting on a customer and before Weed had a chance to say anything. "You can leave the damn dog here, but I don't want to know anything about it… But you're not going to be able to leave her in that shed out back. There's not enough room and it's too hot in there. You can just leave her in the men's room at the side of the building. You can lock the door and put the Out of Order sign on the door. It's locked and out of order most of the time, anyway…And if anyone asks, I'll just tell them to use the women's restroom."

"I appreciate it," Weed said, feeling somewhat relieved that one of his problems had been solved. "Wouldn't work if I couldn't leave her here, and I'll take all the blame if anything goes wrong…which it won't."

It would have to do, Weed thought as he walked around to the back of the Quick Fix and unlocked the door to the men's room to have a look. He held open the heavy door as he looked inside at the small, smelly, graffiti-filled room that looked like it hadn't been cleaned in years. Wasn't the Waldorf…but it would have to do, he imagined as he came back around to the front of the store.

"Looks fine," he told Bob, even though he didn't really like the thought of leaving the dog in a place like that for probably close to three hours. Seemed like too many chances for something to go wrong.

"I want to make a test run to see just how long it's going to take me tomorrow," Weed told Bob as they both got into his car.

"I'll have maybe an hour and a half tomorrow. Maybe more, but I don't know for sure since Hileman pulled her little charade…

might delay things…so I just want to see how long it will actually take…and try to factor in anything that might go wrong," he said as he started the drive back toward the courthouse.

When he got there, he had Bob check the time and then drove what he was sure was the quickest route out of town…driving just under the speed limit to make sure that the cops didn't pull him over tomorrow.

"I'm going to have to call Liz tomorrow on my way out to her house," Weed said. "I think I know where she keeps her spare key, but it's been a while, and I'm afraid she might have hidden it somewhere else like she has a habit of doing. If I get out there and I can't find the key to get into the house, then the plan's finished. And that bothers me. That's a real unknown. If she doesn't answer and I can't find a key, I'm screwed," he said as they moved further down the highway.

He could see Liz's car parked in the driveway and the two large LOST DOG signs she had put up as they slowly drove by.

"Twenty-four minutes," Bob said, looking at his watch.

A little longer than Weed had expected. Wouldn't take any longer than ten minutes to get the dog out of the house if things went as planned, he imagined as he started the drive back to town… driving first past the Quick Fix before driving through the city and back to the courthouse. Just under an hour and twenty minutes total. Add ten minutes to get the dog out of the house, and maybe another ten minutes here or there for unforeseen circumstance. Was cutting it pretty close, he knew.

"Plenty enough time…You could almost stop for a drink," Bob said with a laugh as he got out of the car in front of the Quick Fix. "And remember, I don't know a thing about any of this."

Would be pretty tight on time, but it could be done, he thought as he pulled into Walgreen's to get a stronger antibiotic and some pain pills for his hand. Hand looked a little better, but he couldn't risk having a swollen hand slowing him down tomorrow when he was trying to get things done quickly. Including trying to get an unpredictable dog out of the house and into his car, he thought as he stood in line at the pharmacy.

It was when he saw the crayons and the construction paper sitting on the pharmacy shelf beside him that he thought about it. A thought that just sort of sprang into his mind, like the thought that had sprung into his mind the night he had taken Hileman's dog. Might be more believable if he left a note for Liz…a note that looked like it had been written by a child…a note thanking her for caring for their dog…he reasoned as he stood in line. Would add more believability to his story, he thought as he picked up the pack of multicolored paper and then a box of crayons. Physical evidence…tangible evidence was always better…something to verify his story. He liked it…Icing on the cake.

What was he doing? he thought after standing in line for another couple of minutes ridiculously holding the colored paper and box of crayons…like a small child. Was he losing his mind? Maybe it was the fever from his hand causing him to not think clearly. How much more absurd could he get? How much more deviously juvenile could he make the situation? he thought. She would just have to believe what he told her…didn't need some ridiculous crayon note from a child to convince her, he thought as he put the crayons and paper back on the shelf.

But by the time he was ready to leave the pharmacy he had changed his mind again impulsively, and he took the crayons and colorful construction paper back off the shelf. Had to at least leave the option open, he thought as he paid the clerk and then walked back to his car. Give him time to think about it.

Wasn't really all that ridiculous, he thought, putting the crayons and paper under his seat and then taking a drink of bourbon. Might prevent him from having to answer a bunch of stupid Liz questions later. Would sleep on it, he thought.

He would get the dog tomorrow. Tell Liz he had found his wallet and then tell her about the kids and their father waiting on the porch. That they had seen one of the posters she had put up.

And then just hope that Liz would never find out what actually happened. Probably by the time she figured it all out it wouldn't really matter, he thought as he sat in the car and took two of the pills that he had just bought.

Plan wasn't perfect, but should work, he thought as he drove slowly past the animal shelter. The cages were still there beside the shelter, just like he remembered. Could put the dog in one of the cages after the shelter had closed and when it was dark with no one around to see him. Then he would be done with the damn dog, he thought as he finished his drive home.

Sandy and Helen were sitting at the picnic table in the back yard drinking and putting up more decorations when he arrived home...drunk and all excited about the anniversary party.

He talked for a while, telling them about Turzak and Hileman's dog, but they were both too giddy and drunk to care what he was saying.

He was dead tired...would have a big day tomorrow, he thought... going over the plan in his head once and then again...wondering how a grown man could be doing something so perverse and depraved as this...before he finally drifted off into a deep, fitful sleep.

CHAPTER THIRTY-EIGHT

Tuesday, May 18
7:15 a.m.

Sometime during the night he thought he heard a motorcycle in the street outside his window, but when he got up and stood at the window in the dark and pulled back the curtain just a little to look out, he saw nothing for as far down the street that he could see. Maybe it was just his imagination, he thought, or maybe it had all just been a dream...But after that dream, he was unable to sleep.

He held his hand in front of the mirror, as if the reflection of his swollen hand might be easier to accept if he didn't have to look at it directly. Maybe looked a little better, he thought, as he tried to open and close it a couple of times. Antibiotics must be working. Couldn't do the fine work of surgery with a hand that swollen, but he could probably use it to pick up a small dog and to lay his hand on a bible without anyone noticing...he hoped.

Sandy was still sleeping soundly when he left the room. Sleeping off her hangover from the night before. Maybe it was her new medication that was making her act so strange, he thought as he flipped through the morning newspaper...but he couldn't concentrate on anything other than his plans for the day...trying to determine if he should risk it at all...that maybe there was a better, safer solution to his dog problem.

Just one small article in the newspaper about the trial...a recap of each day's testimony including Monday's suspension without any explanation. Nothing really too bad for his side...maybe overall the trial was close to a draw, he thought. But nothing in the newspaper about the shooting...and nothing about the police arresting Pickles. Three days since he had talked to the cops and there was still nothing much about the shooting...maybe it would all just go away, he thought as he drank some orange juice and took one of Sandy's Valium pills and then put a few more in his shirt pocket to take later if necessary.

Bob would be at the Quick Fix by now, he thought as he started his drive into the city. He was going to call and make sure that everything was still okay with him. Didn't want to show up with a dog and nowhere to leave it, he thought as he dialed Bob's cell.

"Everything's fine, but if anything happens, remember, I don't know a thing," Bob answered before Weed could say anything. "I'll tell them that I don't even know who you are," he said, sounding as if he had a lot more doubts today than he had yesterday.

"Don't worry, nothing's going to happen," Weed said as he took a sip of his drink. "I should be there around one thirty. If there's a problem, I'll call," Weed reminded him before he ended the call.

He sipped his bourbon as he sat parked in front of the courthouse.

The idea was probably pretty juvenile, but it was still maybe a good idea, he thought as he tentatively reached for the crayons and construction paper under his seat. Why not? Couldn't hurt, he thought as he ripped the cellophane off the pack and pulled out a yellow piece of construction paper and then took a red crayon from the box. He had to think about the words a six-year-old might use and how a child that age would form the letters to make it all seem believable. Big block letters with overlapping lines and words that drifted off unevenly across the page. And he was going to print at least one of the letters backward. If anyone saw what he was doing they would think he was crazy, he knew, somewhat embarrassed that it had come down to this…to this depravity.

"Thanks for finding my dog," sounded the best, and he could leave the *ing* off the end of *finding*. All words that a six- or seven-year-old was likely to know and use, he thought looking at the sloppy red letters that he had just printed across the yellow paper. Then he signed the name *Adam* in block letters and then in even more primitive letters, he wrote the name *Erin* with the letter *e* backward. He held it up and looked at it. For some reason it didn't look like a note written by a six-year-old. He took it back down and then drew three crude hearts and a couple of sloppy Xs and 0s. That's what it needed but also needed to be a little more six-ish, he thought as he wrote it all out again, a little more sloppy this time, now making some of the lines not meet, and the circles less round and the Xs with unequal lines. He repeated it one more time before laying all three on the seat beside him and picking out the one that he thought looked the best…and then held it up in front of him just to make sure that there was nothing that would give him away, before putting it on top of the stack of paper and then putting them all under the seat, holding them all down with his bottle of bourbon. Maybe he was an artist, he thought wistfully.

Even he thought that the thank-you note was a nice touch, now. Might cheer Liz up a little seeing the note of appreciation and hearing the story he was going to tell her. Anything to prevent her from asking a bunch of inane bullshit questions, he thought…And now he had a failsafe explanation of why the dog was no longer at her house.

He would call Liz when he had almost reached her house. Tell her that he was going out to look for his wallet, and that he had thought he might have dropped it behind the couch…when he had been trying to get away from her…but he wouldn't put it that way. And then he would ask her if she minded him looking around her house, which she wouldn't, and then he would ask her where she kept the extra key to the house to make sure that it was still under the flowerpot. Just hoped that she answered her phone, he thought as he left his car and walked up the street toward the courthouse.

"Morning," a man's voice said from behind him as he stood waiting for the light to change.

When Weed turned, a short man in a cheap-looking suit, wearing a plaid hat and holding a clipboard, smiled and offered him a business card.

"Hank Tucci," he said and then mumbled something about being a licensed private investigator as Weed looked at the card. "Ms. Hileman has retained me to investigate the disappearance of her dog," he said and then held out his hand for Weed to shake.

"Sorry. Had a little accident," Weed answered, holding up his swollen hand to show him and then quickly pulling it back before the man could get a good look…But he felt suddenly shaken by the fact that he now had a private investigator to deal with.

The man unfolded one of the fliers that Weed recognized as the one the Girl Scouts had been handing out two days earlier. He handed it to Weed. Jesus, first the Girl Scouts and now a private eye, he thought as he looked at the poster like it was the first time he had ever seen it, before trying to hand it back to the man.

"I'm sure you've heard about Ms. Hileman's dog by now. Damn dog disappeared at the banquet last Saturday night," he added. "And I understand that you were at that banquet…And I've been questioning anyone that might know anything," he said, waiting for Weed to respond.

"Sorry, don't know a thing," Weed answered, trying to sound as sympathetic as he could. "Wasn't even there when it happened…But my wife told me about it later. I guess I must have left the country club long before it happened," Weed told him as the light changed and they both started across the street.

"At first we thought the dog got loose and ran out the back door and off through the field. But after we spent most of Saturday night and Sunday morning scouring the whole area with a fine-tooth comb, we didn't find a thing...not even one paw print. So we figured something else had to have happened to the dog," he said, somewhat out of breath now and trying to keep up with Weed.

"And then I talked to Hileman's driver...You know him? The guy that takes care of the dog?" he asked as they continued toward the courthouse.

Weed shook his head and shrugged his shoulders and acted like he didn't know what the private investigator was talking about.

"Yeah, says he remembered you. Said he even talked to you once or twice...and remembered seeing you at the banquet. Well, maybe you don't remember him..." he added after Weed didn't respond.

"I don't know. Maybe he has me confused with someone else," Weed mumbled.

"Yeah, maybe. But I got to talking to him, and he's certain that there was no way that the dog could have gotten loose on its own... without someone's help. And the other thing...and I know that you're in a hurry," he said, seemingly having a difficult time keeping up with Weed because of a noticeable limp, "but the other thing is that you might have been the last person to see the dog. Seems that a couple of people saw you leaving about the same time that the dog disappeared. And that you probably had to walk right by the dog on your way out that back door past the restrooms?"

"Sorry. Can't really help you with that. As I recall, I don't remember even seeing a dog that night," he said as they stood in the line to go through security.

"It's just that Ms. Hileman and a few other people have this crazy idea that you might have had something to do with it all. Given the trial and everything...that you had sort of a motive...that you've been pretty upset and pissed off and that you maybe wanted to get back at her somehow. If you know what I mean," he added.

"I mean, her dog ran away," Weed said turning back toward him, irritated, trying to brush off his accusations as absurd. "She's going to blame me for this, too? Blames me for everything else, may as well blame me for losing her dog too," Weed said, shaking his head in disbelief. "It's ridiculous, anyway. I don't care about her damn dog and wouldn't stoop to do something that stupid. I think I'm a little beyond that sort of thing," he added, trying to sound convincing.

"Yeah, that's what I've been telling Ms. Hileman…that she's probably wrong about you. That a grown man and respected surgeon in the community wouldn't do something as…what did you say…'as ridiculous as this,' but that's what she thinks happened. She thinks that you took her dog to get back at her. That you just carried her off…because as hard as we tried, we couldn't find even one muddy dog print anywhere, he repeated. "So she thinks that someone just picked up her dog and carried her off," he said, lighting up a cigarette as they moved closer to the walk-through metal detector. "But we're just hopeful that we can get the dog back before anything bad happens to her. I guess the dog's sick and needs some kind of medication," he said and then took a long drag off his cigarette. "We're just hoping that whatever happened, the dog is still all right."

"Dogs run away all the time. Someone carelessly leaves the door open, and the dog's going to get out. Happens all the time," Weed said, trying not to act like he was in pain as he removed his cell phone from his belt to put through the X-ray machine.

"Well, I do appreciate your cooperation. I know that you're going to have a busy day, so I'll let you get going. I'm pretty sure that we're close to solving it anyway. Could be some serious problems for anyone that was involved though," the private detective said, watching Weed's hand closely as he put his phone in a tray.

"Looks nasty...Looks like it's infected," the private investigator said, trying to get an even closer look at his hand and then adding, "I think that you're an okay guy, and I'm going to tell Ms. Hileman what you told me, but if you think of anything, or pick up any tips where the dog might be, I'll be close by, so give me a call," he said and pointed to the business card that Weed was still holding. "Don't want it to get all ugly. You know, bring up a bunch of other things that someone might not want people to know about. I mean, that's my job, finding out things people don't want other people to know about, if you get my drift," he said as he moved back away from the line.

"Sorry," Weed said.

If he had gotten the "drift" of it? What was that supposed to mean? What else did this guy know about him? he thought as another wave of anxiety moved through him. Could know about the shooting and Candy and who knew what else, he supposed...might even know about Liz.

Weed watched as the private investigator limped away slowly, and for an instant thought about calling him back to tell him the whole ridiculous story and end it all. To tell him that it was all meant to be just a big joke and apologize. Or maybe just to stick with his standby story, that he had just found the dog along the highway and didn't realize whose dog it was. "That was Hileman's dog?" he could say and laugh incredulously at the revelation. But he didn't. Was too risky, and too late for that, and he wasn't sure that the investigator wouldn't arrest him right on the spot, he thought as he moved toward the courtroom.

Now he would have to worry about what the private investigator knew about his life, and to make damn sure that he was nowhere around when he started his drive out to Liz's house to get the dog. His life was almost getting too complicated to keep it all straight, Weed thought.

Less than seventy-two hours and there was already a detective on his ass...watching his every move...who probably knew about the shooting…and probably Candy too. Using that as a veiled threat… that's what it had to be…the only thing that made any sense. He was getting in deeper by the minute, he thought as he awkwardly put his shoes back on using only his good hand.

Weed sat in the courtroom, watching and listening to Morgan question another of their expert witnesses, but he couldn't concentrate. He could only think about all the implications of what had just happened and how it was now even more important to get rid of the dog…And everything already seemed out of synch and jumbled with his plan, as if his plan was already doomed, he thought, becoming more anxious as the critical time approached.

It seemed to him that the witnesses were taking too long with their answers and the time was passing too quickly. He had to have at least an hour and a half to safely carry out his plan, but if the attorneys and the witnesses continued to piss around with their stupid redundant questions and answers, then his plan would be screwed and he would have to come up with some other plan to get rid of the dog, he knew as he looked at his watch impulsively again. Almost an hour for the first witness and then a fifteen-minute break before the second witness took the stand…a neurologist who seemed to speak even slower than the first witness while using a small human model to explain things in detail. But he looked more like a bad ventriloquist's act than an expert witness, Weed thought as he tried to mentally move him along more quickly.

He had to be out of the courthouse by twelve thirty at the latest and everyone was just pissing around, he thought. And worse, he felt like he was going to have to urinate soon…something that he had failed to take into account when he had made his trial run yesterday…and something that could use up some of his precious time.

If he had to he would just urinate outside Liz's house when he got there, he thought as he watched the second-hand turn on the clock behind the judge's head, realizing he hadn't heard much of anything that had been said all morning.

But at exactly 12:21 p.m., somewhat unexpectedly and to Weed's relief, Turzak turned to the judge and told him he was finished questioning the witness.

He had made it with a little time to spare, he thought as he crossed the street against the light…checking over his shoulder for any signs of the private investigator before getting in his car and driving off. He was on the clock now, he thought, pressing the accelerator down as the car groaned to life.

CHAPTER THIRTY-NINE

Tuesday, May 18
12:43 p.m.

He hadn't thought about the possiblity that his crappy car might not make it out to Liz's house and back again. Would just have to hold his breath and pray, he thought as he listened to it rattle on, sounding worse than usual.

He was making good time through the light traffic and was encouraged by the fact that he was getting mostly green lights. If everything else went as smoothly he would be okay, he thought as he took out his phone and called Liz.

No answer…just her voice mail. That's what he was afraid might happen. He left a message for her to call as soon as possible, trying to make it sound as urgent as he could.

Liz usually picked up her messages pretty quickly, he knew. Wasn't absolutely necessary that she call back anyway…if he was lucky. He could still maybe find the key without her help, he imagined, but it would be a whole lot easier if he knew exactly where to look.

Was going to have to piss soon, too…but didn't want to waste precious time stopping somewhere now. He would just urinate in Liz's yard somewhere when he got to her house. Could hold it that long, he imagined as he repositioned himself in the seat in hopes that it would lessen his urge.

He had made good time, he thought as he finally made the turn into Liz's driveway, checking the rearview mirror to make sure that there was still no sign of anyone following him. He urinated as fast as he could behind one of the bushes in Liz's yard.

At least Liz wasn't home, he thought as he started up the sidewalk toward the house.

There were at least fifty potted plants lining the front porch… more than he had remembered, he realized as he began his search for the key. Going up one side of the porch lifting pots and then down the other side as fast as he could go, until he had lifted them all without finding a thing. Standing alarmed for a few seconds before starting his search all over again but wondering now if he might have to risk it, break a window to get inside, and then just hope that no one called the police or that he didn't set off some kind of screwy alarm system that she might have. He could tell Liz that it had been a real emergency, and that he would pay her to have the window replaced…She would understand, he imagined just as his cell phone began to vibrate with Liz's number coming up on the screen.

"Got your message…You okay?" she asked, sounding alarmed.

"Yeah, I'm fine, but I think I might have lost my wallet out at your house when I was there the other night. Looked everywhere else, and your house is the last place I can remember having it, and of course I need it now for some paperwork at the courthouse," he told her.

"Oh, I thought that something really bad had happened to you."

"No, just the wallet, but I thought I would drive out and look and then realized that you were probably at work today. Actually,

I'm almost at your house now and thought if you didn't mind, I would take a look around inside to see if I could find it.

"That's fine. But if you want to wait ten or fifteen minutes, I can come out and help you look…I'm not very busy here anyway, and it only takes me about ten minutes to get home."

"Yeah, that would be great if I wasn't in such a hurry. I have the trial, you know…And have to be back in town in less than half hour…So I really don't have that much time. Just going to take a quick look and then leave," he told her, hoping that she wouldn't persist. "You still keep your spare key under the flowerpot?"

"Actually, I moved the key to one of those key holders that looks like a rock, and it's lying right next to the sundial by the steps…You should be able to find it pretty easy when you get there."

Luck was on his side, he thought, already spotting the sundial and the stone.

"And If you can't find it, I'll look around later when I get home," she added. "And remember the dog is there…So don't let her get out," she added before they ended their conversation.

She seemed to buy it, he thought. As he unlocked and pushed open the front door, the dog began to jump around and bark vigorously.

No way that she could make it out here from where she worked in less than then, and by then he would be long gone…and the dog would be gone too, he thought, relieved now that the main concern of how he was going to get into the house was behind him. He could just scoop up the dog now, leave the note, and head back to the city.

The dog barked harder as he approached, jumping forward and then sliding back, growling and baring her teeth a couple times.

"You remember me," Weed said softly, trying to calm her, and then he called her by her name that he had seen on the poster… Pepper…and then offered her a small piece of candy that he had broken off a candy bar.

The dog looked fine, he thought as he watched her eat the first piece of chocolate and then another. Dog definitely didn't look like it was sick, he thought, breaking off another piece of chocolate and then another until he was close enough that he could reach down and pick her up.

He lifted her gently and then petted her softly one the head as he repeated her name, and then carried her, without incident, to the car. He sat her on the seat beside him like he had done before, but this time she just sat there calmly waiting for him to break off another piece of chocolate. At least he hadn't gotten bitten this time, he thought.

The hard part was over, he knew as he took the bottle of bourbon off the note he had written for Liz and carried it back to the house.

He stood in the living room for a moment looking around, trying to decide the best place to leave the note before placing it in the middle of the coffee table. He stood back to see if it looked authentic and then turned it slightly to a better angle. Note looked good, he thought…checking it again to make sure that he had not made any glaring mistakes that would give him away. But he was convinced that it looked authentic…like a note written by a young child…feeling satisfied that the note would add credibility to his story.

She would definitely believe his story now, he thought as he replaced the key.

The hard part would be calling her back and giving her his explanation of why the dog was no longer at the house. She would be upset, maybe even a little pissed at him, but he didn't care. Wasn't her dog anyway…and he would just tell her he would get her another mutt if he had to. He wanted to end the relationship anyway, and this could only help, he imagined.

No one in sight, he thought, looking around at a few distant houses. No one had seen what he had done, he was almost certain as he backed down the long driveway to the main road and then started his drive back into town with the dog calmly beside him.

"You'll never guess…"he said, saying it out loud, practicing what he was going to tell Liz as the dog looked at him strangely…trying to sound as convincing and believable as he could…but he would have to wait until he dropped the dog off at the Quick Fix before he made the call. Didn't want to risk having to explain why a dog was barking in the background after he had already told her that the owners had driven off with Pepper.

Good thinking…for once, he thought as he checked his speed and the rearview mirror and then his watch. And what could he have done? They wanted their dog, and he didn't know what else to do, but to just let them take her…and legally there was probably nothing else he could have done. "They had pictures of the dog and everything, and the kids were so excited, and the dog was excited to see them…" he would tell her. And that they had been waiting there on her porch for almost an hour. "Yeah…they had seen one of the posters in front of the house." And then he could tell her about the two kids and the note that they had left her. She would buy it, he thought…especially with the kids and the note.

It was always difficult for him to make his lies seem believable to others, he knew…his stories always sounded like lies…even when they weren't. A conditioned guilty reflex always gave him away… thanks to his mother never believing him probably, he thought as he approached the halfway mark back to the city, checking the time. Still had plenty of time, he thought as he dialed Bob's cell phone.

Now, unless the car quit running or fell apart he was going to make it, he thought, surprised that everything had gone so smoothly and then thinking that maybe he should say a short prayer for the car…a prayer that it didn't quit running at such a critical time in his life…and then he did. He had made many ridiculous prayers in his life, he knew as he listened to Bob's cell phone ring.

"You ready?" he asked when Bob finally answered.

"You got the dog?"

"I have her, and I'm on my way. Should be there in about fifteen minutes," Weed told him.

"Fine," Bob said with disgust in his tone. "And you'll be back before five?"

"Before that, if the trial ends sooner."

"Good. When you get back, just take the dog, and keep the key. I don't want to get any more involved…already kicking myself," he said. "I know nothing, and I'm going to deny everything," he added.

"Fine. Don't worry. Nothing's going to go wrong," he told Bob… and for once, he felt that he might be right.

CHAPTER FORTY

Tuesday, May 18
1:09 p.m.

He drove slowly past the Quick Fix to make sure Hileman's private investigator was nowhere in sight before pulling his car around to the back of the store and out of sight.

But when he tried to open the restroom door it was locked, and someone grumbled that he would "be out in a minute," before Weed walked around to the front of the store.

"You're just going to have to wait until he comes out," Bob said before Weed could even say a word.

"You let someone use the restroom when you knew how critical it was that I get this thing done?"

"Well, what can I say...he's a good customer, and he's already been in there twenty minutes so he should be out any minute...I mean, how was I supposed to know he was going to be in there half the day? And anyway, you're early."

"I got exactly twenty-three minutes to get back to the court-house," Weed said, irritated.

"Jesus, then just knock on the damn door and tell him to get a move on," Bob said softly, acting as if he wasn't talking to Weed as a customer walked by…and then mumbled something about ingratitude and getting screwed.

Weed wanted to say something to Bob about stupidity but instead just walked around to the back of the store and waited.

Knew it was going too smoothly to go off without some hitch, he thought as he sat in the car with the dog. Might all come unraveled because of some asshole taking a dump, he thought as he took a sip of bourbon and checked the time.

How long could someone stay in that smelly place? Weed thought as the dog sniffed around at the candy bar in Weed's shirt pocket. He broke her off another piece and laid it on the seat in front of her and then went back to watching the restroom door.

He would drive back to the Quick Fix as soon as the trial ended and get the dog, he thought, and then he would drive out to the abandoned reservoir and wait there with the dog until it was dark. Was a safe place to wait…no one went out there anymore, he knew. Then he could drop the dog off at the animal shelter when it was dark and no one was around to see him. That was what was left to his plan…the easy part, he imagined. Then it would all be over… then he wouldn't have to worry anymore about Hileman and her dog or her damn gimpy private investigator.

Weed waited for another couple of minutes before walking over and rattling the restroom's doorknob loudly once and then again, hoping that whoever was in there would get the idea that someone was waiting to use the restroom.

"Be out in a second, buster," a gruff voice complained from inside the restroom after the third time he pulled at the doorknob. But it was nearly another five minutes before the door opened and a large, overweight man with a sweaty red face came lumbering out, carrying a newspaper under his arm and picking at the seat of his pants as he walked.

"Finally," Weed said, disgusted and loud enough for the man to hear. The man looked vaguely familiar, Weed thought as the man slowed to take a better look inside his car, before suddenly stopping all together.

"I know you...you're doctor Weed," the man said, smiling and holding up his finger as if he had just remembered...and then handed the restroom key to Weed through the open window.

"Didn't realize it was someone important waiting...got interested in this newspaper story and lost track of the time, he added, holding the newspaper out in front of him for Weed to see. "I'm Carson Realto...they call me Kit. I'm related to your second wife Sandy," he said, staring back at Weed for some acknowledgement. "Peg Stimson is my aunt, and Sandy's my first cousin. You know," he said as Weed shook his sweaty hand and acted like maybe he remembered who he was.

"How you been doing?" the man asked with a slight southern accent, acting as if they were old friends.

"Real good," Weed answered, but all he could think of was that someone who knew him had just witnessed him with Hileman's dog. What were the chances of him running into someone he knew? Bad luck, and now he was more pissed at Bob, he realized as the man bent down to get a better look at the dog while Weed tried to block his view by getting out of the car.

"Cute little pooch," he said, backing away from the car as Weed got out. "I didn't know you and San had a dog," he added before offering the newspaper to Weed.

"My wife tells me to use the bathroom down here when we're having company...says I stink up the place," he continued as they both moved toward the restroom. "Commode doesn't flush right either, so be careful..."

"Yeah, well, thanks for the warning…and it was real good seeing you. And I'll tell Sandy I saw you," Weed said as he opened the door and stepped inside, happy to finally get away from the man. And then he stood there quietly listening for the man to leave. Would just have to tell Sandy that he didn't know what the hell she was talking about if she ever ask him about seeing him, he thought. He would tell her that the man must have been confused about who he had seen.

Smell inside the small cubicle was overwhelmingly nauseating, Weed thought. Another world inside, torture, the smell so bad, the room the size of a broom closet, the walls marred with graffiti…standing wedged between the door and the dirty commode as unflushed turds raced hopelessly around the inside of the brown-stained bowl…spinning slowly like a horse race, he imagined…he didn't want to take one more breath.

He didn't need to get into a long conversation with one of Sandy's hick relatives, he thought as he just stood quietly for a while, trying to take as few breaths as possible, reading the graffiti on the walls, and waiting long enough to make sure that Sandy's cousin… or whoever he was…was gone.

Little poems and phone numbers and a crude pencil drawing of a penis drawn across the back wall…all looking like a poor Salvador Dali etching. Wonder what Frank would say about that art work, he thought.

But for some reason it sounded like Sandy's cousin was still standing outside the door…rocking slowly back and forth on the loose gravel.

Weed against his better judgment flushed the commode to make his visit sound legitimate, but the commode just filled slowly with more water and started the crap spinning again…and rising slowly to the top as if it might jump ship, he thought as he held his breath and watched apprehensively. Didn't need shit on the floor to deal with, too, he thought. He finally gave out a sigh of relief as the turds slowed and the water began to fall. What a life, he thought. Could it get any lower than this? Not likely, he imagined.

But he had been right…when he opened the door to leave, Sandy's cousin was still standing outside.

"Didn't I tell you? Pretty nasty in there," he laughed. "And I been complaining about it for months, and they still haven't fixed the damn thing," he added. "But I just wanted to tell you that we're going to be coming to your anniversary party this Saturday, and if there's anything you want us to do to help out, just let us know… Tina makes a pretty fair macaroni salad. And that reminded me that she has an appointment to see you next week about her gallbladder," he said as they started walking around to the front of the building.

Weed didn't know if he should get back in the car and drive off with the dog and come back later when the man was gone or just wait for him to leave. But whatever, the man was wasting his precious time.

"What do they charge to have your gallbladder out these days?" he asked as they entered the Quick Fix, but Weed didn't answer.

Bob looked surprised when they entered together talking.

"Sandy's cousin," Weed said, giving him a dirty look.

But Bob just shrugged his shoulders as if he didn't have an answer.

"You want one," the man asked Weed, holding out a bottle of Coke.

Weed shook his head that he didn't and then told him him he had to get going.

"Yeah, you got that trial thing going on, and I wouldn't want you to leave that dog in that hot car back there for very long," he added as Weed left the store.

Weed drove around the block and then called Bob on his cell. "Is he gone yet?" I got to get back to the courthouse and I still have the damn dog."

"He's leaving right now," Bob told him.

"You see, I told you something was going to go wrong," Bob said, coming around to the back of the station with a yellow Out of Order sign after Weed had returned. "Now he knows I'm part of this fiasco."

"Yeah, well, you should have thought of that before you gave him the key…and now he knows that I had Hileman's dog," Weed added as he took the sign from Bob and hung it on the restroom door.

"Shit, see, I told you not to bring the damn dog back here."

"Relax, it will all be over in a couple of hours, and no one will find out. So, just keep an eye on the mutt and I'll take care of everything else," Weed told him as he went to get the dog.

"And just hope that he doesn't say anything to anyone about the dog," Bob said.

Weed took the dog out of the car and carried it over to the restroom. He filled a small bowl with water and another with some dog food and then left them on the floor before breaking off a few more small pieces of candy for the dog.

"You lay there for a while, and I'll be back in a couple of hours to pick you up," Weed told the dog as the door closed. Sort of felt bad leaving the dog…for the dog getting caught in the middle of a fight that she had nothing to do with. The dog was really a pretty nice dog…wouldn't want anything to happen to her, he thought.

He made sure the door was locked, checked the position of the sign, and then put the restroom key into the pocket of his suit jacket.

The dog would be fine in there for just a couple of hours, he assured himself as he started his drive back to the courthouse.

As far as he was concerned, he had completed the most critical part of his plan, he thought, feeling relieved as he took a few sips of bourbon. A celebration for a job done well done, and the bourbon would give him a little more nerve to tell Liz the bad news, he figured as he dialed her number.

"I found it. Wallet was laying right there between the end table and the couch," he said when Liz answered.

"That's great. I'm surprised I didn't see it when I cleaned."

"Yeah, but you're not going to believe what happened," he said, pausing to let her ask what he was talking about, but she said nothing.

"When I got to your house there was a car parked in your drive-way, and there was a man and his two small children waiting on your front porch holding one of those lost-and-found posters that you put up the other day. They said they had been looking all over for their dog and had seen the poster."

"You're kidding."

"No, I'm not. But anyway, there was not much that I could do. When they saw the dog and the dog saw them, they just all sort of went crazy. The dog jumped around all over the kids and then the dog just followed them to their car," he said. "Guy was really grate-ful and wanted to leave you some money for taking care of the dog, but I told him he didn't need to," he said, pausing and thinking that Liz might say something, but she just remained silent.

"But anyway, the man wanted me to tell you how thankful he was for what you did for him and his children and told me that he was going to call you later to thank you...So I gave him your num-ber. I hope that you didn't mind."

"No. No. That's what I figured. Someone would eventually come for the dog," she said, sounding somewhat disappointed. "No big deal, I guess. They live close?

"Yeah, not too far...I think."

"They give you their names?"

"Yeah, yeah they did...wrote it down somewhere," he told her but then wished he hadn't. Would just tell her later that he couldn't find the paper or he had lost their phone number or something. "I'll give it to you later when I have more time."

"Kids not in school?"

"Yeah, that's a good question…Don't know…maybe they're too young or something…But they were all really excited. They even wrote you a thank-you note…and left it for you on the coffee table. Sorry."

"Not your fault, but I was sort of getting used to having a dog around. Actually it was pretty nice company," she told him.

He was amazed at how well it had gone. She didn't seem to suspect a thing as far as he could tell.

"But I'm on my way back to the courthouse, so I better get going. Maybe we can get together this weekend sometime," he said and then told her that he would call her later, even though he knew he never would.

She acted a little upset, but not as bad as he thought she might be. At least it was over, and as far as he could tell, she had bought the story.

He had done it, he thought as he arrived back at the courthouse, relieved at what he'd just accomplished. And soon, his dog problems would all be completely behind him…and he'd finally feel satisfied about something that he'd done successfully…had been a long time, he knew.

CHAPTER FORTY-ONE

Tuesday, May 18
1:14 p.m.

Had completed his mission with almost ten minutes to spare, and with only one small glitch. And right in front of their noses, he thought. Now Hileman and her crack private investigator could quit harassing him. She would have her damn mutt back by tomorrow, he thought, taking a drink of bourbon and another Percodan before starting down the street toward the courthouse.

At least he had sort of accomplished what he had set out to do. He had made Hileman's life miserable, even if it had only been for a couple of days, and even if he had suffered just as much as she had...it was worth it, he imagined.

He felt relieved that the worst was over as he approached the steps to the courthouse. Wouldn't be anything to finish up his plan now. Could just drop the dog off at the shelter later, he thought, for the first time noticing Hileman sitting in her wheelchair and her private investigator standing beside her along his path up the sidewalk…and worse, it was already too late to avoid passing near them, he knew as he moved to the far edge of the sidewalk and tried to move by them as quickly as possible.

As he passed, Hileman made some kind of drunken, derogatory comment that he couldn't make out, at the same time moving her cane in his direction as if she might be trying to use it to strike him or trip him…he couldn't decide which…and he felt strangely intimidated. But she was obviously very drunk. He was certain of that.

The detective moved away from Hileman as he passed and then began to follow him up the sidewalk.

"You think about what we talked about?" the investigator asked, limping up beside Weed as Hileman called out another unintelligent but obviously derogatory slur from far behind them.

"Listen. Let's just cut the bullshit. We know you took the dog. We just don't know what you did with her. That's all. You tell us where we can find the dog, and it's all over. We'll forget about everything else. Forget about filing charges against you and making a big embarrassing scene for you to deal with. We'll just start all over with a clean slate. But this is a one-time offer," he added as Weed continued down the street unabated. "She'll understand…You give us her dog back, and she'll give you your life back…might even go easy on you with this trial thing…And the way I understand it, you could use all the help you can get," he continued as he walked slightly behind Weed.

"You know the dog needs medicine, and Ms. Hileman's all bent out of shape over something bad happening to the dog…And anyway, you've proven your point. You had your big laugh, you've gotten your revenge, or whatever bullshit you wanted to prove…So just let us know where we can find the dog," he said as Weed shook his head in a gesture of disbelief before continuing on toward the courthouse. "You see, Hileman's all devastated, thinks you did something bad to her dog…but I told her you're not that kind of person…that you weren't the kind of person that would do something stupid. I told her that it was all just a big joke and that the dog was fine," he said, pausing as they walked a little further.

"And besides that, we could make your life pretty miserable. More miserable than it already is…if you can imagine that. And that's your big problem, because we know a lot of things about you. I mean, that's what I do for a living and I'm good at it. I find out things about people that people don't want me to find out about. You probably think I'm some stupid gumshoe, just standing around doing nothing…But trust me, I've been around. I could find dirt about the pope if you paid me…so this case is a piece of cake," he added as they started up the courthouse steps. "We know about that young stripper that you've been seeing…What's her name? Candy something? The girl your wife doesn't know a thing about," he said, pausing to catch his breath. "And we know all about that shooting thing at that bar that the police are harassing you about too. I even know about that other girl you've been seeing…What's her name?" he said, taking a long drag off of his cigarette and looking at his notepad. "I know a lot of things that could cause you a world of hurt, and all I'm asking is that you tell me where we can find Hileman's dog. You tell us that and it's all over…you won't have to worry about any of this other stuff. But if you don't tell us where we can find the dog, you're probably going to wish you had. Because if you don't, I guarantee we'll destroy what little life you have left," he said, stopping to take another long drag off his cigarette. "You already got enough problems. You don't need all this too. And I just hope for your sake that you didn't do anything stupid with the dog…that the dog's still okay," he said, pausing. "*Is* the dog still okay?" he added, looking over at Weed for the answer.

"Don't know a thing about any damn dog," Weed said but felt anxiously sickened by what Hileman's investigator had just told him…his whole world coming apart because of some stupid prank…his life ruined by his own stupidity, he thought as he stood in line to go through security. Maybe he should say something to give the investigator some kind of a covert sign to let him know that Hileman was going to soon get her dog back unharmed. But didn't know just how to do that.

Weed thought about it for a little while and then turned back toward the investigator to tell him to just be patient, but by then the man had already disappeared somewhere into the crowd.

Might have been a big mistake if he had said something to the investigator, and besides, he still had the upper hand, since he still had the dog, he thought as he stood at the top of the steps. And in less than twenty-four hours, if everything went according to plan, Hileman would have her dog back anyway. Would just have to take his chance until then, and if they thought he had the dog they wouldn't risk doing something to jeopardize getting it back, he surmised as he went through the metal detector and into the court-house. Couldn't worry about it now...He had too many other things on his mind, he thought as he sat down beside Morgan.

"We did all right this morning," Morgan said when he saw Weed. "I think the best day we've had so far," he added as Weed shook his head in agreement. "We have to question two more witnesses today and then just you and Hileman will be left to testify tomorrow...trial should be finished by Thursday, and I think we might make out okay. And even if we do lose the case, the jury might just give her a small award...maybe even less than a million. And then all your money troubles would be over. And I was just thinking...and I mean, I'm not certain...but I was thinking that maybe tomorrow morning when Hileman's on the stand I'll ask her if she's always had to use her wheelchair like she does here in court. And ask her the same thing about the cervical collar too...but not show anyone the photos you gave me. Not until she commits herself, and then I'm going to try and tell them about the country club last year and show them your pictures. Turzak's going to be really pissed and object, but by that time it will be too late. The jury will at least know about it, and Turzak's objection will just make it that much worse," Morgan said. "Might be our coupe de grace," he added as the bailiff led the jurors back into the courtroom. "I've really sort of changed my opinion about the photographs...Maybe it wasn't such a bad idea," Morgan said as the judge called the trial into session.

Weed tried to relax and calm himself down, feeling somewhat satisfied at Morgan's change of heart as Morgan questioned one of their witnesses...a plastic surgeon...going over diagrams of proper methods of repairing facial lacerations and then having the expert witness affirm to the jurors that everything that Dr. Weed had done had been correct and to the highest standards of proper medical care.

Just like they had planned, Weed thought. But they were just more disgusting half-truths and blatant lies, Weed realized...lies that had cost them only five thousand dollars...much better deal than Hileman had gotten for her lies, he thought sarcastically.

He would just backtrack to lose Hileman's investigator and then pick up the dog at the Quick Fix, Weed thought, running his plans over in his mind again as the incessant nonsense continued. Wait with the dog at the abandoned reservoir until it was dark...drop the dog off at the shelter when no one was around...put her in one of the cages outside the shelter and be done with it, he thought.

Would have to stop for something to eat for the long wait, he imagined, and he'd already had enough bourbon, he knew as he tried to think if there was anything that he had forgotten while he listened to Turzak's objection to something Morgan had just said... but he wasn't sure what.

Might even make an anonymous phone call to the shelter in the morning to let them know about leaving the dog. Could even tell the person that answered that he thought it might be the dog that everyone had been looking for. Would have to make it from a pay phone at some remote location he supposed, and even that might be a little risky. Didn't want to do anything stupid to give himself away after all he had put himself through and so close to the end.

And that's when the whole mess with the dog would be officially over…out of his hands…when he drove away from the shelter. One problem solved and put to bed. That's when he could quit obsessing about what had preoccupied his time for the last three days, he thought, excited at the prospect. And unless Bob or Liz or that fat guy or the dog said something to someone about what had happened, then no one would ever be the wiser. They might have suspicions, but who cared about suspicions.

And Liz might be a problem later, but he didn't really care. She might put it all together someday, but by that time it probably wouldn't matter much. It would all be over by then. She could think what she wanted to think and tell whoever she wanted to tell. If she had any suspicions about the dog, he would just tell her that it was all just a strange coincidence or some bullshit like that, he thought. Wasn't going to worry about that possible problem now.

And then just hope that Hileman's investigator found the dog at the shelter before he did anything stupid like letting everyone know about the bar and Candy and whatever else he knew about his secret life.

But he still had to stay focused. Didn't want to screw something up now, he thought as Morgan finished questioning the first witness. And then Turzak for the next hour questioning the same witness…trying to ridiculously undo what had just been done. The truth lying somewhere in the middle, Weed imagined, but he wasn't even sure of that.

Was almost another hour before Turzak finished and Morgan called another witness to the stand. But Weed hadn't heard much of anything that either of them had said. He could only think about what might happen to him if Hileman's investigator started talking.

It was when his hand became too painful to continue holding it hidden under the table that he lifted it slowly like a dead weight and rested it on the table, hoping that the change in position might cause the pain to lessen. But it was then that he noticed for the first time all the dog hairs sticking to the sleeve of his suit jacket. Was alarming how many hairs there were, and how noticeable they were against his light-colored suit...And even more amazing was the fact that no one else had apparently noticed them either...especially Hileman's investigator, who had stood only inches away from him talking to him about the dog. Someone trained to look for evidence...to find clues...that had been aggressively trying to find a dog...and he hadn't even noticed that he was covered with dog hairs, Weed thought, somewhat amused...but realizing more the fact that someone could still notice all the hairs. Little black hairs seeming to fluoresce against his light-colored suit like hundreds of little beacons...And now he could see that the hairs weren't just stuck to his sleeves but were all over his suit...There were even a few stuck around where the dog had bitten him. Not as many as on his sleeves, but noticeable nonetheless, he thought as he tried to pick a few of the hairs off without anyone noticing. Slowly, clandestinely extricating one hair at a time, while acting as if he was still engrossed in the testimony...trying to remove the most obvious hairs. Had to be hundreds, he thought as he took the first small handful of hairs down beneath the table and set them free...imagining how many might find their way to Morgan's suit pants...Might be the subject of a strange conversation between the two of them later and an even stranger explanation, he imagined. But trying to remove them all would be hopeless, he knew...There were just too many, and with his swollen left hand he wouldn't be able to pick them off his left sleeve anyway. He would have to just let those hairs lay quietly undisturbed and hope that no one noticed. He had gone this long without being discovered, so his chances were pretty good that no one would notice them now, he surmised. Trial would be adjourned soon. He would just have to leave the courtroom quickly before anyone had a chance to notice, he thought as he spotted one of the hairs sticking to Morgan's coffee mug...right at the spot along the rim Morgan would likely put his lips if he took another sip of coffee.

And that's exactly what he was talking about...staying focused. He would have had plenty of time to brush the hairs off before he got back to the courthouse if he had noticed. But he hadn't stayed focused. And it was just some little thing like this that could destroy him.

To make matters worse, he thought that it actually smelled like there was a dog somewhere nearby. So he maybe smelled like a dog too, he thought, angered at his carelessness...his stupidity...his life.

How had he gotten to this point in his disgusting life? How had a relatively intelligent individual come to this...sitting in a courtroom fighting a ridiculous lawsuit that was ruining his life, and at the same time worrying about dog hairs on his sleeves and hoping that no one noticed that he smelled like a dog? Seemed almost too absurd to be real...to even consider. He felt like just standing up in front of the whole courtroom full of people and confessing...telling everyone his whole life's story...making it sound amusing and funny...as if it were happening to someone else...to make them all laugh...before just walking off...like a comedian leaving the stage to great applause. No one would believe him, even if he did tell them the truth now.

His life was in shambles, and he was probably going to lose everything anyway...His house, his wife, all his possessions...all up in smoke. And all because of something he had said that had pissed someone off...one little mistake...one little misstep...leading to another mistake...and then another...on ad infinitum...never to stop.

Had already lost his reputation...his practice...maybe even his license to practice medicine. The best surgeon in the city once...when he was young and full of life. People used to come for miles just to see him, just like his mother had told him. Now he had become a pariah, who would best be remembered for disfiguring a well-know socialite...Gertrude Hileman, the Mustard Queen...the face on millions of mustard jars...Didn't seem all that funny now...did it?

One failed marriage and two children that didn't want anything to do with him. His second marriage a mess, and probably his fault mostly. Relationships with women half his age. A shooting that could expose the whole sordid side of his life...and that had already exposed him to the threat of a homicidal maniac shooting him...but a threat that might just solve all his problems.

And if that wasn't bad enough, now he had this dog mess...with an investigator threatening to tell everyone everything about this other life. *This Other Life.* That was a good name for it, he thought... a good name for a book about his life.

The possibilities of his demise seemed almost endless. Couldn't even keep them all straight anymore.

His swan song, his midlife crisis...before descending into the abyss of old age...into the darkness of death. At least it would all be over soon. At least he wouldn't "go gentle into that good night."

And now his whole evening was going to be spent driving a dog around town in his broken-down rat trap of a car while trying to avoid a private investigator and the police and a lunatic and then sneaking around like some petty criminal in the dark to leave a dog at some out-of-the-way animal shelter. Sounded like a fun evening. Never imagined his life becoming so absurd...at his age, at this time in his life.

Life was supposed to be easier going into your twilight years. What had happened? He had self-destructed...He had come unraveled, he thought as he listened to the drone of voices in the background. There was some laughter, but he didn't know why...Maybe over his thoughts or for something else stupid that he had done.

It all seemed surreal. The courtroom, the clowns that he could see dancing around outside the window every day, that now all seemed so well placed in his life, he thought and let out a short burst of laughter as the courtroom became confusingly silent.

Didn't know how it was all going to play out. And the bad thing was that he wasn't sure that he even cared. He wasn't happy before all this had happened anyway…Maybe it was all just a blessing in disguise, or maybe a subconscious effort to self-destruct.

And maybe Candy was right…he needed a change in his life… to move off in a different direction, he thought as Morgan finally became silent with his seemingly endless chatter.

"Well. Not bad," Morgan said, leaning over and whispering in Weed's direction after sitting down beside him. "Not the best, but we held our own, and Turzak was a flop today," he said and then stood and told the judge that he had no further questions for the witness.

"A couple more days and we'll be finished. Hileman's testimony tomorrow morning and then you testify in the afternoon. After that, all we'll have left of the trial are the closing statements," Morgan said as he gathered up all his papers. "So if you have some free time, go over the answers to the questions that I'm going to ask you tomorrow," Morgan reminded him. "And maybe by Friday we'll have a verdict. And I'm actually feeling pretty good about the whole thing…We did pretty well," he repeated as he loaded his briefcase.

Weed shook his head but was more anxious to finish up with the dog than dealing with what debris was left of the trial…and still anxious that no one notice the dog hairs.

As soon as the gavel came down Weed left the courthouse and then took a circuitous route through the festival before doubling back to his car and driving off. Hadn't seen Hileman's investigator anywhere. Investigator wouldn't have been able to keep up with him anyway, he thought as he checked his rearview mirror a couple times just in case.

The hard part was over. Now all he had to do was pick up the dog and wait, he thought as he looked at all the hairs still on his jacket. Hard to believe, he thought, that sometimes people can't see what they're looking for even when it's right in front of them.

CHAPTER FORTY-TWO

Tuesday, May 18
6:53 p.m.

He parked at the reservoir in a place where he could watch for any approaching cars far off in the distance. He took the dog out of the car and then looped her leash around the bumper of his car before sitting down in a shaded, grassy area beneath a large tree. It was almost 7:00 p.m. but still very light outside. He would have to wait another couple of hours before he could safely leave the dog at the shelter, he knew as he broke off a few pieces of his chicken sandwich and then laid them on the grass in front of the dog.

From where he was sitting, he could look down at the city below. Rows of houses and a steel mill with smoking stacks and the river and an amusement park that sat alongside the river. He could see the lights of the Ferris wheel spinning slowly and the roller coaster tracks that ran about the trees. And he could hear the distant music of the calliope and the faint laughter of the people at the park as it drifted toward him on the breezes.

He had been to the amusement park many times in his youth, and the sights and sounds brought back pleasant memories...but painful too, now that those days were gone forever, he knew as he took the rest of the food out of the bag. The smells, the sounds, his friends, his first girlfriend...It was so exciting then...Life seemed so fresh and new with so much still in front of him. It had all gone...so quickly, he thought, taking another drink of the bourbon and Coke mixture as the dog sniffed in the air for more chicken and then looked back at him suspiciously as she carried off another piece that he had given her.

He had come a long way from those days. Past didn't even seem real now. Like maybe it had all just been a dream...that none of those good times had ever really happened. Life was exciting then. No worries. Colors all seemed brighter, sounds crisper he thought. Now the world seemed dull and lifeless...and worn-down, like an old coin. What he wouldn't do to have just one of those days back... one of those summers back, he thought as he watched the dog lick at the lid to his Coke and bourbon cup that he had thrown to the ground.

He gave the dog a few small bites of his cherry pie and then watched a string of barges being pushed slowly up the river. Was relaxing just sitting there. How deep the water looked at dusk with the reflections of light going so deep into the still water.

"Hasn't been all that bad, has it?" he asked turning toward the dog. "Like a vacation for you probably. You probably don't even want to go back...You're having so much fun with me," Weed said, laughing as he watched the dog carry a paper wrapper off into the grassy field, probably thinking he was crazy talking to her and trying to get as far away as possible. "We've been all right together... you and me.

"But they'll all think I'm crazy if they ever find out what we've been doing…what we did. You know that? But that's what happens when you don't think things out," he continued, still talking to the dog. The dog looked at him like she might have understood what he was telling her and that any minute she might start explaining where he had gone wrong. "That's what happens when you drink too much," Weed continued. "Everything seems like a great idea when you're drunk," he said as he gathered up the garbage. "And old and don't much care about life anymore," he added as if he had just remembered the sentiment.

"But it was all sort of fun. Making her suffer a little and then having all those people at the club getting muddy looking for you… You probably would have liked it. Searching for a hot dog," he said, laughing. "That's pretty funny," he said, giving the dog another piece of his cherry pie. "And I might actually get away with it. Odds are looking better by the minute. I get you back, and no one will ever be the wiser. They might think I had something to do with it, but they'll never really know," he said as the dog lay down in front of him on her belly with her head perched between her paws, looking up at him, seemingly now interested in what he was telling her.

"You won't tell anyone about this will you?" Weed asked, rubbing the dog's head.

"Sometimes you just get tired of it all, the shit that life lays on you, and you start doing crazy things. Just to try and maintain your sanity…" he said as he lay back and looked up at the start of a starry night sky and relaxed for the first time all day. He closed his eyes and listened to the distant sounds of the calliope playing the same tune over and over but clearer now…Now that the wind had changed direction…soothing…like it had sounded thirty-five years earlier. The sound wafting in the wind back and forth, like it was coming back from the distant past…Distant memories on the wind, he thought. Like a lullaby.

He had been happy once…then…a long time ago. Really happy…before this long journey started, he knew, before this whole nightmare of his life began. Before his life had led him to this abysmal nadir.

Maybe you could only truly be happy once in your life, when you were young. Maybe once it was gone, it was gone forever…at least real happiness. Maybe like real love, too. Maybe that's what he was searching for. The happiness of his youth…But even that sounded like bullshit, he thought as he lay there a long time listening to the wind and the music and watching the stars before he slowly drifted off into a deep sleep.

When he woke…he realized that he had been dreaming… dreaming about trying to sneak a dog through security and into the courthouse with the dog hidden under his coat. It wasn't Hileman's dog but a much larger dog, and the security guard didn't seem to notice even though the dog was barking loudly…And then a security alarm went off somewhere and woke him.

When he regained his bearings, he realized that it had been Hileman's dog that had been barking in his dream, and the security alarm that he had heard was his cell phone ringing.

It was a lot darker now. He could see the lights of the park much more clearly with all the reds, blues, and greens spinning wildly in the night air…as he fumbled to answer his phone.

He must have been sleeping a lot longer than he realized.

"I'm going to need some cash or they're going to kick me out of my apartment," Candy said before he could say a word. "I should just move," she added, starting to cry softly. "It's all been crazy around here. Tatter owes me this money, but he won't pay…Said he needed all my tip money to pay his hospital bills," she said, sniffling. "Said my contract's null and void now. Acted like the shooting was all my fault."

He could hear her flicking her cigarette lighter.

"I'm thinking about changing my life," she said. "I'm tired of it all, and he owes me six hundred dollars."

"Don't worry about the money," Weed told her, still groggy from his sleep…and then he told her that she should go back to school and make something of herself, he wasn't sure why.

"I don't know. But I'm thinking about goin' to Florida. Jen says there's a lot of work down there for dancers, and I could just live with her until I find a place to dance. Then I wouldn't have to put up with all this bullshit," she told him. They talked for another ten minutes, and he told her that he would bring her money tomorrow. It was almost nine o'clock when they ended their conversation.

Weed finished drinking the last of his bourbon and then stood and ran a few steps forward before throwing the empty bottle as far as he could down the steep hillside and into the trees…almost falling as he lost his balance. He listened as the bottle went clanking and tinkling through the tree limbs before hitting the ground with a thump and without breaking.

"Won't be long now," he told the dog as he cleaned up the papery mess they had made.

This final part would be easy, he thought. Would drive by the shelter to make sure that there was no one around and then just double back and put the dog in one of the cages at the side of the building. Dog would be okay there for one night, he thought before putting the dog back into the car and starting his drive back to the city.

And then his stupid prank would be officially over, he thought as his cell phone rang again, with Liz's number coming up this time. Didn't want to talk to her now, he thought, but he noticed the dog bites on his hand as he held his phone. Hand looked a lot better than it had, he thought…and it might not be all that noticeable tomorrow at the trial when he would have to lay his hand on the Bible to be sworn in.

He drove by the shelter to make sure that no one was around, and then circled back to the parking lot. He didn't like the idea of leaving the dog there all night. Someone could take her, he supposed...but it was unlikely, and the cages had locks. He couldn't risk keeping her any longer anyway. Every minute that he had the dog increased his risk that someone might discover what he had done.

There was only one light on inside the shelter and a dim spotlight illuminating part of the parking lot and the cages...with a scraggly-looking cat already occupying one of them. The cat watched intently as he carried the dog to the cages...He could hear a few muffled barks from the dogs inside the shelter.

He put the dog carefully inside one of the cages before going back to the car for her food and water and a few pieces of chicken he had saved.

He would drive by the shelter in the morning on his way to the courthouse to make sure that she was okay, he thought as he watched the dog for another minute. She circled the cage a couple times before laying down calmly...and then looked up at him with her sympathetic eyes, making him feel worse than he already did.

"You'll be fine," Weed told her, reaching back into the cage and petting her head. "Someone will get you first thing in the morning, and you'll be home in no time," he said as he shut the cage door and then snapped the lock shut.

Wasn't a bad dog...and he had sort of had grown to like her, he realized as he got back into the car and finished his short drive home.

Sandy was sitting in the living room reading a magazine with her glasses pushed half way down her nose when he entered the house.

"How'd it go today?" she asked, looking over the edge of the magazine as he passed.

"Who knows? I mean, they let murderers go free all the time. I guess anything's possible," he said, pouring himself a drink. "Morgan actually thinks that we may have a chance at sort of winning...that even if we lose the jury might only award her a small amount of money instead of the seven million that she wants... could possibly all be covered by my malpractice insurance...I might not have to pay a dime...and it might actually make me look like the winner if they only give her a small amount of money," he said, sitting down in the chair across from her. "If you can believe Morgan."

"You're kidding," she said, putting down her magazine.

"Morgan said that Turzak dropped some real bombs, and his experts have all seemed like high-priced plastic phonies...whatever that's worth," he told her as he finished off his drink. "And Morgan might tell the jury about Hileman not needing her collar or wheelchair last year at the banquet. Going to maybe use the photographs that I gave him too...If he has to."

"That's unbelievable," she said. "So the banquet wasn't a complete waste."

"Yeah, he thinks the jurors might realize that it was all mostly an act that Hileman was putting on."

"Best news that we've had in a while."

"Yeah, but I wouldn't get my hopes up too high just yet," he said as he leaned back in his chair and closing his eyes. "Because you never know what can happen," he said, thinking about Hileman's private investigator and the damage that he could still cause.

"Was strange how Hileman's dog just disappeared into thin air," Sandy finally said, breaking a long silence.

"Yeah, I don't know about that, but I think she may have tried to trip me or maybe even tried to hit me with her cane this afternoon when I walked by her at the courthouse...couldn't be sure...'course she was drunk...so who knows what she was trying to do. Then she just sat there all day in court like a zombie staring at me most of the time…felt creepy…sort of scary, actually," he said before telling Sandy he was going upstairs to bed.

"Morgan said that the trial should be finished by Friday. I testify tomorrow after Hileman's done testifying. Two more days and the nightmare will all be over."

"Well, that will be just one more reason to celebrate at our anniversary party on Saturday. I can't believe it. Everything seems to be coming together so nicely. The trial will be over…and we're going to have a really nice anniversary party…And we could even win the case…the icing on the cake. And the weather is supposed to be just great. It's supposed to be warm and sunny all day Saturday," she said. "And they finally got the pool fixed…And didn't I tell you everything was going to work out fine?" she added as she followed him up the steps.

"I guess a couple of Frank's paintings blew away and landed in some mud. Helen said Frank was all bummed out about it yesterday, and that he came home crying…actually crying…like a little baby. Can you imagine him crying like a little baby?"

"Probably."

When he got to the top of the steps, he could see that the lamp and the table that had been sitting in the hallway were gone. Sandy apparently removed the last light source from the hallway. Now he could hardly see to get to the bedroom. At least she had left the bed, he thought as he entered the room.

He lay flat on his back looking up at the ceiling. He was exhausted. The day had worn him out. But he felt relieved that he had at least gotten one major problem out of the way…and that he had probably gotten away with it scot-free. And he had pulled it all off, right in front of everyone's noses.

It could come back to haunt him later, he supposed, but it was unlikely. And it had all worked out pretty much as he had wanted. He had caused Hileman a lot of heartache and grief and had pushed her to the edge, he imagined. And as far as he could tell, the only down side was that he had to suffer a little too…and that he was forced to deal with Liz for a little while longer…and maybe the bites on his hand and her investigator.

And the trial would be over soon and he might maybe sort of win and be vindicated and get some of his reputation back, he imagined. In a few months, everyone would lose interest anyway… and pretty much forget about it all. And in a year, who would re-member any of it? That's the way life was. People didn't remember anything for too long, he thought as he drifted off to sleep.

He thought he had only been sleeping for a very short time when he heard the motorcycle go by. But it must have been longer because Sandy was sleeping soundly beside him, and he hadn't even remembered her coming to bed. Maybe he had been dreaming or his imagination was just haunting him again like two nights earlier, he thought as he looked out the window at the empty street below.

CHAPTER FORTY-THREE

Wednesday, May 19
6:44 a.m.

Weed fumbled with his ringing cell phone in the dim morning light.

"You see the newspaper?" a voice asked that he knew immediately was Bob's. The clock on the nightstand read 6:45 a.m. "There's something in the paper about that shooting last week at Tatter's Bar," Bob told him.

Weed sat up, wide awake now, turning away from Sandy so she couldn't hear their conversation.

"What's wrong?" she asked as he stood and started walking toward the bedroom door.

"Nothing important...just something at the hospital," he said, telling Bob to hold on for a minute as he walked down the hall and then down the steps and into the kitchen.

"Yeah, it's just a small article, but the headline says that the police are looking for a suspect in that bar shooting you told me about, and it's on the front page," Bob continued.

"Knew that they were going to do something like this," Weed said softly, cupping his hand around the phone as he tried to catch his breath. "It's Hileman's damn private investigator...that's who's responsible...Told me yesterday that he knew all about the shooting at Tatter's Bar and threatened that if I didn't tell them where Hileman's damn dog was that he was going to do something like this. I should have just kept the damn dog."

"Investigator?"

"Yeah, Hileman hired some private investigator to find her dog, and he's been harassing me for the last two days. But he couldn't find the dog if it was taped to his ass. Walked right by him yesterday covered with dog hairs and he didn't even notice," Weed said as he checked the porch to see if the newspaper had been delivered yet.

"You didn't tell me anything about Hileman having a private investigator."

"My paper's not here...Read what it says," Weed asked as he looked out the window at the first muddy rays of a disgusting morning, still trying to talk quietly enough so Sandy wouldn't hear.

"Just talks about the shooting, that's all. Gives your name as a witness though...that's why I called...Says that you're a surgeon at the hospital...and that the police have been looking for that other guy, Pickles, since they questioned you last week...and that this other guy could be armed and dangerous. But the article is sort of confusing...Hard to tell who the police are actually looking for... you or that Pickles guy...I mean, you can tell, but you have to read it pretty close."

"Great. Just read it to me."

"I'm in the car drivin' to the Quick Fix now...So wait until I stop at the next red light and I'll read some of it if I can find the damn article again," he said. "You get rid of the dog yet?"

"Yeah, but if I had known that they were going to pull this bullshit, I wouldn't have...I would have just kept the dog," he said as Bob started reading the article.

"May eleventh...da da da...shooting at Tatter's Bar...then it says that you were there and witnessed the shooting and had already been questioned. That you were apparently the only witness to the shooting. Gives your name and address...and then says that you've been a surgeon at the hospital for over twenty-five years...and that the case is still active and under investigation...and then the article tells about the bar's bad reputation. That's not their words, but that's essentially what it said. I lost my place in the paper anyway, and I don't have the right section of the paper right here in front of me now, and the light's green. But it said pretty much what I just told you."

"Sounds like I'm the one responsible for telling the police that Pickles did it?"

"Yeah, that's the other reason I called you, because I wanted to warn you to be on the lookout because I imagine he'll be pissed when he reads it. They made the bar sound pretty bad too...worse than it probably is...like everyone that hung out there was either a drug addict or a prostitute or some kind of freak...doesn't make it sound very good...looks to me like they were almost intentionally trying to make you look bad...I mean, that's just my opinion though."

"Only makes sense...To make me look as bad as they can...so they can destroy me. No way I'll ever win the lawsuit now...shit. Almost feel like going back to the animal shelter and getting the damn thing...pisses me off...knew that something like this was going to screw up everything. And what am I supposed to tell Sandy— and worse, what am I supposed to tell my mother?"

Had to be Hileman's private investigator responsible for the article...There was just no other explanation, Weed knew...And it had to be one of her cronies at the newspaper that wrote the story...

to make him look as bad as they could…and his address…And now that lunatic Pickles knew exactly where he lived and that he had been responsible for turning him in…may as well have just sent him an invitation, he thought.

"I'll be damn lucky if I make it through the day," Weed said. "I'm just surprised the article didn't say something about me dating one of the strippers."

"Yeah, there wasn't anything about that, I don't think. And who knows, maybe Pickles can't read," Bob said, forcing out a laugh.

"Well, I'm just going to act like it's no big deal. Like everyone else does in this country when they do something wrong…just like all the politicians…doesn't matter what they do wrong, they just act like it's all okay…like they were just a victim of circumstances… And that's what I'm going to do…just become a victim of circum-stances…I mean, what else can I do?" he added, checking the porch again for the newspaper.

"But shit, it could be the start of the end for me…when Sandy reads it or my mother or anyone else for that matter," he said, exasperated.

"No law against being in a bar," Bob said before telling him he had to get going so that he could open up the store.

He sat at the table trying to calm his shaky nerves, thinking about how he was going to handle the problem. Just act like it was no big deal. That he had just gone into the bar for a drink with a friend like he had planned to say before. Or that maybe he had just gone in to help the shooting victim…to prevent the victim from dy-ing after he had been shot. That was a better explanation of why he had been in the bar…surprised he hadn't thought of it sooner, and he was somewhat excited about that solid explanation. Would make him seem like an unselfish, brave hero. Why hadn't he thought of that explanation sooner…he thought, almost laughing with joy as he went back upstairs.

Would have to tell Sandy that explanation and hoped that she believed him…even half believed him…but she probably wouldn't. She knew him too well…She would know that he would never enter a bar and risk his life. She knew he was basically a coward when it came to things like that. Was going to tell her that story anyway… and stick with it, he thought. Regardless, she would be pissed at him for doing something so stupid when they had so much on the line. And pissed that she would now have to explain yet another potentially embarrassing situation to all her friends. And just when there was a ray of hope that things might actually be improving, he thought.

Maybe should just wake her up and tell her his side of the story before she heard it from someone on the street, he thought. Put his spin on it. Tell her that she was making too much out of it, that it was no big deal, and then try to convince her that there was no way that it could affect the outcome of the trial…because of all the legal regulations. And explain to her that jurors weren't allowed to read newspaper articles like that, and even if they did, which was highly unlikely, they weren't allowed to consider it when they made their decisions.

Might make it easier for him later if he told her now, he thought, as he looked over at Sandy sleeping soundly and half hoping that she would wake up so that he could tell her.

Yeah, he knew about the shooting, but was no big deal…was just as surprised as she was that it was even in the newspaper, he could tell her. That he had been in the area or something seeing Bob when it happened and someone knew he was a doctor and called him into the bar…So what was he supposed to do…couldn't let the guy die…could have really gotten in trouble for that. And then he could tell her that he didn't even think that it was worth telling her about the shooting because he knew she would be upset and didn't want to worry her, he thought, trying to make sure that his new story all made sense…before he woke Sandy up and committed…he thought as he rehearsed the presentation in his mind again.

And he didn't even want to think about what his mother would say…what she would do when she found out, he thought as he buttoned the cuff of his shirt. He would just tell her the same thing he told Sandy…make out that he was the hero for saving the guy's life…still surprised that he hadn't come up with that explanation sooner, he thought.

Unless it all started to come unraveled…like if Sandy somehow found out about why he had really been in the bar.

Hand didn't look much better either, he thought, checking it in the mirror before dabbing on some Betadine and then covering the bite with a small, skin-colored Band-Aid.

"Everything okay?" Sandy asked, leaning forward in the bed just as he was about ready to leave.

"Yeah, everything's fine," he said, trying to get up the nerve to tell her, but he couldn't. Didn't need the aggravation this early in the morning, and maybe letting her find out on her own would give her time to cool down before he had to face her. Might be better just to wait, he thought.

"You were talking to yourself again," she said, her muffled voice coming from under the covers.

"Yeah, don't know…Don't really care," he mumbled, but not loud enough for her to hear as he left the room and walked down the hallway. She would be talking to herself too if she had to deal with what he had to deal with, he thought.

The paper was there now. He picked it up as if it were poison… and then reluctantly read the article…and then read it again…hoping that it might not sound as bad the second time. Embarrassing, it sounded like he was a common criminal, and worse, it sounded like he had been totally responsible for single-handedly ratting out Pickles…and it didn't sound like he went in the bar to save anyone's life. Article couldn't have been more poignant. And all this over a shooting where the guy hadn't even died…And if Candy was right, he was already back on the street.

Hileman had to be responsible for the damn article…No one cared about shootings at a sleazy bar in the worst section of the city. It was a good old-fashioned hit job, and he was going to sue her for harassment and defamation of character, he thought. And he was going to sue her over the false accusation that he was responsible for taking her dog too, he thought as he pushed the paper into the inside pocket of his suit jacket so that Sandy wouldn't see it.

And now he didn't even feel safe leaving the house. Police didn't have any trouble finding him and his crummy car, but they couldn't find a raving lunatic on a motorcycle riding around all over town, he thought, having a difficult time believing what was happening. He pulled back the curtain from the kitchen window to check the porch and the path to his car for any suspicious activity before leaving the house. How ridiculous, he thought as he started his drive to the courthouse, imagining what he might do if he ran into Pickles… other than run. If there were no other options, he would just try to talk his way out of it…Explain to Pickles vehemently that it wasn't him…that they thought it was him…and that he hadn't said a word, he thought as he maintained his vigil but knew that Pickles was more likely to shoot first and ask questions later. Would be nothing he could do but run in the opposite direction and hope that Pickles was a bad shot.

Hileman had beaten him again. Had pulled the rug out from under him and turned the whole dog mess inside out. Now he was the victim…and the stakes had gotten a lot higher. Didn't seem like a very good idea now did it? he asked himself again, pissed at the person inside him that had made that rash decision.

Hileman would soon get her dog back and everything would be fine with her, while he would be dealing with some crazed lunatic, he thought as he drove slowly by the animal shelter to check on the dog.

Dog wasn't there. The cat wasn't there either, he thought, satisfied that the animals had already been taken inside the shelter and that the dog thing was finally over. He was going to really let Hileman's private investigator have it now…demand an apology for accusing him unjustly of taking the dog. Tell them that he was getting an attorney of his own to sue them for harassment and defamation, he thought. But how weak…wasn't even worth it, he thought. Threats…who gave a crap about threats anymore…they were more common than mayflies and just about as serious.

And worse, he couldn't find the bottle of bourbon under his seat, he realized as he sat inside his car outside the courthouse…before remembering that he had drank it all at the reservoir the night before…and then recalling the tinkling sound the bottle had made as it fell softly through the trees before making a loud thump at the end of its journey. One of the most important days of his life, and he was booze-less maybe…He didn't have one ounce of bourbon…not one swallow, he thought, before remembering that he had accidentally dropped a few Valium pills between the car seats a week earlier and had been too lazy to go searching for them then. A Valium might help if he could find one of them, he thought, still noticeably shaky from the effects of the newspaper article. Maybe he could fish one of them off of the floor, he thought…kneeling beside the car and then leaning, twisting awkwardly so he could see beneath his seat. Sandy's shoes were still there…He had to remember to get rid of them…Then a box of crayons and some construction paper…and what looked like an empty bourbon bottle far off in the distance under the passenger seat…reminiscent of the last two weeks of his life…keepsakes…a collage of his life, he thought…Pills, booze, party shoes, colorful paper, crayons…like a party…and dust and dirt and bits of food. Could probably tell a lot about a person's life by looking under the person's car seat, he imagined as he felt around the floor for the pills…picking up a few small erroneous white objects before finally finding a pill that he could reasonably be sure was one of the errant Valium. And more exciting, it appeared that there might be a small amount of bourbon left in the bottle under the other seat…a bottle prematurely given up for dead, he thought, lifting the bottle to get a better look at the contents inside…Not a lot, but a start if he drained it completely, he thought as the man pictured on the label smiled back at him…maybe pleased at his good fortune, he thought as he drank what was left in the bottle.

He looked at the newspaper lying on the seat beside him… thinking about all the problems it was going to cause…but didn't have the nerve to read it again. He had read enough, he thought as he dialed Mordicah but hung up before anyone answered…unsure of what he wanted to tell him anyway. He carefully ripped the article from the newspaper and put it in his shirt pocket…but he wasn't sure why.

Weed could see Hileman and her investigator waiting again in front of the courthouse…watching him intently as he walked toward the front door.

"You just stepped in it, asshole," Weed mumbled as he walked quickly past them.

"What are you talking about?" the investigator answered, following Weed up the sidewalk.

"Any chance that bitch ever had of getting her dog back is over. The dog is toast," Weed said loud enough so that Hileman could hear.

"What are you talking about?" the investigator asked as he continued to follow Weed.

"What am I talking about? You had your fun. Now it's my turn. She'll never see that mutt again. I can guarantee you that," Weed said, starting up the steps of the courthouse and satisfied that he was at least getting one last dig in to make Hileman suffer a little bit more before they found the dog.

"What are you talking about?" the investigator repeated as he followed Weed halfway up the courthouse steps.

"You telling me you're not responsible for this?" Weed asked, turning back toward the investigator as he reached into his shirt pocket and took out the article before throwing it up into the air like a piece of confetti.

"What?" the investigator asked, confused, as he chased the small piece of paper as it floated down the sidewalk.

"You want to play nasty? I can play nasty too," Weed said as he stood in the security line and half watched as the investigator read the article.

"We didn't have a thing to do with this," Hileman's investigator said, looking somewhat pale, Weed thought. "Just a coincidence. That's all," he said. "We know all about the shooting, yeah, but we didn't have a thing to do with this article being printed in the newspaper...We never said a word to anyone," the investigator assured him as Weed entered the metal detector.

Let them all sweat a little longer. Let Hileman think that he had done something bad to the dog and that she would never see it again. Would serve her right, Weed thought.

"Getting pretty damn ridiculous out there," Weed told Morgan as he sat down beside him in the courtroom. "Hileman's investigator still thinks I had something to do with her losing her damn dog. Can you believe that?" he asked before letting out a weak laugh. But Morgan sat motionless, as if he hadn't heard a word that Weed had said.

"Yeah, well, forget about that," Morgan finally said, turning toward him. "We need to concentrate on testifying. Might be the most important day of the trial, and we don't need any distractions," Morgan told him, apparently still unaware of the article that had appeared in the morning newspaper.

"Just do what we talked about...Try to stay on task, and don't elaborate unless you have to...And try to act sympathetic and understanding...even if you aren't." The same thing he had told him the first time he had testified, Weed realized as he watched Turzak wheel Hileman past him in her wheelchair.

But he had a strange feeling as she passed...as if he could actually feel her cold hatred for him.

He sat there in the long streams of sunlight coming through the courtroom windows trying to concentrate on testifying, but his thoughts kept going back to the shooting and the newspaper article...and the distracting clowns gathered outside the window. As if they were all waiting for his final performance.

And knowing that soon, when the whole world awoke and read the newspaper, they would realize what kind of a demented pervert he really was, he thought as he tried to read a small, scribbled notation he had written by one of the questions Morgan was soon going to ask him. His attempt to improve his image, to emphasize the good and put a spin on the bad...to make what he did seem as benign and innocuous as possible. Like his life...little notes to improve his life. But his answers all seemed like words without meanings. All half-truths...just like the half-truths of his life, he thought.

And then for the rest of the morning he took the stand, without anyone noticing his swollen hand, and answered all the questions Morgan asked with all the answers they had painstakingly constructed.

When they adjourned for lunch Weed sat in his car, wondering if Sandy had seen the article yet and then tried to call her...but the call went unanswered.

She had probably already seen the article or had learned about it from one of her friends...Probably Helen, if he had to bet. Just as well...More time for her to cool down and for him to fine-tune his alibi...his story. The story about saving someone's life that had been shot...risking his life to save someone else's life...and this was the thanks that he got.

A cool breeze blew through the window as he listened to a band playing in the park. He searched the horizon carefully as he weighed the risks against the benefits of making the short journey down the street to the liquor store.

CHAPTER FORTY-FOUR

Wednesday, May 19
1:12 p.m.

Weed held his cell phone up in front of him to see who was calling as he started back across the street to the courthouse…and then shook his head in disgust when Liz's name appeared on the screen. It was the fifth time she had called since yesterday. Wasn't going to talk to her again, he thought, irritated as he hung the phone back on his belt.

She wanted the phone number of the man whom he had told her had the dog. But when was she going to get the message that he didn't have any phone number to give her?

But strangely, he thought that he could still hear Liz's voice. Maybe he accidently hadn't disconnected the call, he thought, looking at his phone again before realizing that Liz was standing right in front of him. She was holding her phone out in front of her with a disgusted look on her face.

"You told me you did that once to one of your friends," she said, walking up to where he was standing. "Mordy, I think it was."

"What's that?" he said but knew immediately what she was talking about.

"You told me that you called people up when they didn't know that you could see them so you could see their reaction when they saw who it was that was calling. That it was a good way to see how people really felt about you."

"Not me, I don't think," he said, laughing lightly. "Must have been someone else, but it is sort of funny. I'll have to try it sometime," he said, trying to recover and laugh it off. "That was you that just called?"

"Yeah, that was me!" she said, sounding irritated.

"If I would have known I would have answered, but I haven't been answering any of my calls today. Have been so preoccupied with the trial that I can't think straight," he said, trying to give her kiss before she pushed him away.

"Thought I could get that number you told me you had," she said, still sounding irritated. "Since the last phone number you gave me was some pervert that now had my number but knew nothing about any lost dog," she said. "One of your friends, I imagine?"

He forced a laugh as he began searching his pockets as if a slip of paper with a phone number on it might miraculously appear. "Yeah, yeah…It's here somewhere, I think," he told her.

"If I were a reasonable person I would think that you were trying to avoid me, and that the whole story you told me about the dog and the little children being so happy about getting their dog back was all just a bunch of crap."

"That's not true. I've just been busy and preoccupied with this trial. I can't even remember my own phone number," he mumbled, opening up his wallet and looking through a stack of small papers and business cards before unexpectedly finding a phone number written on a small piece of paper.

"Yeah?"

"Maybe this is it," he said, handing her the paper. But he had no idea where it had come from or whose number it was. "I think that's it, but if that's not it, then I think I might know where I left it," he said as she took the paper and dialed the number, rolling her eyes as she continued to listen to his explanation.

"It might still be at the house…if that's not it," he said somewhat awkwardly as he watched her expression and just hope that no one answered.

"Stan's Mercedes Group," she said, closing her cell phone with an angry snap. "Your car's ready," she said after a short, confusing conversation. "Didn't think it would be Jim Johnson, or John Jimson, or whoever the hell you told me you gave the dog to," she added, throwing the paper up in the air like he had done earlier with Hileman's private investigator. He watched as it floated to the ground, somewhat mesmerized by the strange coincidence.

"The whole story is nothing more than one of your fancy lies," she said as they stood in front of the courthouse.

"What's that?"

"What you told me happened. Like the cat that swallowed the bird. It's all just a crock, and that's what I suspected from the very beginning with that lost-wallet excuse. And then I just happened to hear about that woman who's suing you losing her dog. And then when I dug a little deeper, I found out she lost it at the country club last Saturday night. And the description sounded just like the dog you said you told me you found last Saturday night right outside my house…remember?…What a coincidence…which is what I'm sure you're going to tell me…that it was all a coincidence," she said, giving him another disgusted look.

"Yeah, I did hear about her dog, and yeah, it was probably just a coincidence."

"You think I'm stupid?" she asked, waiting for his answer. "And how could you do something so damn heartless," she continued when there was none. "To take that poor woman's dog when you knew she was sick. After you single-handedly ruined her life...wasn't that enough for you? Wasn't making her look hideous and turning her into a cripple enough? And then you steal her dog. That's pretty low."

"That's not true. I knew that you might think that. I was even going to say something, but what I was told was that the dog looked nothing like the dog I found. Her dog has completely different markings, and I mean, the owner with the kids took it! How do you explain that?"

"Then give me the number."

"I told you I have it somewhere...Jesus, give me a chance to find it."

"I should just go to the police. I probably would if I knew that I wouldn't have to get involved with you any more than I already am. If I knew that my name wouldn't get dragged through the mud with you and the rest of your friends...as some kind of an accomplice... or even just as an acquaintance...would be bad enough. I don't need that embarrassment...that aggravation. I don't want anyone to even know that I know you."

"You got it all wrong," he said but felt somewhat relieved that she hadn't already gone to the police. "This has been hard for me too."

"Yeah, well, I don't really want to hear any more of your sad stories. I'm tired of it all. I should have ended our relationship a year ago like I had planned," she added as she continued to move away from him down the street. "You know, you're just an egotistical, self-centered narcissist that doesn't give a damn about anybody but yourself. It's over. I'm finished with it all," she said as she continued walking away.

"And that little note that you left me," she said, stopping suddenly halfway down the block and looking back at him angrily. "That was really cute…a nice touch…" she said, pausing. "You know…that cute little note from those lovely little children. That note that just happened to smell like bourbon…strange that a note from a six-year-old would smell like bourbon, don't you think? And I just hope you didn't do anything stupid to her dog," she said before turning and continuing down the street.

He stood there for a few seconds, watching as she walked away before mumbling the only thing he could think of in the moment: "Am I the only one in this town that drinks bourbon?" But he was hoping that she hadn't heard his stupid explanation…and hoping that no one had heard their conversation.

Wanted to break it off with her anyway…but hadn't seen it happening quite this way, he thought. But at least she hadn't gone to the police.

He felt woozy and lightheaded as he walked up the courthouse steps before looking up to see Hileman's detective standing there at the top like one of the ridiculous-looking gargoyles perched atop the building…watching him intently as he approached. Maybe he had found the dog and was going to thank him or something, he thought as he tried to move around him and into the courthouse.

"You got it all wrong, Ben," the investigator said, walking beside him the last couple of steps. "We didn't have anything to do with that article in the newspaper today. Sure we knew about that shooting but didn't say anything to anyone about it. You think we're stupid? You think we would do something like that when we wanted to get the dog back? She was even thinking about dropping this whole trial mess and offering you a reward," he said.

Unlikely, Weed thought, but the possibility was disturbing.

"And now Ms. Hileman's all upset," the detective said as he continued walking beside him. "She heard what you told me this morning, and she's worried that maybe you did something bad to her dog…and her psychic told her that she thinks the dog might actually be dead," he said as he stood with Weed in the line to go into the courthouse. "I know it's a lot of crap...psychics...Who believes that shit? But Ms. Hileman does, and the psychic told her some bullshit about seeing her dog floating around in heaven...so she's pretty upset. But I can guarantee you that we didn't have anything to do with that article you gave me. And if you can maybe just tell us anything...and I'm not accusing you of anything...but maybe just like where you think the dog might be...or even the general location or direction where we can look, then you won't hear another word from us. And we'll make sure that nothing else appears in the newspapers about you...and all this trial thing will sort of just disappear. Might even be able to help you with all this other stuff you got going on...You know, Ms. Hileman can pull a lot of strings. She has a lot of friends in high places, and she can make things happen... So we're ready to cut a deal."

"Sorry. Can't help you now," Weed told him, but the offer was almost too tempting to pass up...if he could trust them...and he still wasn't sure that he could...the offer could just be a ruse...to make him confess so they could maybe have him arrested...And he wasn't sure that he believed what the investigator had told him about not having anything to do with the newspaper article either, he thought as he went through the metal detector...but thinking that maybe it wouldn't hurt just to tell the investigator that maybe he should just try and look for the dog at the animal shelters around town, but when he turned and searched the crowd...the investigator was nowhere in sight...Another missed opportunity, he knew, feeling more pissed about the fact that maybe he had given up on his plan too soon.

"They're having problems," Morgan said as Weed sat down beside him in the courtroom. "I think Hileman's too drunk to testify, and Turzak's been pleading with the judge for the last ten minutes for a recess," Morgan added.

"Look at her," he said softly so that no one else could hear him. "Took them almost ten minutes to get her out of the car this morning…had to hold her up the whole time, and now she keeps nodding off. There's no way she's going to be able to testify," he added with a smile on his face.

"Didn't I tell you," Weed said. "She's always drunk."

"Not that bad…They can't even keep her awake today. There's no way that she's going to be able to testify," Morgan repeated as Turzak finished talking to the judge and walked back to his desk.

Hileman sat with her head bent, as if she might be sleeping in a drunken stupor, Weed thought. He watched Turzak lean in close to Hileman, speak into her ear, and gently shake her arm, apparently trying to keep her awake, before she finally looked in his direction.

"He wants to take a recess until she sobers up. That's why he was talking to the judge. I'll bet you a thousand bucks, that's what he was doing," Morgan said. "They put her on the stand in that condition, they'll be committing suicide. Especially after you slipped up and told everyone this morning that you thought she had been drinking heavily the night of her accident. She's turning into the exact person you described. I couldn't have scripted it any better," he said, laughing softly again. "We tell them that she was drunk that night and then she comes to court plastered. What a stroke of luck, what a role of the dice…good job," he added, holding out his hand for Weed to shake.

They sat and waited for another ten minutes as the judge looked over some papers, before he finally told Morgan that he could call his next witness.

"I would like to call Ms. Gertrude Hileman to the stand," Morgan said as he stood and looked over to where Hileman was sitting.

Turzak leaned in close to Hileman, telling her something that seemed to startle her awake before wheeling her forward to the witness stand…and then with the help of the bailiff, they lifted her awkwardly out of the wheelchair and into the witness stand.

But she appeared to be dead weight and like a rag doll, Weed thought as Turzak then explained to the court how Ms. Hileman had been taking a lot of pain medication for all her injuries and that the medication was making her very weak and lethargic...but smiling sheepishly at the judge and then the jury before going back to his seat.

Morgan asked her a question and then repeated it when she didn't answer. But she still gave no answer as she looked around, confused and lost, staring blankly into space. And then when she didn't answer a third time, the judge leaned toward her and told her that she was going to have to answer the question.

But what she said didn't make much sense...if any sense at all, Weed knew...Just verbal rambling...a completely disjointed answer...but somewhat arrogant in tone. An answer that didn't even come close to addressing the question that had been asked.

Is that you're final answer? Weed thought, amused and excited about what he was seeing. She was becoming the exact person that he had described to the jury not two hours earlier when he had testified.

Then another question, and another rambling answer from Hileman that seemed to ramble off into obscurity. Then four more questions with equally bizarre and confusing answers.

Vague answers that went nowhere, that answered nothing, and that included some obtuse and strange reference to her lost dog and psychic. Her speech was slurred and she moved her head painfully slowly, as if she was trying to locate where Morgan's voice was coming from...the whole time pulling at her collar as if it was too tight. A performance that could only help his case, Weed knew.

And Turzak objecting almost constantly, telling the jurors that it was the pain medication she was taking that was making it difficult for her to answer Morgan's questions. And then going on to explain to the jury that it was medications she needed to take because of all the injuries she had suffered at the hands of Dr. Weed. But like Morgan had told him before, the objections just seemed to be drawing more attention to Hileman's pathetic state.

"Do you need your collar and wheelchair all the time?" Morgan asked suddenly and unexpectedly as he quickly removed the photograph from his briefcase of Hileman that Weed had given him and then held it up for everyone to see.

"Isn't this a picture of you dancing at last year's Spring Fling… and I would like everyone to notice that she is not wearing her collar or using her wheelchair…and that this picture was taken almost a year after her accident had occurred," he said as he walked the photo closer to the jurors. "You were dancing, weren't you…You were fine last year…no collar, and no wheelchair," Morgan continued as Turzak finally objected vehemently after he realized what Morgan had just done.

"This is ridiculous. I want it all stricken from the record. It's absurd, and the defendant's attorney is just trying to confuse the jury," Turzak added as the judge gave Morgan a dirty look and sustained the objection before Morgan slowly lowered the photo.

But the damage was done and now the jury might realize that it was all just a big act, Weed thought as he watched Morgan and Turzak arguing with the judge in muffled voices in front of the judge's bench, just as Hileman's cervical collar came loose and fell to the floor. Hileman looked around, moving her neck freely, before Turzak hurried over and replaced her collar, just as the judge brought down his gavel loudly and announced angrily that the trial was now in recess.

Hileman looked almost exactly like the person he had taken care of that night. An uncooperative, obnoxious drunk. And the jury had seen it all, Weed knew.

Morgan and Turzak stood in front of the judge talking in muffled voices for almost ten minutes before going back to their seats. And Hileman searched though her purse loudly before finding a cigarette and placing it loosely between her lips while continuing her search…most likely for a cigarette lighter, Weed thought.

"We're going to take a recess for the rest of the day," the judge finally said. "We've all been under a lot of stress, and the witness does not feel that she can testify today due the large amount of strong sedatives and pain medications she has been taking, and I believe it more prudent to just adjourn and hear her testimony first thing tomorrow morning, when she's feeling better," the judge said, addressing the jurors. "And I would like you to all realize that her testimony here today is stricken from the record. That you should ignore the testimony completely, as if it had never been given," he added, looking at them and then pausing as a few of the jurors shook their heads in agreement.

"So we're going to start fresh with Ms. Hileman's testimony first thing tomorrow morning...with a clean slate. And following that, we'll begin closing statements...So be prepared," he added, looking at both attorneys, "because we're definitely going to end this trial by Friday. So if there's no further business, the trial is adjourned until ten o'clock tomorrow morning," he said, bringing down his gavel.

"Great," Morgan said, leaning in toward Weed. "Couldn't have asked for anything better," he said under his breath. "She was a total basket case, and the jury saw it all...made a complete fool of herself, and you had to be blind not to see how drunk she was...couldn't understand a word she said. And we just doubled our chances of winning," Morgan said as the jurors were led out. "How could Turd Sack let her come to trial in this condition? Million-dollar attorney, and he made a five-dollar mistake.

"Can you believe it? You tell the jurors this morning that she was an obnoxious drunk, and what does she do? She comes to court drunk and obnoxious. Excellent," Morgan continued as he up stood and started moving toward the back of the courtroom. "And when her collar fell off...You tell me there isn't a god," Morgan said, laughing. "And showing the jury that photograph of her from last year was a great idea...Glad you thought of it," he added.

"Yeah, I told you she was a crazy drunk...And her psychic told her that I probably killed her dog," Weed said, laughing lightly as they walked outside the courthouse, but Morgan didn't seem interested, Weed thought as he watched as Morgan disappear into the crowd.

CHAPTER FORTY-FIVE

Wednesday, May 19
3:15 p.m.

Weed sat in his car trying to decide what he was going to do for the rest of his day. Didn't want to go home and face Sandy. Still needed to give himself more time to work on his explanation of why he had been in Tatter's Bar that night…he thought as he started to drive somewhat aimlessly before driving by the Quick Fix.

He could talk to Bob for a while. Couldn't get into much trouble doing that, he imagined but wondered if the newspaper article might counter any advantage he had gotten from Hileman's drunken performance in court.

He told Bob about Hileman's meltdown…and then about his conversation with Liz and the dog…and how he had apparently spilled bourbon on the note he had left for her. He talked to Bob for over an hour before driving off aimlessly again but still preoccupied with the conversation he was going to eventually have to have with Sandy…and with his mother too…and everyone else who might bring up the subject of why he had been in that seedy bar. It would be an uncomfortable and somewhat embarrassing conversation no matter how he tried to explain it away, he imagined as a motorcycle whizzed past, breaking his concentration…and sending a wave of fear through him thinking that it might be Pickles.

He tried to call Candy as he drove, but there was no answer. Hadn't been with her since his sexual misadventure almost a week ago, he thought, remembering that he still hadn't picked up anything at the drug store to prevent another embarrassing situation like that from happening again…especially not with Candy.

Made him feel old and depressed just thinking about it, he ruminated as he drove past the animal shelter. Looked almost abandoned, he thought. He parked a short distance down the street from the shelter and then decided to walk in.

There was only one person inside…a young girl sweeping the floor and seemingly disinterested in his presence.

"We're about ready to close, sir," she said, giving him a disgusted look after he had gone down one row searching the cages for Hileman's dog.

"I'll just be a minute," he told her as he started down another row of cages, uncaring that he had just created another potential witness to his crime.

Damn, he thought, finally finding Hileman's dog still lying in one of the cages at the back of the shelter. Almost twenty-four hours since he had left the dog at the shelter, and the hotshot private investigator still hadn't found her, Weed realized, now thinking that maybe he should have already made that anonymous call to the shelter.

Dog looked okay. Was even acting a little excited to see him, Weed thought. "You remember me?" Weed asked quietly as he stuck his fingers through the cage to pet the dog. Dog was fine, he could see as the dog licked at his fingers. Would probably just call the shelter in the morning from some pay phone and tell whoever answered whom the dog belong to, he thought as he made his way back toward the front of the shelter. Enough was enough, and the damage was already done, he imagined, and he didn't need to be harassed any longer.

"You thinkin' about getting a dog?" the girl asked as she followed him toward the exit.

"Maybe, but I'll stop back tomorrow," he said as he pushed open the door and left the shelter.

Real crack investigator. Didn't have any trouble finding out everything there was to know about his miserable life, but couldn't find a dog in broad daylight at probably one of the most logical places to look, he thought as he finished his drive home just as it started to get dark.

Sandy was gone, but she had left a note on the kitchen table. The opening salvo, he imagined as he reluctantly unfolded the paper and read.

"Ben, you disgusting piece of shit," was all that was written on the paper, and it looked as if she had probably been pretty drunk when she had written it...probably too drunk to think of anything better to write, he thought, crumpling the note and tossing it into the trash. Sweet and simple...He was a piece of shit. After all this, that was the best she could come up with. He was too tired for another fight anyway, he thought as he fixed himself a drink before going into the living room and sitting on the couch. He would just tell Sandy that he had gone into the bar to give medical treatment to the man that had been shot. And then just hope that Hileman's investigator hadn't told her anything more...like about his relationship with Candy, he thought, almost too exhausted to care.

Hopefully, in a couple weeks it would all be behind him anyway...if he didn't get shot first, he thought as he lay back on the couch and turned on the television. But instead of a TV station appearing on the screen, *Silky's Revenge* started to play. He had almost forgotten about the DVD, and he watched a few more minutes of Hileman dressed in her psychedelic bell bottoms and Silky with his afro running down some dark alley chasing two criminals. She wasn't bad-looking then...sort of sexy...and her acting wasn't horrendous, he imagined as he switched off the movie and closed his eyes, wondering what had transformed her into such a bitter old woman. Probably the same thing that had transformed him into a bitter old man. Was life, he imagined...inevitable consequence of growing old, he thought as he closed his eyes.

He had been sleeping when he finally heard Sandy's car pull into the driveway.

"It's not as bad as it sounds," he said as she came storming through the kitchen and into the living room. "They made me sound like I'm some kind of a criminal, but that's not what happened at all," he told her, trying to sound incredulous.

"I wasn't even going into that bar...I was just driving by when I noticed all the commotion, and when I stopped to see what was going on, they told me a man inside the bar had been shot...that's why I even went into the bar in the first place...and I mean, what else was I supposed to do? Just drive away...and let the man die? That would have been worse yet if I hadn't stopped. There's laws again doctors abandoning patients. You know that," he pleaded as he watched her search the refrigerator in silence, but he could tell that she had already been drinking very heavily.

"So I go into this bar...that I don't know a thing about...and save this guy's life...And the police...for some unknown reason... write this article in the newspaper like I actually know what happened...like I'm their lead witness...when I don't know a thing... didn't see a thing," he said and paused, hoping that she might say something. "But there's nothing about that...nothing about me risking my life to save this poor bastard's life...No...just that I was in the bar and witnessed something...But I didn't witness anything, and I told them that...and the police are just trying to cover their asses...I guess...And that's the whole story...and that's the thanks I get," he pleaded as he stood and followed her into the kitchen, as she began to sob. "Knew it was going to be a problem."

"Yeah, nice story that you came up with," she finally told him. "But I don't believe any of it...And to tell you the truth, I don't really care why you were in that bar...other than I always suspected that you were some borderline closet sexual deviate...I mean why should I expect anything less...And actually, I'm scared to even know the real reason why you were in that place...prostitutes and drug addicts and perverts...that's the only people that ever go in that bar," she said, stopping to blow her nose as he continued to try and plead his case.

"And who cares what great story you make up to tell people why you were in that bar...because everyone already knows...everyone has already made up their minds, no matter what crazy story you try to tell them," she said, almost hysterically in a panic now. "They already know," she said, turning toward him with tears flowing down her checks, expressively shaking her arms in front of her. "They've already made up their minds why you were in the bar...because you're some perverted sex addict," she said, throwing her purse and keys down hard on the counter before looking for a bottle under the sink.

"And now we're truly finished...I thought there was a slim chance that we might recover...that we might get our dignity back... our respect...but now that's over...the exclamation point at the end of your destructive story...the laughing stock of the town. The town jesters," she told him with her head still buried under the counter.

"See, I knew you wouldn't believe me...You never believe me. So believe what you want...whatever that is...that I'm some kind of a sex pervert...that's fine...Thanks for your support."

"And that's pretty funny...because you would never go into any bar to save anyone's life...or go anywhere that someone had a gun. That's probably the most unbelievable part of your whole story..."

she said, laughing sarcastically. "You're afraid of your own shadow," she said, crying but laughing hysterically at the same time as he tried to convince her of the veracity of his story with more details of how he had saved the victim's life, but in the back of his mind he could only think of the note that he had left Liz.

"And I know why you were in there…You don't think I see the way you look at all those stripper ads in the newspaper every Sunday? No, you fit right in a place like that," she said sarcastically, holding up a half-full bottle of gin that she had fish from beneath the sink.

"And what, you haven't humiliated us enough yet? You haven't embarrassed me enough? I can't even face my friends anymore… even Helen…I'm just too damn embarrassed to even try to explain… just feel like jumping off a bridge somewhere," she said, pouring the gin into a wine glass as Weed watched now, quietly…and somewhat resolved that his well-crafted cover story was falling apart.

"And what's next…What's the next perverted surprise I'm going to have to deal with? You single-handedly destroy the life of the most important person in the city and then you go off and let everyone know that you hang out at the most notorious dive in the city…You've become one of them," she continued before downing the entire glass of gin. "My life is ruined anyway…Wouldn't matter what you did now…it could only pale in comparison," she added, sniffing back tears and wiping her eyes. "What did I ever do to you to deserve this?"

"You're just too upset to understand," Weed said, finally able to get a word in. "I'm the victim…I tell you…I try to save some poor guy's life that gets shot…and put my own life in danger…entering a bar with a crazed lunatic with a gun…and that's the thanks I get," he told her, giving it one last try.

"And now we've lost everything…'cause there's no way you can win your case now…everything's gone…out the window…Hell, they'll probably give her twice as much as she wants," she added. "Give her the shoes off my feet."

"Big deal...So I'm in a bar where there's been a shooting...I can't help what happens in this world...and I didn't even know that the bar was that bad," he added as he looked over for a rebuttal, but she seemed too preoccupied with something floating in her wine glass. "And what was I supposed to do, let the guy die? I couldn't do that...If I had done that, I would have been charged with abandonment...They put that in the newspaper? No. And what, I get no credit for putting my neck on the line? And I don't even know what you're talking about, me looking at something in the newspaper some way...Don't even know what you're talking about," he added as she started to cry again.

"And I knew if I told you about it, that it would upset you... And I knew that this is exactly how you would react...and that's exactly why I didn't say a thing to you...I didn't want you to have to worry about it...I was looking out for you, and that's the thanks I get," he said, pausing as he watched her continue to cry and act disinterested in what he was telling her. "And I'm so happy that you're so concerned about my well-being...You know, I could have gotten shot...you ever think of that...I mean, the guy's crazy...and I was the only one brave enough to go into the bar to help the other guy...the only one brave enough to talk to the police...Everyone else, I heard, was too scared to say anything to the police...ought to get a medal just for that...But that's fine. I just apologize again for any inconvenience I may have caused you or anyone else for saving someone's life and doing what was right."

"You just don't care about anyone but yourself...never have... don't care who you hurt," she said, sobbing more deeply now. "And frankly, I think you're going crazy...talking to yourself...obsessing over some damn old pair of smelly sneakers...and some little toy cars...That's the exact definition of crazy...or nervous breakdown or some kind of a bizarre midlife crisis...the whopper of all midlife crises," she added as she started up the steps slowly...finally stopping halfway up to turn back, point in his direction, and yell at him that he was crazy. She then stumbled and nearly fell backward down the steps before catching hold of the railing, her dark make-up now smeared eerily down both her cheeks.

"And I just hope something like this happens to you someday..." she said as she continued up the steps. "We're going to lose everything now anyway...and then I can move into the YMCA with other people just like us...bag ladies and derelicts," she said as she slammed her bedroom door shut.

He stood at the top of the steps for a while trying to determine if it would help to continue...but knew that anything he told her now probably wouldn't help...And as far as he was concerned, he had done pretty well and it seemed like a good place to stop. She was too drunk and out of control to be reasoned with. Would just let her finish venting, he thought as he stood outside her door and listened to her mostly disjointed tirade and hysterical sobbing before he walked back down the steps.

He sat at the kitchen table and drank and half listened...first to Sandy's sobbing and then her laughing and then back to talking to herself about different things...money and her mother and eventually getting around to yelling something about Hileman and her dog...but none of it made much sense. And then, toward the end, speaking as if he were in the room and telling him how he needed to see a psychiatrist...a small pause of silence...and then the sound of her wine glass breaking against the wall...seemingly the sign that ended her disjointed tirade...the bell for the end of round one, he imagined.

Just let her burn herself out. Could smooth things out some in the morning, maybe...tell her how well the trial was going, and about Hileman's breakdown on the witness stand and how Morgan felt that they had a pretty good chance of winning the case. Might make her come to her senses, he thought. At this point, he was not even sure that he really cared.

When he turned on the light in the guest bedroom...where he thought there might still be some furniture...there was none...no bed...no night stand...no nothing...everything gone but the paint, he could see. Last extra bed in the house gone like the wind. Would have to sleep on the couch downstairs, he thought as he started back down the stairs.

He had gotten off pretty easy so far...at least for the first salvo, he imagined. Hadn't been more than a ten-to-fifteen-minute tirade, and he had come up with a pretty good story that still might have some life left in it. And Sandy would be calmer in the morning when she was sober and had regained her reasoning, and he could smooth things out more then. And then just hope that she didn't find out anything more about what really happened at the bar, he thought as he lay down on the couch and covered himself with an afghan that was way too small, and tried to sleep. But all his conflicts rolled around confused in his thoughts as if they had nowhere to go, like a villainous nightmare refusing him escape.

CHAPTER FORTY-SIX

Thursday, May 20
6:45 a.m.

The first good sleep that he'd had in weeks, he thought as he sat on the edge of the couch. Felt good about the fact that, for all intents and purposes, the trial would be ending today. Soon another major problem would be behind him. And more, the trial might not turn out as badly as he had expected...especially after Hileman's major meltdown yesterday.

Sandy was probably still sleeping it off, he thought as he quietly passed by her bedroom door.

He dressed in one of his better suits and one of his most expensive silk ties. Wanted to at least look good for the last day, he thought as he checked his appearance in front of the hallway mirror.

Even the pain and swelling in his hand had subsided, he realized as he stopped briefly in front of Sandy's bedroom door to listen for any sounds that she might be awake. But there was nothing but silence.

He made coffee and ate a cold waffle as he read the newspaper...but for a change there was nothing about the trial. Would have been nice if the newspaper had printed something about Hileman's drunken performance on the witness stand yesterday... how confused she had been...or even something about how she had been able to dance freely at last year's Spring Fling...but there was nothing.

If it had been anyone other than Hileman, the newspaper would have had it all...and embellished, Weed knew as he slid the paper aside, disgusted.

The hottest day of the month...for the year for that matter, he supposed, taking a quick look around for any signs of Pickles as he left the house. Felt like a sauna, he thought as he drove toward the courthouse with all the car windows down.

When he got to the courthouse, he sat in the shade of some trees and sipped his Coke and bourbon, wondering if Hileman would be in any better condition today.

He didn't see Hileman's private investigator anywhere around the front of the courthouse. Good sign...Maybe he had found the dog, and he wouldn't have to put up with any of his harassment today, Weed thought as he got out of the car and walked across the street to the courthouse.

Morgan, Hileman, and Turzak were already in the courtroom when he entered. Turzak was leaning in close to Hileman, talking to her like he had been doing the day before, and she didn't really look much better than she had yesterday, Weed thought. Maybe a little more awake, but she still looked like she had already been drinking heavily.

"Well, this is it. Should be our last agonizing day," Morgan said, looking over at Weed before handing him some papers. "It's our closing statement. You can look it over to make sure I didn't leave anything out," he said as Weed reviewed the paper that Morgan had given him.

"She looks a little better today, but I still think she's had a few too many," Morgan said after a long pause. "They still had a lot of trouble getting her out of the car this morning. And she's been acting sort of strange, like maybe she's taking some other kind of medication to keep her awake...maybe a stimulant or something... but I'm not sure. And she keeps looking over here too," Morgan added. "Like now," he said as Weed looked up to see her turned awkwardly toward them. "Sort of freaky," he added.

"I feel like going over and telling her what I think about all this mess. Tell her that she owes me an apology for all this harassment over this dog thing," Weed said, looking up from the papers.

Morgan shrugged his shoulders. "Maybe later...And we don't need any more distractions or trouble this morning."

"Might be my last chance. I have to confront her and tell her what I really think...and make her apologize," he said and went back to reading over Morgan's closing statement as the courtroom continued to fill with a standing-room-only crowd. And maybe more reporters than he had ever seen in the courtroom, Weed thought.

And then he watched as the bailiff led the jurors past him and into the jury box. A different bailiff than before, and he had brought the jurors in through a different door, before the judge had even been seated. Seemed strangely...out of order, he thought as he watched the fans move lethargically overhead, wobbling, moving the hot air from one place to another but not offering any relief. He could already feel the sweat running down his back.

He didn't know when it all started. One minute, he was sitting quietly at the desk reading Morgan's closing statement and not thinking about much of anything. Only anxious that the nightmare would soon be over and not really able to concentrate on what he was reading, when he noticed a commotion in the general direction of where Hileman and Turzak were sitting. Voices, saying something louder than he would expect, arguing sort of...A confusing, unexpected disturbance in an otherwise relatively calm courtroom.

And then to his right, a blur in his peripheral vision, like a floater. When he looked, Hileman, still in her wheelchair, was now ominously close to where Weed was sitting. Closer than she should have been, and wheeling even closer. Turzak was turned awkwardly in his chair, calling her name, seemingly confused himself about what she was doing but not making any attempt to stop her progress.

Hileman moved even closer to where Weed was seated before attempting to stand...once falling back into her wheelchair and then a second time successfully...but precariously teetering, as if she were about to fall off a narrow ledge of a tall building...and now standing not ten feet from where he was sitting...blocking the rays of light coming through the windows...her shadow now being cast partially across him.

Puzzling, confusing behavior, Weed thought, thinking that maybe she wanted to talk to him about getting her dog back or even maybe wanting to apologize to him for not harming the dog. She stood there swaying, as if she might soon fall, clutching her purse with her left hand while she searched the purse with her right.

Turzak standing behind her, looked confused and called her name quietly...trying to get her attention.

Weed looked up at her and smiled but felt strangely intimidated by her scarred face and closeness.

Her hair and pink suit were disheveled, and her look was more ominous than friendly now, Weed could tell.

He was almost tempted to stand and steady her, and to help her find whatever she was looking for in her purse, just as she took a step backward before pulling something out of her purse. Something shiny and metallic, Weed could see, but mostly hidden beneath a piece of colorful fabric. An object that with a little imagination might almost look like a gun peeking out from beneath the colorful fabric that she was holding, he thought.

She was probably crazy enough to do something like that, but it was a pretty absurd thought, he imagined as he felt his heart start to race.

"What the hell is she trying to do?" he asked, turning toward Morgan, who apparently hadn't noticed her standing there.

But when Morgan looked up at him and then at Hileman, he got a shocked look on his face before quickly moving away…falling awkwardly to the floor under the table in a semifetal position, without uttering a word or explanation.

And when he turned back to see what Morgan had seen, he could now see that he had been right and that what Hileman was holding was indeed a gun…a gun that she was now holding firmly between both hands and pointing directly at him. Hileman looked down at the gun, seemingly trying to determine that it was pointed in the right direction…before looking directly at him with glazed over eyes…and trying to take better aim, he imagined…as he stood frozen, fearful of making any sudden movements. It was a point-blank shot. There was no way he could escape now without getting shot, he knew, trying to rack his brain for a solution.

To talk her out of it…by telling her that her dog was fine and where she could find it seemed like the most logical solution.

Hileman stood there wobbling slightly and inebriated, holding the gun unsteadily. A gun that seemed to almost be levitating out of focus in front of him…but was pointed directly at him.

"She's got a gun," Weed could now hear someone shouting in the background and someone else yelling, "Oh my God," in a frightened squeal and then a collective gasp of the crowd, accompanied by the sound of chairs sliding across the floor and more gasps as people scrambled to escape. A wave of people disappeared from his peripheral vision, leaving only Hileman and himself standing alone at the front of the courtroom.

Hileman teetered even more precariously now, staring menacingly at Weed and holding the gun as if her target was moving erratically.

Weed was frozen. He couldn't move, even if he had wanted to... frozen in fear. And not a single route to escape without being shot, he knew. And with the way the gun was bobbing around aimlessly, he probably had a better chance of not getting shot by standing as still as he could, he realized, mortified...even though he still had a strong urge to run wildly away.

Hileman was now sort of bent forward, with her collar twisted awkwardly around her neck, still wearing her sunglasses, holding the gun with both hands, and shaking uncontrollably as she shrieked almost hysterically...trying to say something with slurred words. Turzak was standing behind her now, looking confused and still unable to see the gun, shaking his head and calling her name calmly but maybe realizing that something drastic was happening.

"People think I'm crazy. Well, I'm not crazy," Hileman finally said with her speech more clear but still slurred, pausing for what seemed like a long time before mumbling something more about her psychic and her dog...not really making much sense...but Weed understood completely.

"You're as crazy as me!" she finally shouted.

The gun still levitated erratically in front of him, as if she had no real target or any real control over it...that it might go off at any second, whether she intended it to or not. And she was obviously very drunk.

"You hear what I said, Weed?" she said, shaking the gun like a pointer. "You're as crazy as me!"

He could hear, but he was more aware of other people in the courtroom yelling hysterically as they continued to scramble toward the exits, the whole scene seemingly being played out in slow motion. He was going to have to do something fast, he knew.

And then out of nowhere, he had the bizarre thought that the whole situation was nothing more than some old *Saturday Evening Post* cover of a perverted Norman Rockwell painting...a colorful painting of jurors, security guards, the judge, and Hileman holding her gun to shoot a well-dressed man standing in front of her. Was a disturbing and troubling image, Weed thought.

"Calm down," he finally told her as he held out his hands in front of him. "Your dog's fine. It was just a big joke anyway. What's the big deal...She's fine," he said, having trouble finding the right words but even then hoping that no one could hear his confession. "She's at the shelter right down the street," he blurted out as quickly as he could, but the words seemed heavy and sticky and were coming out slow, some of them seeming not to come out at all...And he wondered if any of it was making any sense. Just then, Hileman lost her balance and stumbled slightly backward before righting herself.

It was just after that. Just after he heard the security guard tell everyone to calm down...that it was nothing more than a toy gun that Hileman was holding...and that it was impossible to get a real gun into the courthouse...And just a split second after he felt some small sense of relief and comfort from the guard's words that it all happened. When the old security guard tentatively tried to snatch the gun from Hileman, Weed heard the gun shot and felt the sharp pain in the middle of his chest. A direct hit...right over his heart, he realized. He had been shot.

There was a low thumping, snapping sound of the gun as Hileman lost her balance and the old security guard flinched, turning away from Hileman and crouching in the opposite direction, apparently now no longer interested in capturing the toy gun. Hileman fell backward from the recoil of the gun, trying to catch herself before missing the seat of her wheelchair but hitting it with enough force to send it spinning aimlessly in circles...around twice, before it rolled backward and slammed into the jurors' box as Hileman continued to the floor. All witnessed in slow motion, before the bullet had had any of its lethal effects. Hileman hit the floor with a thump and a blood-curdling scream as the gun slid across the floor and a different security guard chased after it on his hands and knees.

The sound was not loud, but nothing like that night at Tanner's Bar when the gunshot had been deafening, he remembered. He felt the sharp pain in the middle of his chest and grabbed for the wound, twisting in agony, trying to make sense of it all in his confused mind.

Couldn't believe that he had been shot. That this was the way his life was going to end. Couldn't believe he had been shot over some stupid mutt, he thought and then did what he thought someone should do when you got shot and were about to die: he stumbled backward slightly, like he had seen thousands of times in the movies, sort of turning and catching himself on a chair before continuing his fall to the floor…joining Morgan, who was already curled in a fetal position under the table.

He could feel the blood now as he lay there on the floor, breathing deep, sucking for air, trying to get all the air he could, and realizing that this was what it was like to die. But there wasn't much pain. He was more just short of breath, and weak, as if the life was slowly being sucked from his body one breath at a time…and the faster he breathed, the harder it became. The bullet must have torn through a major blood vessel in his chest or collapsed one of his lungs, he imagined as he continued to try to suck in as much air as he could, to breathe deep, but now feeling lightheaded and numb… as he pressed harder on his chest to try and slow the bleeding, he realized that any chance that the bullet had bounced harmlessly off a rib were behind him…and then he wondered if someone might have a ballpoint pen that he could use to shove into his chest and reinflate his collapsed lung and save his life. His last hope down to a ballpoint pen…a thought that seemed absurdly ridiculous, he knew.

So this is what it was like to die. All the things unsaid, undone, he thought...saying a quick prayer, to see him through this one last crisis, to not let him die. To forgive him for all his sins and all the mean things he had done in his life and for all his doubts about religion...just in case, he thought. Trying to come into the flock at the last minute...in the bottom of the ninth...through the back door...And if he lived, he would be more religious and a much better person, he swore.

But annoyingly, the one thing he was aware of as he lay there near death...the one thing that he could hear over everything else in the courtroom...distracting him even from his prayers...even as he lay dying...was Gertrude Hileman's incessant moaning...in a high-pitched, annoying screech...repeating over and over the lancinating words, "I broke my fuckin' hip...I broke my fuckin' hip..." Out of all the din and commotion of the courtroom, out of all the screams and yells of the security guards and whoever else was screaming and yelling, the only sound that he could really perceive and concentrate on was her endless moaning...that she had broken her fuckin' hip.

Those words could be the last words that he ever heard, he imagined. "I broke my fuckin' hip," coming from the person that had just shot and killed him because he had stolen her dog. Didn't seem right, he thought. Didn't seem like the words you would want to end your life on, he knew.

And then in his line of vision with his head on the floor, he could see the soles of Hileman's shoes, one pointing up and the other turned out awkwardly at ninety degrees, and he realized that she was probably right...that she had broken her fuckin' hip.

And then just before he was sure he was about ready to lose consciousness...when he could no longer take one more breath... when his vision was getting fuzzy and distant...his hands getting numb...and thinking that he might actually see a white light approaching him, to lead him into the afterlife or somewhere else...

he could hear and see someone in the distant light laughing, saying something again about the gun just being a toy gun. Maybe an angel playing a trick on him, he thought as he tried to concentrate on the glowing image.

Then the angel floated forward before leaning down close to Weed's face and asked if he was all right, or told him that he's all right, or something that he wasn't sure of. An angel that looked surprisingly like one of the jurors he had seen every day for the last two weeks, telling him that she had once been a paramedic and that he was going to be okay.

"I have a chest wound. I need an ambulance," he gasped up at her blurry figure.

"I don't think...they're saying that it's just a toy gun," she repeated as he continued to resist her attempts to remove his hand from his chest so that she could examine his wound.

"Toy gun...I can feel the blood...and I can hardly breathe. If I take my hand off my chest, I'm going to die! That's the only thing preventing me from bleeding to death!" he added, still in a panic.

"Well, they're telling me that it's just a toy...And I think the reason you can't breathe is because you're hyperventilating."

"Trust me, I have my hand over the bullet hole and I can feel blood. My hand is the only thing that's keeping me alive. What I need is an ambulance, now," he pleaded, feeling even more dizzy and lightheaded.

"There's an ambulance on the way," someone shouted as others gathered around to look down at his curled up body on the floor.

"It's just a paintball gun. You just got hit with a paintball," the security guard said, laughing and holding the gun down so that Weed could see it more closely. "And I was right the first time. There's no way anyone could get a real gun into this courthouse."

"You're going to be just fine...So let me see where it hit you, Dr. Weed," the woman insisted, pulling his hand gently away from his chest as the paramedics moved toward him with a stretcher.

"Just a little green paint," one of the paramedics said with a laugh as he looked at where Weed had been holding his chest. "It's not blood that you're feeling, unless the color of your blood is green," he added as he continued to try to get him to take his hand away from his chest.

Weed reluctantly moved his hand away as the paramedic folded Weed's tie back, exposing the clean white shirt.

"I don't think that it even ruined your shirt," the paramedic said. "But your tie is toast...and you need to slow your breathing... you're hyperventilating," he added as he looked back over his shoulder and then asked another paramedic to bring him a paper bag.

The paramedic placed the paper bag over Weed's mouth and then helped him up from the floor and into a chair.

He felt relieved as he took a few deep breaths into the paper bag, but he still wasn't certain that he wasn't going to die. He felt like an idiot as he watched the judge pounding his gavel and yelling out orders for everyone to come to order. But no one seemed to be listening or care what he was saying, Weed realized as he continued to watch the chaos unfold around him.

Cops, security guards, paramedics, and other individuals moved around chaotically...until it seemed that there was little space left inside the courtroom.

Then a SWAT team in full riot gear entered the courtroom and progressed cautiously down the center aisle toward the front of the courtroom, making quick jerking movements with their guns as they searched for other dangers...another gunman in the crowd who might still want to shoot him. And maybe there was someone else, Weed thought.

"I told them they couldn't get a real gun into the courtroom," the security guard told the judge proudly.

"I don't give a damn, I just want to know what the hell just happened here," the judge shouted as he stood behind his bench, looking out at the chaotic courtroom scene.

"She shot him because she thinks he stole her dog," Weed could hear someone shouting to the judge, sounding incredulous and ir-ritated at the question…as if the judge were the only person in the courtroom who didn't know what had happened.

But Weed couldn't believe that that had been the first explana-tion, and that the explanation had come so quickly.

"You just ruined your tie, but that's all. The shirt looks fine to me," the paramedic repeated as Weed tried to calm himself and slow his breathing.

He could still feel his heart racing…thumping hard inside his chest…and he was still visibly shaking…but he hadn't been shot, he concluded as he was finally able to take some normal breaths. The paramedic continued to urge him to slow his breathing.

"She shot him with this paintball gun that looks almost real," Weed could hear the security guard telling a police officer as he held the gun in front of him on the end of a pen. The officer finally took hold of the pen and dropped the gun into a plastic bag but seemed pissed that the security guard had been tampering with the evidence.

"And the jury saw everything?" the judge asked, seeming con-fused and just now realizing that most of the jurors were still seated in the jury box.

"Great…all this bullshit, and it's going to end up being nothing more than a mistrial…I can't believe it," he said, running his hands through his hair. "And so close the end…All this aggravation and bullshit for a mistrial," he said, sounding completely exasperated.

"So just clear the whole goddamn courtroom," Wisensee shout-ed and then repeated it as he banged his gavel hard against the desk. "I want everyone out of my damn courtroom," he said, this time looking at Morgan. "And I'm going to have the whole bunch of you ingrate clowns charged with contempt and pull your licenses," he said, pointing a finger in the direction of Morgan and then at Turzak, who was now kneeling down beside Hileman.

Weed continued to watch it all as he rubbed the small sore spot on his chest and tried to control his breathing, still trying to make sense of it all. Still not certain that it had all been real or just a bad dream that he would wake from at any second. But he was feeling better and no longer had the feelings of numbness in his hands or shortness of breath, and his fear of dying had passed.

"Probably hid it in her wheelchair somewhere when she came through security," Weed could hear a police officer explaining to another group of police officers as they all inspected the gun and Hileman's wheelchair.

"I think my client may have broken her hip," Turzak said, looking up at the judge as if the trial was still in progress and he was trying to make a motion. Hileman was still lying flat on her back on the floor, continuing to moan and yell annoyingly that she need a shot of morphine.

"Well, what do you want me to do?" the judge said to Turzak rhetorically and with biting sarcasm. "And give her something to quiet her down before she drives everyone in the courtroom crazy," he added as another group of paramedics arrived at the back of the courtroom and wheeled their stretcher down to where Hileman was lying.

There was still chaos and confusion everywhere. People trying to get into the courtroom to see what was happening and others trying to get out, afraid of what might happen.

"My son plays with these paintball guns all the time...and they can really knock the wind out of you...can put your eye out," the paramedic continued, laughing lightly as he checked Weed's blood pressure.

"You want to maybe let us take you to the hospital Doc?" the paramedic asked when he was finished taking Weed's vitals.

"I'm okay," Weed answered. "I'm feeling better now, and I think you were right...I was probably just hyperventilating some," he told the paramedic.

He was still sweating slightly but was not feeling as lightheaded as before, and his vision seemed to be almost back to normal.

"Maybe you should...Your pressure's still pretty high...one ninety over one ten," the paramedic told him as he took his pressure for the third time.

The police and security continued to move around the courtroom, taking names and asking questions and clearing the courtroom...and arguing with the judge intermittently about who was actually in charge as Weed watched, in disbelief over it all.

Then he watched as the paramedics picked Hileman up and put her onto a stretcher...her leg turned awkwardly outward and her stocking torn...her hair a mess and her dress disheveled...with her make-up smeared across her face as she winced in pain at any sudden movement...as the paramedics pushed her past where he was sitting.

She gave him one last glance as they wheeled her out of the courtroom. And for once, he felt truly sorry about everything that had happened...everything that he had caused.

The paramedics had been right...he had just hyperventilated. He felt fine now, he thought as he took the brown paper bag away from his face.

"I think that you should let us take you to the hospital with a blood pressure that high," the paramedic repeated but sounded less insistent.

"I'll be fine," Weed told him as he sat watching the crowd thin, now wondering if anyone had overheard what he had told Hileman about where she could find her missing dog...or if in his excitement he had told her something even more incriminating. It was hard to even remember what had actually happened now, or what he had told Hileman...It already seemed like it had happened a long time ago. And if what he thought had happened had happened, then it was all pretty damn crazy, he imagined. But in the excitement and confusion, maybe no one had heard much of what he had actually said to Hileman. Was going to have to deny it anyway, or admit that it had just been a wild guess that had been right.

At least everyone had witnessed firsthand what kind of a nut Hileman was…That was at least some consolation to what had just happened, he imagined.

"You okay?" Morgan asked, coming over to where Weed was seated and resting his hand on Weed's shoulder.

"I guess. Just shaken a little. But didn't I tell you that she was crazy?"

"Yeah, can't argue with you about that point now," he said, sitting down beside Weed. "She scared the crap out of me too. I just dove for cover when I saw her pointing that gun at you…thought that she might just start shooting," he said, seemingly somewhat embarrassed at his reaction. "And I really thought that you had been shot, the way you fell back and landed on top of me like dead weight," Morgan added as he inspected the green spot on Weed's tie. "Sprained my ankle pretty good when you fell," Morgan said, pushing his sock down so that Weed could see his swollen ankle.

"But you should probably go to the hospital like the paramedic told you with a blood pressure that high."

"I'm fine," Weed said and laughed as he watched Morgan take a few tentative steps on his injured ankle before moving further away to shake someone's hand…shaking his head in disbelief and wiping his brow in a gesture that it had been a close call.

Weed sat there, still stunned, and watched the judge fight with the police officers about how piss-poor the security had been…that someone could have gotten killed…and then arguing with them about who really had authority…pointing his finger at them accusingly before one of them told him that they had the authority to arrest anyone, including a judge, and that he needed to keep his mouth shut.

"You hear what the judge said? Going to declare it a mistrial," Morgan said as he sat down beside Weed again, sounding disgusted.

"Really nothing else he can do, I guess, after what the jury saw and heard," he told Weed. "All this work and aggravation down the drain in an instant...been almost two years," he said, sounding reflective. "And gone in two minutes..." he said and laughed. "Such is the world...And just when I thought we might actually win this thing...especially after yesterday. But now nothing...just a case lost in purgatory," he said, looking off in the distance contemplatively.

"I guess they're going to have to try the whole case all over again...from square one," Morgan said as he started to gather up some of his papers that had fallen to the floor. "New jury, new witnesses...new lawyers...But not me...I'm finished...No offense to you, but I don't want to have anything to do with this thing anymore," Morgan added. "But why couldn't she have done this on the first day of the trial instead of the last?" Morgan added.

"On the other hand...at least we didn't lose...and who knows, maybe she saved you from losing everything. A verdict could have gone the other way just as easily, I imagine...Jury could have given her a ton of money and then where would you be. Never know about these crazy juries these days. So that's maybe a good thing," he added, finally getting all the papers off the floor and into his briefcase. "And Hileman might not want to go through with another trial anyway...Maybe she's had enough and will just settle," he said, pausing to look around at the courtroom scene. "One thing...I will never forget this day as long as I live."

Weed watched as the police continued to move around the courtroom interviewing witnesses.

Courtroom seemed to be getting back to normal, Weed could see. The SWAT team had left, as had most of the police officers and security guards...as had most of the other people that had been in the courtroom. But the jurors were all still sitting in their seats as a police officer went down the line, questioning each one of them. And the judge was sitting quietly now, his head bent in his hands, looking down at papers scattered in front of him.

When Weed finally calmed down enough to think about what had just happened, his relief of still being alive and uninjured quickly turned into anger. Now, he felt pissed at what Hileman had done...what she had committed...an assault and battery...plain and simple. Hileman had assaulted him with a potentially deadly weapon, he realized, and there had to be serious legal ramifications for someone doing something like that. Police should have arrested her already, Weed thought. They should have read her rights to her and put her in handcuffs and taken her away in a police car instead of an ambulance. If he had been the one who had done the shooting, that's exactly what they would have done to him, he thought, growing even more incensed.

And he was going to sue Hileman. Sue her for assault and battery and for all the injuries she had caused him for everything she was worth. He could probably come up with some pretty good fabricated injuries himself that she had caused him to suffer. He was hit in the chest and fell hard to the ground...back and neck injuries maybe...not to mention the mental anguish he would likely suffer for the rest of his life. He could accuse her of all kinds of physical and psychological trauma, just like she had done with him. See how she liked it when the tables were turned...He could lay it on just as thick as she could, he knew...but the plan seemed cheap and hollow for some reason.

Might just go to the hospital anyway to have it all documented... couldn't hurt. Get X-rays, wear a collar, the whole nine yards, just like she had done, he thought. Was definitely going to press criminal charges, he knew as an officer came over and told them both that they were going to have to remain until an officer had questioned them.

"Isn't this an assault? I mean, didn't she technically assault me, and couldn't I have her arrested?" Weed asked, turning toward Morgan as the officer moved away.

"Yeah, probably...I guess," Morgan answered.

"I might just do that. Have her arrested for assault and battery."

"What'd you say about her dog, anyway?" Morgan asked after a long silence, as if he had just remembered.

"What?" Weed asked, upset that someone had heard his mini-confession and trying to think how he was going to answer.

"You said something to her about the dog right before she shot you."

"Don't even know what I said now," Weed said with a laugh. "I said something?"

"Yeah, I think I heard you tell her that her dog was fine and in a kennel somewhere."

"Don't even remember, but I could have said anything with a gun being held on me," he answered. "I probably would have told her that I had the damn dog in my back pocket if I thought it would have prevented her from shooting me," he said and laughed again. "Just told her anything that popped into my head I guess…What did you think I said again?" he asked Morgan, trying to act confused.

"I think you said that the dog was fine and was located at the an-imal shelter down the street or something…But I could have been wrong," Morgan told him.

"Don't even remember."

"Yeah, well, it was pretty quick thinking."

Weed watched as the judge started yelling again at the para-medics and then the security guards before the police reminded him that they didn't need his help, that if he didn't calm down they were going to have to remove him from the courtroom, that they were responsible for carrying out a thorough investigation, and that they didn't need his help.

Weed dabbed at his tie with a paper towel as he stood in front of the bathroom mirror after the police agreed to let him leave the courtroom to use the restroom. He didn't really want to talk to the police. If Morgan had heard what he had said to Hileman, then there was a good chance that others had heard what he'd said too. And he was going to have to come up with some explanation, he thought, stopping to look at his flushed face in the mirror. He held out his hand to see if he was still shaking, but instead he only noticed the dog bites.

He watched someone in the mirror as he entered the restroom and stepped to the sink beside him.

Would just have to tell the police that it was all just a coincidence when they found the damn dog at the shelter. That he knew that she was upset about losing her dog, and it seemed like the most logical thing to tell her so that she wouldn't shoot. And then he could tell them that it had just been "a strange coincidence" when they found the dog.

"You hear some guy just got shot in the courtroom across the hall?" the man standing beside Weed asked. "That's what all the excitement was about...killed him, I guess," the man added after a long pause. "Heard that it was all over some kind of strange dog tale...that he stole her dog or something. Ever hear of anything as crazy as that?" the man added, laughing as Weed smiled and pushed his stained tie inside of his shirt. "A lot of crazy people out there these days," the man added as Weed moved toward the exit.

"Another dog joke," Weed thought, disgusted, as he walked back to the courtroom. "A dog tale..." Wasn't any more funny than Bob's hot dog joke was, but he would have to tell Bob anyway.

Weed sat in the courtroom for almost an hour as the police moved painfully slowly around the courtroom questioning witnesses before telling them they could leave.

Someone brought over coffee for both of them, and the paramedic checked his blood pressure one last time before leaving.

Weed sat there for almost an hour before almost everyone else in the courtroom had been interviewed. He tried to relax and figure out what he was going to tell the police to make it all sound believable...realizing that they may have already found the dog...

and that this was the second time in just a week that he had been questioned by the police.

Should probably just tell them the truth, he thought. But he wasn't going to. Not now. Not this close to the end. Not to make him look like the guilty party again. Didn't want to face the consequences now, he thought, and the chances were small that they could prove anything even if they had heard what he'd said, he thought as he sat there and wiped the sweat from his forehead... and rubbed his chest.

He was just going to tell the police that he didn't have any idea what he had said or where the dog was, but that he wanted to file charges against Hileman...distract them and turn the tables...that she had been psychotically harassing him about her lost dog all week, and he didn't know a thing about it. That's what he was going to tell the police.

The whole thing was pretty ridiculous. The kind of story you read about in the *National Enquirer*. The kind of story that no one ever believes...just an embellished fairy tale from someone's creative imagination...that it was all so crazy that someone had to have made it all up. That he had been shot by some deranged lunatic with a toy gun because he had stolen her dog. Jesus, how much more ridiculous could a story get...How much more ridiculous could his life become?

Couldn't imagine what the newspapers would print about it tomorrow, he thought as he finished his coffee and watched as one of the police officers started walking in his direction.

CHAPTER FORTY-SEVEN

Thursday, May 20
11:43 a.m.

"You okay?" the officer asked, smiling, as he adjusted his laptop and started typing. "Guess it was quite a scare for you. Just lucky it wasn't a real gun," he said as he looked at the green stain on Weed's tie.

Weed nodded in agreement.

"Guess that she was upset about the trial...with her scars and her neck injuries," he said as the investigator brought up a small homunculus-like figure at the bottom of his laptop. "And also upset about losing her dog or her dog running away or something...that she thought that maybe you had something to do with that too?" the officer asked, looking over at Weed for an answer.

"Pretty crazy, isn't it? Weed said, shaking his head in disbelief.

"So she thought that you took her dog and then with all this other stuff going on with the trial, I guess she just sort of snapped?"

"I guess," Weed answered. "Her and her private investigator have been sort of harassing me all week about that dog...especially her private investigator. Didn't even know what they were talking about until someone explained it to me," he said, trying to sound believable.

"That's what I understand," the officer said as he looked over some papers. "So you were sort of having a disagreement with Hileman all week about her dog."

"She was, not me."

"But you didn't have any idea what they were talking about with the dog?"

"I didn't have a clue what they were talking about until they told me."

"So she got a little more upset every day when she couldn't find her dog, and I guess that was her basic motivation for shooting you today?"

"I guess that's probably part of it. That and all the other things that she blamed me for over the last two years...the scars on her face and her back and neck pain and then a bunch of other things she claimed I was responsible for causing her," he said, pausing as he watched the officer type the information into his laptop.

"My honest opinion is that she's got some really deep-seated psychological problems, and she just snapped. That and the fact that I think she's an alcoholic who's been drinking pretty heavy today."

"Yeah, it is pretty strange," the officer said as he turned the laptop so that Weed could see the screen. "I guess they were going to get her a psychiatric evaluation after they took care of her hip," the officer added.

"And you got hit with the paintball about right here?" the officer continued as he pointed to the small chest area on the diagram of the man displayed on his laptop.

"Yeah, that's about right, I guess," Weed answered as he looked at where the officer was pointing.

"Would you mind standing at the spot you were standing when she shot you?" he asked.

Weed stood and then moved to the approximate spot where he thought he had been standing when he had been shot.

"And would you say that this is about where Ms. Hileman was standing when she shot you?" the officer asked, standing in front of Weed but a little further away than Weed thought that Hileman had been standing.

"A little closer, I think."

"So she's standing about here," the officer said after moving forward. "That close," he said, seeming surprised at how close they had been standing to each other. "So she wheels herself over here in her wheelchair to about right here and then gets out of her wheelchair, fumbles with her gun for a couple of seconds, says something to you about being upset about you taking her dog...and then you tell her something about her dog...and then shortly after that...that's when she shoots you?" he asked as Weed shook his head in agreement.

"Then she sort of lost her balance and fell backward to the floor, and that's when you fell to the floor too?"

"Yeah, I guess that's about right."

"You sure you're okay? You still look a little pale," the officer said, telling Weed that he should sit down, and that he was sorry if he had upset him any more by putting him through his bad experience all over again.

"So she's upset over the dog and the scars and maybe a lot of other things...and that you're both at this banquet where her dog turns up missing, and she just assumes that since you were already fighting it out in court and that you don't like each other that you might have taken her dog?"

"Pretty crazy, I know...But I figure that's about it in a nutshell," Weed answered.

"Well, I can sort of understand her thinking it, but it is sort of crazy. A grown man...a physician no less...doing something as crazy as that," he said, laughing, as he continued to type his report into his laptop. "But people get crazy ideas in their heads. Do crazy things like this all the time," he added, pausing to make a correction. "So she thinks that you have her dog. She wheels over to where you're sitting, stands, pulls out the gun...and then says something to you about 'where's the dog' or something? And then you said something like, 'your dog is at a shelter down the street somewhere'?" he said, looking at him as if he were watching more for his reaction than for his answer.

Weed shrugged his shoulders. "Don't even really remember what I said, now."

"A couple people thought they heard you tell her something like that, that the dog was okay, and that it was at one of the shelters around here somewhere," he said, looking up at him after reading from the screen. "Something like that?"

"Yeah, I think I probably said something like that, I guess. To tell you the truth, I don't know what I said to her. You say most anything when someone's holding a gun on you," Weed said, sort of laughing. "I just made up some kind of story and hoped that she would buy it and wouldn't shoot."

"Yeah, that was good thinking," the officer said with a touch of sarcasm, Weed thought, but wondered if someone had already found the dog at the shelter.

"Yeah...well, that explains it. So you really didn't have any idea where her dog was...I mean, how could you...but you were just making up some kind of story to prevent her from shooting you?"

"Yeah...I guess I'm not even sure what I was thinking...or what I was telling her. I mean, I'm still sort of in shock over the whole ordeal," Weed said, holding up his hand to show the officer that he was still shaking, realizing too late that he had just exposed the dog bites.

"Understand completely," he said. "And I think that about does it for now," the officer said as he closed his laptop. "If you think of anything else later you want to tell me, give my office a call," he said, handing Weed a business card. "And I would strongly recommend that you get checked at the hospital. I heard them tell you that your blood pressure was way too high, and you still look a little pale," he added with a smile.

"I might," Weed said and then thanked him, before asking him if Hileman was going to be charged with anything.

"Don't really know right now. Bringing a gun into a courtroom is pretty serious business…even if it is just a toy gun…with all the crazy things going on in the world today. But then, if she was under a lot of stress and not thinking right…probably not much we can do, and she was saying some pretty crazy things when they wheeled her out of here. Didn't really make much sense. Sort of feel sorry for her, actually."

"Just seems that if someone pulls a gun and shoots someone that it would be enough to have them arrested."

"Yeah, I understand your concerns completely…but that hasn't been determined yet. But she is an old lady with psychological problems who now has a broken hip. Seems like that's almost punishment enough, if you know what I mean, and anyway, it's all up to the DA to file any charges. I don't have anything to do with that. But if it was me, I would forget about it for now and relax and let us take care of everything…Let us complete our investigation and find out exactly what happened…and then we'll make our decision. And you take care of yourself," he added as he moved away.

Figured as much. If he had been the shooter they would have arrested him on the spot, put him in handcuffs, and hauled him off to jail…and his picture would be on the front page of every newspaper in the county, he was sure.

But at least the interview had gone pretty well…Officer acted satisfied with his answers…and he didn't act suspicious with any of his answers about Hileman's dog, Weed thought as he left the courtroom.

Morgan was waiting for him outside the courthouse.

"You still doing okay?" Morgan asked as he approached.

"I guess. Who knows? The whole thing's just a big, confusing blur," Weed answered.

"You want me to drive you to the hospital?" Morgan asked.

"I'm fine."

"Anyway, I wanted to tell you that Judge Wisensee wants to talk to us all tomorrow morning. Can hardly wait for that. But his secretary is supposed to call and tell me when and what's up with the trial. Has to be a mistrial though…after the jury saw what happened today. Can't salvage any of the trial now," he repeated, shaking his head in disbelief. "So I'll call you when I find out what's going on," Morgan said as they continued walking toward the exit.

"You *sure* you don't want me to drive you to the hospital?" Morgan asked as he started walking off in a different direction.

But Weed shook his head that he didn't as Morgan continued on his way.

Weed stood at the top of the courthouse steps for a minute, looking out at the street and the people, and all the police vehicles and ambulances, and the SWAT team vans and reporters, before starting down the steps.

"Would you like to give a statement, Dr. Weed?" one of the reporters asked when he got to the bottom of the steps just as all the other reporters swarmed around him like flies to a dead carcass…holding microphones in front of him as a few cameras moved around in front of him.

"No, don't think so," he said emphatically, trying to move around them all.

"Why'd she do it?"

"'Cause she's crazy," he mumbled reflexively but wasn't sure he should have. They would likely twist his words and make it the front-page headline in the morning paper, he imagined as he continued past them.

"We heard that you swiped her dog last week and wouldn't give it back."

"That's ridiculous," he laughed, shaking his head in a gesture of disbelief. "Do I really look like someone who would do something that stupid? Just another one of her delusions," he mumbled as he jogged across the street to his car.

Might be in a shitload of trouble when they found the dog at the shelter, he thought as he sipped at what little bourbon was left in the bottle, not even particularly caring who saw him now.

Would stick to his story that it was all just a coincidence, and that it had been a different dog he had found that night, and it was just a lucky guess that the dog was in a shelter somewhere, he thought as he sat in his car and then tried to make up his mind about whether he should go to the hospital to have his injuries documented for when he sued Hileman.

He started the drive toward the hospital, but he felt so tired of it all. Tired of even dealing with Hileman...It was all getting too crazy. He just wanted to be done with it all, he thought as he turned the car and drove instead to the Venus Lounge. He needed a drink a lot more than he needed an X-ray, he knew as he tried to call Sandy. Could tell her what had happened and tell her not to worry, that he was all right, he thought, but before she answered he ended the call. She probably wouldn't have answered or even cared how he was doing anyway, he imagined. She would have probably been just as happy if it had been a real gun.

And so the trial was over that quick...almost two years of misery and aggravation...ended in a split second...to be continued some time later, he imagined. And nothing resolved...do not pass go...do not collect two hundred dollars...go directly to jail...all just a game anyway, he knew.

CHAPTER FORTY-EIGHT

Thursday, May 20
2:17 p.m.

He sat at the bar and drank most of the morning and into the afternoon trying to come up with some reasonable story to explain it all away. As if the trial hadn't been embarrassing enough, he thought as he tried to call Sandy again. Three times and she still hadn't answered...didn't know what he would tell her or if it would even matter, anyway. She was already pissed about the newspaper article, and now he had to come up with some explanation for the fiasco at the courthouse.

He felt calmer now. His heart rate was lower, and the shaking in his hands was gone, he could tell as he held the phone up in front of him to see who was calling. Mordy.

"You okay?" Mordicah asked when he answered. "Was worried about you when I heard about all the commotion at the courthouse."

"I'm fine," Weed told him and then went into a long, detailed explanation of what had happened and how ridiculous it all had been. "Every time I think about it, it's like having a flashback. I get nervous and my hands start to shake. And Mordy, I swear it looked like a real gun," he said, not wanting to sound too much like a wimp. "Thought that with the way she was moving the gun all around that my best chance of not getting shot was just to stand as still as I could," he added, thinking that Mordy might find his statement funny. "And when the paintball hit me in the chest, I thought I was going to die," he said with as much emotion as he could muster...But his explanation just seemed to come out flat...as if he had already rehearsed too much.

"Well, I'm just glad to hear that you're okay and thought that I might be able to help."

"Yeah, well, thanks, but I think I'm fine...But do you realize that you're the first person who has called to find out if I was okay?" Weed said, feeling good that at least one person was concerned about his welfare...just surprised that of all people it had been Mordy.

"But I'm seriously thinking of suing the bitch. Been thinking about it all morning, and the more I think about what she did, the more pissed I get. Just have her arrested for assault and battery...just considering whether I should go to the hospital to have all my injuries and emotional distress documented...My blood pressure's sky high. And I injured my neck when I fell... You know, just to have it all documented if I decide to sue her... just like she did to me. My opportunity to get even...to see how she likes it."

"Yeah, I guess you could sue her," Mordy said with some hesitation and no enthusiasm.

"But I still can't believe it. Pretty damn ridiculous and embarrassing. The SWAT team and the police...was all just one big circus. And all because of this crazy idea that I had something to do with her losing her dog at that damn banquet we were at last Saturday night."

"Yeah, I did hear something about that."

"Her psychic told her some crazy story that she saw the damn thing floating around in heaven somewhere and that I had something to do with it. Anyway, she was so drunk that when she shot me she lost her balance and fell backward and broke her hip. So I guess she made out just as bad as I did...I'll probably end up getting blamed for her broken hip too. Anyway, you think that I have a case...assault and battery with psychological and physical injuries?"

"Maybe, but I'd have to think about it awhile, and that's not really my legal expertise."

"Bad thing is, I don't know if I want to get involved with her again...would really just like for it all to go away," Weed told him but was thinking more about all the trouble it might cause him. Especially with what Liz already knew about the dog...didn't want to really push it any further, he imagined.

"The bad thing is that Morgan thinks the judge is going to declare a mistrial, and I might have to go through this mess all over again," Weed continued.

"Yeah, probably with what happened...But at least you're not going to lose...and then you can go back to the way it was before all this started...at least for a while," Mordy explained.

"Hey, Ben," Mordy said, changing the subject abruptly as if he might not even be interested in what Weed had been telling him. "I have someone in my office right now, sort of busy, but the other reason that I called you was because I needed to talk to you about some leftover legal paperwork we need to get caught up on. I need a couple of signatures and thought that maybe we could meet up somewhere tomorrow. Like Starbucks for lunch or something?"

"Yeah, I guess that would be fine. That important?"

"No...nothing really important," he answered. "Just some legal real estate paperwork that I forgot about that needs the loose ends tied up on. But nothing really important," he repeated.

"I'll tell you, Mordy. I'm getting pretty fed up with everything... the trial, the shooting at the bar...my miserable life. "I'm seriously thinking about just giving it all up. Been thinking about it all after-noon. Just closing my practice and quitting medicine all together. Find something else to do with my life. Something easier...something uncomplicated with no stress. Just changing my life and mov-ing off in a completely different direction."

"You think you can start over that easy...just wipe the slate clean? You wouldn't last a week," Mordy laughed. "With your life-style...your obligations. You're stuck in the mud just like everyone else is stuck in the mud."

"Doesn't matter. At least I wouldn't have to put up with all this. Actually, I might not do anything for a while. Just lay back and take it easy. I mean, I have some retirement money...you know that...and I could live off that money for at least a couple years."

"Sounds pretty naïve to me. Doesn't sound feasible with all your responsibilities. You have an ex-wife, and kids to support, and a big mortgage, and bills...and hell, you haven't even paid off your MG yet. People would start coming out of the woodwork, taking you to court right and left to get their money if you did something like that. And to me it sounds like you could come out of this trial smell-ing okay, for the time being at least...maybe not like a rose, but not bad...I mean, there's a lot of things worse than a draw. You just might be able to go back to doing what you have been doing all your life...just like nothing ever happened...just like it was before."

"That's great. 'Like it was before.' That's what I'm saying. I don't want to go back to the way it was before. That's what I'm telling you. I'm tired of my life the way it is. I need something different. Something more...a change...I need a new life. That life is stale like an old loaf of bread that I should have thrown out years ago."

"You'll come to your senses when all this is behind you. And if I were you, I would think it out before you make any rash decisions. Anyway, I'll meet up with you tomorrow at Starbucks and we can talk about it then...but got to get going now, friend. I have clients, but I'm really sorry about what happened to you today. Just happy that you're okay, and if you need anything, just give me a call," he added, hanging up quickly before Weed could even respond.

Didn't seem to be taking him seriously, Weed thought. Sounded like Sandy giving him the same lecture when he had told her about his plans. But at least someone cared enough to call to see how he was doing, he guessed. But no calls from anyone else...Sandy, Frank, Bob, or even his mother...all gone missing...even though he was sure that at least some of them had heard about the shooting by now, he thought before taking out his phone and looking for any messages that he might have missed.

He sat at the bar and drank and watched the start of the news, wondering what Mordy wanted to talk to him about that was apparently so urgent.

Behind him the TV blared and reflected in the back bar glass in front of him pictures of a SWAT team moving wildly up the courthouse steps and into the courthouse...as a reporter described the action. Giving the story in fine detail...with lights flashing and Benjamin Weed being mentioned again and again...the reporter acting amused and sarcastic at the same time over the fact that it was nothing more than a paintball gun shooting...laughing before he began to interview an eyewitness, and just as Morgan's number came up on his cell phone screen.

"Judge is really pissed off," Morgan said before Weed could say a word. "He went ballistic and told me that we made a mockery out of his courtroom. That it was an attack on his good name and the impeccable reputation of his courtroom or some bullshit like that...he was so upset I couldn't understand what he was telling me half the time," Morgan added. "But he thinks that you were a big part of Hileman losing her mind...because you had something to do with the dog...But anyway, he wants us all back in court tomorrow at ten a.m. Says that he's going to fine us and then sentence us all to community service or some bullshit like that, since he can't really throw us in jail...which he said he would do if he could…but who knows what he's going to come up with by tomorrow. So come prepared."

"Yeah, well, I figured as much. I'm the victim, but I get the punishment."

"But anyway, he's already declared it a mistrial. So I guess you get to start all over again," he added, laughing, before ending the call.

The fresh air felt good as he walked along the river, sitting on one of the benches for a while to watch a couple of tugs pushing barges slowly up the river…trying to find something good about his life to think about. He walked aimlessly through the city and then through the festival, looking mindlessly at all the art…as the lights flashed…feeling more drunk than usual…and sort of looking for Frank. Someone to talk to…to bounce his story off of…but Frank was nowhere in sight.

When he got home, the house was silent and empty…echoing Sandy's name when he called out to her. Just made it easier for him that she was gone, he thought.

He lay down on the couch and thought about what he had told Mordy about giving it all up. Changing his life and just leaving it all behind, and how great it would be. To just get away from all this… from this crazy, unsatisfying life he had created, and back to the freedom and the excitement of youth.

He tried Sandy one last time before closing his eyes. Trying to sleep…but too anxious…images of Hileman standing in front of him with her gun…bizarre, confusing thoughts dancing around in his mind, not letting him rest…not setting him free. He felt spent and exhausted, old and long lost before he finally drifted off into a deep sleep.

CHAPTER FORTY-NINE

Friday, May 21
6:15 a.m.

He woke early, laying in the darkness and listening for any sounds to let him know that Sandy had returned, but there was nothing but dead silence. And her car was still gone from the driveway, he could see as he looked out the bedroom window at the first shades of morning. Already seemed lonely. She would probably return soon, but he wondered how much she had discovered about his other life...Candy, Liz, the dog...She might know about it all, he imagined.

He noticed the small bruise on his chest as he dressed in front of the mirror...and then his paint-stained tie hanging over the chair behind him. Made him anxious to think about the shooting all over again. The whole incident would be a source of embarrassment for a long time, he imagined. Immortalized forever...what people would remember about him. Wouldn't remember anything about all the people he had taken care of over the years...No, the only thing that

435

anyone would really remember was that he had been involved with some bizarre incident at the courthouse...that would likely morph into hundreds of even stranger stories. The rest of his life would be nothing more than a footnote. "That's the guy who the famous mustard lady shot," people would explain to their friends, he knew as he made the last adjustment to his tie. Consequences that lasted forever. "You're finished with the past, but the past's not finished with you," he thought, remembering and thinking how true that statement was. Of all the words of wisdom that he had been given over the years, those words seemed to be the truest and the most poignant.

After he had finished dressing he looked at himself closely in the mirror. He looked different today...older, yes...but wiser...he doubted it. Reflection always seemed like a stranger staring back at him...recriminating...judgmental...he didn't know what...but someone whom he didn't really recognize or know how to explain. Where had that other person gone...and when did this other person arrive? he thought, now staring mesmerized into his own eyes. Fixated by those two dull, brown, lifeless eyes...looked much older than just last week. An old face on a young-person psyche. And when did it happen? When did he get old? he asked himself, wishing that he was still young and full of life. He didn't want to get old. But he was. He had been young just yesterday it seemed, but now he was just another cranky old man that drank too much and mostly got in the way. An old man that was not only slipping physically but mentally too, he knew, finally looking away from the disturbing image. All of this his swan song.

Downstairs, he sat at the kitchen table and looked at the newspaper, but like every other morning he had a difficult time concentrating on what he was reading. Didn't really care anyway, he thought as he read about the courthouse shooting...almost detached. In the center of the front page, again, a large picture of the SWAT team climbing the courthouse steps and below the picture, two small pictures of himself and Hileman, both smiling about better times. Old pictures of them, when both were much younger, like old friends in a yearbook, together forever. AFA, he imagined.

Couldn't read anymore, he thought as he slid the paper aside. Was too annoying...and he knew what it would say. His mother would read it for him, he knew. So would Sandy and everyone else he knew. They would tell him what it said, he was certain as he added a little more bourbon to his orange juice.

He left the house and drove to the courthouse, uncaring of his safety now...feeling emboldened by his frustration...almost hoping Pickles would show up so he could tell the asshole about all the trouble he had caused him.

At least he had gone out with a bang, he thought, only slightly amused at the sick pun. He had shined brightly and burned out quickly.

He was going to quit drinking...he told himself as he took another drink of bourbon and then held the bottle out in front of him. As soon as this was all over, he vowed...Caput, he thought as he took another sip. Would get rid of his old friend...the only friend that had stood by him and had gotten him through most of this mess. That little man on the bottle with the smile on his face.

There were two police cars, and he counted seven police officers strategically placed outside the courthouse. Two officers looking though purses and briefcases, and two others going over people entering the courthouse with long, black wands as another seemed to be taking names and asking questions. Too little too late now...it was all over, fellows, Weed thought...unless Pickles was somewhere near. Just like everything these days. Nothing was done until it was too late, he thought as he got out of his car and walked across the street to the courthouse.

"Pretty good guess," he heard someone shout from behind him as he went up the steps of the courthouse...and then repeated the statement, this time more emphatic. "They found the dog at the

D. M. Baker

shelter…right where you said they would find it," the female voice insisted, sounding more sarcastic this time as Weed turned to see that the person speaking was one of the reporters that he had seen at the trial every day.

"Yeah, well, where did you expect they would find a dog? he said and then paused before adding, "What, you thought they would find it at a Jack in the Box?" he asked with dripping sarcasm.

"That's a good one," the reported answered, feigning a laugh as Weed continued up the steps. "I'll have to put that one in my next column."

The courtroom was empty but for Turzak, Morgan, and a court reporter…and two security guards standing solemnly at the back of the courtroom, their legs spread and their arms crossed in front of them…guns strapped to their waists, attentive, watching every move, like something might happen any minute.

"You were right, she broke her hip," Morgan said when Weed sat down beside him. "And Turzak's all bent out of shape…and they found the dog."

"That's what I heard," Weed said as the judge came into the courtroom.

"Yeah, found it at a shelter across town," Morgan said but made no incriminating statements.

Wisensee sat behind his desk and looked over some papers for a short time, acting disgusted and distressed before looking up and speaking.

"You don't know how pissed off I am. In twenty-five years, I've never seen anything so hideous," he said and then continued on for the next twenty-five minutes…in a rant that didn't always seem to make much sense, like some kind of a mad, disheveled scientist, and then finally getting around to telling Weed how cruel and heartless he had been.

"You shouldn't even be allowed to practice medicine. You're a menace to society. And if I had my way, I would have the state take

438

your license away from you and then I'd throw you in jail. You leave Ms. Hileman a paralyzed, disfigured invalid confined to a wheelchair and that wasn't good enough. Then you had the stupidity to pull off some idiotic sophomoric stunt like this to cause her to break her hip and suffer a nervous breakdown. You're a real John Dillinger," he added, shaking his head in disbelief. "And I know you had something to do with it, so don't even try to deny it. You're just lucky that you didn't harm the dog. And I know that you're responsible because they found the dog right where you said they would find it. And trust me, you haven't heard the last of that stunt...I have the police looking into it right now," he said, pausing as if he was waiting for Weed to say something. "But I'm tired of even looking at all of you...I want you all out of my sight...out of my life...out of my courtroom as soon as possible, before I do something irrational," he said and then paused for a long time, shuffling papers as if his thoughts were lost.

"So first, I'm charging you all with contempt of court and fining you each ten thousand dollars...the maximum fine permitted by law. And to make matters more interesting, I'm going to assign each one of you to two hundred hours of community service. I had planned to throw you all in jail for a while, but they tell me that's not possible. But at least I'll now have the satisfaction of knowing that you're all going to all suffer a little, spending time at some miserable job...that I've personally picked out for you.

"So each of you are going to spend four hours a day for the next ten weeks working at the worst possible place I could find to send you. I wanted to send you all down to the City Sewage Authority to work, but the last group of convicts screwed up something that cost the city over fifty thousand dollars to fix, and that's still not working right...so they don't take criminals anymore...But I found out that the Parks Department needs criminals just like you to scrub down their outhouses at all the city parks and to pick up garbage along all the highways around town. Seems appropriate...so I'm sending you all down there to work," he said, looking at them for any reactions. "So you're scheduled for Monday morning at ten a.m. sharp...so don't be late, or I'll send the police to look for you and then you'll be able to spend your two hundred hours down at the jail instead... and I *mean* ten a.m. sharp," he added, before bringing his gavel down hard one last time.

"She tries to kill me...shoots me in the chest...and I'm the one that gets screwed. That's how my life goes. Probably give her an award," Weed said to Morgan as they watched as the judge leave the courtroom.

"Your put her in the psych ward for the second time in less than a week, and caused her to break her hip. What more do you want Weed?" Turzak complained after overhearing what Weed was telling Morgan. "And I'm going to have you arrested when the police get to the bottom of this little dog stunt of yours...whatever it was," Turzak said as he went by Weed.

"Screw you," Weed said as Turzak continued out of the courtroom.

"Don't worry...no one's interested in her damn dog," Morgan told Weed when Turzak was gone.

"Well, I guess this is it for the trial," Morgan said, holding out his hand when they arrived at the top of the courthouse steps. "I can't say that it hasn't been exciting, and maybe it did work out for the best...who knows. There are worse things than a mistrial, and you might even consider the outcome a small victory," he said as he stood silent for a few seconds. "But I'll probably have more paperwork for you to sign, so I'll give you a call later...and the office will keep you informed if they ever get around to rescheduling a second trial," Morgan added before walking down the courthouse steps and disappearing into the crowd as Weed stood there and watched.

He didn't want to get into trouble over the dog this far out, Weed thought as he walked back across the street to his car, wondering if he should call Liz and try to smooth things out with her so she might keep her mouth shut…at least for the time being, while the heat was still on with the dog. An unforeseen consequence of his misadventure…restarting their miserable relationship. Would have to think about that for a while, regardless of the possible consequences.

At least for the foreseeable future, the trial was over…Should celebrate, he thought, but he didn't feel much like celebrating. Community service…cleaning toilets, picking up garbage, he thought as he sat in his car. He had seen the scraggly-looking men in orange uniforms in the park and out along the interstate picking up garbage. White bags dropped at the side of the road marking their route. They mostly looked like recovering drug addicts down on their luck. And now he was one of them. Couldn't be all that bad, and no one would likely recognize him zipping by in a car going seventy miles an hour, he figured as he started walking down the street toward Starbucks and his meeting with Mordy.

But he couldn't imagine going through another trial. Sitting there across from Hileman with her menacing stares for a second time. Listening to all the scathing accusations and innuendos. All the aggravation…all the embarrassment repeated…all the agony back for a standing ovation. Held over for a second performance, he thought just as Frank came up behind him.

"I read about the shooting. You okay, buddy?" Frank asked, patting him on the back. "We were all worried sick and then when we couldn't get you or Sandy to answer your phones, we got concerned. Helen wanted me to wait for you down here and talk to you and find out if you're all okay," Frank said, looking at him as if he were searching for bullet holes.

"I'm fine. But didn't I tell you she was crazy?"

"Yeah, you certainly did…I heard you say that on TV, but what's this crazy thing about you and her dog disappearing?"

"She's delusional is all that I can tell you. Psychic told her that I had something to do with her losing her dog. Doesn't that tell you something…a psychic?" Weed said, moving away from Frank and telling him that he was in a hurry but to tell Helen hello and that he and Sandy were just fine, and that he would have Sandy call her later.

"Just takin' it like an old trooper," Frank added, still walking behind him but having a hard time keeping up. "And remember, you need anything, you call me, and remember that big kick-butt fireworks display I told you about at the end of the festival. Supposed to be better than last year's. You should bring Sandy. Will take your minds off all these other problems you're having…cheer you up," he said nauseatingly as he turned and waved and then disappeared back into the crowd as Weed continued down the street.

CHAPTER FIFTY

Friday, May 21
1:15 p.m.

Weed sat at the table across from Mordy as they drank their coffee.

"Can you believe this weather? Rain, sun...doesn't know what it's going to do," Mordy said, making nervous conversation.

"Yeah, next thing you know it'll be snowing again...snowing in May," Weed responded as Mordy told him about a day in May he remembered when it snowed six inches.

"So Wisensee gave you two hundred hours of community service...Didn't I tell you he was crazy? But that's not too bad, I guess...considering," Mordy said, shaking his head in disbelief. "Going to cut into your free time for a while, I imagine. And it would have been nice to get the case out of the way once and for all...instead of having it linger for who knows how long now...especially when Morgan said it was looking pretty good for you guys," he added before putting his briefcase on the table and taking out some papers.

"What do you think about me filing charges against Hileman for assault and battery?"

"Yeah, don't know about that...maybe later when the dust settles," Mordy answered.

"Would give her a dose of her own medicine," Weed added, but he didn't think Mordy was listening. He seemed more interested in the papers he was shuffling nervously on the table in front of him... as if he were trying to put a puzzle together.

"What's up with all this, anyway?" Weed finally asked, looking over at the papers.

"Yeah, well it's sort of painful to bring it up now, Ben...I mean, with all you've been going through lately," he said, for the first time not making eye contact with Weed when he spoke. "And then we've been friends for so long...probably since...what, the ninth grade? Ms. Hycuk's math class," he said, smiling and finally looking across the table at Weed. "Where did the time go?"

"Yeah, were did the time go?"

"But I may as well not beat around the bush any longer and just come right out and tell you why I'm here," he said, hesitating and taking a deep breath before he continued. "But Sandy wants me to start drawing up divorce papers...and she wants me to be her lawyer..." he said before sliding one of the papers he had been shuffling toward Weed. Which brings up sort of a small dilemma for me...that basically I can't have both of you as clients...wouldn't be ethical...and a conflict of interest. And basically, it would be illegal. That's why I did a lot of soul searching before I made up my mind to agree to do something like this...Normally, I would never even consider it," he said as he took a sip of his hot coffee and again fumbled nervously with his papers. "And I certainly don't want to lose you as a friend, he said, smiling weakly as Weed looked shocked at the paper Mordy had just slid across the table.

"I mean, that's the real reason I had to meet with you today. I needed you to just sign a release form to release me from any legal responsibility for representing Sandy...and to attest to the fact that I'm no longer your attorney," he said and pointed to the bottom of the paper where he wanted Weed to sign. "It's all kosher...just says that, for the time being, I'm no longer your attorney...that I'm exclusively Sandy's attorney now...and that you're releasing me from any legal responsibility or any other issue that might arise from having her as my client," Mordy assured him. "Just a formality, really... Actual written form doesn't mean all that much," he added, laughing nervously.

"That's bullshit, Mordy...You think I'm an idiot? I'm not going to sign anything like this...that's bullshit. You already know too much about my personal life," Weed said, sliding the paper back across the table to Mordy. "There's no way I'd ever sign anything even remotely like that. It's unethical...even I know that."

"Not unethical, Ben...and like I said, a signed paper copy doesn't mean all that much anyway...all that I'm legally obligated to do is to inform you that I'm no longer your attorney...so a verbal agreement is sufficient. And so I guess I'm formally telling you now that I'm no longer your attorney...and I have officially made you aware of the situation," he said, taking the paper and putting it back in his briefcase. "And trust me, Ben, I did everything I could to try to talk Sandy out of it...told her that things were going to improve... that you were just going through a rough spot in your life...but she wouldn't listen...And then with all this other stuff with the trial and the shooting...it has really put her in a difficult position...pretty much forced her hand," he said, nervously taking another sip of coffee. "I mean, Ben, what did you expect her to do?"

"I don't know that much about the law, Mordy, but I think the whole thing stinks...seems pretty unethical to me...to have someone who knows all about you representing the other side in a divorce...I mean, you know all about Tatter's Bar...and about that girl down there," he said quietly, leaning forward so that no one else could hear his anger. "I've been confiding in you for over twenty years. You know everything there is to know about my life, and you could use it all against me in court...that can't be legal."

"That's the thing, Ben...I can't use any of that stuff...that's all privileged information from when you were my client...So you don't have to worry about me divulging one iota of any of that information...and I wouldn't anyway...You know that. I can only use what Sandy tells me now, or what's in the public record."

"You expect me to believe that? That's ridiculous."

"Frankly, Ben, I think that she probably knows about most of that other stuff anyway...Not much that I could tell her that she doesn't already know about you. This Tatter's Bar shooting thing...I mean, everyone knows about it now that it's been in the newspaper...that's one of the big reasons that she wants me to do this... Said that that was the final straw...and frankly, Ben, I think it might even be a good idea to just go ahead and tell her about everything that went on at the bar. Be honest and get it all off your chest...start out with a clean slate and instill some trust into her."

"Yeah, that would be real helpful," Weed answered sarcastically.

"And I may as well tell you up front, she already knows all about that girl at the bar...Wat's her name...Candy? And she was pretty devastated when you had been going through marriage counseling at the time you were seeing that other girl," he added. "She was really upset...and Ben, I can swear on a stack of bibles that I had nothing to do with her finding out about any of it. She came into the office with that information," he said, nervously taking another bite out of his donut. "You know me better than that. And she was bound to find out all about it sooner or later anyway. Women always find out about things like that."

"I mean, Ben, she is really upset this time. Wanted me to even file a protection from abuse order against you...to keep you away from her...Can you believe that?" he asked but didn't wait for Weed to answer. "But luckily, I was at least able to talk her out of that... told her that I could get you to stay somewhere else for a while until things cool down...that I didn't think a PFA order would be necessary right now...that I could talk to you about staying somewhere else for a while...maybe with your mother or something...and then we wouldn't have to worry about getting involved with any messy PFA. And luckily, she agreed to that," he said as he slid another paper across for Weed to read...the PFA paperwork. "And you should thank me for that...because a PFA can look pretty bad on a person's record. And you don't want something like that...airing all your dirty laundry and getting into the newspaper. You've had enough of that already."

"That's crazy...I never laid a hand on her."

"I know, but there's verbal and mental abuse and other things like that...You know, threats and things that can be just as bad... The judge would give her the PFA anyway...They always do...even if it was just temporary. Just standard with most divorces these days."

"Kicking me out of my own house?"

"She needs a place to stay, and she doesn't want you around. Jesus, Ben...give me a break on this...What don't you understand? I mean, I am doing you a big favor...And technically, it is her house too. I'm doing you a favor, because if one of these high-priced lawyers got hold of this case, they would destroy you. They wouldn't hesitate to file for a PFA...and maybe in a couple of weeks I can talk her out of it, because if she goes through with this divorce, I don't think you stand a chance. She'll likely get everything and probably a lot more."

"That's ridiculous...vacate the property...What's that supposed to mean? You throwing me out of my own house?" Weed said as he read the PFA paperwork that Mordy had pushed in front of him.

"I said I wasn't going to file it unless I absolutely had to...drew it up just in case...but just forget it...I'll file the damn thing and let the chips fall where they may. You're going to have to move out one way or the other anyway, Ben. So it's your funeral," he said as he took back the paper.

"Ben…go stay with your mother for a couple weeks…and don't turn this into some federal case…Get off on a good note, and Jesus, just give her this one small consolation…I mean, she deserves it for all the bullshit you put her through. You look bad enough already… You don't need a PFA hanging over your head."

"'Due to stress and verbal and mental abuse,' what the hell is that supposed to mean?" Weed asked as he continued to read the PFA.

"I couldn't really make it read any better…just routine…and to tell you the truth, most of it is true…I mean, dating two women while you're undergoing marriage counseling…Doesn't that meet the criteria of stress and mental abuse? You want people to know about that instead?"

"Seventy-two hours…" he said, looking up at Mordy. "I get seventy-two hours to get the things that I need out of the house or be cited for trespassing and possibly arrested…Doesn't sound very routine to me," Weed said, pushing the paper back toward Mordy's side of the table.

"That's just if I file the papers. You can have more time if you need it," Mordy said, snapping closed his briefcase. "You know legal documents always sound worse than they are…Just a bunch of bravado that doesn't mean much…Seventy-two hours is just a vague estimate anyway."

"That's comforting. You really like throwing me under the bus, don't you? Never really liked me, did you?"

"Think about it, Ben…think about what you're saying…I've always been your friend…I've always looked out for you…and I'm doing the same thing right now…you just don't realize it. And you're just lucky that she didn't go out and hire some high-priced attorney from the city…they'd rob you blind, and to tell you the truth, I'm damn near doing the case pro bono…so try and think about that… Would I do this pro bono if I didn't like you? Because in the end, the money's coming out of your pocket. So try and understand that

I'm really just trying to do you a big favor," he said, tapping his index finger against his temple. "Understand that I'm looking out for you too...as a friend. And relax...my gut feeling is that you're both going to work this out and get back together before the week's out...and then I won't get a dime...So just stay calm...and let the dust settle," he said and paused. "And I feel just as bad as you...I don't like to see things like this happen...especially to my friends... Everyone thinks that lawyers are just a bunch of heartless bastards, but that's not the case. I feel bad for you too, Ben," Mordy added. But it didn't sound sincere in the slightest, Weed thought.

"Fine...I'll leave...was never a bowl of cherries for me either. I'll vacate the property in seventy-two hours...And there's nothing left for me to take anyway...she already took most of it."

"Fine, now you're thinking...And Ben...maybe you should go back to counseling for a while...but by yourself this time...Talk to that lady you've been seeing...Helen or whatever her name is...she seemed to be really concerned about your well-being...so see if she can help," he said.

"Help...she only made things worse. And anyway, Mordy, I don't really think I need any more advice from you. Always been rotten advice anyway."

"I knew you would be pissed. I told Sandy, 'Ben's going to be pissed when he finds out I'm going to be your attorney,'" he said, taking a sip of his coffee and putting some papers back in his briefcase before telling Ben the papers he was trying to forcibly give back were his copies to keep.

"I'll pay," Mordy said, grabbing at the check as Weed got up to leave. "And calm down. You knew that this was coming," he said as Weed started toward the door.

"And I'm going to need some things from you as soon as you can get them to me. Things that Sandy doesn't have access to... like your last four or five tax returns from your office," he added as he followed Weed through the store. "So call me when you get an attorney so I can talk things over with him...And remember, Ben, try not to take it personally...things like this happen," he added as he followed Weed out the door and onto the sidewalk.

"You know, Mordy, you can just kiss my ass. I'm going to fight you every inch of the way...So if you want something, you're going to have to subpoena it or talk to my attorney or whatever...and you'll have to find out who that is on your own," Weed said as he continued down the street.

"What did you expect, Ben?" Mordy said, following him down the street. "You knew this was coming. How much did you expect her to put up with? Going to some dirty strip bar and having an affair with a teenager. I mean, for Christ's sake, what did you expect? You had to know this would eventually happen...that you would eventually self-destruct," he said as he continued down the street a couple steps behind Weed before giving up.

Never really was his friend...had known it from the start. Betrayed, all for a few bucks. And Mordy knew everything about his life...probably knew more about his than he knew about his own life, Weed imagined...and he would use it all against him if he had to. He was going to call the State Bar Association first thing Monday morning and file a complaint against Mordy and find out just how legal all this was, he thought.

Kicking him out of his own house...fine...might be better off anyway. Wouldn't have to put up with Sandy for a while. And it would give him time to think, he knew as he walked another two blocks before realizing that he was walking in the wrong direction. That he had parked his car at the other end of the street.

So, the trial was over and so was his marriage...all happening on the same day...the daily double, he thought, turning and walking back toward where he had just come from. Maybe it was best this way...had been a pretty crappy marriage...and maybe the marriage was unsalvageable...worn out...he didn't know...didn't know if he even cared anymore…and it might be nice to get away for a while from the daily hassles of his marriage.

He could move some things over to his mother's house Sunday, he imagined. Wouldn't need that much, he thought, getting back in his car. A couple of suitcases full of clothes would probably be all he'd take…He could buy whatever else he needed.

Would have to make some excuse up to his mother for why he was moving back in after all these years…Probably would just tell her the truth and then have to endure her moral lectures about his failed life. He was used to it anyway…no real change.

And in a way it would be a relief just to get away from it all and back to where it all started. To get back home…to his room…for maybe a new start, he thought as he pulled his car into the parking lot in front of the Quick Fix.

CHAPTER FIFTY-ONE

Friday, May 21
6:43 p.m.

"Jesus, what the hell happened?" Bob asked when Weed entered the Quick Fix.

"She blew a fuse, I guess. Told you she was crazy," Weed said, taking a Coke out of the cooler. "Scared the crap out of me...and all over that damn dog."

"Didn't I tell you...that dog was going to cause you trouble? That's why I didn't want anything to do with it in the first place. So don't say a word. You sure no one knows about anything?"

"Don't worry. It's all over. They found their damn dog...So it's not going to be a problem...and I'm not going to say anything anyway."

"Yeah, well I'm still worried about it."

"Don't worry. But it was still crazy. Pretty damn embarrassing too."

"Yeah, sounded real crazy...and it was sort of funny...about the gun and all, and how you fell and then thought you were going to die…Read all about it in the newspaper. You sure you're okay?" Bob said as he waited on a customer.

"Just pisses me off, that's all. She shoots me and I'm the one that has to pay. Judge fines me ten thousand dollars for contempt and then sentences me to do two hundred hours of community service…Can you believe that? Wasn't even my fault…and as far as I know, he didn't say a word about Hileman."

"Yeah? She has immunity in this town."

"Supposed to clean outhouses in the parks and pick up garbage along the highway as punishment for allegedly screwing up his damn trial. You know those guys you always see in the orange jump suits along the roads…criminals? Well, I'm going to be one of them come next week."

"Sounds like fun."

"Pisses me off that she shot me, and I'm the one that gets shit on. He'll probably give her an award, but I get to clean outhouses. Anyway, I might eventually just sue her for assault and battery…just fabricate all kinds of physical problems that she caused me to have when she shot me…emotional distress, nightmares, neck pain… anything that I can think up to sue her for. See how she likes it. Should be worth something," he said, pausing. "Bad thing is that I'm not sure I want to get involved with her again. You know, with the dog as an issue, and who knows what Liz might do. I'm tired of dealing with it, and the way things are going I might end up losing again…and then I still might have to go through another trial with her."

"Yeah, I see what you mean…Might end up getting the death penalty if you don't watch it. I guess they could say it was sort of your fault anyway…I mean, if they found out you stole her dog."

"Yeah, I guess. But anyway, the reason I stopped was to ask you if you could help me out Sunday. I want to move some things from my house over to my mother's house. Thought that maybe you could give me a hand. That I could borrow your truck for a couple hours."

"Yeah, shouldn't be a problem," he said as another customer entered the store. "You movin' back home with your mom?"

"Yeah, that's the other good news. Sandy kicked me out. Out of my own house. She's filing for a divorce. Which is fine, I guess, but that SOB Mordy thinks he's going to be her attorney...which actually makes me more upset than the divorce. He already threatened to file some kind of a PFA if I don't leave the house... gave me seventy-two hours, or the police could arrest me...Can you believe that? Forty years of paying him for bad legal advice and acting like he's my friend, and now the bastard's throwing me out of my house. Said the PFA was Sandy's doing, but I don't believe him."

"Yeah, that's crazy. He never did seem to like you all that much... even I noticed that...probably something you did to him when we were in high school."

"And he knows too much about me already, and I'm sure he'll use it all against me if he has to. Told me that Sandy already knows about Candy...that stripper down at the bar. Said that she found out on her own, but I'll bet he's the one that told her. I'm just lucky I never told him anything about taking Hileman's dog," Weed said before waiting for Bob to finish with another customer.

"Yeah, well, doesn't sound very good, I guess. Maybe Sandy will change her mind. And then you stay miserable like the rest of us," Bob said.

"Well, to tell you the truth, I don't really give a damn. I'm tired of it all. Tired of all the heartache and aggravation. I just might up and quit my practice and do nothing for a while. Maybe just move away and leave this life all behind. Maybe could even get a job here with you at the Quick Fix...I see the Help Wanted sign is still in the window," Weed said somewhat jokingly, even though he wasn't really sure he was. "If I quit working, then no one gets another dime from me...let all the vultures fend for themselves," Weed said, pausing for Bob to wait on another customer.

"But anyway…thought that you could help me move some things over to the house Sunday."

"Yeah, shouldn't be a problem."

"Maybe around one or two…sometime after church…Shouldn't take long."

"Your mom okay with it?"

"I don't know. I didn't tell her yet. I just got the news myself. Probably tell her as little as possible. She doesn't need to know all the specifics anyway."

Weed stood at the end of the counter and talked to Bob for almost an hour about the trial and the divorce and then about Liz and her dog, and Pickles and Candy, and a few other topics as Bob waited on customers. He talked until he felt like maybe he was becoming a nuisance to Bob and decided he would leave.

"Yeah, I'll come by Sunday around one o'clock with the truck," Bob said, coming out onto the sidewalk as Weed started toward his car.

In the distance, Weed could see the glowing lights of the festival. Too early to go home and risk the possibility that he might have to deal with Sandy now. Would stop for a few drinks and unwind, he thought as he drove back toward town feeling exhausted. He called Candy but got no answer. He could drop by her place, he imagined. Had been a while since he had seen her…not since the last time he had tried to have sex with her, he thought, disgusted, as he turned his car and started the drive to her apartment.

CHAPTER FIFTY-TWO

Friday, May 21
8:21 p.m.

H e looked through a few magazines as he waited for the phar-
macist to fill his prescription. Seven times at last count...and
he wasn't going to let it happen again. No more awkward, embarrassing excuses, he thought as he put the magazines back into the
rack, but for an instant thinking that the count might actually be
eight.

Just needed a jump start, he thought while watching his distorted imagine in the security mirror overhead as he moved slowly
around the store.

Was almost an hour before someone in the pharmacy texted
that his prescription was ready.

He sat in the car and read the long list of the possible complications of taking the medication written on the back of the box...
temporary blindness, hearing loss, an erection lasting longer than
four hours, heart attack, stoke...they seemed to be getting worse

the further down the list he got...was half scared to read much further, he thought as he popped one of the pills in his mouth and then washed it down with a few sips of bourbon.

And then he remembered a joke Bob had told him once a long time ago about a little boy whose mother caught him masturbating...telling him that if he didn't quit masturbating, he was going to go blind. But the boy told his mother that she didn't have to worry because he would stop when he needed glasses. Still thought the joke was pretty funny, he thought as he started his drive toward Candy's apartment.

Tatter's Bar looked abandoned as he drove past. No signs of anyone, including Pickles. Maybe the police had finally arrested him and put him in jail, he thought as he pulled into the lot behind Candy's apartment building.

"Tried to call you," he said when she pushed opened the door. He gave her a quick kiss before she moved away.

"Yeah, I think my phone's not been working right," she said, yelling out from the kitchen.

"You hear about the fiasco down at the courthouse?" he asked, sitting down nervously on the couch and already sexually aroused.

"The what?"

"That fiasco down at the courthouse...the shooting?"

She shook her head that she hadn't as she came back into the living room and handed him a drink. She sat down on the couch across from him...pulling her long, sensuous bare legs up beneath her loose-fitting nightshirt she was wearing, exposing her lace bikini panties.

"The woman that was suing me went berserk yesterday at the courthouse," he said but was already too excited about having sex to concentrate on the details of his story...and satisfied that he already had a useable erection...and amazed and gratified at how well the medication was working, he realized as he reached out and touched her thigh as he made some inane comment about the paintball gun Hileman had used.

Was a good erection…harder than he had experienced in a long while…He would finally be able to reestablish his manhood… that he wasn't some washed-up old pervert, he thought as he moved over to the couch before kissing her passionately on the lips as he lifted her nightshirt over her head. He kissed her neck and breasts and stomach before realizing that if he didn't pick up the pace a bit that he might climax before he even got started.

He kissed her a couple more times before somewhat awkwardly and abruptly making penetration, but it was only a minute or two before he had lost control completely and was unable to stop his premature climax. Only a minute or two of actual sex and it was already over, he knew, as he continued to fake it for a while…moaning and moving his hips, telling her how much he loved her…and faking another orgasm before his erection completely disappeared. Maybe two minutes max of actual sex, he thought as she put on another poor act of having an orgasm.

Bottle hadn't said a word about that complication, he thought, pissed but satisfied.

He let out a long sigh and rolled to the side, as he caressed the side of her face while she stared up at the ceiling.

Two minutes max…but probably less…maybe a lot less, he thought. What happened to "an erection lasting four hours" like the bottle had warned? he thought to himself as he tried to come up with an explanation of what had just happened…Wasn't even certain that she'd realized that he had an erection and that they were having sex.

"You don't know how much I love you," he said, giving her a kiss.

"Could have been a little bit longer, I guess," he resisted telling her…but the long silence needed filling. "Excited me so much tonight that it was pretty quick," he said, trying to laugh it off…but pissed that he was still making excuses about his sexual performance.

"It was fine," she said with a sexy slur in her voice as she caressed the back of his hand before getting up and putting her nightshirt on and lighting a cigarette. "You worry too much."

At least it hadn't been a complete embarrassment…At least he had had actual sex even if it had been for only been for a couple of minutes…and so far he hadn't gone blind or had a stroke, he thought…but *pathetic* was the thought that came to mind.

Maybe next time it would be better now that he knew what to expect, he thought as he lay on the couch in the darkness and half listen to Candy jabber incessantly about the bar as she moved around her bedroom.

"I'm still thinking of leaving," she finally said as she moved from her bedroom and into the bathroom before turning on the shower. "Although I haven't made up my mind definitely. This town is dead. You can't find any good places to dance. Just a bunch of old cripples trying to stick a dollar in your bra. Has to be the cheapest town in the country," she said, pausing as she stuck her hand in the shower to check the temperature of the water. "Sue is making tons of money dancing in some real nice club down in Florida…told me some guy gave her a fifty-dollar tip," she added as she took a long drag off her cigarette and he listened to the soothing sound of the shower. "She told me that I could stay with her until I found a place of my own. Until I get my feet on the ground," she said, putting her cigarette in the ashtray beside him before giving him a quick kiss and going back into the bathroom. "Lot of young guys down there too…you know, with a lot of money…not old, tight guys…if you know what I mean," she asked, not waiting for an answer. "I always wanted to change my life anyway. I've been in this rut for too long…I deserve more," she added. "Maybe take a few college courses somewhere…" she said, poking her head back out of the bathroom. "I always thought that would be interesting. Make something out of myself. I mean, I'm really not all that stupid…just never applied myself, they told me. And I always wanted to go someplace warm," she said while he watched her in the bathroom mirror as she stepped into the shower.

"Yeah, you should," he said, laying there relaxing as a cool breeze blew through the open window, and for some reason feeling sorry for her. "That's what I've been telling you. Make something out of your life," he shouted over the din of the running water. "Like me," he added, somewhat amused at the irony.

"Cops always hassling me," she said poking her head out of the shower. "You know, when you hang around a place like Tatter's Bar, you get a bad reputation. Doesn't matter what you do. I could be a registered nun, and they would still treat me like a whore...which there's no way I am," she said and paused. "'Course, I'm not a hundred percent sure about leaving yet," she said as she disappeared back into the shower.

Probably never leave, Weed thought. She never seemed to do anything that she said she was going to do, he thought as he watched her image move behind the glass shower door.

"You should come with me," she said after a long pause, and it was hard to hear what she was saying over the running water...but it sound melodic and mesmerizing as he closed his eyes and tried to relax.

"What?"

"If I leave, you should come with me. Come to Florida with me."

"Yeah, maybe," he said, now having to almost shout for her to hear what he was telling her. "That's not so crazy. I've been thinking about doing something like that anyway. Giving up my practice and just going somewhere and starting over."

"Quit being a doctor? How could you do that?"

"Wouldn't be hard...All seems to have become one big pain anyway. Patients, hospital...stupid, embarrassing lawsuits and crazy patients...Getting tired of trying to act like I care...that's the real problem. I don't care anymore. I've cared long enough...about everything. My caring is all worn out...all used up," he said, feeling strange that he had said something like that to her. "There's not one thing in my life that's not one big pain in the ass...besides you and us."

"I love you too," she said, coming over and giving him a kiss.

"And I just found out that Sandy's leaving...filing for a divorce."

"You're kidding," she said as she dried her hair standing completely naked in front of him.

"No...told me today. Actually that son-of-a-bitch Mordy told me. Said she's all upset about the trial and the bar shooting, and probably us."

"She knows about us?"

"That's what he told me. Could have been Hileman's investigator that told her, but it was probably Mordy...Doesn't matter now, I guess. I was going to tell her about us soon anyway," he told Candy but wasn't sure he ever would have.

"Now we don't have to sneak around anymore. We can go and do whatever we want whenever we want and we won't care who sees us together."

"That's right. That will be great," he said, trying to act excited. "Yeah, I could give up my practice and take the money I have saved and take it easy for at least a while...maybe travel...until I decided what I really wanted to do...maybe to some tropical island."

"That would be freaky," she said as she dried off and then wrapped the towel around her head before going back in the bathroom.

"I have enough money. Have almost a half million put away in my retirement account. That would last us for a while," he told her.

"Yeah...and then maybe we could move to Florida when we get back. You could make a million dollars down there, with all the sick old people...those old farts have tons of cash. I'll bet you would like it there, and you would like my friend too. She used to work in a doctor's office once. Until she got in trouble for something. I don't know if they fired her or what, she never said...but I think it was drugs or something," Candy said, looking at herself in the mirror before telling him that she was working on a new dance number for the club. "We could get a place on the beach," she said, lighting up another cigarette as she stood looking out the windows holding her hands out and letting the breeze blow across her nude body.

"Must not have been a very good psychic," she added after a short break in their conversation.

"What?"

"Must not have been a very good psychic if the psychic told Hileman that you had the dog and you didn't," Candy said before going back in the bathroom. He watched her silhouette in the light coming from the bathroom. He felt tired, but relaxed as he closed his eyes and thought about what they had been talking about... leaving it all behind. Go back to the life he had when he was young. When life was easy and simple. Everything alive and bright, more distinct and real, emotions tangible...and no expectations. Maybe that was his story...No Expectations. Where had that gone, he thought as he listened with his eyes closed, mesmerized by a song that Candy was singing softly. "When the world was a lot smaller and the stars a lot closer," she sang...but he didn't think he had ever heard it before.

He might have dozed off for a few seconds, he thought, but wasn't certain as he opened his eyes. The last thing he remembered was yelling into the bathroom to ask Candy if she wanted to get something to eat...but there was no answer, and now the apartment was completely silent. He must have been sleeping for a lot longer than a few minutes and Candy must have left...he thought, hearing only the muffled sounds coming up from the street.

It was as if she had just disappeared into thin air, he thought as he sat on the edge of the couch. It was a lot darker too, and the bathroom light was turned on...silence as he called for her once more.

Now he could hear the fireworks at the festival...must have been what had awoken him, he thought as dressed and then read the note that Candy had left on the coffee table: Didn't want to wake you...You were sleeping like a baby...Will ttyl. And think about it. Call. Love, Candy.

The Venus Lounge was abandoned when he got there but for an old drunk couple arguing in the corner and the bartender who was mopping up a spill. He sat down at a booth near the window and looked out at the crowds and the flashing lights of the fireworks overhead reflecting deep into the river.

"What a zoo," the bartender said, sitting a drink down in front of Weed. "Must have been three hundred people in here a half hour ago...now just you and those two drunks. Fireworks sent them all out into the street," he added. "You don't like fireworks?" he asked as he moved away before getting an answer, but feeling that the question was somehow well placed.

Weed sat there drinking for a long time, talking to the bartender and thinking about his life. Thinking about Sandy and all the good times they had had together. He had loved her once, he was certain. Maybe he still loved her...didn't know. How did you ever know? Maybe Helen was right...he just didn't know what love was...maybe never had...that he didn't have the capacity to really love...just another flaw in his character. Maybe they would eventually work things out...but he wasn't sure that he even wanted that, he thought as he left the bar. He stood in the night air, somewhat dazed and disoriented...realizing that he'd had way too much to drink and trying to remember in which direction he should walk to find his car.

CHAPTER FIFTY-THREE

Saturday, May 22
11:43 a.m.

The distant sounds of splashing water and laughter woke him...
part of a dream he was having. Young people swimming on a
warm sunny day at the pool at the end of the street of his boyhood
home...the cool water against his hot skin, the fresh smell of chlo-
rine...the girl that he had always been in love with, sunning herself
nearby...his last chance at love...his whole life in front of him...all
ending when he woke...lost youth and lost love forever. His recurrent dream...his recurrent nightmare in reverse.

But he wasn't at his mother's house and the pool hadn't opened
for the summer season yet, he knew, but he could still hear the
people's laughter and the splashing of water even though he was
now wide awake...he realized...now trying to get his bearings. It
sounded like it was all taking place just outside his window.

He lay there for a short time listening, clearing his thoughts,
trying to tell what was dream and what was reality.

He was still dressed in the clothes that he had been wearing the night before when he had left the bar, he realized, sitting up on the edge of the bed, still groggy and with a bad hangover. Wasn't even certain how he had gotten home.

But the explanation came to him easily. That if yesterday was Friday, and he was pretty certain that it had been, then today had to be Saturday…and Saturday was the day of their anniversary party. He had forgotten all about it until this very moment.

And all the noise in his dream was just the laughter and splashing coming from that party in his back yard, he realized.

How could he have forgotten about the party? Couldn't even remember when he had thought of it last…had too damn much on his mind and too much to drink to even remember, he thought as he tried to stand.

He sort of assumed that Sandy would just take care of everything and remind him of it later. Maybe she had, he thought as he stood tentatively, feeling dizzy and catching himself once on the nightstand before proceeding to the bedroom window.

Maybe Sandy had changed her mind and decided to come back for the party, he thought.

He stood at the window and looked down at all the decorations and tables of food in his back yard and all the people dressed in their colorful Hawaiian outfits…amazed at how he had been able to sleep right through a party already in full swing just outside his window.

He searched the two large tents and around the pool and then where people were playing volleyball to try to locate Sandy. But if she was there, he couldn't find her, he thought as he scanned the crowd a second time.

Helen and Frank were there…He could see them standing by the pool, holding some kind of a pink drink in one hand and a small plate of food in the other. Both dressed in shorts and stupid-looking, oversized Hawaiian shirts. And Mordy, the bastard, was dangling his feet in the water at the edge of the pool, wearing a straw hat and drinking something blue, his feet barely touching the water. What was that SOB doing here after what he had just done to him yesterday? he thought, searching the grounds again for Sandy with somewhat more desperation this time...realizing how awkward an anniversary party could become without Sandy.

There were people everywhere, eating and drinking and swimming and playing volleyball. Had to be over two hundred, he imagined, still amazed that he had slept through it all. Over two hundred curious pains in the ass who had come for the show. To see how he was holding up after all the bullshit that had happened to him over the last two weeks, he thought. To find out the latest rumors, he imagined. To see if he had lost everything and had been evicted from their house yet. To watch the Weeds squirm with embarrassment and humiliation. Wouldn't be this many at his funeral, he knew as he showered and dressed as quickly as he could, putting on the goofy Hawaiian shirt and Bermuda shorts and sandals that Sandy had bought for him months earlier. There was no way that he was in any kind of a mood for a damn party, he thought, checking to see just how goofy he looked in the hall mirror.

Should go down and tell them to all to just go home. That the party was over. Give them even more to talk about, he thought as he stood at the window and searched for Sandy one last time before starting down the steps. She definitely wasn't there, he thought.

Now what the hell was he supposed to do? She hadn't shown up for her own anniversary party, he thought as he tried her cell before going outside.

She had gotten him good this time...left him high and dry to do all the explaining, he thought, standing on the patio and looking out at the crowd...and for a moment thinking that maybe his best option might be to just keep walking. No explanations...just walk through the crowds to the bar down the street...and then just drink until the party was over. Let them think what they wanted...

At this point, it really didn't matter much anyway, he imagined. Just let the party burn itself out, he thought as he walked into the back yard.

He could cover for Sandy for a while, he imagined. Tell everyone that she just wasn't feeling well and was lying down upstairs until she felt better, and that she would be out later. And then tell all the people to just go ahead and enjoy themselves. That's what he would tell them, he thought as he walked toward one of the tents... navigating around a few groups of people, smiling and nodding as they did the same.

"I've been looking all over for you two," Helen said, coming out of nowhere. "Thought something might have happened," she said. "Where's San, anyway? Haven't seen her yet...and I've been here for almost an hour," she said as she walked beside him.

"Yeah, well, she's not feeling all that well. That stomach virus that's been going around...I think Mordy had it...maybe gave it to her...She's upstairs resting, but she should probably be down in a little while," he said, hoping that would be enough of an explanation to hold her until he could track her down.

"She hasn't returned any of my calls. That's why I was concerned...and then when she wasn't here...well, that's when I really got concerned. Started to worry me that she might be upset about the trial or that horrible thing down at that bar. I'm sure she was upset about that...I was shocked myself when I read about it," she said, pausing...probably waiting for him to explain, Weed thought. "You know what kind of bar that is?" she added after he didn't answer.

"No, no. She wasn't upset about that. She knew about that a long time ago...a victim of circumstances...in the wrong place at the right time was all that was," he said, trying to move around her. "Just went in to save that guy's life that got shot. Lucky that I was there, or he probably would have died. Should be a hero," he said, excusing himself and then telling her he would talk to her later and to enjoy herself.

"I might go up and check on her," she continued as she followed. "Thought she might need my help...You know, I could give her one of my pep talks...I don't want you two slipping...not after all we've accomplished so far."

"No, I don't think she really wants to be bothered with another one of your pep talks," he said sarcastically. "I'm supposed to go up and check on her in a few minutes...So I'll tell her that you're here," he added before finally losing her in the crowd.

For the next half-hour he shook hands and welcomed people to the party like nothing was wrong and then told them about Sandy being sick. He tried to call Sandy three more times without an answer, before he finally left a message...telling her that she was overreacting and that all her friends were looking for her, and it was getting pretty embarrassing. "At least we can act like we're happy for one more day...What's one more day?" he said before ending the message abruptly.

He milled around the crowd for a while longer. Shaking more hands and laughing and explaining what had happened at the courthouse and then about the shooting at Tatter's Bar and how he had saved the man's life and how crazy and funny that it all had been. Trying to make a big joke out of most of his explanation. Then telling them about how Hileman couldn't stand the fact that she was going to lose her flimsy case and so she just snapped...that it had all been just a bunch of lies from the start anyway...and that he didn't have a clue about her crazy dog story. And then explaining again about the bar shooting to a larger crowd about how he had actually gone into the bar because they had needed a doctor and he had just been driving past...and that's how he had come to be sort of a witness to the shooting. And then he told them about how he had heroically saved the victim...even though he was concerned that he might get shot himself.

Just spin it all...he thought as he moved away from the crowd. Simple and easy...just spin it all.

"Mordy, you have any idea where Sandy is?" Weed asked quietly as he sat down beside Mordy at the edge of the pool.

"Not sure, Ben. Couldn't tell you if I did, but she said something about staying at her sister's until you were out of the house, but I didn't tell you that," he said, pausing before asking, "You know the water in your pool is low and the grounds all muddy here?" and pulling up a piece of loose sod. "You bury someone here recently?" he said, laughing at his joke.

"Glad you're enjoying yourself…Maybe her Judas attorney could call her and tell her that she needs to get her ass over here and face the music too…that it's her anniversary party…that she had to have…and that ninety percent of the pain-in-the-ass guests are her pain-in-the-ass friends anyway…So let her explain…she created this damn spectacle, so let her come over and deal with it," he said as he stood and started to walk away.

"I don't know, Ben. If she doesn't want to come to the party, then she doesn't have to come. I mean, can you really blame her… If it was me, I probably wouldn't come either."

"You know Mordy, it really takes a lot of balls to show up here after what you did yesterday," Weed shouted as he started walking away.

"Yeah, well, that's what Karen said you would say…told me that we shouldn't come because you would be pissed that we were here…So if you want me and Karen and the kids to leave, just let me know…but we're taking all these damn chairs we lent you with us," he said. "And you know, the water in your pool is pretty damn low, Ben," Mordy repeated as Weed continued to walk away.

He moved through the crowd for a little while longer talking… shaking hands and socializing…before giving it all up. He was tired of making excuses, smiling, feigning laughter, acting like he was having a good time…his fabrications. It was all getting to him and he had had enough.

"Just want to make an announcement," he said, finally standing on a chair and using one of the band's microphones. "Everyone has been asking about Sandy," he started, and for an instant thought about telling everyone the truth before continuing. "We were hoping Sandy would be feeling better by now, but she has been under the weather the last couple of days. Some intestinal flu thing that she's been trying to shake. She's maybe feeling a little better now and is supposed to be out a little later, but she thanks you all for coming and told me to tell you all to enjoy the party," he told the crowd, smiling, before walking around to the side of the house and trying to call Sandy one last time. When she didn't answer, he went back inside the house and upstairs to his bedroom, lying there and thinking about his miserable situation as he listened to the annoying din of the crowd and music.

He would wait up in his room for as long as he could, he thought, and hope that Sandy returned...But it probably didn't matter... the rumors had already started, he was sure. "A rumor is halfway around the world before the truth gets it shoes on," he knew. Didn't matter anyway...rumors might be more kind to him than the truth, he imagined, getting up from the bed and walking to the window to watch all the people eating and swimming...just as the five-piece band starting playing again.

He lay back on the bed, shut his eyes, and tried to relax just as his cell phone started to ring...Had to be Sandy, he thought as he answered...but it was Mordy's voice instead.

"Where the hell did you get to? There's two cops down here, and they want to talk to you."

"Two cops?"

"I'm sorry...What, I'm not speaking clear enough? Yeah, two cops. Something surprising about that?" Mordy answered, sounding overly irritated.

"'Bout what?"

"I don't know ''bout what.' Who knows ''bout what' with you. Could be 'bout anything," he said sarcastically before hanging up the phone.

He stood at the window and looked around the crowd to locate the two cops...two uniformed officers that he didn't recognize. Great. What the hell did they want now...had to be something about Hileman's damn dog or the shooting. Or maybe they had come to arrest him...to take him away in handcuffs in front of all his friends...couldn't have scripted it any better. Perfect timing: "Murder Suspect Arrested at Own Anniversary Party." That would stop any rumors that things weren't going well, he knew.

Then there wouldn't be either of the happy anniversary couple present at their own party, he thought as he walked down the steps, hoping to end it quickly before it became any more of a spectacle.

"Yes, can I help you?" he asked as he approached the two officers, holding out his hand for them to shake as the whole crowd seemed to silence and move closer as if they all had become a whole lot more interested in what was happening. And he could hear someone trying to shush the band.

"You're Dr. Weed?" the officer asked as he shook Weed's hand. "I recognize you from downtown," the officer said and laughed as he turned toward the other officer. "Hey Mack, this is that Weed guy from down at the courthouse...Didn't I tell you...you know, the Pickles guy," he told the other officer. "Glad to meet you," he added as he continued to shake Weed's hand. "You're quite a celebrity these days."

"Yeah, quite a celebrity," Weed answered sarcastically.

"You know, we arrested that asshole two nights ago," the officer continued. "He pulled an Evel Knievel just down the street...ran a red light and ran right into the side of a pick-up...broke every damn bone in his body. Paramedics had to put him in a bag to take him to the hospital," they continued, stopping only to laugh. "Should be dead...But you know that assholes like him never die. But he had the gun that he used to shoot Tatters...so you won't have to worry about him for a long time. "We figured that maybe he had come

471

way over here to see you…so maybe you lucked out," the officer added.

"But anyway, the reason we stopped was because someone called about a couple of cars blocking a driveway down the street that need to be moved," he continued, turning toward the other officer and asking him for the license plate numbers.

The other officer handed Weed a slip of paper with the license plate numbers and the makes of the cars written on it.

He was probably supposed to feel relieved, but he wasn't sure that he did, he thought as he moved over to the band's loudspeaker. For an instant, he felt like telling the crowd some wild story about the police coming to arrest him as a suspected murderer…and that he would appreciate it if the last person to leave would turn out the lights. But he didn't. Instead he just announced the license plate numbers…laughing as he did…but thinking that he probably sounded a little too upbeat about some illegally parked cars. But he did sense disappointment from the crowd as he returned the microphone to the band leader.

Another lunatic after him with a gun captured…twice in one week. Something minor to be thankful for, he imagined…as he walked back toward the house, wondering just how long "a long time" for Pickles might be.

It was almost 2:00 p.m. before he left the party. The excuses had grown weak and too detailed and hard to maintain. No one seemed to believe him anyway, and the questions were getting more annoyingly involved. He told Mordy just to tell everyone the truth when he was gone if the crowd got too overbearing…and he was sure Mordy would…Mordy would fill them in on all the colorful details of his life and eminent divorce as soon as he was out of sight…with added embellishments at no extra cost, he was sure.

Would talk to Bob for a while, he thought as he drove toward the Quick Fix. He wouldn't return until the party was over and everyone had gone. They could party without him. None of the pains in the ass cared about either of them or their anniversary anyway, he thought as he pulled into the parking lot outside the Quick Fix.

"Thought you would be at the party?" Bob asked as Weed entered the store.

"Couldn't stand it any longer. Just too much fun...And Sandy was a no-show. She left me holding the bag. Didn't even call...Didn't even try to cancel the damn thing...Everybody just showed up while I'm upstairs sleeping. Now I have all these people at the house and neither of us is there for our own anniversary party. Don't know what the people will think. Don't really care, but I'm sure Mordy will fill in the details. Sort of funny when you think about it...if it's not happening to you."

"Really?"

"I'll tell you, Bob...my plan sounds better all the time. Just leave all this behind...this miserable life...and just start over...to live...to do what I want for a while. Not what everyone else wants me to do. Live like we lived when we were young. Warm summer days without a care in the world. That's what I want. Those days back."

"I told you...I think about doing that same thing all the time too," Bob said as he stopped lining soup cans up on the shelf. "Just up and leaving it all behind...my job...my wife...my kids...but never gets any further than the thinking-about-it phase. It's science fiction...never happens...can't happen. Kids and wives and jobs are like anchors. Holding you down...preventing you from sailing off to calmer waters. Just takes the life right out of you. Every man thinks about leaving, but no one ever does it. Once you're in the rut, you can't get out. Too many obligations and responsibilities to ever do something so irrational. There's always a catch that pulls you back in," he said as a clerk came back to where he was standing and ask him the price of the can she was holding in front of him.

"Be nice to be free though," Weed said before Bob left to wait on a customer.

"Kill yourself and then you'll be free," Bob said with syrupy sarcasm.

"You still all right with tomorrow?" Weed asked after their conversation had emptied. "I'll wait at my mother's house after church," Weed said as he started out the door.

"Yeah, it shouldn't be a problem. I'm going to stop at the party later when I'm finished here," Bob said as Weed held the door open and Bob followed him into the street. "Wife and kids wanted to go eat and swim...I think they should be there by now, so maybe I'll see you then," he said.

"Yeah, that would be fine, but I don't know when I'll get back to the party or if I'm going back at all until it's over. Maybe we can shoot some hoops after we're finished tomorrow?" Weed added as they walked toward his car.

"Yeah, I don't know. My back's been killing me lately. I'm not sure I can," Bob told him before Weed got into his car. He pulled away, watching Bob in his rearview mirror as he got smaller and smaller.

He sat in a corner booth at the bar down the street and drank until it was dark. Trying to determine when it would be safe to go back home. Wondered what had happened at the party...at the wake. Could only imagine...probably pretty strange, he thought, amused at the thought that neither of them was there for their own anniversary party. Wondering if, in all of history, anything like that had ever happened.

CHAPTER FIFTY-FOUR

Sunday, May 23
6:58 a.m.

He hadn't slept well and woke early.

He looked out his bedroom window at the mess in the back yard...paper plates and torn streamers and half-eaten food scattered everywhere. The large tents flapping in the wind, and some flowers pulled out of the ground where someone might have slipped in the soft mud. Total destruction, he thought as he packed some shirts and pants into one suitcase and then some jeans and underwear into another. Could get most of what he needed later, he supposed.

Their relationship hadn't been all that bad. They had had some good times together but never really knew if they loved each other. Probably like most couples. And he still wasn't sure that he even knew what that meant. He was never able to get a good grasp on the concept. To him, it had been elusive...just a thing that everyone talked about but no one seemed to be able to explain. Like Helen had told him, he didn't know what love was, he thought as he removed a few suits from his closet before laying them neatly across one of the suitcases.

Back to the old grind on Monday, he thought as he looked at the suits. Would have to make up his mind what he was going to do about the office...to continue on like he had been for the last twenty-five years, or to move off in a new direction...to just give up his medical practice and find something else to do...something easier...or maybe he would just retire for a while like he had told Candy, he thought as he showered and dressed and then went downstairs to the kitchen.

Had plenty of time before he had to pick up his mother and drive her to church, he thought as he sat down at the kitchen table. He could already smell the leftover food in the back yard starting to spoil as he fixed toast and coffee and read the newspaper.

Nothing but one small, almost unnoticeable article about the trial on page three. Apparently, Mordy was right about something. That the public had already lost interest. Didn't take long, he thought as he carried his suitcases downstairs to the front door. He could get the suitcases later when he came back with Bob, he thought as he removed the TV from his study and carried it out to where he had left the suitcases.

Might not say a word to his mother about moving back. Might be just as easy to simply show up with his suitcases without any explanation. What could she do anyway? Couldn't throw him out of his own house...he didn't imagine...not for a second time. He would probably have to listen to a lecture or two about his moral character and his failed life, but so what...He was used to that, he thought as he drove toward her house, passing a few leftover dog posters still stuck to the telephone poles...still chasing him through the neighborhood...their secret. Sort of missed the dog.

He could see his mother looking out the front door as he pulled up in front of the house, but by the time he got out of the car she had gone.

He called out for her when he entered the house, but there was no answer. Probably really pissed at what had happened at the trial and about the newspaper article about the shooting, he thought. But he wasn't going to say anything…Wasn't going to validate any of his life to her, he thought, noticing the wilted flowers he had bought her still resting on the dining room table…wondering, annoyed, why she hadn't yet thrown them out. Probably some kind of a cryptic message she was trying to send him about himself and wilted flowers…maybe how much they were alike.

"You about ready?" he yelled out again.

"I guess," she said with disgust in her voice as she came out of the kitchen, stopping to check her hat in the hall mirror as he had watched her do for the last fifty-four years.

"You hear about all the commotion at the courthouse Thursday?" he finally asked to break the dead silence as he helped her down the steps and into the car, but she just grumbled something undecipherable, though he thought that she probably had tears in her eyes.

"Didn't I tell you she was crazy? Was lucky that she didn't kill me," he said, but still not a word from her. "Didn't I tell you I was going to win the case? Well, that's why she did what she did…She couldn't stand to lose. Put me through all this for nothing…put us all through this for nothing," he added. "Didn't I tell you that the whole trial was about nothing more than a bunch of lies?" he said as if he might be talking to himself…and uncertain if his spin was even helping. "But at least now everyone knows…And now all your friends will know that I'm not such a bad person after all," he said, but she still remained silent and looked straight ahead.

"Hileman knew she was going to lose, that's why she did what she did," he repeated, but there was still no response. "I guess that's just the burden I'll have to bear. But then no one understands my burdens, do they?" he added with a tone of disgust.

"You can leave me out in front of the church," were her first words as he drove near the church. At least he wouldn't have to explain the shooting at the bar to her, he thought. At least not yet.

He pulled up in front of the church, but before he could get around to the other side of the car to help her out, she had gone off on her own and had started up the church steps. She didn't even want to be seen with him now, he knew…too embarrassing. Every Sunday for over twenty-five years the same routine, helping her slowly up the church steps so everyone could see how proud she was that her son was the infamous Dr. Weed. Now she ascended the steps like an Olympic athlete…She didn't want to even be seen with him…her own son…Cast out like someone from the Bible… but he couldn't remember who…maybe Job or Saul, he thought as he pulled the car into the lot before jogging back across the street to the church, catching up to his mother just as she was about to enter the church.

"I'll be here when you come out," he said, but she still didn't acknowledge his presence as he walked into the church behind her before going off in the general direction of his Sunday school room. But he wasn't going to listen to some juvenile Bible babble this morning, he thought as he went out the back door of the church without slowing. Was too nice of a morning to be stuck in a stuffy room at the back of some musty-smelling church anyway, he thought as he started up the alley behind the church that led back up the hill to his mother's house.

Didn't really understand any of it anyway…what it was all about. Religion had always been reluctantly wasted on him, he knew.

He would come back and drive her home after the church service was over, he thought as he walked along the path, enjoying the fresh air and the rays of sunlight streaming down through the canopy of leaves overhead.

It was when he was almost to his house that he heard the children. Two small girls and a boy in the back yard of the house next to his mother's house, fighting and cursing like they were adults. The two girls pulling at something that looked like a piece of cardboard as the boy pushed a small, orange object along the ground. Another family that had moved into the neighborhood that he didn't know anything about other than they seemed to be pretty crude, he thought as he continued unnoticed up the alley.

But the closer he got, the more it looked like the small, orange object the boy was pushing was one of the missing Matchbox cars he had been looking for all winter. The 1967 fluorescent orange Mustang…He knew it well. And the cardboard box the girls were tearing apart was the box to his Flying Matchbox Circus Set…now lying face down and lifeless in the mud with one flap missing…the girls no longer interested.

Now he could see it all. All the cars from his priceless collection strewn hopelessly across their back yard…with missing parts and chipped paint, he could see…near worthless now, he knew as he stood shocked for an instant, not knowing what to do.

They had destroyed his cars. The crappy little bastards had stolen his cars and had destroyed every last one of them, he realized as he reached over the fence and carefully picked the tattered box off the ground…before trying to brush it clean…assessing the damage as he did.

"Son of a bitch!" he shouted, looking up at the kids as they stared back at him mortified…only now noticing his presence.

He twisted and turned the torn cardboard box, attempting to fit it all back together but realizing it was hopeless.

"What the hell do you think you're doing?" he yelled as he opened the gate and entered their back yard. "You're all in trouble…'cause I'm calling the police and having you all arrested, he said as moved around the back yard hastily picking the cars up off the ground but realizing his statements were ridiculous. The children stood motionless…shocked. "Dirty kids have no respect for anything these days."

"These are mine!" he told them emphatically as he continued to pick up the cars...mumbling to himself or to the kids, he wasn't sure which...about how valuable they were...so upset that he wasn't really sure what he was saying...before they all darted off toward their house, screaming for their mother.

"Can I help you?" an angry voice coming from somewhere near the house asked seconds later.

"Yes, you can help me," Weed said even more pissed, looking up at the woman with her arms crossed standing on the back porch. "These are my cars and they're worth a lot of money," he said, trying to catch his breath...but more trying to regain his composure and recover from his apoplectic exhibition. "And I'd like to know how your kids got these cars."

"Oh, I think that I know who you are now," she said. "Sorry, I didn't recognize you at first. You're Dr. Weed from next door. I've seen you over at your mother's place, but I guess we've never had a chance to speak," she said, wiping her hands on her pants and reaching across some bushes to shake his hand.

"Your mother gave those cars to the kids a good while ago. And I told the kids to be careful with them because I thought some of them might be valuable. But you know kids...I think I even said something to your mother about it...that maybe she should check with you first...you know, before she gave them all away...But I guess she didn't seem to think it was necessary," the woman added as she gathered up a few of the remaining cars. "See what I told you, kids...See what you did...I told you to be careful," she said, holding up one of the broken cars for the children to see. "They never listen to me anyway," she added, shaking her head and trying to hand the cars back to Weed.

"Yeah, I mean some of them are pretty valuable," he told her and then tried to explain but realized the ridiculousness of the whole situation. A grown man dressed in a suit arguing with a bunch of kids over some muddy toys. He had actually thought that maybe in his frenzy he had pulled one of the cars right out of one of the little girls' hands...like a flashback...but he wasn't sure and just hoped that their mother hadn't seen or heard most of his embarrassing tirade.

"I know what you mean. My boyfriend has his ashtrays locked up in the basement. Says that someday they're going to be valuable... You know, since no one smokes anymore," she added, wiping her hands on her pants again.

"Doesn't matter, I guess. Most of them look in pretty bad shape now," he said disgusted but trying to act calm as he examined the cars. "Probably not worth much now. And I guess your kids may as well keep them," he said, smiling weakly and trying to save as much face as possible as he unsuccessfully tried to give one of the cars back to one of the children.

"Yeah, well, what I'll do is clean them all up and see if I can find some more of the missing parts and then bring them all over to your mother's house later. I'm tired of listening to them fight about the damn things anyway. Yeah, your mother gave them to the kids a couple of months ago," the woman repeated. "Maybe longer... She said that you wouldn't mind," she added as she bent over to dig another one out of the mud. "This one's not too bad," she said, holding out a car for him to take.

But it was all a waste of time, Weed knew. Cars wouldn't be worth more than a couple of dollars now.

"You don't have to do that. Just let your kids keep them. I mean, technically, they're their cars now anyway. And I guess I just sort of overreacted. You know I just saw them playing with them. Sort of shocked me," he said, smiling.

"I'm going to bring them over anyway, and it was nice meeting you" she added, holding her hand out for him to shake.

"Was nice meeting you too. Sorry it wasn't under better circumstances," he said, feigning laughter and then apologizing again for scaring the children. But now he could only think about how pissed he was at his mother.

"How is your mother, anyway?" the woman asked as he continued his walk up the alley.

"She's just fine," he answered but felt like telling her that she was a crabby old pain-in-the-ass bitch and that she had done this all on purpose just to get revenge for his lawsuit.

"I try to keep an eye on her. Just in case anything would happen to her...You know, like if she fell or something," the woman continued.

"I appreciate that."

"Very nice woman. You're lucky to have her as your mother," she added as he continued up the alley.

"Don't I know that," he said, trying not to show any sarcasm or disgust in his voice but thinking that he hadn't done such a good job.

He could just faintly hear one of the small girls telling her mother that she didn't like "that old man" just as he stepped into his own back yard.

Forty damn years down the drain. Those cars were a part of his life for over forty years, and his mother knew it. One of the few things in his life that he could still cling to from the past...that hadn't changed, that offered some enjoyment, some pleasure. He knew the history of each one like they were his children. Now they were just worthless pieces of junk, he knew. Just like himself.

He was pissed as he sat down on the porch, only then realizing that he was still clinging to one of the cars. The fluorescent blue 1969 Cougar...barely recognizable now, he thought, looking down at the chipped paint and missing tires. Sort of felt sorry for the car...for himself.

Could probably get replacements, but it would take years and be damn expensive...and it really wouldn't be the same, he knew as he took a closer look at the car.

And all because he had embarrassed her...that he had let her down. Just to get revenge...he thought as he tried to calm himself.

She was a vindictive person…but he was never really sure why she had disliked him so much. He had always been a disappointment to her, he was sure…maybe it was that way with all families…that parents always felt their children were failures…disappointments. Didn't know, he thought, but wasn't going to let his mother get away with it again without getting at least some revenge…his pound of flesh.

For starters, until he could think of some better way to get even, he would let her walk home from church. Just let her walk up the long hill from the church, he thought as he hurried back down the hill to the church and then drove his car home. See how she liked it when no one showed up to haul her ass back up the hill. Let her wait there until hell froze over, as far as he was concerned.

He almost felt like crying, he realized as he sat down on the porch swing and anxiously waited for his mother to appear.

It was almost two hours before he finally saw her limping slowly up the sidewalk toward the house, and for an instant he felt sorry for what he had done…guilty for what he had just made his mother do…But he wasn't going to give up that easy…not this time, he thought as he watched her slowly move up the sidewalk toward him…resting every so often…and then grabbing for the wrought iron hand railing to help pull herself along.

She was moving like a turtle, he thought, anxiously waiting to say something nasty to her when she got close enough to hear.

"Found out what happened to all those cars that I've been looking for every damn Sunday for the last two years," he said when she was almost at the front gate.

"Where were you, anyway?" she said, looking up at him as if she had just realized he had been sitting there. "And don't cuss on Sunday," she said, stopping again and grabbing for the railing as if she might have lost her balance.

"All that I'm saying is that it was pretty damn rotten what you did…You knew how much those cars meant to me…You knew how valuable they were and then you go and give them away…to a bunch of snotty-nosed kids to destroy…that you told me last week were nothing more than a bunch of hoodlums. Well, you got your wish… they destroyed every last one of them…turned them all into junk… and just to get even for the trial…and God knows what else," he said as she opened the gate and started up the steps. "And just how long were you going to let me look for them before you told me?" he added when she didn't respond.

"Those little cars…that's what you're all upset about? That's why you made me walk home? Well, that's what I figured…had to be something really stupid," she said, reaching down and rubbing her foot. "Your whole life is coming apart at the seams and you're worried about a bunch of little toy cars," she said, shaking her head in disbelief. "That's the story of your whole life."

"How about all those little souvenir spoons you collected over the years that you have hanging on the wall in the kitchen…that we had to drive twenty miles out of our way to get on every damn vacation that we ever took? Beautiful beach, and what were we doing… swimming, having fun? No, we were driving all over the place looking for some damn little souvenir spoon. Why didn't you give those spoons to the little bastards…or better yet, why didn't you give them my damn accordion…it's still in the basement…maybe one of them can learn how to play the damn thing."

"You could have been good…if you would have practiced," she said as she stood on the porch, loosening the lace in her right shoe. He could see that her foot was swollen and red…more than usual.

"And maybe I did give your cars to those kids. I don't even remember now. I'm not thinking as clear as I used to," she said, but he wasn't going to let her play the senile card again. "Maybe if I got a little help around the house, I wouldn't do things like that. Maybe if my kids treated me like most kids treat their parents, things like that wouldn't happen," she added as she limped noticeably toward the front door. "You don't know how hard it is getting old. I'm miserable every day of my life. Some days, I just wish I could die. No one wants me around anymore," she said as he followed her into the kitchen. He had heard that spiel many times before.

She sat down in the kitchen and took off her shoe and exposed the large, red spot on her foot.

"No one cares about you when you're old. You know that. They just let you walk home when you're old. And someday you'll understand that. Someday soon...when you're old...you'll understand... they'll let you walk home," she added, rubbing her foot.

He shook his head in disbelief. As usual, she had changed the whole subject of the argument. Always the same...could never win and argument with her...just a waste of time, he thought, but now he was suddenly more interested in the nasty-looking red spot at the base of her large toe...His plan had already backfired...he was already backpedaling...already a catch and always consequences to your actions, he thought as he kneeled down in front of her to take a closer look at her foot.

"Just a little blister...I'll bring some cream home for you tomorrow...But it's your shoes that are the problem...they're way too small," he said as he picked up one of the shoes and then acted as if he were examining it closely. "You need a bigger-sized shoe...I told you about that a couple months ago," he scolded faintly, but she remained silent.

"And that bar story in the newspaper was a complete misunderstanding," Weed added. "Newspaper never said anything about the real reason that I was even in that bar...Well, I went in to save the guy that had been shot...I saved the guy's life...but not a single word about that...Made it sound like I was actually in the bar...like I was some kind of a lowlife," he said, disgusted. "Would never go into a place like that...Didn't even know about it," he said as he got her a bowl of warm water to soak her foot in before she told him to take the roast out of the oven before it burned.

They sat in silence and ate the tasteless meal as he tried to come to grips with what had just happened...hoping and praying that the blister on her foot would heal without any serious complications... and realizing that he had once again ended up the loser.

CHAPTER FIFTY-FIVE

Sunday, May 23
1:25 p.m.

Weed was sitting on the porch waiting for Bob when the woman from next door came around the corner of the house carrying a shoebox filled with all his toy cars.

"This was the best that I could do," she told him. "Most of them look okay," she continued, handing him the box as she came up the steps.

All of them were clean and nicely parked in the bottom of the shoebox, Weed could see. And a few of the cars actually looked like they might be salvageable, he thought.

"And I just want to apologize again. If I would have known how valuable they were, I wouldn't have let the kids play with them," she added.

"Not your fault. I was just shocked when I saw them...that's all," he told her. "Didn't mean to scare the kids either. Sort of embarrassing."

"No…no…they're fine," she said, stepping back off the porch.

"To tell you the truth, you can just let your kids keep them," he said, offering her the shoebox. "I'm getting a little too old for them anyway," he said and laughed, trying to make light of the situation but finding it hard to even look at the cars.

"No. I wouldn't feel right keeping them," she said, starting back down the steps…just as Bob pulled up in his pickup truck.

"Here, then," he said, offering her two twenty-dollar bills that he had taken out of his wallet as he followed her down the steps. "Buy your children something else that they can play with."

"That's nice, but I wouldn't feel right," she said, hesitating for a moment before taking the money. "They'll be excited, and if I find any more of the cars lying around the house, I'll make sure that I bring them over," she said, stuffing the money in her pants pocket as she continued down the street toward her house. "Tell your mother I said hello," she turned back and yelled once before waving and going into her yard.

"You sure your mom's okay with this? I don't want her getting pissed off at me for hauling all your shit back over here," Bob asked as Weed walked down the steps and got into the truck, still holding the box of cars.

"She's okay with it. She's already pissed about something else anyway."

"What's that?" Bob said, looking at the box that Weed was holding as they slowly drifted down the street in the truck.

"It's what's left of that Matchbox collection I've been looking for all winter," he said, tipping the box so Bob could look inside. "My mother gave them to the kids next door. That's why I couldn't find them…and they destroyed every one of them," he said, taking one of the cars out of the box and holding it up for Bob to look at. "Did it just to get even with me for this trial, I guess," he said as they drove. "She was upset that I embarrassed her in front of all her friends at church. I condemned her for all my sins. Would probably be pretty funny if it wasn't so damn sickening," he said, dropping the car back into the shoebox and then telling Bob to pull the truck up in front of a garbage can that was sitting alongside the street.

When they were close enough to the garbage can, Weed leaned out the window of the truck and took the lid off the garbage can. "Not much of a sendoff," he said as he watched the cars slowly roll out of the shoebox and into the garbage can.

"Yeah, not much of a funeral," Bob added as they drove on.

"Now what will she have to bitch about?" Weed said, looking straight ahead. "Pissed me off so much that I made her walk home from church this morning...Can you believe that?" he said. "And now she's limping around with this big blister on her foot...that I'm worried might get infected. Knew that it would all backfire...just like with Hileman's dog...everything I do backfires. Think I'm getting the upper hand but end up always losing in the end. Like that catch thing you always talk about...that there's always a catch," he said as Bob shook his head in agreement.

"Sandy going to be there?" Bob asked when they had almost gotten to the house.

"I doubt it...She wasn't there all night or when I left this morning...so she probably won't come back until she's sure I've left."

"What a mess," Bob said, looking at all the trash in the back yard as he pulled the truck into the driveway.

"Sort of fitting, I guess...it all ending in a big mess," Weed answered, noticing the large Happy Anniversary Sandy and Ben sign torn into pieces and lying twisted on the ground.

"Glad I don't have to clean it up," Bob said as he got out of the truck.

"Yeah, well, that's Sandy's problem now," Weed said as they entered the house.

"I'm not sure what I should take. Not much left to take anyway," he said, looking around at the mostly empty house. "She took most everything already."

They carried the flat-screen TV out of the house and loaded it into the back of the truck...and then searched the garage for something to secure it in the back of the truck...but all that Weed could find was a ball of string.

"You think that's going to work?" Bob said as he watched Weed winding the string around the TV like a complex spiderweb.

"If we wrap it around the TV enough times, it will probably hold it. We only have a couple miles to go, and we can take it easy," Weed added.

"I don't know," Bob questioned. "I don't want to be responsible if it falls out of the truck, and there's that one steep hill in front of your mother's house."

"Don't worry. The string will hold it," Weed said. "And I can't find anything else to use, anyway," he said, standing back and looking at what he had just created.

They loaded the suitcases and a few other boxes into the truck, wedging them up against the TV to give it more support, and then they both drank a couple of warm beers that were left over from the party that Bob had found in one of the abandoned coolers in the back yard.

"Sort of feel bad," Weed said as he stood in the foyer when they were about ready to leave. "Good ten years, I guess. Don't know where it went. Remember moving in. We were really happy then. Thought we owned the world and that it was only going to get better," he said. "But where did it go? Just vanished. Like everything else in your life, just seems to vanish right before your eyes," he said as they started walking down the driveway toward the truck.

"Wish I could get it all back...maybe do it differently."

"I know what you mean," Bob said as they got into the truck. "Unfortunately, you can never go back. Life doesn't wait for you... it just passes you by."

"Was mostly my fault that she left anyway. Maybe it was all my fault."

Bob shrugged his shoulders. "Who knows?"

"She was the one that kept us together," he added. "Never knew what love was...I guess. Still not sure that I know. I sometimes think that it's mostly all a bunch of crap. That there is no such thing as love...just a made-up word that means...well, I don't know what. That it's all just a tangled mess of emotions. With a man, it always seems to end up being about sex. That's what love is at the start. Then the love part seems to end up getting tangled up with the lust and physical attraction. The excuse you use for having sex or something. Or maybe it's just me. Maybe it's just the way I am...a personality flaw. That I'm not capable of really knowing what love is...of loving anyone...like Helen told me," he added but could tell that Bob wasn't really interested in all his philosophical babble.

"Yeah, probably. I never really thought about it all that much," Bob finally said after a long silence, nodding his head in agreement.

"Yeah, I don't know. I think that I maybe love Candy a little. I don't think that I really ever felt any stronger about anyone than that one girl way back when we were in high school...that one girl that Candy sort of reminds me of."

"You said that about Sandy too. That she reminded you of that girl too."

"Yeah, I guess I did."

"She said that she might be leaving," Weed said after a long pause.

"I thought she already did?" Bob answered and looked over at Weed, confused.

"No, not Sandy...the other girl from the bar...Candy. She told me that she's thinking about moving to Florida. Wants me to go with her. Can you imagine that? And old man like me with someone like her? Did sound pretty inviting though. Just leave all this shit behind and run off with her. Wouldn't have to deal with any of this bullshit any longer. Wouldn't have to listen to all the whining from the hospital and nurses. No more frivolous law suits. No more obnoxious, malingering patients…bitching about their damn dogs. No more Sandy and her goofy-assed friends to deal with…no more Mordy…and no more mother…Wouldn't have to deal with any of that anymore. I could just loaf around all day on a beach somewhere and live off the land. Not a worry in the world," he said, pausing to think about what he was telling Bob. "You don't know how close I am to doing something just like that. I'm not really interested in this life anymore…I already screwed it up badly…irreparable…probably. My career is mostly over anyway. Won't have any patients left after all this, and my reputation is shot. I was never much of a surgeon…just average at best…that's all," he said, pausing for a short time. "It's the freedom that I want. Free from all this. I want to live like we used to live. That feeling you have when you're young. When it was all new and exciting…and not a care in the world…when anything was possible…and we had our whole lives in front of us…and nothing to tie us down. That's what I want back. I want that life back," he said but was unsure if he even knew what he meant… or if any of it made any sense.

"Yeah, you tell me that all the time. You're a broken record. But it ain't going to happen," he said. "We're old now. You can't go back there. You can't get that life back. It's just a dream…a memory, that's all…and it's over. Just like basketball. We're old men trying to act young…trying to preserve our youth. Everyone knows it but us. Time to move on."

"I'm serious. I'm this close to leaving it all behind," he said, somewhat irritated at Bob's frivolous attitude. "Just closing the office and living off the land," he added, but this time as if he were talking to himself.

"Yeah, would be a nice life," Bob said, slowing the truck to make a turn as he watched the TV wobble in his rearview mirror. "But like I told you, there's always a catch…a catch that always stops you from doing something crazy like that," he said.

"You know all the people at the anniversary party yesterday thought you got arrested?" Bob said, laughing loudly and breaking the silence after long pause.

"What's that?"

"At the party, when I finally got to the party yesterday. The rumor was that the police had arrested you. That those two police officers that were at your house came to arrest you and that was the reason you left the party. That their story about moving some cars that were blocking a driveway was just a distraction...a cover story... and that they were really there to arrest you."

"You're kidding."

"No. Was your friend Helen, I think. She came up with this story that it was because Sandy was missing, and that the police had taken you in for questioning. That Sandy hadn't been seen or heard from all day, and that you had lied to her about her being upstairs at the house, resting...and then she told everyone that things like this happen all the time...that doctors are all a little crazy and always doing strange things," he said and laughed again. "It was pretty wild, and that Helen lady was really drunk and funny."

"You're kidding! You tell them that none of it was true?"

"No, not really. Didn't really think that it was my place...And what made the difference...I don't think anyone really believed her," he added.

"Jesus, Bob, you should have said something. What...they think I'm Jack the Ripper now?"

"I don't know. Does it really matter what they think? It was just all sort of funny, that's all. And everyone was so drunk and laughing and having a good time, you know how people get when there's free booze. I'm not sure that anyone cared or would even remember now...So I wouldn't even worry about it...And really, they all seemed to know that you were getting a divorce over that stripper thing at the bar...and that's why Sandy never showed for the party. That, and the trial, and about Liz too. Just seemed like they all knew everything about your life anyway…that's always the way it is. Even seemed to know about Hileman and her dog…that you had taken her dog for a couple days," Bob said as the truck stalled when he stopped for a red light. All those gyrations you went through and then everyone knew anyway…was all just sort of funny."

"Should have expected as much."

"We'll be damn lucky if the TV makes it," Bob said, looking at its reflection in his rearview mirror. "It wobbles back and forth every time we hit a bump. Wouldn't take much to send it into the street."

"It's fine," Weed said, looking over his shoulder at the TV but pissed about what Bob had just told him and more pissed that his best friend hadn't said a word to defend him…One true friend and even he had abandoned him in the end, he thought…But he wondered, like Bob, if any of it really mattered.

"Drive down this next street," Weed said abruptly as they approached an intersection. "I want to see where I have to be tomorrow."

"Past the City Garage?"

"Yeah, past the City Garage…that road right up there. Maybe seeing it now will make it easier to stomach in the morning. I'm not going to tell anyone about the community service. Might be pretty embarrassing standing out in the street picking up garbage…Don't want to be a spectacle. People probably already know about it anyway…seems like everyone knows everything about my life even before I know it," he said, looking over at Bob.

"No. I don't think anyone said anything about that at the party."

"Might be able to come down here every day and do my four hours without too many people finding out about it. Get it all done and out of the way before anyone even realizes that I'm cleaning toilets and collecting garbage," Weed said as they sat in the truck in front of the City Garage for a few minutes before driving off.

"Supposed to rain tomorrow," Bob said after a long silence.

"Thanks…that will add to my enjoyment," Weed answered as they continued on their journey.

"Sort of excited about moving back home," Weed said as they pulled up in front of the house. "Will be like a vacation from everything else…might be invigorating. Like an adventure. Like when we were young," he said as they got out of the truck and started to unload the suitcases and boxes.

Weed could see his mother standing by the window, watching.

"She looks a little pissed," Bob said as he looked up and waved to her.

"Yeah, well, she'll get over it," Weed said as they carried the suitcases up to the steps and sat them on the porch.

"You want to shoot some basketball later?" Weed asked when they were about finished unloading the truck.

"Maybe, if my back doesn't start acting up in the meantime… and Kim lets me. If I can, I'll meet you at the courts," Bob said as he got back in his truck.

Weed unpacked the suitcases in his room, putting most of his stuff in the same drawers that he had used when he was young, and then he pushed the other boxes to one corner of the room. Would unpack them later, he thought, standing at the window looking down at his old neighborhood.

He sat in his room enjoying the feelings of being back home and remembering how it used to be, before he changed into shorts and put on his tennis shoes.

At least for now most of the crap was behind him, he knew. The trial, the shooting, Sandy…He was starting off fresh…almost from square one, he thought as he dribbled the basketball down the street toward the basketball courts.

Maybe he could get it right this time. Sort of just start the game all over again, he thought.

When he got to the basketball court he started shooting…long shoots, lay ups, jump shots…as he waited for Bob. It felt good. Felt young and alive. He could stay here forever, he imagined. This was the place most of the good in his life had taken place. This was his heaven, he knew.

He played a pick-up game with a bunch of younger guys until it started to get dark...before Bob finally showed up carrying two bottles of beer...and then they sat on the curb and talked and drank until it was dark.

"Where'd the days go?" Weed asked. "Seems like it was just last week that we were young and sitting here doing the same thing."

"Yeah, well, it's all gone and there's no sense getting philosophical again...We've done that enough...and anyway, I'm tired of it," Bob said, standing as he finished his beer.

"One day you're young and full of life and before you know it, you're a beaten-down old man, like us," Weed said as he leaned back and sipped at the beer. "Best years of my life and I never realized it until now, until it was over."

"You're right about that. Probably the same for everyone though," Bob said as he knocked the ball out of Weed's hand and took a long jump shot that hit the rim and bounced away before he sort of just jogged away down the road toward his house waving back as he did...and saying nothing.

Weed waiting until Bob was out of sight before starting home... going out of his way to walk past the garbage can where he had thrown his toy cars earlier in the day. He lifted the lid and then reached way down inside the can and separated the cars from the garbage before stuffing them all into his pockets. Would maybe hold on to them awhile longer, he thought as he continued on his way, strangely feeling a sense of relief.

He stood at the sink in the kitchen and drank a glass of ice water as his mother soaked her foot in a pan of soapy water on the floor in front of her.

"You want me to look at it?"

"It's fine," she answered.

Anything to make him feel guilty, he thought as he walked up-stairs to his bedroom.

He lay there a long time, thinking about his life, thinking about how all the years and all the journeys he had taken had brought him back to where it had all started…his fifty-four-year migration. Like traveling around the spaces of a board game and ending up back at the start. His life had been a board game…but he wasn't sure if he had been the winner or if he had even finished. Do not pass Go. Do not collect two hundred dollars.

Maybe he would have better luck next time…with the next game, he thought before he finally drifted off into a deep sleep.

CHAPTER FIFTY-SIX

Monday, May 24
7:05 a.m.

He remembered when he was getting ready to go to the office that sometime through the night he had had a dream. The dream had awoken him, and after that he couldn't get back to sleep.

The dream was something like this...He had taken his mother to the emergency room because of an infection on her foot. He saw her foot at the house, but by the time they had gotten to the hospital, her foot was twice as big and twice as red.

A goofy-looking doctor, who could have possibly been himself, wearing glasses that were too small and a white coat that was way too big, was examining her foot. The foot looked even worse now, and it was making the doctor sick. And then the doctor turned and told him that there was no hope, that his mother was going to die a miserable death and that he didn't want to be around when it happened...and that it had been mostly his fault for letting her walk home from church. Then the doctor sort of just vanished...as his mother looked up at him, with a look that blamed him for every-thing bad that had ever happened in her life.

"What happened," the doctor asked him, suddenly reappear-ing, but for some reason in the dream, he started telling the doctor about his sexual relationship with Candy...that he had been impo-tent for a while but thought that he was probably okay now. But the doctor told him that he already knew about that but wanted him to start over at the very beginning. But in the dream, what he was wor-ried about was that somehow someone might find out that he had been responsible for his own mother's death.

And then off in one corner of the ER...in his dream...Bob was sitting eating a candy bar at the Quick Fix, looking over at him and telling him that "you never get all the kinks worked out...and there's always a catch...to love." And a dog barking in the corner, and maybe Candy and Pickles somewhere around in the dream ar-guing. And then when he looked back at his mother, it was Hileman lying there on the stretcher instead of his mother, with her legs crossed, holding a remote and looking up at the TV screen. That's when he woke up. Sort of a nightmare...maybe worse than a night-mare. He felt nervous and couldn't get back to sleep for a long time after that.

He thought about the dream as he shaved. "There's always a catch," always something pulling you back into your crappy life.

Even his sleep had turned against him, he thought as he dressed in one of the suits he had brought to his mother's house.

His mother was standing at the stove cooking scrambled eggs and bacon, and for a moment, he thought that he might still be dreaming.

"Morning," he said, but she only made a sort of guttural sound of acknowledgement, saying, "Yes it is," as if it had been a ques-tion. Slight limp but otherwise she looked okay, he thought as he watched her move around the kitchen. Foot was still a little red but didn't look near as bad as it had in the dream.

He drank his coffee as he looked at the newspaper but couldn't quit thinking about the dream. Still shocked him to think that his mother might die because he had let her walk home from church... that he would be the direct cause of her death...had to be some kind of a religious parable that would free him from what he had done, he thought.

"You want some bacon?" his mother asked as she put some scrambled eggs on the plate in front of him while he read the newspaper.

"Yeah, that would be good. Haven't had a good breakfast for a long time," he said and then tried to apologize for making her walk home. "I had so much on my mind that I forgot all about the time and then the hospital called, and before I knew it, you were coming up the sidewalk," he said. "Might have seemed that it had something to do with those toy cars, and I was upset, but that really didn't have much to do with anything else. I'm getting a little old to be worrying about things like that, anyway," he said, trying to act unconcerned about his loss.

"That's what I thought," she answered, but he was sure he detected sarcasm in her voice.

"I probably shouldn't have given them away before I asked you first..." she added, and then went on to explain to him again how her mind was slipping.

Nothing...not a single thing about the trial or the shooting at Tatter's Bar in the newspaper that he could see. Old news already. But in section D...the Family section...a picture of him and the rest of the Committee to Clean Up City Neighborhoods. The picture that the newspaper had taken almost a week earlier...but the faces were mostly unidentifiable and the names at the bottom almost unreadable. Even when he took off his glasses and looked closer at the faces, he couldn't tell who many of them were. Could hardly pick himself out of the crowd...out of the lineup, he imagined. Just a group of anonymous men standing in front of a church, he thought, and wondered what all the others had to hide...wondered if anyone else in the picture had a girlfriend that was a stripper and half his age, or anyone who had been attacked by a washed-up actress, or who had almost been shot by a psychotic biker. Unlikely... but probably most of them had something they were trying to hide.

He was going to say something to his mother about the picture but decided against it...No telling where she might go with it... Something better left alone, he imagined.

He felt bad watching her hobbling around the kitchen. And felt even worse thinking about how big a failure he had been in her eyes.

He tried to make small talk as they ate. Trying to keep her busy with other thoughts so she wouldn't start asking questions that he didn't have any good answers for...about Sandy or the trial or the shooting. Would be too exhausting and fruitless to try to come up with good lies this early in the morning. But by the time he was ready to leave for the office, she hadn't said a word about any of it. Probably, like everyone else, she already knew most of the story. She just didn't know the details yet, he imagined.

"You going to be home in time for supper?" she asked as he started out the door.

"Yeah, probably. I'll give you a call later. Have some things at the hospital to do after office hours and I don't know how long they will take, but I should be home in time for supper."

"I'll make some hot roast beef sandwiches and some potato cakes with the leftovers from yesterday," she added as he left the house.

Something he hadn't had to eat for a long time, he thought.

He stopped on the front porch for a minute to breathe in the fresh air and to smell the lilac bushes...to take in the sights around him. Not much had changed over the years. And Bob had been wrong about the rain. It was a beautiful day. Not a cloud in the sky. Would be a great morning to be out in the fresh air...cleaning up garbage along the highway or cleaning toilets, he thought, suddenly amused and unthreatened by his predicament. Wouldn't even mind doing that on a day like today, he thought. Seemed almost invigorating...therapeutic.

And he had come out of it all relatively unscathed, he imagined as he started the drive toward his office. And like Bob had told him, it was maybe what he really wanted all along...to leave that life and move back home where it had all started...to get away from it all... and maybe start over.

Didn't know what he would tell the nurses at his office about closing the office. He wasn't even sure what he was going to do yet. In the light of the day, that plan didn't seem quite as good as it had the night before. Didn't seem that easy to just up and drop it all...to jump ship on this life. Seemed frivolous and irresponsible, and who knew what was behind the next door that he opened. Wasn't easy to just change your life...to change the direction you've been headed all these years. Never did have enough nerve to pull the trigger anyway. All talk and no action. Would probably just keep muddling along through this miserable and meaningless life, he imagined.

He could still feel where the dog had bitten him on the forearm, and he could still feel the pain in his right knee that he had hurt at Tatter's Bar that night...but neither pain was bad...just reminders. Hand looked almost healed, he thought, holding it out in front of him in the sunlight as he pulled up in front of his office.

All three of his nurses were standing together, smiling and clapping their hands, giving him a big cheer when he entered the office...like a returning victor. And then one after the other, the nurses all gave him a big hug and patted him on the back. Behind them, draped across the waiting room, was a large Welcome Back Dr. Weed banner with streamers and balloons. And on the table, a box of Panera bagels and coffee...and huddled somewhat inconspicuously in the corner, two drug salesmen.

Definitely not the time to tell anyone about thoughts of closing the office. Would have to wait and think about it awhile longer, he thought as he thanked them all and then lied and told them how happy he was to be back.

They all sat and ate bagels and drank coffee and talked about how bizarre the whole mess had become, and how he had come out the victor...but none of them believed any of it, he could tell. And nothing said about the even more touchy issue of the shooting at Tatter's Bar. They were trying to make him feel good and put some kind of a good spin on it all...but the lies were hard to take. There were so many elephants in the room that it was difficult to move, he thought.

"We love you, Dr. Weed...I don't know...You're so...something that's hard to describe...You just make us all feel good...and we're all happy that you're back...and we're going to be just as busy as we were before all this started," one of the nurses assured him. "Maybe even busier," one of the other nurses added and then told him about how many people had called the office for appointments while he was gone. But he suspected that was a stretch too.

"Was all pretty ridiculous, wasn't it," Weed laughed...as they all started to laugh...even the drug salesmen. "A real spectacle," he added, shaking his head in a false gesture of amused disbelief.

When they were through eating and the conversation had faded and the drug salesman had left, he told the nurses about his schedule change and then went back to his office and tried to work. But he couldn't concentrate on much of anything he was doing, only on what he was about to do. So he just sat there and watched the clock until it was time to leave for the City Garage.

He sat in the garage with the smell of oil and grease and a bunch of mostly younger men who looked for the most part like recovering addicts...with stringy hair and countless tattoos. And two women who looked pretty much the same. And Morgan and Turzak at both ends of the room...sitting quietly, blank-faced, staring straight ahead...and Morgan distant now, only nodding with a slight smile as he walked past.

They all sat on creaking old folding chairs and listened to a fat supervisor…wearing a dirty shirt that was stretched opened between the buttons, exposing an even dirtier undershirt…talk to them about what they were going to do and what they weren't going to do…as he pointed to the blackboard behind him…to the faded chalk words: "No drugs. No booze. No weapons. No fighting. No wise asses." Words that looked as if they had been written there a long time ago…like maybe they had been leftover commandments given to him by Moses, Weed thought.

Could his life become any more pathetic? Only up from here, he thought as they all got changed into bright-orange, oversized jumpsuits and then hopped into the back of a dirty orange work truck…like the chain gang from the movie *Cool Hand Luke.* "What we have here is a failure to communicate," Weed thought as the truck moved down the highway, dropping off groups of men…before dropping Turzak and a couple more men left to clean the outhouses at the park…Turzak jumping down from the truck this time. At least one small proverbial victory, Weed thought…Turzak left to clean dirty outhouses.

And then a few more stops before the driver finally called out his name and someone named Merle Smousy.

They jumped off the truck and then moved slowly through the morning haze down the highway in their baggy orange jumpsuits and with their black bags under a baking sun, picking up garbage as the cars whizzed by…some blowing their horns in warning, or more likely as entertainment…candy wrappers and half-eaten hamburgers and old shoes…picking up things that neither of them could identify and shoving them into the bags. Then stopping long enough to drag someone's discarded mattress and portable TV up through the weeds to the side of the road, like the supervisor had told them to do.

And the other man, whose name Weed could no longer remember, talked almost incessantly as they moved along the highway.

Small talk, mostly…that did nothing but fill the dead space as Weed thought about his life. The youth that had vanished like magic… as if it had all just been smoke and mirrors. And then he thought about the mistakes he had made in his life…and how he had ended up being pretty much of a failure. But concluding that maybe everyone in the end sort of wound up being a failure…that a person could always do better. But it all sounded like more philosophical gibberish…and he was tired of that, he knew.

They had worked just a little over an hour when the other man yelled that this was all "bullshit" and he was tired of picking up "other people's shit." He spun around like a shot put thrower with his bag of garbage in front of him before letting go and tossing his garbage bag as far down the highway as he could.

Then they both sat down in the grass in a shade spot.

"I remember my mom used to take us to you when we were kids," he said, pulling up his shirt and showing Weed a long scar running across his abdomen. "You took my appendix out when I was about twelve," he said as he took a long drag off of his cigarette. "She told me that I almost died. So I want to thank you now," he said, holding out his hand for Weed to shake.

"Before or after the surgery?" Weed asked laughingly, but the other man didn't seem to get the intent of his humor…or maybe he had and just didn't think that it was funny.

Then the man took a long drink from a bottle that had magically appeared from somewhere under his orange jumpsuit. "Just a little whiskey for later," he said, looking intently at the bottle…probably to judge just how much he had left, Weed imagined, before he offered him a drink.

Then he leaned back against a tree and started telling Weed about all his problems…about his life of petty crime…that he had robbed three convenience stores, but the police only knew about two…and then seemed to be pleased with that percentage. Then on about his personnel misfortunes and failures…but they all seemed to be the apparent fault of someone else in his life...his friends...his wife...his family...the police not understanding him...or the way he had been raised...But none of his failures were ever directly his fault. A victim of circumstances...an innocent and misunderstood bystander of life...like everyone else in this world, Weed knew.

Weed took a drink from the bottle and then for some unknown reason, began to tell the man about all his problems...about the trial and the dog and Hileman and the shooting...but it all sounded almost boring and lifeless now...barely interesting even to himself...And worse, it sounded uncomfortably similar to the tale that the other man had just told him. That all his problems had been more or less caused by someone else in his life. That he had no part in any of it...that he too had been nothing more than an innocent bystander drawn up into the milieu.

And then there was silence, as if neither of them were interested in talking to each other anymore.

It was almost one o'clock when the car pulled off to the side of the road ahead of them not far from where they were working. Weed watched as the door opened and Candy got out of the car and came running back to where he was standing.

"Can you believe it? I finally made up my mind. I'm on my way to Florida, Ben," she said excitedly, coming up to him and giving him a hug and a long kiss as she sort of jumped around with excitement. "I tried to call you yesterday but couldn't get you on your cell...but I'm so excited," she said. "Philomena called. She has a job all lined up for me and a place to live. Only three blocks from the beach...Says there's all kinds of really good-looking guys," she said but quickly changed it to "good-looking people."

"You could come too. There's plenty of room in the car...I left you a little space in the backseat for your things," she added.

"Yeah, I wish it was that easy," he said, sort of laughing.

"You've been talking about leaving...how long now? This is exactly what you wanted to do. Change your life. Get away from all this," she said, putting her arms on his shoulders and giving him another kiss. "You could come with me...and we could start all over down there. You could open another doctor's office where there are a lot of rich people," she said, standing back and looking at him as if she were waiting for him to answer. "I could drive you back to your mom's house. You could get some things...and we could just leave now. Because if you don't do it now, you never will...This is your big opportunity," she said as he stood there and thought about it for a moment.

But for some reason he knew that he didn't have the courage or the energy or the youth to do anything like that. He was beyond those days.

"Would be nice. But I have things to do here before I could leave." The catch, Weed thought. "I mean, I have to do this," he said as he opened his hand, exposing a gum wrapper that he had just picked up off the ground. "I don't do this, they're going to come looking for me and lock me up," he said, laughing. "But maybe later when I get things finished up here I could come," he said, giving her a kiss and then slowly walking her back to her car, where she wrote out her new address on the gum wrapper he had shown her.

"Wanted to tell you good-bye, anyway," she said, handing him the wrapper and then giving him another long kiss and hug. "Knew you wouldn't come," she said, acting maybe a little disappointed.

She gave him another hug and a long kiss, before walking backward, throwing him multiple kisses in the air, and getting back into her car...and then sticking her head out the window and waving as she pulled away, driving slowly down the highway...still waving until she was far down the highway.

Probably would be the last time he ever saw her, he thought as he watched the car disappear into the distant traffic...murmuring to himself, "Good-bye, my love," and feeling empty like he always did when someone he loved left him.

He stood out in the baking sun, half listening to the other man tell him how crazy he was for not going off with a hot chick like that…but thinking more about his own life as he moved a little further down the highway…realizing that, in the end, he had probably gotten pretty much what he had deserved.

THE END

ABOUT THE AUTHOR

D. M. Baker was born in Dunbar, Pennsylvania, on October 30, 1950. He graduated from the University of Pittsburgh in 1972 and from Des Moines University in 1976. *Oceans Rising* is his first published novel.